Dear Readers,

Many years ago, when I was a kid, my father said to me, "Bill, it doesn't really matter what you do in life. What's important is to be the *best* William Johnstone you can be."

I've never forgotten those words. And now, many years and almost 200 books later, I like to think that I am still trying to be the best William Johnstone I can be. Whether it's Ben Raines in the Ashes series, or Frank Morgan, the last gunfighter, or Smoke Jensen, our intrepid mountain man, or John Barrone and his hard-working crew keeping America safe from terrorist lowlifes in the Code Name series, I want to make each new book better than the last and deliver powerful storytelling.

Equally important, I try to create the kinds of believable characters that we can all identify with, real people who face tough challenges. When one of my creations blasts an enemy into the middle of next week, you can be damn sure he had a good reason.

As a storyteller, my job is to entertain you, my readers, and to make sure that you get plenty of enjoyment from my books for your hard-earned money. This is not a job I take lightly. And I greatly appreciate your feedback— you are my gold, and your opinions *do* count. So please keep the letters and e-mails coming.

Respectfully

WILLIAM W. JOHNSTONE

CREED OF THE MOUNTAIN MAN

GUNS OF THE MOUNTAIN MAN

PINNACLE BOOKS
Kensington Publishing Corp.
http://www.kensingtonbooks.com

PINNACLE BOOKS are published by

Kensington Publishing Corp.
850 Third Avenue
New York, NY 10022

All Kensington Titles, Imprints, and Distributed Lines are available at special quantity discounts for bulk purchases for sales promotions, premiums, fund-raising, and educational or institutional use. Special book excerpts or customized printings can also be created to fit specific needs. For details, write or phone the office of the Kensington special sales manager: Kensington Publishing Corp., 850 Third Avenue, New York, NY 10022, attn: Special Sales Department, Phone: 1-800-221-2647.

Pinnacle and the P logo Reg. U.S. Pat. & TM Off.

First Pinnacle Books Printing: May 2006

10 9 8 7 6 5 4 3 2

Printed in the United States of America

CREED OF THE
MOUNTAIN MAN

1

Smoke and Pearlie were leaning on a corral fence, watching Cal try to break one of the horses Smoke had bought for the Sugarloaf remuda.

"Ride 'em, Cal boy," Pearlie shouted, grinning from ear to ear. "Don't let that cayuse show you who's boss."

The boy in his late teens was holding on to the hurricane deck for dear life, shouting and waving his hat in the air as if he were at a county fair competition. The bronc was crow-hopping, swallowing his head, and generally giving the young man fits.

Smoke Jensen smiled and tilted his hat back. "I know Cal is pretty good with most horses, but I think this one has his number."

Just then, the horse bent almost double and gave a quick double jump and twisted sideways at the same time. Cal went flying head over heels to land in a pile of horse apples in the middle of the corral.

"He's forked end up, Smoke," Pearlie hollered as he quickly scaled the fence and shooed the still-bucking animal away until Cal could climb shakily to his feet and make his way over to the fence.

"Jimminy Christmas, Smoke, that there broomtail acts like he's got a burr under his saddle," Cal said.

He brushed the seat of his pants with both hands, grimacing as he touched areas bruised by the fall. After a moment, as if the idea had just occurred to him, he narrowed his eyes and glanced over his shoulder at Pearlie. "You didn't do somethin' nasty like that to me, did you, Pearlie?"

Pearlie sauntered over, holding his hands out in front of him. "No, Cal, I didn't put no sticker under your saddle." He gave a short laugh. "I didn't figure I needed to since there weren't no way you was gonna be able to stay in the saddle nohow."

"Whatta you mean, Pearlie?" Cal said, sticking his jaw out. "You think I can't break that hoss? Just gimme another try and we'll see."

Smoke said, "Hold on, Cal. We all know you're a pretty good rider, but breaking horses takes some specialized knowledge. Pearlie, show him how it's done."

Pearlie pulled his hat down tight and walked to the snorting horse, ignoring the way it was pawing the ground and looking walleyed. He bent down and picked up the reins, bringing the horse's head down toward his face. He grabbed its ear, bent it over, and swung into the saddle. As the mount kicked up its heels, Pearlie threw his weight forward, wrapped his arms around its neck, and squeezed and twisted the animal's ear almost double. It immediately quieted down, rolling its eyes back and trying to see what was happening. Pearlie dug his spurs in and made the bronc trot around the corral a time or two.

After a few minutes, he let go of the horse's ear and continued to ride in peace, the horse trotting as if wearing a saddle and rider was the most natural thing in the world.

Pearlie grinned, took his hat off, and swept it in front of him as he took a bow toward Cal while riding the now-docile animal.

"Well I'll be gosh-darned," Cal said, wonderment in his voice.

"That's an old-timer's trick, Cal," Smoke said. "The old trail hands used to tell the tenderfeet they were whispering in the horse's ear when they did that, but they were really just putting all their weight on the animal's neck and using the ear to cause it enough pain to make it forget all about bucking."

He shrugged, and inclined his head toward Pearlie. "It doesn't always work that well, but you had already tired the animal out enough that he was about ready to quit bucking anyway. Course, Pearlie's going to try and take all the credit for it—you just watch."

Pearlie trotted his mount over to the two men and said, "See, Cal boy, it's easy when you're an old hand at breakin' hosses like I am."

"That's bull an' you know it, Pearlie. I already had that crazy animal plumb tuckered out so's he couldn't hardly walk, much less buck you off."

"Okay, boys, that's enough jawing," Smoke said. "Let's get the rest of this sorry bunch of animals broken so we can get some lunch."

Pearlie, an acknowledged chowhound, grinned and said, "Yes, sir!" at the mention of food. He walked his bronc over to the gate and put it in with the ones already broken. He and Cal managed to saddle another of the wild horses, and he walked back over to stand next to Smoke as Cal once again tried his hand.

As the young man leaned forward on the horse's neck and twisted its ear, Pearlie said, "Smoke, I can't hardly believe the changes in Cal since Miss Sally brought him back to the ranch a few years ago."

Smoke's eyes crinkled as he smiled at the recollection. "Neither can I, Pearlie. . . ."

Calvin Woods, going on eighteen years old now, was just fourteen when Smoke and Sally took him in as a hired hand. It was during the spring branding, and Sally was on her way back from Big Rock to the Sugarloaf. The buckboard was piled high with supplies; branding hundreds of calves made for hungry punchers.

As Sally slowed the team to make a bend in the trail,

a rail-thin young man stepped from the bushes at the side of the road with a pistol in his hand.

"Hold it right there, miss."

Applying the brake with her right foot, Sally slipped her hand under a pile of gingham cloth on the seat. She grasped the handle of her short-barreled Colt .44 and eared back the hammer, letting the sound of the horses' hooves and the squealing of the brake pad on the wheel mask the sound. "What can I do for you, young man?" she asked, her voice firm and without fear. She knew she could draw and drill the young highwayman before he could raise his pistol to fire.

"Well, uh, you can throw some of those beans and a cut of that fatback over here, and maybe a portion of that Arbuckle's coffee too."

Sally's eyebrows raised. "Don't you want my money?"

The boy frowned and shook his head. "Why, no, ma'am. I ain't no thief. I'm just hungry."

"And if I don't give you my food, are you going to shoot me with that big Navy Colt?"

He hesitated a moment, then grinned ruefully. "No, ma'am, I guess not." He twirled the pistol around his finger and slipped it into his belt, turned, and began to walk down the road toward Big Rock.

Sally watched the youngster amble off, noting his tattered shirt, dirty pants with holes in the knees and torn pockets, and boots that looked as if they had been salvaged from a garbage dump. "Young man," she called, "come back here, please."

He turned, a smirk on his face, spreading his hands. "Look, lady, you don't have to worry. I don't even have any bullets." With a lightning-fast move, he drew the gun from his pants, aimed away from Sally, and pulled the trigger. There was a click but no explosion as the hammer fell on an empty cylinder.

Sally smiled. "Oh, I'm not worried." In a movement every bit as fast as his, she whipped her .44 out and fired, clipping a pine cone from a branch, causing it to fall and bounce off his head.

The boy's knees buckled and he ducked, saying, "Jim-miny Christmas!"

Mimicking him, Sally twirled her Colt and stuck it in the waistband of her britches. "What's your name, boy?"

The boy blushed and looked down at his feet. "Calvin, ma'am, Calvin Woods."

She leaned forward, elbows on knees, and stared into the boy's eyes. "Calvin, no one has to go hungry in this country, not if they're willing to work."

He looked up at her through narrowed eyes, as if he found life a little different than she'd described it.

"If you're willing to put in an honest day's work, I'll see that you get an honest day's pay, and all the food you can eat."

Calvin stood a little straighter, shoulders back and head held high. "Ma'am, I've got to be straight with you. I ain't no experienced cowhand. I come from a hard-scrabble farm and we only had us one milk cow and a couple of goats and chickens, and lots of dirt that weren't worth nothing for growin' things. My ma and pa and me never had nothin', but we never begged and we never stooped to takin' handouts."

Sally thought, *I like this boy. Proud, and not willing to take charity if he can help it.* "Calvin, if you're willing to work, and don't mind getting your hands dirty and your mus-cles sore, I've got some hands that'll have you punching beeves like you were born to it in no time at all."

A smile lit up his face, making him seem even younger than his years. "Even if I don't have no saddle, nor a horse to put it on?"

She laughed out loud. "Yes. We've got plenty of ponies and saddles." She glanced down at his raggedy boots. "We can probably even round up some boots and spurs that'll fit you."

He walked over and jumped in the back of the buck-board. "Ma'am, I don't know who you are, but you just hired you the hardest-workin' hand you've ever seen."

Back at the Sugarloaf, she sent him in to Cookie and told him to eat his fill. When Smoke and the other punchers rode into the cabin yard at the end of the day, she introduced Calvin around. As Cal was shaking hands with the men, Smoke looked over at her and winked. He knew she could never resist a stray dog or cat, and her heart was as large as the Big Lonesome itself.

Smoke walked up to Cal and cleared his throat. "Son, I hear you drew down on my wife."

Cal gulped, "Yessir, Mr. Jensen. I did." He squared his shoulders and looked Smoke in the eye, not flinching though he was obviously frightened of the tall man with the incredibly wide shoulders standing before him.

Smoke smiled and clapped the boy on the back. "Just wanted you to know you stared death in the eye, boy. Not many galoots are still walking upright who ever pulled a gun on Sally. She's a better shot than any man I've ever seen except me, and sometimes I wonder about me."

The boy laughed with relief as Smoke turned and called out, "Pearlie, get your lazy butt over here."

A tall, lanky cowboy ambled over to Smoke and Cal, munching on a biscuit stuffed with roast beef. His face was lined with wrinkles and tanned a dark brown from hours under the sun, but his eyes were sky-blue and twinkled with good-natured humor.

"Yessir, boss," he mumbled around a mouthful of food.

Smoke put his hand on Pearlie's shoulder. "Cal, this here chowhound is Pearlie. He eats more'n any two hands, and he's never been known to do a lick of work he could get out of, but he knows beeves and horses as well as any puncher I have. I want you to follow him around and let him teach you what you need to know."

Cal nodded. "Yes, sir, Mr. Smoke."

"Now let me see that iron you have in your pants."

Cal pulled the ancient Navy Colt and handed it to Smoke. When Smoke opened the loading gate, the rusted cylinder fell to the ground, causing Pearlie and Smoke to laugh and Cal's face to flame red. "This is the piece you pulled on Sally?"

The boy nodded, looking at the ground.

Pearlie shook his head. "Cal, you're one lucky pup. Hell, if'n you'd tried to fire that thing it'd of blown your hand clean off."

Smoke inclined his head toward the bunkhouse. "Pearlie, take Cal over to the tack house and get him fixed up with what he needs, including a gun belt and a Colt that won't fall apart the first time he pulls it. You might also help pick him out a shavetail to ride. I'll expect him to start earning his keep tomorrow."

"Yes, sir, Smoke." Pearlie put his arm around Cal's shoulders and led him off toward the bunkhouse. "Now the first thing you gotta learn, Cal, is how to get on Cookie's good side. A puncher rides on his belly, and it 'pears to me that you need some fattenin' up 'fore you can begin to punch cows."*

As Smoke grinned at his memory of the day Cal arrived, his thoughts turned to his foreman, Pearlie, standing next to him.

Pearlie had come to work for Smoke in as roundabout a way as Cal had. He was hiring his gun out to Tilden Franklin in Fontana when Franklin went crazy and tried to take over Sugarloaf, Smoke and Sally's spread. After Franklin's men raped and killed a young girl in the fracas, Pearlie sided with Smoke and the aging gunfighters he had called in to help put an end to Franklin's reign of terror.†

Pearlie was now honorary foreman of Smoke's ranch, though he was only a shade over twenty-four years old himself— boys grew to be men early in the mountains of Colorado.

Sally, Smoke's pretty, brown-haired wife, appeared next to him, breaking his reverie. "Howdy, boys. I thought you might like to take a little break and have a snack before lunch."

She was carrying a platter of still-steaming bear sign,

*Vengeance of the Mountain Man
†Trail of the Mountain Man

the sweet doughnuts that cowboys had been known to ride ten miles for.

Pearlie's eyes widened and he let out a whoop. "Hey, Cal, Miss Sally's got some bear sign for us!"

As Cal looked over, he let his concentration slip and released the horse's ear. It immediately began to crow-hop and jigger around the corral, finally throwing Cal in a heap in a far corner.

The boy sprang to his feet, slapped the bucking horse out of his way with his hat, and ran to jump over the fence. "Boy howdy, I could sure use some nourishment, Miss Sally."

Sally laughed and handed the platter of doughnuts to Pearlie and a pitcher of lemonade and some glasses to Smoke. She shook her head and started back toward the cabin. "You boys don't work Smoke too hard breaking those broomtails. He's getting on up in years and may not be able to take it."

Smoke called out to her retreating back, "Dear, you notice I'm not the one sweating here. It's these two young bucks who're doing all the work. I'm busy supervising."

She called back, "Good, then that means they can have all the bear sign."

"Like hell," Smoke muttered, as he hurried to grab a handful before they were all gone.

2

The day was finally over, and Smoke and Sally were sitting at the kitchen table, having a cup of after-dinner coffee. "Sweetheart," Smoke said, "I'm going to make a trip to Wyoming."

Sally put her mug down and stared at Smoke for a moment before asking, "Why?"

"Seven, the Palouse stud Preacher gave me, is getting old, and even though he's bred us some good crosses for our remuda, they aren't Palouses. I want to find some pure Palouse stock mares and maybe another stud or two and carry on Seven's line."

Smoke didn't have to say any more, for Sally to understand this was his way of keeping alive the memory of the man who meant as much to him as his father. Back when Smoke's name was Kirby Jensen, just after the end of the Civil War, he and his father came west from their crab-apple farm in Missouri with all they had strapped to one mule. Soon, they met Preacher, an old mountain man, who saved their lives from a band of marauding Indians. During the fighting, young Kirby killed his share of the attackers, and was given the name Smoke by Preacher, both for the thin trail of smoke from his Colt Navy .36 and for the color of his ash-blond hair.

After traveling with the mountain man for a spell, Smoke's father was killed by three men who had stolen some gold from the Confederate Army. Preacher took Smoke in and raised him for the next several years, teaching him all the lore of the strange breed known as mountain men.*

Sally asked, "What about Horse?" referring to the Palouse Smoke had been riding since putting Seven in his own pasture on the Sugarloaf to run free and enjoy his old age.

"I'd like to carry on his line, too. I ran across a trapper coming down from the mountains for supplies last week. He said the Nez Percé tribe that used to live there was gone. He didn't know where, but he'd heard there was still a small band of them camped up near Buffalo in northern Wyoming."

Smoke drained the last of his coffee and reached across the table to take Sally's hand.

"The Nez Percé are the ones who developed the Palouse breed, Sally, and they always keep a good supply of breeding mares and studs on hand. I plan to go to Wyoming before the tribe gets killed off, or mixes with another and loses their identity. I'm going to carry on the Palouse line here on the Sugarloaf, starting with Seven and Horse."

"But Smoke, it's the middle of winter. Don't you think this will wait until spring, at least?"

He shook his head. "No, I don't want to be gone during the spring calving and branding. That's too heavy a load to leave on Pearlie and Cal. I'm going to get on the Union Pacific Line train and take it all the way to Casper, a little range town at the foot of the Big Horn Mountains. From there I'll pack by horse up into the mountains north of Buffalo and see if I can find out where the Nez Percé are now."

He sat back and shrugged. "Then it's just a matter of doing some good old-fashioned horse trading."

Sally got the pot off the stove and poured him another cup of coffee. "I don't like the idea of you traveling halfway across the country in the dead of winter by yourself. Why don't you take Cal or Pearlie with you?"

"There's too much work here they need to be doing."

*The Last Mountain Man

He glanced out the cabin window at their ranch. "Fences need mending, corrals have to be built, and the cattle have got to be taken care of." He hesitated, a slow grin crossing his lips. "Besides, do you think this old beaver is getting too old to make a trip by himself? You think I need taking care of?"

She stared at him for a moment without speaking, as if she was considering that possibility. Finally, she got up from the table and took the coffeepot off the stove, putting it on a counter to cool. She stoked the fire in the stove, sending waves of warmth through the chilly room. When she was finished, she took her apron off and began to walk toward their bedroom.

After a few steps, she glanced back over her shoulder and smiled. "Oh, I don't think you're getting old at all, but why don't you come to bed and show me how young you're feeling?"

And he did just that.

3

Cheyenne, Wyoming

Hubert Teschemacher and Frederic O. deBillier swung their identical gold-headed walking sticks to and fro as they approached the Cheyenne Club through a light snowfall.

They swaggered as they walked, tipping their top hats at other prominent citizens as they passed. Having come to Wyoming from Boston a few years back with five hundred thousand dollars to invest, they were well aware of their place in Cheyenne society as two of the wealthiest men in the state capital.

"Freddy," Hubert said, "we've come a long way since we roomed together at Harvard."

DeBillier glanced at his friend, a sardonic smile on his face. "Yes, Hubie, this western country is certainly different from Boston, wouldn't you say?"

Teschemacher shrugged. "Yes, of course. There is no culture at all out here, and the food is generally atrocious."

He paused, before grinning and smoothing his handlebar moustache with the flick of a forefinger. "But then, there is always the Cheyenne Club to relieve our boredom," he said with a wink at his friend.

DeBillier smiled back, adjusting his silk cravat as the

two men entered the three-story Cheyenne Club, described in its charter as "a pleasure resort and place of amusement."

A doorman in formal attire took their overcoats and hats and walking sticks, saying, "Good evening, sirs. The others in your party are awaiting you on the third floor."

The first floor of the Cheyenne Club was the kitchen and storage area for the vast supplies of liquor and wine and other culinary delicacies the members maintained.

The second floor was the "communal" room, where the prettiest whores in the state would arrange themselves in various small cubicles and rooms, to play pianos or other musical instruments, sing, and otherwise amuse their wealthy clients. All of the girls were handpicked by Teschemacher and deBillier, who as co-founders of the Cheyenne Club, retained certain perks for themselves.

The third floor was the dining and meeting hall. Dozens of overstuffed leather chairs and tables were arranged around the room in the manner of the English men's clubs that Teschemacher and deBillier had seen on their travels abroad. In a separate room was a dining table made of carved oak, over twenty feet long, with chairs to seat forty diners.

Butlers and maids were everywhere, and the floors were connected to the kitchen by a series of dumbwaiters, so the members were never without food or drink for very long.

As Hubert and Frederic climbed the stairs, Hubert said, "Now remember, Freddy, we must handle Hesse with extreme care in our discussion tonight."

"I know, Hubie. That damned pompous limey bastard won't agree to anything unless he's made to feel it's his idea."

Hubert nodded. "Exactly. So the trick is simply to lead him in the right direction, so that he'll decide things our way."

"What about Bill Irving?" Frederic asked.

Hubert snorted, "Oh, William is just a midlevel manager for his investors back in Omaha. He'll do whatever

we tell him to do, since it's his butt on the line if his
ranch doesn't make a profit every year."

Slightly out of breath from their climb, they finally
reached the third floor and walked into the anteroom,
where they saw their friends standing in small groups,
with Cuban cigars in their hands and holding crystal
goblets filled with brandy and Kentucky bourbon.

Teschemacher and deBillier had spared no expense in
decorating the room, making use of a French decorator
brought over for just that reason. There were paintings
on every wall, and a twenty-five-foot gilded mirror behind
a massive, ornately carved mahogany bar that ran the
length of the room, stocked with thousands of dollars'
worth of expensive whiskeys and wines and brandies. A
billiard table was in a corner, underneath a fancy French
chandelier with hundreds of small candles arrayed
around the crystal glass it was made of. The polished
wooden floors were covered with hand-woven rugs of the
finest wool.

Hubert and Frederic had invited a group of the rich-
est and most influential men in the county to attend the
meeting, all owners or managers of the largest cattle
ranches in the area.

William Irving managed a large ranch owned by mil-
lionaire backers from Omaha, and served as a director of
the Cheyenne and Northern Railroad and other corpora-
tions. Fred Hesse, an Englishman, had worked (swindled,
Hubert often said) his way up from foreman to manager
of a ranching system that grazed tens of thousands of
cattle on far-flung Wyoming ranges. Major Frank Wolcott was a former Army officer from Kentucky who still
wore puttees and maintained his military bearing despite
a twisted neck—acquired in a tussle with a Laramie
cowboy—that left his head permanently cocked to one
side. Wolcott's jaw, Frederic had observed, "closes with a
snap after every sentence he utters."

Most of the plutocrats in the group had spent less time
in the saddle than in the state capital, spending most of

their nights in the plush and exclusive surroundings of the Cheyenne Club.

Tonight, there were forty-one members attending the club banquet arranged by Hubert and Frederic. Some were playing billiards, while others nibbled at pickled eels and French hors d'oeuvres while waiting for the dinner to be sent up. Hubert had ordered twenty bottles of wine and over sixty bottles of champagne for his guests tonight. There would be none left by night's end.

After greeting each of the cattle barons, Hubert signaled the head butler that dinner was to be served.

Later, as the men sat around with more brandy and cigars, he addressed them from his station at the head of the table.

"Gentlemen, we are at a crossroads here in Wyoming. As you know, the smaller ranchers in the area are getting more and more brazen about stealing and rustling our cattle."

Several of the men nodded in agreement, while others scowled and sniffed their disapproval of the subject.

Hubert continued. "We are suffering unacceptable losses to our herds from the depredations of these thieves, and some drastic measures may have to be undertaken."

Even as he spoke, Hubert knew that most of the losses of the big ranchers were due to poor management practices such as overstocking the range, unpredictable whims of nature in the form of prairie fires and plagues of feed-destroying grasshoppers, and sieges of bad weather. But he also knew that whenever lean dividends had to be explained to far-off investors, rustlers provided the best excuse.

William Irving spoke up. "But Hubert, what about our cowboy blacklist, where we agreed not to hire cowboys who owned their own spreads and cattle. Isn't that working?"

Hubert shook his head. "No, in fact our scheme has actually backfired on us, and has driven many of these cowboys who can't find work with us to strike out on their own with small ranches that further eat into our profits."

Fred Hesse stood and adjusted his vest before speaking. "How about the law we arranged to be passed by the legislature, the 'maverick' law, making every unbranded stray calf on the range the property of the Wyoming Stock Growers Association, which we control? In my annual report, I see that we are making huge profits on the cattle that we auction off under the law."

Hubert nodded. "Yes, we're making a profit, but most of that is being spent to hire stock detectives and pay them two hundred and fifty dollars for every rustler convicted or killed." He paused to relight his cigar, then continued. "Furthermore, the small ranchers are calling these detectives bounty hunters and assassins and are making a lot of noise in the legislature to get the maverick law repealed."

He pointed down the table at Albert Bothwell, one of the wealthiest and most arrogant of the cattle barons present. "And it didn't help matters any when Al lynched those two homesteaders on the Sweetwater range last summer."

Bothwell stood up, his face red and flushed from several bottles of wine. "Dammit, Hubie, you know Jim Averell and Ella Watson were squatting on my land illegally, and that whore Watson was known to take her pay in cattle rustled off my range."

Hubert nodded and held up his hand. "I know, Al. That's why we spread the rumor in the newspapers that her name was Cattle Kate and that she was a gun-toting rustler queen. But it's harder to explain to people how Jim Averell, who owned not a single cow, was a rustler."

Bothwell waved his hand. "Doesn't matter," he slurred. "He deserved to die for tryin' to settle on my land."

Hubert shook his head, trying hard not to laugh. He knew the land Bothwell claimed as his own was actually free range, owned by the state of Wyoming, and was open to anyone who chose to settle on it. Of course, since all of the men present did much the same thing, he wasn't about to quibble over small details.

"All right, Al," Hubert said, holding his hands up to soothe the big man's temper, "but what I'm trying to say is all of these things have not served to stop the rustling. I want to propose something a bit more . . . severe."

Fred Hesse called out, "I'm sure for anything that'll stop those damn rustlers from stealing me out of house and home!"

He looked around at the others, waving his cigar in the air. "And now they've had the effrontery to form their own association, calling it the Northern Wyoming Farmers and Stock Growers Association," he said, his voice heavy with sarcasm. "Hell, I think it's just a fancy name for a den of thieves and footpads and rustlers to hide behind."

Hubert's lips curled in a small smile. The group was right where he wanted them, ready to do anything to make more money. He glanced at Frederic and gave a small wink before he continued with his talk.

"Gentlemen, what I propose is to completely wipe out that organization and exterminate the rustlers once and for all."

William Irving, who wasn't as drunk as the others, arched an eyebrow and stared at Hubert thoughtfully. "Just how do you plan to go about that, Hubie? Especially since Sheriff Red Angus in Buffalo, up where most of the rustlers operate, is openly sympathetic to the small ranchers."

Hubert took a sip of his hundred-year-old brandy and puffed deeply on his Cuban cigar, letting the smoke trail from his nostrils. This was going to be the hardest part of his scheme to get the men to accept.

He leaned forward, his knuckles on the table. "First, we must recruit a force of gunfighters from outside the state, and send them in force against Johnson County, which is the headquarters of the rustlers . . . home to men like Nate Champion, who is the head of the Northern Wyoming Farmers and Stock Growers Association."

He paused for a moment, letting the idea sink in, then continued. "Then we cut all telegraph wires that link the county to the rest of the state, thus isolating the citizens while our attack gets under way. Next, we take over the town of Buffalo, which is the county seat, and assassinate the sheriff, his deputies, and the three county commissioners, thereby stripping the county of its leadership."

He had their full attention now, as talk of a full-scale range war usually did. "And finally, we dispose of all the men on this 'death list' I've got here that our WSGA detectives have put together." He held up a fistful of papers with over seventy names printed on it.

At first, as the idea sank in, there was stunned silence from the men sitting before Hubert. It wasn't the fact that they would be breaking the law; they did that most every day. It was the sheer magnitude of the thing that gave them pause. None of the others had thought on such a grand scale before.

Slowly, they began to talk excitedly among themselves, and Hubert knew he had them. He sat down and leaned back, enjoying the double bite of brandy and cigar smoke on his tongue as he watched them assimilate his grand scheme.

After a moment, Mike Shonsey, a local rancher who was talking quietly to Charley Ford, foreman of the TA ranch, looked up and said in a loud voice, "Hubie, your idea sounds good on the surface, but just who do you have in mind to lead this expedition against the Johnson County rustlers, and where are you going to find enough gunfighters to carry out your plan?"

Hubert stood up and signaled the head waiter to his side, whispering in his ear.

The man left the room and returned a few minutes later with two men in tow. They walked over to stand at the head of the table next to Hubert Teschemacher.

Hubert put his hand on the first man's shoulder. He stood a couple of inches over six feet tall, had a wide moustache curled around the corners of his mouth, and wore a grim, serious expression.

"I'm sure most of you know Frank Canton, former sheriff of Johnson County and now one of WSGA's best stock detectives," Hubert said.

Several of the men at the table nodded and smiled at Canton, knowing him to be a stone killer who had already murdered several rustlers in his duties for the Association.

Hubert pointed to the other man, somewhat shorter than Canton, also sporting a dark moustache. He was broader, with a stocky body, and wearing a black coat, with twin Colt .45s strapped to his belt.

"This is Tom Smith, another of our fine stock detectives, ex-deputy U.S. marshal from Texas, who is going to lead our recruiting drive by going back to his old stomping grounds and finding us some of the toughest men in the country to help us in our war against the rustlers in Johnson County."

Robert Tilsdale, another rancher, called out, "Tom, just how are you going to convince these men to come all the way up here in the dead of winter to fight our war for us?"

Smith stepped to the head of the table, a small smile on his face. "I'm going to offer them wages of five dollars a day, a bonus of fifty dollars to every man for each rustler killed, no matter who kills him, and a three-thousand-dollar accident policy for each volunteer. I figure I'll need between twenty and thirty hardcases to get the job done."

"Jesus," Charley Ford said, "that's going to come to a lot of money, Hubie."

Hubert nodded. "That's right, and I'm going to ask each member of the WSGA to donate one thousand dollars to the war fund. With over a hundred members, that'll be more than enough to get the men and equipment we need."

He glanced over at William Irving. "Bill, I'm going to need the cooperation of the Cheyenne and Northern Railroad to send Tom and Frank down to Texas and to bring the Texicans back up here. There's no other way to get them here with the weather so bad right now, and we need to get this done before the spring calving or we're going to lose a lot more head to the rustlers."

Irving nodded. "That'll be no problem. I'll arrange for a couple of cars to be added to the southern run. But what about horses and weapons for the gunmen?"

Hubert said, "I plan to send a couple of our men over to Colorado to buy what we need there. If we try to round up that many extra mounts from our local ranches, it would raise too many questions and the rustlers might get wind of our plans. I've already arranged to buy three heavy freight wagons, and I've placed orders for tents, bedding, guns, pistols, and ammunition enough to see us through this war."

He waved the men toward the parlor. "Now, if any of you have any further questions, Tom and Frank will be glad to answer them over coffee and cigars."

As they made their way to the elaborate bar at the other side of the room, Canton and Smith looked around at the expensive furnishings. This was quite a change from the saloons they used to frequent when they were deputy U.S. marshals.

4

Big Rock, Colorado

Smoke stood on the porch and watched lazy snowflakes dance and weave as they fell from a leaden sky while he had his morning coffee. He heard a noise and turned. Sally stood in the bedroom doorway, her hair tousled and her face sleep-puffy. Smoke thought he'd never seen a lovelier woman in his life.

Sally rubbed her eyes and smoothed back her hair. "Smoke, I hate saying good-bye to you in a train station. Why don't you come back in here and let me tell you how much I'm going to miss you in private?"

She didn't have to ask him twice.

A while later, Cal and Pearlie accompanied Smoke into Big Rock, the town he had founded a few years back after the Tilden Franklin affair. He had packed his buckskins and moccasins and most of his guns in a large valise, and was wearing his traveling clothes—a flannel shirt, corduroy pants tucked into knee-high leather boots, and a rawhide coat with fur on the inside to protect against the harsh winter of northern Wyoming. His only weapons were a Colt Navy .36 carried in a shoulder holster under the coat and a bowie knife in a scabbard on his belt.

"Smoke, I sure wish you'd let one of us go with you," Pearlie said as they entered the city limits of Big Rock.

"Now don't you start on me, Pearlie. I've already hashed this out with Sally. I don't need you trying to play nursemaid to me too."

"How are you planning on gettin' those horses back here, Smoke?" Cal asked. "You can't hardly drive them here by yourself over those mountain passes in the winter."

"I'm not going to drive them here at all, Cal. I'm going to hire a special boxcar on the train and ship them by rail."

"Hell, Smoke, it's just not gonna be the same around here without you," Pearlie said.

"Pearlie, I need someone I can trust to look after the Sugarloaf, and to make sure Sally's all right. I'm depending on you and Cal to keep things going until I get back."

Cal pulled his hat down tight, a serious expression on his young face. "You can count on us." He glanced at Pearlie. "At least, I'll try not to let Pearlie eat you out of house and home before you get back."

Before Smoke could answer, there came a whistle from a doorway, and a voice called, "Well looky who's comin' down the road. Is that some Eastern dude, perhaps a tenderfoot who's lost his way?"

Monte Carson, the sheriff in Big Rock, was leaning against the doorjamb of his office, a cigar in one hand and a steaming tin of coffee in the other.

Smoke and Monte Carson had become very good friends over the past few years. Carson had once been a well-known gunfighter, though he had never ridden the owlhoot trail.

A local rancher, with plans to take over the county, had hired Carson to be the law in Fontana, a town just down the road from Smoke's Sugarloaf spread. Carson went along with the man's plans for a while, till he couldn't stomach the rapings and killings any longer. He put his foot down and let it be known that Fontana was going to be run in a law-abiding manner from then on.

The rancher, Tilden Franklin, sent a bunch of riders

in to teach the upstart lawman a lesson. The men killed Carson's two deputies and seriously wounded him, taking over the town. In retaliation, Smoke founded the town of Big Rock, and he and a band of famous aging gunfighters cleaned house in Fontana.

When the fracas was over, Smoke offered the job of sheriff in Big Rock to Monte Carson. He married a grass widow and settled into the job like he was born to it. Neither Smoke nor the citizens of Big Rock ever had cause to regret his taking the job.*

Smoke frowned. "There's men planted all over this country for talking to me like that, cowboy. You looking for trouble?"

Carson laughed so hard he almost spilled his coffee. "Oh, no, sir, Mr. Gunfighter, sir. I just didn't recognize the famous gunhawk Smoke Jensen in those fancy city duds." He bowed low. "I apologize if I offended your delicate sensibilities, sir."

Smoke grinned. "I'll forgive you if you've got some more of that coffee cooking on the stove in your office."

"Come on in, light and sit and talk a while, Smoke. It's been too long since we've had a palaver."

Smoke got down off Horse, and asked Pearlie and Cal if they'd like to have some breakfast over at Longmont's saloon while he talked with Monte.

Pearlie didn't even answer, just spurred his mount and galloped off in a cloud of dust.

"You know you have to be careful when you ask Pearlie if'n he wants food, Smoke, or you're liable to get trampled in the stampede," Cal said. He followed Pearlie at a more sedate pace, shaking his head at Pearlie's legendary appetite.

Smoke stepped into the sheriff's office and poured himself a cup of coffee from the pot on a corner stove. After taking a sip, he made a face. "Damn, Monte, this stuff is thick enough to float a horseshoe."

*Trail of the Mountain Man

Carson shrugged. "Hell, Smoke, nobody's forcin' you to drink it, an' you shore can't argue about the price."

The two men sat on opposite sides of Carson's desk, and Smoke began to tell his friend about his plans to travel to Wyoming in search of suitable horseflesh to replenish his remuda.

After he caught up on all the news about his friends in town, Smoke stood and stretched. "How would you like some breakfast over at Longmont's? It's on me."

Carson grabbed his hat. "You don't have to ask me twice, Smoke. Let's see if we can get Louis's fancy chef Andre to cook up some regular food for a change, none of them frog legs or whatever."

As they walked down the street toward the saloon, Cal came flying backwards out of the bat-wings, landing sprawled on his back with blood streaming from his nose.

Smoke ran and squatted next to the semi-conscious boy. "Cal, Cal, can you hear me? Are you all right?"

Cal shook his head and gently felt his rapidly swelling nose. "Uh, I guess so. Jimminy but that fellow packs a mean punch."

Smoke gently wiped blood off Cal's cheek. "Seems like every time I bring you to town, Cal, you end up bleeding on me." He sighed. "Well, at least this time you haven't been shot," he said, referring to the fact that Cal seemed to get wounded in every fracas he'd ever been in. Then, Smoke's eyes turned dark and he stood up and walked into the saloon. Pearlie was standing next to a table, twin Colts in his hands pointed at two large men with heavy beards dressed in dirty buckskins. He glanced over his shoulder at Smoke. "Is Cal all right?"

Smoke didn't take his eyes off the two men as he answered, "Yeah. What happened here?"

"These two galoots were talkin' bad 'bout you, Smoke. They was saying they heard you got your reputation by bein' a back-shootin' coward. Cal told 'em to take it back, and they walloped him without any warnin' whatsoever."

Smoke glanced over to an adjacent table where Louis Longmont sat, smoking a cigar and drinking brandy out of a large crystal snifter. The gambler had a slight smile on his face, but Smoke noticed the rawhide thong was off his Colt and his right hand was lying on his thigh, indicating Louis was ready to step in if Pearlie needed any help.

"That about the size of it, Louis?" Smoke asked.

"Yes, Pearlie has reported the events that transpired with amazing clarity and accuracy," Louis answered. "These . . . gentlemen were being very disparaging of you, Smoke, and I was on the verge of asking them to depart when Cal took them to task for their remarks."

Smoke frowned as he took a pair of black gloves, padded over the knuckles, out of the back of his belt and walked toward the two trappers. "You assholes have something to say about me, you can say it to my face instead of picking on someone half your size."

One of the men stuck out his chest and pulled up his pants, his expression belligerent. "We got a right to our opinion, Jensen. We was jest sayin' what we heared, that's all. Ain't that right, Asa?"

"Jesse's right," said the one called Asa. "It was jest a friendly little fracas. Weren't no need to git pistols involved."

Smoke shook his head. "No such thing as a friendly fight, mister. Fighting is deadly serious, especially when your opponent is only a boy."

"Well, he shouldn't oughta have called me a liar," Jesse said. "I don't let nobody, boy nor man, talk to me like that."

Smoke smiled. "Oh, is that so? Well, I don't only think you are a liar, but I think you stink. I could smell your rotten carcass from across the street."

The two men looked nervously at Pearlie and his twin Colts. "You wouldn't dare to talk at me like that if'n you didn't have those six-shooters backin' yore play," Jesse mumbled.

"Pearlie, holster your weapons," Smoke said without looking at him as he pulled his gloves on tight. "I'm going to teach these ignorant bastards a lesson in manners."

Jesse grinned and suddenly swung a meaty fist in a roundhouse right cross at Smoke's head, trying to surprise him. The mountain man ducked easily under the punch and stabbed a quick right jab square into the man's nose, flattening it and spreading it all over his face. The trapper grunted in pain as his head snapped back, and Smoke kicked sideways into his knee, snapping it inward where it hung for a moment at an awkward angle until the man fell over screaming.

Asa growled and rushed forward, wrapping his huge arms around Smoke's chest in a bear hug. He squeezed until his face turned red, but Smoke flexed his muscles and just smiled at the straining man. After a moment, Smoke head-butted Asa in the face, splitting his nose in two and breaking it with a loud crack.

As Asa let go of Smoke and grabbed at his ruined face, Smoke drew back and hit him in the stomach with all his might, lifting all two hundred pounds of the man off his feet and slamming him back against the bar, where he leaned bent over, moaning and gasping for breath. Smoke stepped up and threw a left cross, catching the man in the temple and knocking his lights out. He crumpled in a heap on the saloon floor, dead to the world.

Smoke turned in time to see the other trapper struggle to his feet, his face screwed up in rage and his fists doubled at his sides. "I'm gonna kill you, Jensen," Jesse snarled.

"I don't think so," Smoke said and planted the toe of his boot in Jesse's mouth, shattering his teeth and knocking him unconscious.

Smoke bent, took a gold double-eagle coin from the trapper's poke, and handed it to Louis. "This should pay for their drinks and any damage they caused."

Louis smiled and pocketed the coin. He glanced at the bartender. "Jake, drag this trash out back and pile it in the alley, will you? And open the windows and let some of their stench out, please. I'm beginning to feel a bit nauseated at the odor."

Smoke looked up as Cal stumbled in, holding a bandanna to his face. "Where are they? I want another shot at that big bastard."

Monte Carson laughed. "You're just a tad late, son. Smoke's already taken care of that for you."

Smoke put his arm around Cal's shoulder and led him to a table. "Come on, Cal, let's have that breakfast you came here for."

Louis clapped his hands. "Andre, fresh coffee and buns for our guests, then burn five steaks and scramble some hens' eggs with chopped tomatoes and onions. These men look hungry."

As Cal and Pearlie and Monte Carson sat at their table, Smoke walked over to shake Louis's hand. "Thanks for the backup, partner, I appreciate it."

"You noticed?" Louis answered as he put the rawhide hammer thong back on his Colt.

"Even if I hadn't, I always know you've got my back, *compadre.*"

Louis nodded and raised his brandy glass in a salute to his friend of many years. The gambler owned this saloon and considered it his home. It was where he plied his trade, which he called teaching amateurs the laws of chance.

Louis was a lean, hawk-faced man, with strong, slender hands and long fingers, nails carefully manicured, hands clean. He had jet-black hair and a black pencil-thin moustache. He was, as usual, dressed in a black suit, with white shirt and dark ascot—something he'd picked up on a trip to England some years back. He wore low-heeled boots, and a pistol hung in tied-down leather on his right side. It was not for show, for Louis was snake-quick with a short gun, and was a feared, deadly gunhand when pushed.

Louis was not an evil man. He had never hired his gun out for money. And while he could make a deck of cards do almost anything, he did not cheat at poker. He did not have to cheat. He was possessed of a phenomenal memory, could tell you the odds of filling any type of poker hand, and was one of the first to use the new method of card counting.

He was just past forty years of age. He had come to the West as a boy, arriving with his parents from Louisiana. His parents had died in a shantytown fire, leaving the boy to cope as best he could.

He had coped quite well, plying his innate intelligence and willingness to take a chance into a fortune. He owned a large ranch up in Wyoming Territory, several businesses in San Francisco, and a hefty chunk of a railroad.

Though it was a mystery to many why Longmont stayed with the hard life he had chosen, Smoke thought he understood. Once, Louis had said to him, "Smoke, I would miss my life every bit as much as you would miss the dry-mouthed moment before the draw, the challenge of facing and besting those miscreants who would kill you or others, and the so-called loneliness of the owlhoot trail."

Sometimes Louis joked that he would like to draw against Smoke someday, just to see who was faster. Smoke allowed as how it would be close, but that he would win. "You see, Louis, you're just too civilized," he had told him on many occasions. "Your mind is distracted by visions of operas, fine foods and wines, and the odds of your winning the match. Also, your fatal flaw is that you can almost always see the good in the lowest creatures God ever made, and you refuse to believe that anyone is pure evil and without hope of redemption."

When Louis laughed at this description of himself, Smoke would continue. "Me, on the other hand, when some snake-scum draws down on me and wants to dance, the only thing I have on my mind is teaching him that when you dance, someone has to pay the band. My mind is clear and focused on only one problem, how to put that stump-sucker across his horse toes down."

Smoke tipped his hat and went back to join his friends at their table, where Pearlie was telling Cal how Smoke had whipped the two trappers.

5

Nate Champion tugged gently at the reins of his big dun stallion and stopped in the shade of a copse of piñon trees. He pulled a pair of battered binoculars out of his saddlebags and began to look over the herd of milling cattle spread out in the valley below him.

Sure enough, he didn't have to search for very long before he found what he was looking for. There, mixed in with the other cattle, were over fifty of Nate's own beeves.

He put the binoculars back in the saddlebag, pulled out his old Winchester Model 1873, and levered a round into the chamber. He shoved the carbine in the saddle boot and then flipped open the loading gate on his Colt Army and checked his loads. He knew Shonsey was going to be plenty pissed when he braced him about the cattle, and he wanted to be ready for anything.

Nearing thirty years of age, Nate Champion had been born in Round Rock, Texas, and was considered a top cowboy by all who knew him. With a fierce moustache, he was a solid, good-looking man, noted for his honesty and forthrightness. He had many friends among the punchers and small ranchers in northern Wyoming.

Until he was blacklisted six months ago by the Wyoming Stock Growers Association for starting his own small herd, he'd been the kind of cowboy every ranch owner wanted. Now that he was persona non grata to the big ranchers of the Association, it was a different story. Nate was not a man they could scare. He was handy with a gun and was never far from his weapons.

He didn't plan to back down from Shonsey, or any of the other cattle barons for that matter, no matter how many hired guns they had riding for their brands.

Nate slipped his Colt in his holster, but left the rawhide hammer thong off, and rode down the slope of the hill toward the group of men tending Shonsey's herd below.

Johnny Garfield slapped the rump of a cantankerous steer with the end of his lariat, and had leaned to the side to spit tobacco juice when he noticed Nate Champion riding over.

He settled back against the cantle of his saddle and waited to see what Champion had to say.

"Howdy, Johnny," Nate said as he pulled his horse to a stop in front of the wrangler.

Garfield spat again, then nodded. "Howdy, Nate. What're you doin' over here? I thought your spread was 'bout ten mile the other side of the crick over there."

Nate crossed his leg over his saddle horn, pulled a bag of Bull Durham tobacco out of his shirt pocket, and began to build a cigarette.

He struck a lucifer on the hammer of his Colt and lighted the butt, then left it in the corner of his mouth as he spoke, the smoke trailing up to make his eyes squint.

"Well, Johnny, it's true my spread's over to the east, but damned if about a fourth of my beeves aren't right here with yours."

Garfield narrowed his eyes, shifting his butt in his saddle just a bit. "You don't say?"

He looked out over the herd for a few moments, then nodded and spat again. "Now that you mention it, I did see some beeves that didn't look familiar to me this mornin'. I just put it down to some mavericks having drifted into the herd during the night."

Nate took a deep drag of the cigarette and tilted his head to let the smoke out. "Yeah, Johnny, 'cept mavericks don't generally have brands on 'em, and these do . . . my brand."

"I can see that, Nate, now that you point it out."

"How about I ride on in there and cut my cattle out of yours, and then I'll drive 'em back to my place?"

Garfield's face screwed up in a frown. "I don't know, Nate. Ever since you been blacklisted by the Association, Mr. Shonsey been talkin' bad 'bout you something fierce."

Garfield hesitated, glancing at Nate out of the corner of his eyes, as if afraid to look him in the face. "Matter of fact, he's kind'a spreadin' the word that you were black-listed for rustlin' cattle."

"That so?" said Nate, his lips and jaws tight.

"Yeah. He said that's how you managed to put your herd together, by takin' mavericks off the range that belong to the Association and puttin' your brand on 'em."

Nate took a deep breath, trying to control his temper, which typically had a short fuse anyway.

"Johnny, how long you been punching cows here in Wyoming?"

"'Bout five year, why?"

"Then you know that most of the land around here is owned by the government, and mavericks have always belonged to whoever took the trouble to round 'em up and brand 'em. Just because the Stock Growers Association bribed the legislature to write a nonsense law sayin' they belonged to the Association don't make it so."

"That may be, Nate, but it's still the law."

Garfield pointed at Nate's clothes. "Mr. Shonsey says that sash you're wearin' is the mark of your gang of rustlers, even says it's called the Red Sash Gang."

Nate, who was something of a "dude" in his dress, was wearing black corduroy pants, a red and black check-ered flannel shirt, and a red sash tied around his waist.

He laughed and shook his head. "Now I've heard everything. Hell, half the cowboys I know wear these things, Johnny," he said, pointing to his sash. "They get 'em from the Sears and Roebuck catalog and wear 'em 'cause the ladies seem to like 'em."

Garfield shifted his cud of tobacco from one cheek to the other. "Well, anyways, Mr. Shonsey won't like it much if I let you cut some beeves outta his herd." He paused a moment before adding, "I'll tell you what, Nate. We're gonna be movin' this herd tomorrow, an' I'll have the boys cut any beeves with the KC brand on 'em out and leave 'em here for you. How's that?"

Nate shrugged. "I'll take your word on it, Johnny, an' I'll be back just after dawn with a few of my men to pick 'em up."

The next morning, Mike Shonsey was out on the range with his men when Garfield and the others culled Champion's beeves from his herd. After Garfield and the other drovers drove Shonsey's cattle over the hill toward another range to feed, Shonsey turned to the two men with him.

"Bob, I want you and Curly to scatter those cattle all over the range."

Bob Cartwright looked at his boss in disbelief. "But Mr. Shonsey, those are Nate Champion's cattle. If'n we do that, it'll take him two days to round 'em up."

Shonsey gave him a hard look. "Bob, I don't recall askin' your advice on the matter. I'm foreman of this spread, an' long as you ride for this brand you'll do what I say. Is that clear?"

"Yes, sir, Mr. Shonsey," Bob replied.

He pulled his hat down tight, pulled his pistol out, and put the spurs to his mount. He and Curly charged toward the small group of cattle, then fired into the air and whooped and hollered, causing the grazing cattle to stampede off in several directions.

Ten minutes later, as Shonsey and Bob and Curly were

riding toward Shonsey's herd, Nate Champion came riding after them, leaning over his saddle and raising a cloud of dust.

Shonsey pulled his mount to a stop and waited. He looked at the two men with him. "All right, boys, here he comes, and he looks madder than a wet hen."

Nate pulled his horse to a stop next to Shonsey's.

"Why'd you scatter my beeves, Shonsey?" he asked, his face red as a beet.

"Because they were grazing on my land, eating feed that belongs to my cattle, that's why."

"This ain't your land, asshole," Nate said, his voice low and hard. "This is free range, in case you've forgotten, and it's open to anybody's cattle that wants to use it."

Shonsey gave a nasty grin. "Well, Champion, seein' as how there's three of us an' only one of you, just what do you intend to do about it?"

Nate cut his eyes to the two men with Shonsey. He straightened in his saddle and let his hand hang near his Colt.

"You boys want some of this?" he asked, his eyes cold as the water in the nearby stream.

Bob and Curly looked at each other, then at Shonsey, their eyes wide. They both knew Champion's reputation as a fast gun.

"We ride for Mr. Shonsey, Nate, but he don't pay us for no gunplay. This is between you and him."

Nate glanced back at Shonsey. "Looks like it's you and me, Mike. You want to make your play?"

Shonsey's face began to gleam with sweat, though the temperature was barely above freezing. "Now wait a minute, Champion. I don't intend to draw on you," Shonsey said, his voice rising into a whine. "You can't shoot a man down in cold blood over a few head of cattle."

Nate shook his head, his expression disgusted at Shonsey's cowardice. "No, you're right, Mike. I can't shoot a coward who won't back his play."

Without another word, Nate swung a backhanded

blow and knocked Shonsey out of his saddle, to land on his butt on the frozen ground with a loud grunt.

Nate swung out of his saddle and walked over to stand before the man on the ground.

"Get up, you spineless cow flop," he said.

Shonsey rubbed his reddening jaw and shook his head. "I'm not gonna fight you, Champion."

Nate, who stood a couple of inches over six feet and had broad shoulders and wiry muscles from years riding the range, reached down and grabbed Shonsey by the front of his shirt, lifting the man to his feet as if he were a child.

He held his shirt with his left hand and began to slap his face with his right, back and forth, snapping his head with each blow.

Finally, Shonsey tried to fight back, swinging a wild punch at Nate's head. Nate ducked the blow, twisted his shoulder to the side, and swung with all his might, catching Shonsey flush in the face with a fist hardened by years of hard work.

Shonsey's nose cracked with a noise like a rifle shot, flattening over his face, sending blood and teeth flying in the chilly air. His eyes crossed and he dropped like a stone to the ground, unconscious.

Nate rubbed his fist, his first two knuckles already beginning to swell. Then he bent, picked Shonsey up, and threw him face-down across his saddle.

"Take this piece of crap back to his ranch and get him doctored up," Nate said to Bob and Curly.

As he stepped into his saddle, he pointed a finger at the two punchers. "And spread the word that the next time any of your men touch or mess with any of my beeves, I'll kill 'em."

He touched the brim of his hat. "If any of your men have a problem with that, you know where to find me."

After Nate rode off, Bob glanced down at Shonsey where he lay over the saddle.

"Jesus, Curly. Look at his face. It looks like he's been kicked by a mule."

Curly watched Nate's back as he rode off to round up his strays. "You know, Bob, I think I may just mosey on down south an' see if there's any work down there. Mr. Shonsey don't pay me enough for this. That Champion's meaner'n a two-peckered billy goat, an' I don't want to be on the receiving end of that fist of his."

Bob nodded. "Yeah, an' unless I miss my guess, things around here are gonna get a whole lot worse 'fore they get better."

6

Nate Champion pulled his dun to a halt on a ridge overlooking a wide, flat range that stretched as far as the eye could see.

He nodded at his friend, George "Flat Nose" Curry, sitting on a horse next to him.

"George, see those beeves down there?"

Curry inclined his head before leaning to the side to spit a wad of Bull Durham onto the ground. "Yep."

"Those are the cattle Bob Tilsdale stole from my herd the other day."

Curry pursed his lips. "Let me get this straight, Nate. Tilsdale put two thousand cattle onto a range where you was already grazing your herd, then had the balls when you braced him about it to drive his cattle and yours over to this range?"

"That's about the size of it," Nate answered.

"That sumbitch is too dumb to know who he's messin' with, ain't he?"

Nate grinned. "Tell me, George, what would your old pals in the Wild Bunch or the Hole in the Wall Gang do about something like that?"

Curry—who wore two pistols on his belt, butt first for cross-handed draws, and a double bandolier of Winchester rifle shells across his chest—pulled his rifle out of its saddle boot and levered a shell into the chamber.

"They'd probably do what we're gonna do in a few minutes."

Nate glanced back over his shoulder at the twelve hardcases riding with him and Curry.

"Load 'em up six and six, boys," he called as he pulled a Colt from his holster.

A few minutes later, the fourteen men put the spurs to their horses and charged down the hill in a cloud of dust toward the cattle milling below.

Robert Tilsdale's men minding the herd looked up and saw them coming. Joshua Barlow, Tilsdale's foreman, almost swallowed his chewing tobacco when he saw the group of heavily armed men riding down on him.

He cupped his hands around his mouth and shouted, "Rustlers comin'! Draw your guns, boys!"

The other six men riding herd glanced at each other, then pulled their reins around and headed their horses away from the fracas, wanting no part of gunplay to save a few cattle that didn't belong to them.

Barlow, seeing he was standing alone against the men, held up his hands as Nate and his group approached.

He relaxed a little when he saw it was Nate Champion riding down on him.

"Howdy, Nate," he said as the gang reined to a halt next to him.

"Howdy, Josh," Nate replied, holstering his pistol and signaling his men to put their guns away.

"What're you boys doin' way out here this mornin'?" Barlow asked, breathing a bit easier with all the firearms out of sight.

"We come to get my beeves, Josh."

"The ones your boss stole from Nate the other day," Curry added, his heavily bearded face screwed up in a scowl.

Barlow shook his head, but couldn't bring himself to look Nate in the eyes. "We didn't mean to take your cattle, Nate. But Mr. Tilsdale wouldn't give us time to cut them outta the herd. He said to drive 'em all over here and he'd make sure you got yours back later."

"That's bullshit, an' you know it, Josh," Nate said angrily. "You know as well as I do he never intended to give me my cattle back."

Barlow shrugged. "Hey, Nate. I'm just a hired hand, doin' what I'm told. I don't never mix in politics nor other people's business."

"Good," Curry said, "then you can just ride on over to that stand of trees over yonder and sit your butt down and take a little siesta while we get Nate's beeves."

Barlow hesitated just a moment, as if weighing his chances against Curry, before he nodded and jerked his horse's head around to ride away.

"Mr. Tilsdale ain't gonna like this very much, Nate," he said over his shoulder.

"Good," Nate growled, "I hope he chokes on it."

Nate turned to the others. "Okay, boys, round 'em up and move 'em out."

Billy Black, a youngster of no more than sixteen years, yelled back, "You want us to just take the ones with your brand on 'em, or you want us to get the calves too?"

Nate pursed his lips, thinking for a moment, then called back, "Take everything with my brand on it, an' everything without any brand on it, and scatter the rest all over the range."

Curry grinned. "We're gonna get a lot of calves that belong to Tilsdale then."

"Maybe it'll teach him not to mess with the other small ranchers around here," Nate said. "Especially ones that belong to the Northern Wyoming Farmers and Stock Growers Association."

"You a man after my own heart, Nate, tough as nails and hard as steel."

Nate spurred his horse. "Only way to be and still survive out here, George."

Early the next morning, Nate was having coffee and pan dulce in his cabin with an old friend, Ross Gilbertson.

"How do you feel about the men electing you president of the Northern Wyoming Farmers and Stock Growers Association the other night, Nate?"

Nate smirked. "Other than the fact that it's kind'a like hanging a bull's-eye on my shirt, I guess it's all right."

Gilbertson frowned. "You don't really think the other cattlemen's association will try and do anything against you, do you?"

"I think it's only a matter of time, Ross. The big ranchers can't allow us little ranchers and independents to organize. Otherwise they won't have any power over the cattle business in Wyoming."

"What do you mean?"

"Well, for instance, if enough of us gather together, we can get the legislature to repeal the maverick law, an' that's where the WSGA gets the money to finance their stock detectives and hire the bounty hunters to shoot down innocent ranchers."

Gilbertson was about to reply, when suddenly the door crashed open, splinted by a man wielding a sledgehammer.

As Nate slapped at his thigh, he realized his pistol was hanging on a post next to the wall, behind his head. He was unarmed.

Three men, wearing bandannas over their faces, stormed into the room, pistols in their hands.

"Put 'em up," one of the men called, aiming his gun at Nate.

Nate and Gilbertson raised their hands.

"What do you men want here?" Nate asked, seemingly cool as a cucumber under the circumstances. "I don't have no money nor valuables for you to rob."

"We ain't robbers, Champion. We came to drill you through and through for all the rustlin' you been doin' of the Association's stock."

Nate nodded slowly, staring at what he could see of the men's faces over their kerchiefs. He saw one of the men had a crooked scar over his right eye, running through his eyebrow, and knew he was Joe Elliot, a stock detective for the Association.

"I ain't no rustler, an' you boys know it."

One of the men with Elliot turned to the detective. "What 'bout this other feller? They didn't say nothin' 'bout killin' anybody else."

"Shut up, you idiot!" Elliot said.

He pointed his pistol at Gilbertson. "Who might you be, mister? You a rustler like your friend here?"

"My name is Ross Gilbertson, and neither one of us is rustlers."

"Are you a rancher?" the third man, who had remained silent until now, asked.

Gilbertson shook his head. "No, I'm not. I own a general store over in Buffalo. Me and Nate been friends since we was pups."

"Well," the man Nate recognized as Elliot said, cocking his pistol, "you're gonna die with him anyway."

The third man put his hand on Elliot's arm. "Just a minute. We ain't got no call to be killing innocent shopkeepers."

While Elliot was distracted, Nate pretended to yawn and stretch, extending his hands back over his head toward the post holding his holster and Colt.

When Elliot turned his eyes to the third man, Nate grabbed his pistol and drew and cocked in one fluid motion. He swung the Colt Army down and pulled the trigger, his slug taking the second man in the upper chest, next to his shoulder and spinning him around.

When Nate's gun exploded, blowing smoke and flame out into the room, the other two intruders ducked and dove through a door into another room in the cabin, just as Nate fired two more rounds, chipping wood from the door frame.

Gilbertson dove to the floor, while Nate flipped the table over and the two friends got behind it, using it as partial cover.

Elliot stuck his head around the door and fired into the room, drilling holes in the thin wood of the table.

Nate didn't bother to duck, but aimed and shot back,

his slug hitting Elliot in the forehead, burning a shallow furrow along his scalp and piercing his hat.

"Goddamn," he shouted, grabbing his head and ducking back out of sight, "I'm hit, Frank, I'm hit!"

"Come on," the third man yelled, "let's get out of here."

He stuck his hand around the corner of the door without looking and fired off three or four shots.

While Nate hid behind the table, the two men scrambled on hands and knees into the front room, all three, including the wounded man, ran out the front door.

When the door slammed, Nate bounded up and ran out the side door, aiming and firing as fast as he could at the retreating figures as they jumped into their saddles and rode away.

He saw Elliot grab at his shoulder as if one of his shots had hit home, but he couldn't be certain just how bad the man had been wounded.

"Holy Mary, Mother of Christ!" Gilbertson said as he walked out of the cabin, unconsciously crossing himself as he spoke. "That was a close call, Nate."

"Yeah, it was," Nate replied.

"You think that was men from the WSGA come to kill you?"

"I know it was, Ross. The man doing most of the talking was Joe Elliot, one of the men the Association hired as so-called stock detectives. Hired killers is more like it."

"What about the other two?"

Nate wagged his head.

"I don't know. I didn't recognize either one of them."

"Cowardly bastards," Gilbertson said, "bustin' in on a man's house, wearing masks like common stage robbers. They ought to be hanged."

"Yeah, they should, but you and I both know with the power of the WSGA behind them, there's slim chance anything will ever come of it."

"What are you gonna do now, Nate?"

"First off, I'm going into Buffalo and file a formal complaint with Sheriff Red Angus. He's pretty much on our side in this range war, but even his hands are tied, especially since we can't testify we saw any faces on the men."

"Then what's gonna happen?"

"Then, I'm going to call for a roundup by our Association, and we're gonna start rounding up mavericks on our own, and we'll just see what the WSGA tries to do about it."

7

Big Rock, Colorado

Smoke boarded the train, stuffed his valise under his seat, and leaned out the window to wave good-bye to his friends on the platform.

"Ride with your guns loose," Pearlie said.

"Keep 'em loaded up six an' six," Cal added as he tipped his hat.

Smoke smiled to himself, thinking, *It's hell getting old. Everyone starts worrying about your hide all of a sudden like you can't take care of yourself.*

With a rush of steam and a series of small jerks, the train pulled out of Big Rock, heading north, straight into the face of a chilly wind blowing southward from the arctic regions of Canada.

Smoke shivered and pulled his coat tight. The railroad passenger cars were unheated, and the temperature in the drafty coach was barely above freezing. He cracked his window, pulled a long stogie out of his pocket, and sat back in his seat to relax and enjoy his journey northward. As ice crystals formed on the window and wind-driven sleet and snow pounded the glass, he was grateful he wasn't trying to make the trip on horseback.

After lighting his cigar, he took out a small map and

used his finger to trace his path to where he'd heard the Nez Percé had been sighted.

It was about 125 miles straight north from Big Rock to Casper, Wyoming, and then another eighty miles or so up to Buffalo, where the Indians were supposed to be camped. His trip would take him through Boulder, cut back south to Denver, then head north to Greely. From there, it was a short hop to Cheyenne and then Laramie. From Laramie, the Union Pacific ran north to Medicine Bow and finally Casper, where he would change trains for a ride up into the Big Horn Mountains and Buffalo on a spur line.

He knew he was traveling in the worst of the winter weather, and expected many delays as tracks would have to be cleared of snowdrifts at times, especially in the higher elevations of the many mountain passes they were to traverse.

He wondered briefly if he was, as Sally had hinted, being foolish to head north this time of year. Sally, an ex-schoolteacher, was exceptionally smart, and Smoke had found she was not often wrong about such things. No matter. He loved Sally deeply and had never regretted giving up his traveling ways to marry her and settle down. But lately, he had been feeling hemmed in by civilization, crushed by the weight of humanity all around him.

Since his teen years, when he had lived with Preacher, Smoke had loved the high lonesome of the mountains. He was more used to going months without seeing another human being than being in their company on a daily basis.

Old Hoss, he thought, *you just need to get up into the high country for a while, stretch your legs, and get away from people before you explode like dynamite too close to a campfire.* He had a feeling Sally understood more of his motives than she let on, but loved him enough to give him free rein when he felt he needed it. Not many women were that understanding or insightful about their mates.

He flipped his cigar out the window, pulled his hat down over his face, stuck his hands in his coat pockets, and settled back for a nap as the iron horse pulled him through the blizzards toward a much-needed adventure in the mountains.

The trip was uneventful until he reached Denver, where the conductor announced there would be a lay-over due to the heaviness of the snowfall. The passengers were told the train would leave at dawn with a snowplow engine preceding them through the mountain passes north of the town.

Smoke took his valise and walked two blocks down the main street to check into the Alhambra Hotel. He had need of a hot bath to get the cinders and ash from the engine off his clothes and out of his hair and skin after traveling all day.

Once in his room, he unpacked fresh clothes and took them, his money belt holding two thousand dollars in greenbacks, and his Colt Navy pistol with him to the room where the hotel had several tubs set up and an attendant keeping water heated on a wood-burning stove.

Smoke set his clothes, gun, and the money belt on a chair next to the tub, and eased down into the steaming, soapy water with a sigh of relief. He lay back and let the heat soak some of the soreness out of his muscles.

Smoke smiled as he thought how ironic it was that he could ride horseback for days at a time and never get stiff or sore, but twelve hours in a rocking and rolling passenger car and he felt like someone had beaten him with ax handles.

After ten minutes, the young boy acting as attendant poured more hot water off the stove into Smoke's tub. Smoke opened sleepy eyes to thank him, and heard foot-steps approaching outside the door. He realized with a start he could also hear the jangle of spurs on boots. *Damn,* he thought, *men coming for a bath seldom wear their spurs.* He sat up a little in the bathtub and reached over to pick up his Colt and slip it under the suds, resting it on his knee just above the water while he waited.

Seconds later, the door opened and three rough-looking men stepped into the room. They were all wearing trail clothes that looked and smelled as if they hadn't been washed for weeks.

The attendant muttered, "Uh-oh," as his face paled at the sight of the men.

Smoke gave a lazy smile. "Come in, gentlemen. The water is hot and soapy and just right to take that stink of the trail off you."

The man in the middle, who seemed to be the leader of the trio, narrowed his eyes and glared at Smoke. He took a few steps forward and leaned over to pick through Smoke's clothes, cutting his eyes at his friends when he fingered the money belt. "Say, boys, look what we got here. A bunch of fancy city duds and a big ole thick money belt."

One of his friends said with a sneer, "Maybe you ought'a ask real polite-like if the gent soakin' over there minds you pawin' through his stuff, Carl."

"Yeah, that's a good idee, Johnny," Carl answered. "Say, mister, you don't have any objection to my lookin' at your clothes, do you?"

Smoke's smile faded and his eyes grew cold as ice. Evidently the men were too stupid to notice Smoke's empty holster lying on the floor next to the chair. "As a matter of fact I do mind. Your hands are filthy and you stink. Please put my things down and leave the room."

"And what if I don't?"

"Then I'll just have to get out of my nice hot bath and make you, and I promise you won't like that one bit," Smoke replied, his voice low and hard.

Carl, too dumb to notice the warning signs, ignored him and opened the belt, his eyes widening at the sight of thick stacks of bills lying inside. "Jesus," he said, "Johnny, Sam, come here and take a look at what the dude is carryin'."

As the two men rushed over, the attendant tried to sneak out the door behind them. Carl drew his pistol and pointed it at the young man. "Hold on there, ace. You ain't goin' anywheres, just stay put where you are."

Johnny reached down and fingered the greenbacks,

his mouth hanging open in wonderment. "Jeez, Carl, I ain't never seen so much money in one place at a time!"

Smoke shifted in the water, steam rising from his bare shoulders. "Gentlemen, I worked hard for that stake. Do you really think I'm going to sit here and let pond scum like you take it from me?"

Carl stepped back, still holding the belt in one hand and his pistol in the other. Johnny and Sam drew their Colts and waved the attendant over to stand next to the tub with Smoke in it.

"Well, Mr. City Dude," Carl snarled, "I don't see you have much choice in the matter. I think we'll just tie you and the boy up and head on out of town. By the time somebody finds you, we'll be long gone."

Smoke grinned, but the smile didn't reach his eyes. "I want you to think on it real hard, Carl. Is that money worth dying for? 'cause I'm giving you one last chance to put it down and walk out of here. Otherwise I'll see that you're carried out on a board."

The words were spoken softly but rang with tempered steel.

Carl threw back his head and laughed, along with Johnny and Sam. Carl eared back the hammer on his Colt. "Maybe I won't tie you up after all, pilgrim. Maybe I'll just drill you instead."

Smoke sighed and glanced at the attendant. "Boy, you can see they just don't give me any option."

Without another word, he let the hammer down on his Navy and it exploded, blowing suds and gunsmoke out of the tub all over the men standing in front of him. His first slug took Carl high in the forehead, blowing his scalp and half his head off and throwing him backward to land sprawled on his back, a pool of blood forming under his ruined skull.

Before Johnny or Sam could react, Smoke fired twice more, the shots sounding like dynamite in the confined room. One bullet punched a hole in Johnny's chest; the other tore through Sam's neck, almost tearing his head off. Johnny bounced on the floor, holding his hands over the hole in his chest, his eyes hurt and surprised at the turn of events. He groaned once, then died quietly, bloody froth on his lips.

Sam was dead before he hit the floor.

The attendant stood there, his hands over his mouth, his eyes wide and tearing from the acrid gun smoke in the room. He stared at the dead men for a moment, then looked at Smoke, his face paling as if he might faint.

Smoke carefully wiped his pistol on a towel before placing it gently on his clothes. Then he sighed and lay back in the water.

"Boy, open that window over there and let some of the smoke out of the room. Then get me some more hot water. All this jawing has let my bath cool down." He laid his head back and closed his eyes, relaxing again, as if nothing had happened.

As the smoke whirled out the open window and the room began to clear, a man wearing a sheriff's star on his vest came running into the room, his gun in his hand. "What the hell's goin' on in here?" he shouted.

A younger man, carrying a shotgun and sweating in spite of the cold, ran into the sheriff's back as he stopped short just inside the doorway, staring at the carnage lying around him. The sheriff glared at Smoke, turning his pistol to point at him. "Are you responsible for this, mister?"

Smoke opened his eyes and sat up a little to look over the edge of the tub, as if noticing the dead bodies for the first time.

After a moment, he shrugged and lay back in the water, his expression calm. "No, Sheriff, those men are. They started the dance, and I just reminded them someone had to pay the band. As you can see, it ended up being them."

The attendant nodded his head rapidly. "That's right, Sheriff Thomas. This man was just sittin' there in his bath when those three tried to rob him of his money. Said they was gonna tie us up and take it all."

The sheriff walked over to stand before Smoke, his pistol still pointing at his chest.

"What's your name, mister?"

"Smoke. Smoke Jensen."

The sheriff took a step back, his mouth open. "*The* Smoke Jensen?"

Smoke smiled. "I wasn't aware there was more than one. And Sheriff, would you mind pointing that hogleg away. I get a mite nervous when someone aims a gun at me."

Thomas hastily holstered his pistol. "Yes, sir, Mr. Jensen."

He looked over his shoulder at his deputy. "Dewey, git somebody in here to clean up this mess so Mr. Jensen can finish his bath."

Dewey glanced at Smoke, his mouth open, his eyes wide, his knuckles white where they gripped his shotgun.

"Dewey, dammit, git a move on!" the sheriff shouted, finally spurring the young man into action.

Sheriff Thomas turned back to Smoke, spreading his arms wide. "I'm sorry about all this, Mr. Jensen. Ever winter we git a bunch of white trash come into town when the blizzards blow. It's hard to keep a handle on things when the town's full like this."

"No problem, Sheriff Thomas."

"Uh, Mr. Jensen," the sheriff asked, rubbing his chin and staring at Smoke from under bushy eyebrows, "you plannin' on stayin' in town long?"

Smoke grinned. He knew his presence in their towns usually made lawmen nervous, because there always seemed to be a surplus of gunplay and dead bodies wherever he went. Such was the price of fame, of being known as the deadliest gunfighter in the West. Someone was always trying to build a reputation on Smoke's back.

"Just long enough to get a steak in the dining room and grab a few hours shut-eye until the train to Wyoming pulls out in the morning, Sheriff. I'd appreciate it if you'd keep the fact that I'm here quiet until then. Otherwise you're liable to have more bodies to clean up."

The sheriff said to the attendant, "Jeremiah, go tell

the cook to get Mr. Jensen's steak ready so's he don't have to wait in the dining room too long."

"Tell him to just cook it long enough so it doesn't crawl off the plate, and it'll be just fine," Smoke told the boy as he stood to get out of the tub.

The sheriff's eyes widened at the sight of Smoke's body. He stood six feet two inches tall, with broad shoulders and huge, heavily muscled arms. His waist was lean and his ash-blond hair was cut short and neat. The sheriff couldn't help but notice the many scars covering Smoke's skin, mementos of hundreds of fights with guns, knives, and fists.

The sheriff shook his head. "You shore look like you been to the river and back again, Mr. Jensen."

Smoke glanced down at the scars as he pulled on his pants. "Just one of the many prices of fame, Sheriff, just one."

As he tucked in his shirt, Smoke asked Thomas, "Are there any Indians in town?"

The sheriff laughed. "In Denver? There are dozens, especially in the winter."

"Would you do me a favor, Sheriff Thomas? Would you ask around to see if any of them know anything about a small tribe of Nez Percé, supposed to be camping up near Buffalo in northern Wyoming?"

Thomas nodded, and said to the attendant just as he was leaving the room, "Jeremiah, after yore done talkin' to the cook 'bout Mr. Jensen's steak, head on over to the cantina at the other end of town and do what Mr. Jensen asks. If any of the braves or breeds knows anything, bring 'em on back to the hotel. You'll have to stay with 'em or they won't let 'em in to talk to him."

Smoke smiled. "Mighty obliged, Sheriff."

"Least I can do, Mr. Jensen, after you helped clean some of the trash out of my town for me."

8

Smoke was half through with his steak when the bath attendant, Jeremiah, appeared in the hotel dining room, followed by a rail-thin Indian dressed in dirty buckskin rags. From the way the brave licked his lips and eyed Smoke's plate, Smoke knew he hadn't eaten for some time.

Smoke flipped a coin to the young man and said, "Thanks, Jeremiah."

Jeremiah grinned and pocketed the money as he walked out of the hotel, his chest stuck out as if he was proud to have helped the famous gunfighter Smoke Jensen.

Smoke gestured for the Indian to take a seat next to him and called to the waiter, "Bring my friend a steak, some potatoes, and a pot of coffee."

The waiter looked flustered, glancing over his shoulder at the dining room manager, who was standing next to a table with several local men eating, giving the Indian and Smoke a hard look. "Uh, Mr. Blake don't allow no Indians in here, sir."

Smoke turned cold eyes on the boy. "He's with me. Now bring him some food, or call your boss over here and I'll deal with him myself."

The young man's face blanched, and he walked quickly over to the manager, speaking to him in low tones while looking over his shoulder at Smoke.

The manager scowled, hitched up his pants, and swaggered over to Smoke's table.

"I don't know who you think you are, mister, but this here is my hotel and I don't allow no dirty redskins to eat in it."

Smoke got slowly to his feet, towering over the shorter man by six inches, and leaned over to put his face right next to the manager's.

"My name is Smoke Jensen, Mr. Blake. I'm a paying customer, and this gentleman sitting with me is a friend of mine, and I intend to feed him whatever he wants. Have you got that?"

Blake's eyes widened and he took a step back, tilting his head to look up at Smoke. What he saw in Smoke's eyes must have convinced him that he was treading on thin ice.

"You be Smoke Jensen the gunfighter?"

"One and the same," Smoke answered, his voice flat and hard.

"Well, uh, I guess if you say he's a friend of yours . . ."

"He is. Now either get us our food, or I'll be forced to go back into the kitchen and get it myself, and you don't want that, do you?"

"No, sir. I'll see that it gets right out," Blake said, his head bobbing up and down with a fine sheen of sweat covering his face. He turned on his heels and walked quickly back into the kitchen, the back of his neck red and flushed.

Once he was gone, Smoke spoke to the man sitting next to him. "My name is Smoke Jensen."

"I am called Walking Bear."

Smoke took in the beads and markings on his buckskins. "You appear to be of the Kiowa people."

"Yes, I am Kiowa."

"You know anything about a small tribe of Nez Percé, supposed to be camped up near Buffalo?"

The Indian nodded. "There may be thirty . . . forty Nez Percé in the mountains just outside the town. Been there maybe four or five moons."

"Do you know if they have any Palouse with them?"

Walking Bear smiled, showing cracked, yellow teeth

and reddened gums, signs that spoke to Smoke of malnutrition.

"The Nez Percé always have the spotted ponies. It is their way."

After a few minutes, the waiter put a plate of steaming meat in front of Walking Bear. The hungry man bent his head and began to tear into the steak, using a knife from his belt and ignoring the fancy silverware the hotel provided.

While he ate, Smoke poured him a mug of coffee, to which Walking Bear added large helpings of sugar from the silver service on the table.

Smoke took out his map and had Walking Bear show him where the Nez Percé were camped, just north and east of the town called Buffalo. As they were talking, a pair of cowboys who'd obviously been drinking their dinner walked up to stand next to Walking Bear.

"Hey, mister," one man said to Smoke. "We don't 'preciate havin' to eat with a dirty redskin in the room."

"Yeah," the other one added, swaying on his feet as if he was about to tip over. "They smell like dog shit an' it ruins our appetite."

Walking Bear hung his head and started to get up from the table. Smoke put a hand on his shoulder and motioned for him to continue eating. Then Smoke leaned back in his seat and looked at the pair standing before him.

"You gents just go on back to your drinking. We'll be through here in a minute."

One of the men made the mistake of putting a hand on Smoke's shoulder. "Maybe you didn't hear us, dude. . . ."

Smoke grabbed the man's fingers and bent them back, driving the man to his knees with a short scream. As the other reached for his pistol, he stopped, mouth hanging open as Smoke's Navy appeared in his hand as if by magic with the barrel two inches from his face. "I heard you just fine. I just didn't think I needed to pay any attention to what a couple of cow-flop drunks had to say."

He eared back the Navy's hammer with a loud click

and pressed the barrel against the man's lips. "Now, are my friend and I going to be allowed to finish our supper in peace, or am I going to have to blow your teeth all over this room to do it?"

When the hotel manager appeared, wringing his hands and sweating at the thought of bloodshed in his establishment, Smoke said, "You'd better escort these men out of here, Mr. Blake. One of them appears to have broken some fingers and is in need of medical attention."

He narrowed his eyes and glared at the other man. "And this one may need a dentist if he doesn't shut his mouth and get on his way."

When the manager said, "Yes, sir, Mr. Jensen, I'll see to it right away," the man looking down the barrel of Smoke's Navy paled even more.

"Jensen? You be Smoke Jensen?"

Smoke nodded, his expression not changing.

"I'm awful sorry, Mr. Jensen. Me and Roy didn't mean no harm—we was just funnin' is all."

He grabbed his friend by his collar and yanked him to his feet, hustling him out of the room without looking back.

As Smoke holstered his Colt, Walking Bear began to eat again. "I have heard of Smoke Jensen, called Man Who Walks on Mountain. It is said he is friend of Kiowa."

Smoke nodded. "The Kiowa are brave warriors, men of honor."

Walking Bear used a piece of bread to sop up the last of the gravy off his plate, then stood up. "The chief of the Nez Percé is called Gray Wolf. If any braves going north, I send word Man Who Walks on Mountain is coming."

"Are there any more of your people in town?"

Walking Bear nodded. "We come in for food, but trapping not good this year. No furs to trade, so many go hungry."

Smoke took a hundred-dollar bill out of his money belt and pressed it into his hand. "Take this—it will feed your people until the spring brings the beavers out of their houses and into your traps."

"My people will sing your song around our fires."

"You're welcome, Walking Bear. Thanks for the information."

Walking Bear walked from the hotel and into the driving snow.

Smoke settled back for another cup of coffee, thinking about the spotted ponies of the Nez Percé.

He took a long cheroot out of his pocket and struck a lucifer on his boot. As he bent over the flame, he noticed a group of twenty or twenty-five men enter the hotel dining room.

A tall, broad-shouldered man, who was evidently the leader of the group, waved Blake over to them.

"My name's Tom Smith, an' me and my boys need some food. We been on that train all the way up from Texas and we haven't eaten anything worth spit in two days."

"Yes, sir, Mr. Smith," Blake said, waving his hand at a group of tables in the corner. "Tell your men to have a seat and I'll get the cook working on your food. What will you gentlemen be having?"

"Steaks for everybody, with plenty of potatoes and gravy and some sliced peaches or tomatoes if you have 'em." He hesitated a moment, then added, "An' plenty of beer, but no hard liquor 'cause we got a ways to go yet an' I don't want 'em to get too drunk to travel."

"Yes, sir, I'll get right on it."

Smoke watched the men scramble to the tables. He noticed all the men carried rifles and wore six-shooters on their belts. Most of the men he could hear talking spoke with thick Texas accents, and they were still dressed as if they were in the heat of the Texas flatlands. None of the men had coats thick enough for the Colorado winter, and several were clad only in thin shirts and worn trousers, with boots more suited for horseback than walking.

When all the available seats in the room were filled, there was one man left standing, looking around as if confused by the lack of a seat for him. He stood a shade over six feet and must have weighed at least 250 pounds, Smoke thought.

He was clad in nothing but a summer undershirt,

trousers with suspenders, and shoes without any socks. As he stood there, snow and ice melting in his hair and running down his neck to soak his shirt, Smoke waved him over.

"Looks like you need a place to light and set, partner," Smoke said, liking the good-natured smile the man had.

"Thank ye kindly, stranger," the man said, holding out his hand. "My name's Jim Dudley, an' I'm from Texas. What's yore handle?"

Smoke smiled again, thinking, *This man is obviously from the deep backwoods of Texas, and this is probably the first time he's ever traveled outside his county, much less across several states.*

"My name is Smoke Jensen, and you're welcome to sit here while you eat your supper."

Smoke was relieved when the Texan's expression didn't change at the mention of his name. *Perhaps there's still some people in the country,* he thought, *who haven't heard of my reputation.*

Dudley nodded his thanks and pulled out a chair and sat down. As he crossed his arms and shivered from the cold, Smoke poured him a large cup of still-steaming coffee from the pot on the table.

"Here you go, Jim, drink some of this. It'll help take the chill off."

Dudley took the cup and drank half of it down in one huge swallow, moaning with pleasure at the heat of the dark liquid.

"That's mighty good. Ain't had no decent coffee for three, four days now."

Smoke took a drag from his cigar and tilted smoke out of his nostrils as he asked, "What are you boys doing way up here from Texas? Don't they have enough cattle down there to keep you busy?"

Dudley grinned in his happy-go-lucky way. "Hell, yes, we got plenty of beef in Texas, but this is a different sort'a job."

"Oh?" Smoke said as he took a drink of his coffee.

"Yep. Marshal Smith over there done hired us to come

up to Wyoming and help get rid of some cattle rustlers up there."

"Marshal Smith?"

"Oh, he ain't a marshal no more, but he used to be a U.S. marshal down Texas way, an' that's where some of the boys know him from."

He leaned forward and added in a hoarse whisper, "Hell, he arrested most of 'em more'n once."

Smoke nodded and glanced over at the tables containing the men from Texas. He could see that most of them had a hard look about them, as if they had all spent some time riding the owlhoot trail. It was in their eyes, an almost-vacant look, as if there was nothing of civilization behind them.

Smoke thought Dudley seemed different from the rest of the men. "How about you, Jim? You ever been arrested by the marshal?"

"Shucks, no," Dudley replied with his ever-present grin. "I ain't no gunhawk. Me and my wife started a little spread down on the Rio Bravo, near Del Rio." His face clouded. "We didn't have enough money to buy good beeves so I got me some Mexican cattle from across the river, only they turned out to have tick fever and every one of 'em took sick and died."

The big man shrugged, his grin returning. "So I decided to join up with Marshal Smith's group an' come on up to Wyoming and earn me enough money to go back and start a new herd."

Smoke glanced at Dudley's clothes. "Well, Jim, if you plan to survive the winter up here, you're going to need some better clothes and a heavy coat."

Dudley shook his head. "I plan to buy some up in Cheyenne. That's when we'll get our first payday."

Smoke leaned over, opened his valise, and took out two thick flannel shirts and a buckskin coat, one slightly thinner than the fur-lined one he was wearing.

He handed them across the table. "Here you go, Jim. Take these until you get some pay under your belt, then buy a coat with some fur in it."

"Shucks, Mr. Jensen, I can't take yore clothes."

"Sure you can, Jim. I've got plenty more up in my hotel room, and I'm headed up to Wyoming too, so if you see me later you can give them back to me."

The waiter appeared with a tray covered with plates of food. Jim reached up and took two plates and a knife and fork.

When he saw Smoke staring at the amount of food he took, he grinned again. "My wife tole me 'fore I left to eat plenty of food to keep up my strength."

Smoke laughed. "That much ought to take you all the way to Wyoming before you need a refill."

The next morning, on the way to board the train, Smoke found a dime novel on a chair in the hotel lobby. He picked it up, glancing at the cover with a smile. It showed a man dressed all in black, with a large handlebar moustache, menacing a cowering young girl who looked terrified. Smoke stuck the penny dreadful in his pocket. Reading about the adventures of Deadwood Dick and Hurricane Nell would keep his mind occupied on the long, slow trip through mountain passes covered neck-deep in snow.

On the way to the train, he thought about when he'd met Erastus Beadle, who wrote the dime novels under the name Ned Buntline. The adventures they'd had together rivaled anything the imaginative writer ever conjured up in his mind.*

*Battle of the Mountain Man

9

Cheyenne, Wyoming

Smoke stretched and yawned, thinking he felt like he had been beaten with a barrel stave. Every muscle in his body ached from riding for two days and nights on the hard wooden bench of the railroad car.

The trip from Denver to Greely hadn't been too bad, the mountain passes having received less snow than expected, but the run from Greely to Cheyenne was horrible. The Union Pacific engine was only able to go at a snail's pace, depending on the smaller engine with the snowplow attached to clear a way through drifts as high as ten or more feet.

To make matters worse, Smoke hadn't been able to catch much shut-eye, since the group of Texans in the next car had managed to smuggle aboard a prodigious supply of whiskey, and were using the cold as an excuse to fill their bodies with as much liquor as possible. This, of course, led to the inevitable rowdiness and fighting that went with cowboys and liquor as sure as stink went with a skunk.

Several times, Smoke was on the verge of walking to the Texans' car and pounding some sense into their heads, but then he remembered how it was to be young and away from home for the first time, and was able to laugh at the antics of the youngsters as they discovered the blinding pain of hangovers caused by too much liquor and too little food.

At one point, Jim Dudley stumbled through Smoke's car, his hand over his mouth, looking for someplace to unload his swollen, bloated stomach. Without too much pleasure, Smoke pried open a window frozen stuck with two inches of ice and stuck the big man's head out into the freezing snow and sleet.

Dudley sobered up surprisingly fast, and was kind enough to thank Smoke for his efforts before heading back for more of the same with his newfound friends.

Smoke breathed a sigh of relief when the train finally pulled into Cheyenne in the dead of night. The conductor told him he would transfer to the Cheyenne and Northern Railroad in the morning to continue northward to Laramie, Medicine Bow, and finally on into Casper. There he would change trains yet again, switching to a spur line for the ride up into the Big Horn Mountains and Buffalo.

At least, he thought, he would have a chance to get a room in a hotel, preferably one other than that chosen by Tom Smith and his Texas vigilantes, and he might be able to get some much-needed sleep.

As he climbed down off the train, his valise and suitcase swung over his shoulder, Smoke saw Dudley and the other Texans exiting their car further down the tracks. Most of the men looked like death warmed over, heads hanging, some bending over to throw up in the black snow next to the railroad car, while others walked with arms around friends' shoulders for support.

He noticed Tom Smith walk up to a man dressed in Army puttees and carrying a swagger stick, and watched as the two men exchanged what seemed to be angry words, wondering briefly who the martinet was and what he had to do with the Texans.

Smoke shook his head, chuckling softly to himself. *I sure hope they have a chance to sober up before they run into those rustlers they're looking for,* he thought. *Otherwise, it'll be Texas's worst defeat since the Alamo.*

After consuming a thick steak, sauteed in fresh-cut onions and sliced tomatoes, with canned pears as a dessert, Smoke finally was able to slip between the covers of a hotel bed, his last conscious thoughts of Sally and the Sugarloaf and how much he missed them both.

While Smoke was sleeping, the Pullman containing Tom Smith and the Texans was shunted into the switching yard and joined to a train that included a baggage car, three stock cars, a flatcar bearing the three big freight wagons the cattlemen had equipped with camping gear, weapons, and ammunition, and a caboose.

Of the one hundred stockmen who had put up the money for the expedition, nineteen had chosen to go along with the gunfighters.

With their cattle detectives and a few guests, they boarded the Pullman for their first look at the Texans.

As a Union Pacific locomotive was readied for a fast run to Casper, a little range town at the foot of the Big Horn Mountains, the expedition's commander, Major Wolcott, issued his first order.

"Hurry up," he barked at the railroad superintendent. "Put us at Casper and we will do the rest."

Shortly thereafter, with a hiss of steam and the squeal of brakes being released, the train chugged off, due at Casper before dawn.

As the train pulled out of Cheyenne, the Texans were in the passenger car, bunched together at one end. Some of them were playing cards, while others dozed and tried to suffer through their headaches and stomach cramps.

At the other end of the car, Wolcott and Smith and the Wyoming stockmen were gathered, talking over their plans for the upcoming battle with the small ranchers. It was evident that while the cattlemen valued their hired gunfighters, they would never dream of admitting them to the society of gentlemen.

The Texans, for their part, showed no interest in pressing the matter, content to play cards, smoke, and try to get over their hangovers.

After a while, plans having been made, Wolcott walked two cars back to the baggage car, intent on rearranging the supplies to expedite unloading at Casper.

He was surprised when Frank Canton entered the car, since he had expressly forbidden anyone else to come there.

"Canton, I thought I told you to stay out of my business. Now get your ass back to the others and stay there, like I told you."

Canton arched an eyebrow, a slight grin tugging at the corners of his mouth.

"Kiss my ass, you sawed-off little runt," Canton replied, standing a bit straighter to emphasize the difference in their heights. He knew the major was sensitive about his shortness, and he couldn't resist a chance to rub it in, especially when the man dared to give him orders like a common soldier under his command.

Major Wolcott fairly sputtered. He wasn't used to being talked to in this disrespectful manner.

"Mr. Canton, need I remind you I am in complete command of this expedition." He squared his shoulders and stuck his chest out. "Now, you'll follow my orders or I'll have you removed from the train."

Canton stared back at Wolcott with an insolent grin on his face.

"We'll see about that, Wolcott. You won't have an expedition to command without my men and me."

He turned to go, calling back over his shoulder, "Before this is over, you'll be apologizin' to me, just wait an' see."

Canton walked rapidly back to the passenger car, grabbed Tom Smith by the arm, and took him to a far corner, away from the other cattlemen. In a quiet voice, he told Smith what had transpired in the baggage car. Smith, an old cowboy like Canton, didn't appreciate the way the Army, or its officers like Wolcott, looked down on their abilities. He slapped Canton on the back.

"I'm with you, Frank. Now, let's go on back with the Texicans and let the major stew in his own juices for a while."

He winked at Canton. "I'm sure 'fore the train pulls into Casper, he'll see the light."

During the night, Canton and Smith hung out at the end of the passenger car with the Texans, laughing and joking and playing cards with them. Every effort by Wolcott and the cattlemen to engage them in conversation or to tell them of the plans for the upcoming fight was rudely rebuffed.

Finally, at breakfast the next morning, Wolcott grandly resigned his command, and Tom Smith took charge of the Texans, while Frank Canton assumed leadership of the expedition as a whole.

While on the way to Casper, Canton had the engineer stop the train at a small junction, where he attempted to telegraph the town of Buffalo. He was delighted when the telegraph operator reported he couldn't get through. To Canton, that meant the cattlemen's allies in Johnson County had done their job and the wires to the county seat were down.

Once they arrived in Casper, the plan had been to unload their gear and pick up their horses for the 150-mile ride to Buffalo. The cattlemen had planned it this way to insure the element of surprise, rather than take the quicker and much easier ride the rest of the way by rail.

The problem was the Texans were in no shape for a long jaunt through snow-covered mountain passes. They needed some sleep and food, and most of all a couple of days without liquor.

Major Wolcott was furious when Canton hired an entire hotel in Casper and ordered the Texans to eat and then go to bed, but since he had resigned his command, there was little he could do about it.

10

Smoke carefully wrapped his money belt around his waist and pulled his buckskin shirt down over it after paying the man at the livery stable in Buffalo.

He'd bought a large, black stallion with plenty of muscles through his shoulders, figuring the horse would have to have lots of stamina to carry him through the deep snow up into the mountains toward the camp of the Nez Percé.

He'd also purchased a somewhat smaller, but still sturdy packhorse to carry what supplies he thought he might need on the trip up into the high lonesome.

Glancing up at a leaden sky filled with dark, roiling clouds, he knew he was only hours ahead of a fierce snowstorm. If he was going to make any time, he needed to get on the trail pronto.

Jake, the livery man, shook his head. "You sure you want to take off 'fore that storm hits, mister? It shore looks like it's gonna be a doozy."

Smoke stepped into the saddle of the stud and lightly touched him with his spurs, wrapping the dally rope to the packhorse around his saddle horn.

"If I wait for it to quit snowing, I'll be here until summertime. Thanks for your help, Jake. When I come back through Buffalo with the horses, I'll stop in and say hello."

Jake scratched an unruly beard. "You do that, mister. I'll be lookin' for you in a couple of months."

Smoke pointed the horse's head straight north and started up the trail, large, wet snowflakes already starting to fall. He wasn't worried overly much, having wintered in the higher elevations of Colorado since he was in his teens. He wondered briefly if there were any mountain men in these mountains, hoping if there were he might be able to find out about some old acquaintances among the breed he hadn't heard of for years.

It felt good for Smoke to be out of his traveling clothes and back into his mountain duds. He wore a buckskin shirt and buckskin trousers, tucked into knee-high moccasins such as the Apache wore. He carried a .44 Colt on his right hip, and a .44 Colt on his left hip, butt-first. A large bowie knife rested in a scabbard on his belt, and a tomahawk was stuck in his belt at the small of his back. He had a Greener ten-gauge shotgun in his left saddle boot, and a Winchester Model 1873 carbine in his right saddle boot.

The livery man, seeing his armament, had asked if Smoke was going to war. Smoke had laughed, saying, "You never know what you're going to come across in the high lonesome, Jake, and I've always found it's better to be prepared for the worst than to hope for the best."

Smoke made better time than he'd figured, and was twenty miles or more from Buffalo by the second day.

As he traversed a wide range between two mountain peaks, a man rode out of the mist and light snowfall toward him. Even though Smoke saw the man had his hands empty on the reins, he reached down and loosened the rawhide hammer thong on his Colt.

"Howdy, mister," the man called as he approached.

Smoke smiled and nodded as he pulled the big black to a halt.

"I hope I'm not trespassing on your property," Smoke

said, crossing his leg over the saddle horn to take a rest from his riding.

The man grinned and looked around at the range surrounding them. "Hell, no, you're not. This here is government property, free to anybody wants to make use of it."

Smoke took a pair of cheroots out of his shirt pocket and offered one to the cowboy.

As they lighted them, the man said, "My name's Nate Champion, an' I'm bunkin' at the old KC ranch, just over the hill yonder."

Smoke took a deep drag of the stogie, enjoying the bite of it on his tongue.

"My name's . . ." he started to reply as suddenly several gunshots rang out in rapid succession.

When one ricocheted off his saddle horn, Smoke dove to the side, landing in a snowdrift and immediately rolling to his knees, both hands filled with iron.

Nate jumped to the same side, grabbed Smoke by the shoulder, and pulled him out of the clearing behind a small group of Aspen trees next to the trail.

Two slugs tore holes in the bark of the trees as Smoke and Nate ducked.

"Can you see where the shots are coming from?" Smoke asked, peering around the side of the trees.

"Naw, not just yet," Nate answered, rearing back the hammer of his pistol.

As the snowfall slowly increased and the gathering dusk brought semi-darkness, a voice called out, "Come on out and face us like a man, Champion! You've rustled your last steer in this county!"

Smoke glanced at Nate. "You one of the rustlers I've been hearing so much about?"

Nate chuckled. "Only if rounding up stray mavericks on the open range is rustlin', which it ain't."

"Are those lawmen out there?"

"Not hardly. Most probably bounty hunters hired by the big ranchers in Cheyenne. They're offerin' a reward of five hundred dollars for each of us small ranchers they can kill, claimin' we been shootin' their beeves out on the range. They've been pickin' off one or two men 'bout near every week."

"And *have* you been shooting their cattle?"

Nate shook his head. "Not this cowboy. I run a few hundred head of my own." He hesitated, grinning sideways at Smoke. "Supplemented by the occasional stray that wonders into my herd, and I don't believe in wastin' beef. If I wanted their cattle, I'd take 'em, not shoot 'em."

A rifle shot screamed as it ricocheted off a nearby rock, and Smoke said, "I got that one sighted, saw the flash of his rifle." He pointed toward a clump of trees about two hundred yards away, barely visible in the gloom of the storm and dusk.

Their horses had wandered a few yards away, frightened by the gunfire, and neither Nate nor Smoke had rifles with them.

"Give me some covering fire, and I'll see if I can't get us some rifles off those mounts," Smoke said.

Nate looked at him. "Are you crazy? They've got us pinned down here like fish in a barrel. You'll never make it."

Smoke gave a tight grin. "You have any better ideas, Nate? The temperature's dropping pretty fast, and I don't relish sitting here freezing while we wait for them to decide what to do with us."

"You got a point, mister," Nate said, and he rose up and began to fire his pistol as fast as he could cock and pull the trigger.

Smoke leaped over the rocks in front of the trees and sprinted for their horses, zigzagging as bullets began to pock the snow by his feet and buzz by his head.

When he got to the horses, he jerked his rifle out of its saddle boot and grabbed his saddlebags with his extra ammunition.

As he stepped quickly to Nate's horse, a bullet took the animal in the neck, knocking it to its knees with a terrible scream of pain.

Smoke pulled Nate's rifle out and ran back toward the

trees, ducking as a slug nicked the back of his neck, burning a tiny furrow in the skin and stinging like hell.

He handed Nate's rifle to him and levered a shell into his own Winchester at the same time.

"Can't hardly see nothin' to aim at," Nate observed.

Smoke peered over the rock in front of them, laying his rifle across the top of it and sighting down the barrel.

"The trick is to wait for the flash as they shoot and aim a couple of inches over it. If you're quick enough, you might get lucky and nail one of them."

Nate cut his eyes at Smoke. "Course, that means you got to sit there with your head stuck out and let them fire first, don't it?"

Smoke nodded. "Yes, but they can't see us any better than we can see them, so I figure it's worth a try. If more than one fires, I'll take the first, you draw down on the second."

"All right, mister," Nate said, sounding as if he still wasn't sure about it.

Suddenly, there came a flash from the distance, followed a second or two later by the thunder of a rifle shot. Smoke's answering fire was almost immediate, his carbine exploding and slamming back into his shoulder just as another wink of light appeared to the right of the first one.

Nate, his ears ringing from the blasts, pulled his trigger, aiming just above the flash in the distance as Smoke had told him to.

A loud scream rang out, followed by a harsh grunt and a muttered curse.

"God damn you, Champion!" a voice called. "You kilt my partner, you son of a bitch!"

"Sounded like another one got hit, too," Smoke whispered to Nate. "Get ready—they'll probably try again in a minute."

They both levered shells into their rifles and settled down to wait, the increasing cold seeping through their clothes to make them shiver and ache with fatigue.

Twin flashes blinked in the darkness, and Smoke im-

mediately returned fire. He had time to hear a distant
yelp of pain, and the whine and crack of a bullet rico-
cheting back and forth between the rocks next to where
he and Nate lay, before a sudden pain in the side of his
head was followed by a flash of light and then all-encom-
passing darkness.

Nate heard the slap of the bullet striking the stranger
next to him, and saw his head snap back as he dropped
to the ground. Nate fired several quick rounds toward
where the flashes had come from, and heard a horse
nicker and then hoofbeats as someone took off.

He bent quickly and felt the stranger's head, unable
to see in the darkness, but afraid to light a lucifer and
perhaps draw fire.

There was a knot on the man's head as big as a goose
egg, but no hole, and not much blood, considering he
had taken a bullet just moments before.

When there was no further sound from across the
clearing, Nate scrambled to his right and snuck up on
the ambushers' hiding place as quietly as he could, ready
to shoot should they still be there.

He found one man lying on his stomach, still holding
a rifle, half his head blown off, face-down in a wide pool
of blood as black as tar in the darkness.

To his left was more blood, so either Nate or the
stranger had hit another of the men, evidently wound-
ing but not killing him.

He struck a lucifer, shielding it from the wind with his
hands as he rolled the dead man over. He recognized
him as one of the stock detectives, a man called Zack
Renfield, who worked for the Wyoming Stock Growers
Association. There was no horse, so the others must have
taken it with them as they fled.

He grabbed the man's rifle and took his pistol out of
his holster, and trotted back toward where the stranger's
body lay.

Striking another lucifer, he examined the man's

wounds. Imbedded in his hair, just under the skin of his scalp, Nate felt a flat, metallic object. He pried it loose and looked at it. It was a lead slug, flattened out by where it had hit the rocks before striking the man in the head.

He whistled under his breath. "You are one lucky hombre, friend," he whispered to the unconscious man. "If that rock hadn't taken the point off that bullet, you'd be a goner for sure."

Working quickly, before the cold finished the job the rifle bullet started, he managed to get the man across his saddle. He covered him as best he could with a blanket from his own gear, then took his own saddle and saddle-bags off his dead horse and put them on the stranger's packhorse. Finally, Nate took the reins of the big, black horse along with those of the pack animal, and started across the range toward his ranch house, leading both of the wounded man's horses behind him. It promised to be a tough walk in the storm, but he had no choice but to try.

He bent his head against the driving snow, hoping the frigid air would keep the man from bleeding to death, but not kill him on the journey.

He desperately wanted to save the stranger, for the man had certainly saved Nate's life. Nate knew if he had been alone when the detectives ambushed him, he'd be lying back there forked end up, as dead as Zack was now.

He owed the man a great debt, and he intended to do all in his power to pay him back, though he didn't even know his name or where he came from.

If he survived, and with a head wound as serious as this one he might not, perhaps he would tell Nate just what he was doing up here in this country during the dead of winter.

One thing was certain. He didn't look or act like a cowboy, at least not any that Nate had ever met. There was something about him, something that spoke of greater things.

11

Nate Champion made it back to the KC ranch just as the winter storm let loose with all its fury. Visibility dropped to a few feet and the temperature plummeted deep into the minus figures, while the wind howled, blowing snow and ice almost sideways in the worst storm of the year.

Nate bundled the stranger, who was still unconscious, into bed and piled on plenty of covers, before getting the horses into the barn where they'd have food and shelter from the weather.

While he heated some beef stew on the wooden stove, Nate conjectured to himself on the stranger's background and purpose in being in Johnson County.

He knew from the way the man talked that he was well educated, and his accent was different from the people from Wyoming, but didn't have the soft, slurred vowels of a man from the Deep South either.

Fellow, Nate mumbled to himself, *you got to be from out west, or somewhere in the middle of the country, Kansas or Colorado maybe.* He spooned himself a generous portion of stew onto a plate, took a handful of cold biscuits he'd made that morning, and began to eat.

He was ravenous and felt as if he hadn't eaten for days. *Battle's like that,* he thought. *It seems fighting for your life, and winning while taking another man's living away from him, stimulates all the appetites.* During the big war between the states, he'd known men who looked for whores after large battles, while others wanted to eat or drink themselves sick. He shook his head, thinking it must be a body's way of celebrating the fact that it was alive, rather than true hunger for food or whiskey or women.

Nate jumped to his feet and ran back into the bedroom when he heard loud moaning and what sounded like talking coming from there.

The man with the head wound was thrashing about on the bed, rolling his head back and forth, talking and mumbling, though still unconscious.

Nate got his coffee from the kitchen and sat across from the bed, lighting a cigarette and sitting back to listen to what the man said. Might be there'd be some clues to who he was and why he was in the area.

He heard the stranger mention the name Kirby several times, and he even seemed to be talking to a man he called Preacher, as if he were asking advice or asking for help. Nate couldn't make out all the words, and the sentences were often garbled, not making any sense. Sometimes there were shouted warnings to look out for the Indians, or sometimes, there were tender words obviously meant for the man's wife or sweetheart that made Nate blush with embarrassment at listening in.

Nate finally shook his head and got up to fix himself a place to sleep in the other bedroom. He put extra wood in the fireplace and settled in, burrowing deep under his own covers to get warm, wondering if he'd get some answers when his new friend awakened in the morning—that is, if he awakened at all. Nate had known men in the war who'd had serious head injuries that never came out of the sleep the doctors called a coma, but stayed forever in the twilight between sleep and wakefulness.

While Nate slept, the stranger tossed and turned in bed, his body feverish, his mind reeling with sleep images and dreams that were at times real as life and at other times as blurry as images seen through a thick fog. In his dreams, he was sixteen, a gangly, skinny kid tall for his age with wide shoulders that his body hadn't yet grown into. . . .

He knew his name was Kirby, and that the man riding with him was his father, but he couldn't bring his father's name to his mind. They rode westward, edging north. Several weeks had passed since they rode from the land of Kirby's birth, and already that place was fading from his mind. He had never been happy there, so he made no real effort to halt the fading of the images.

Kirby did not know how much his pa had gotten for the land and the equipment and the mules, but he knew he had gotten it in gold, and not much gold at that. His pa carried the gold in a small leather pouch around his neck with a piece of rawhide.

His pa was heavily armed: a Sharps .52-caliber rifle in a saddle boot, two Remington army revolvers in holsters around his waist, two more pistols in saddle holsters, left and right of the saddle horn. And he carried a gambler's gun behind his belt buckle, a .44-caliber, two-shot derringer. His knife was a wicked-looking, razor-sharp Arkansas Toothpick in a leather sheath on his side.

Kirby never asked why his father was so heavily armed. But he did ask, "How come them holsters around your waist ain't got no flaps on them, Pa? How come you cut them off that way?"

"So I can get the pistols out faster, son. This leather thong run through the front loops over the hammer to hold the pistol."

"Is gettin' a gun out fast important, Pa?" He knew it was from reading dime novels. But he just could not envision his father as a gunfighter.

"Sometimes, boy. But more important is hittin' what you're aimin' at."

"Think I'll do mine thataway."

"Your choice," the father replied.

Kirby knew, after hearing talk after Appomattox, that the Gray were supposed to turn in their weapons. But he had a hunch that his father, hearing of the surrender, had just wheeled around and taken the long way back home, his weapons with him, and the devil with surrender terms.

His dad coughed and asked, "How'd you get the Navy Colt, son?"

"Bunch of Jayhawkers came ridin' through one night, headin' back to Kansas like the devil was chasin' them. Turned out that was just about right. 'Bout a half hour later Bloody Bill Anderson and his boys came ridin' up. They stopped to rest and water their horses. There was this young feller with them. Couldn't have been no more than a year or so older than me. He seen me and Ma there alone, and all I had was this old rifle."

He patted the stock of an old flint-and-percussion Plains rifle in a saddle boot. "So he give me this Navy gun and an extra cylinder. Seemed a right nice thing for him to do. He was nice, soft-spoken, too."

"It was a nice thing to do. You seen him since?"

"No, sir."

"You thank him proper?"

"Yes, sir. Gave him a bit of food in a sack."

"Neighborly. He tell you his name?"

"Yes, sir. James. Jesse James. His brother Frank was with the bunch, too. Some older than Jesse."

"Don't recall hearin' that name before."

"Jesse blinked his eyes a lot."

"Is that right? Well, you 'member the name, son. Might run into him again some day. Good man like that's hard to find."

As the days rolled past, Kirby and his father winged their way ever westward. As they rode on, across the seemingly endless plains of tall grass and sudden breaks in the earth, a pile of rocks, not arranged by nature, came into view. Kirby pointed them out.

They pulled up. "That's what I been lookin' for," his father said. "That's a sign tellin' travelers that this here is the Santa Fe Trail. North and west of here'll be Fort Larned. North of that'll be the Pawnee Rock."

"What's that, Pa?"

"A landmark, pilgrim," the voice said from behind the man and his son.

Before Kirby could blink, his Pa had wheeled his roan and had a pistol in his hand, hammer back. It was the fastest draw Kirby had ever seen—not that he'd seen that many. Just the time the town marshal back home had tried a fast draw and shot himself in the foot.

"Whoa!" the man said. "You some swift, pilgrim."

"I ain't no pilgrim," Kirby's dad said, low menace in his voice.

Kirby looked at his father, looked at a very new side of the man.

"Reckon you ain't at that."

Kirby had wheeled his bay and now sat his saddle, staring at the dirtiest man he had ever seen. The man was dressed entirely in buckskin, from the moccasins on his feet to his wide-brimmed leather hat. A white, tobacco-stained beard covered his face. His nose was red and his eyes twinkled with mischief. He looked like a skinny, dirty version of Santa Claus. He sat on a funny-spotted pony, two pack animals with him.

"Where'd you come from?" Kirby's dad asked.

"Been watchin' you two pilgrims from that ravine yonder," he said with a jerk of his head. "Ya'll don't know much 'bout travelin' in Injun country, do you? Best stay off the ridges. You two been standin' out like a third titty."

He shifted his gaze to Kirby. "What are you starin' at, boy?"

The boy leaned forward in his saddle. "Be durned if I rightly know," he said. And as usual, his reply was an honest one.

The old man laughed. "You got sand in your bottom, all right." He looked at Kirby's dad. "He yourn?"

"My son."

"I'll trade for him," he said, the old eyes sparkling. "Injuns pay right smart for a strong boy like him."

"My son is not for trade, old-timer."

"Tell you what. I won't call you pilgrim, you don't call me old-timer. Deal?"

Kirby's dad lowered his pistol, returning it to leather. "Deal."

"You pil . . . folk know where you are?"

"West of the state of Missouri, east of the Pacific Ocean."

"In other words, you lost as a lizard."

"Not really. You heard me say where Fort Larned was."

"Maybe you ain't lost. You two got names?"

"I'm Emmett. This is my son, Kirby."

"Pleasure. I'm called Preacher."

Kirby laughed out loud.

"Don't scoff, boy. It ain't nice to scoff at a man's name. If'n I wasn't a gentle-type man, I might let the hairs on my neck get stiff."

Kirby grinned. "Preacher can't be your real name."

The old man returned the grin. "Well, no, you right. But I been called that for so long, I nearabouts forgot my Christian name. So, Preacher it'll be. That or nothin'."

"We'll be ridin' on now, Preacher. Maybe we'll see you again."

Preacher's eyes had shifted to the northwest, then narrowed, his lips tightening. "Yep," he said smiling. "I reckon you will."

Emmett wheeled his horse and pointed its nose west-northwest. Kirby reluctantly followed. He would have liked to stay and talk to the old man.

When they were out of earshot, Kirby said, "Pa, that old man was so dirty he smelled."

"Mountain man. He's a ways from home, I'm figuring. Tryin' to get back. Cantankerous old boys. Some of them mean as snakes. I think they get together once a year and bathe."

Kirby looked behind them. "Pa?"

"Son."

"That old man is following us, and he's shucked his rifle out of his boot."

Preacher galloped up to the pair, his rifle in his hand. "Don't get nervous," he told them. "It ain't me you got to fear. We fixin' to get ambushed . . . shortly. This here country is famous for that."

"Ambushed by who?" Emmett asked, not trusting the old man.

"Kiowa, I think. But they could be Pawnee. My eyes ain't as sharp as they used to be. I seen one of 'em stick a head up out of a wash over yonder, while I was jawin' with you. He's young or he wouldn't have done that. But that don't mean the others with him is young."

"How many?"

"Don't know. In this country, one's too many. Do know this: We better light a shuck out of here. If memory serves me correct, right over yonder, over that ridge, they's a little crick behind a stand of cottonwoods, old buffalo wallow in front of it."

He looked up, stood up in his stirrups, and cocked his shaggy head. "Here they come, boys . . . rake them cayuses!"

Before Kirby could ask what a cayuse was, or what good a rake was in an Indian attack, the old man had slapped his pony on the rump and they were galloping off. With the mountain man taking the lead, the three of them rode for the crest of the ridge. The packhorses seemed to sense the urgency, for they followed with no pullback on the ropes. Cresting the ridge, the riders slid down the incline and galloped into the timber, down into the wallow. The whoops and cries of the Indians were close behind them.

The Preacher might have been past his so-called prime years, but the mountain man had leaped off his spotted pony, rifle in hand, and was in position and firing before Emmett or Kirby had dismounted. Preacher, like Emmett, carried a Sharps .52, firing a paper cartridge, deadly up to seven hundred yards or more.

Kirby looked up in time to see a brave fly off his pony, a crimson slash on his naked chest. The Indian hit the ground and did not move.

"Get me that Spencer out of the pack, boy," Kirby's father yelled.

"The what?" Kirby had no idea what a Spencer might be.

"The rifle. It's in the pack. A tin box wrapped up with it. Bring both of 'em. Cut the ropes, boy."

Slashing the ropes with his long-bladed knife, Kirby grabbed the long, canvas-wrapped rifle and the tin box. He ran to his father's side. He stood and watched as his father got a buck in the sights of his Sharps, led him on his fast-running pony, then fired. The buck slammed off his pony, bounced off the ground, then leaped to his feet, one arm hanging bloody and broken. The Indian dodged for cover. He didn't make it. Preacher shot him in the side and lifted him off his feet, dropping him dead.

Emmett laid the Sharps aside and hurriedly unwrapped the canvas, exposing an ugly weapon with a potbellied, slab-sided receiver. Emmett glanced up at Preacher, who was grinning at him.

"What the hell you grinnin' about, man?"

"Just wanted to see what you had all wrapped up, partner. Figured I had you beat with what's in my pack."

"We'll see," Emmett muttered. He pulled out a thin tube from the tin box and inserted it in the butt plate, chambering a round. In the tin box were a dozen or more tubes, each containing seven rounds, .52-caliber. Emmett leveled the rifle, sighted it, and fired all seven rounds in a thunderous barrage of black smoke. The Indians whooped and yelled. Emmett's firing had not dropped a single brave, but the Indians scattered for cover, disappearing, horses and all, behind a ridge.

"Scared 'em," Preacher opined. "They ain't used to repeaters; all they know is single-shots. Let me get something outta my pack. I'll show you a thing or two."

Preacher went to one of his pack animals, untied one of the side packs, and let it fall to the ground. He pulled out the most beautiful rifle Kirby had ever seen.

"Damn!" Emmett softly swore. "The blue-bellies had some of those toward the end of the war. But I never could get my hands on one."

Preacher smiled and pulled another Henry repeating rifle from his pack. Unpredictable as mountain men were, he tossed the second Henry to Emmett, along with a sack of cartridges.

"Now we be friends," Preacher said. He laughed, exposing tobacco-stained stubs of teeth.

"I'll pay you for this," Emmett said, running his hands over the sleek barrel.

"Ain't necessary," Preacher replied. "I won both of 'em in a contest outside Westport Landing. Kansas City to you. Besides, somebody's got to look out for the two of you. Ya'll liable to wander round out here and get hurt. 'Pears to me don't neither of you know tit from tat 'bout stayin' alive in Injun country."

"You may be right," Emmett admitted. He loaded the Henry. "So thank you kindly."

Preacher looked at Kirby. "Boy, you heeled—so you gonna get in this fight, or not?"

"Sir?"

"Heeled. Means you carryin' a gun, so that makes you a man. Ain't you got no rifle 'cept that muzzle-loader?"

"No, sir."

"Take your daddy's Sharps then. You seen him load it, you know how. Take that tin box of tubes, too. You watch out for our backs. Them Pawnees—and they is Pawnees—likely to come 'crost that crick. You in wild country, boy . . . you may as well get bloodied."

"Do it, Kirby," his father said. "And watch yourself. Don't hesitate a second to shoot. Those savages won't show you any mercy, so you do the same to them."

Kirby, a little pale around the mouth, took up the heavy Sharps and the box of tubes, reloaded the rifle, and made himself as comfortable as possible on the rear slope of the slight incline, overlooking the creek.

"Not there, boy." Preacher corrected Kirby's position. "Your back is open to the front line of fire. Get behind that tree 'twixt us and you. That way, you won't catch no lead or arrow in the back."

The boy did as he was told, feeling a bit foolish that he

had not thought about his back. Hadn't he read enough dime novels to know that? he chastised himself. Nervous sweat dripped from his forehead as he waited.

He had to go to the bathroom something awful.

A half hour passed, the only action the always-moving Kansas winds chasing tumbleweeds, the southward-moving waters of the creek, and an occasional slap of a fish.

"What are they waiting for?" Emmett asked the question without taking his eyes from the ridge.

"For us to get careless," Preacher said. "Don't you fret none . . . they still out there. I been livin' in and 'round Injuns the better part of fifty year. I know 'em better—or at least as good—as any livin' white man. They'll try to wait us out. They got nothing but time, boys."

"No way we can talk to them?" Emmett asked, and immediately regretted saying it as Preacher laughed.

"Why, shore, Emmett," the mountain man said. "You just stand up, put your hands in the air, and tell 'em you want to palaver some. They'll probably let you walk right up to 'em. Odds are, they'll even let you speak your piece; they polite like that. A white man can ride right into nearabouts any Injun village. They'll feed you, sign-talk to you, and give you a place to sleep. Course . . . gettin' *out* is the problem.

"They ain't like us, Emmett. They don't come close to thinkin' like us. What is fun to them is torture to us. They call it testin' a man's bravery. If'n a man dies good—that is, don't holler a lot—they make it last as long as possible. Then they'll sing songs about you, praise you for dyin' good. Lots of white folks condemn 'em for that, but it's just they way of life.

"Point is, Emmett, don't ever let them take you alive. Kirby, now, they'd probably keep for work or trade. But that's chancy, he being nearabout a man growed." The mountain man tensed a bit, then said, "Look alive, boy, and stay that way. Here they come." He winked at Kirby.

"How do you know that, Preacher?" Kirby asked. "I don't see anything."

"Wind just shifted. Smelled 'em. They close, been easin' up through the grass. Get ready."

Kirby wondered how the old man could smell anything over the fumes from his own body.

Emmett, a veteran of four years of continuous war, could not believe an enemy could slip up on him in open daylight. At the sound of Preacher jacking back the hammer of his Henry .44, Emmett shifted his eyes from his perimeter for just a second. When he again looked back at his field of fire, a big, painted-up buck was almost on top of him. Then the open meadow was filled with screaming, charging Indians.

Emmett brought the buck down with a .44 slug through the chest, flinging the Indian backward, the yelling abruptly cut off in his throat.

The air had changed from the peacefulness of summer quiet to a screaming, gunsmoke-filled hell. Preacher looked at Kirby, who was looking at him, his mouth hanging open in shock, fear, and confusion. "Don't look at me, boy!" he yelled. "Keep them eyes in front of you."

Kirby jerked his gaze to the small creek and the stand of timber that lay behind it. His eyes were beginning to smart from the acrid powder smoke, and his head was aching from the pounding of the Henry .44 and the screaming and yelling. The Spencer Kirby held at the ready was a heavy weapon, and his arms were beginning to ache from the strain.

His head suddenly came up, eyes alert. He had seen movement on the far side of the creek. Right there! Yes, someone, or something, was over there.

I don't want to shoot anyone, the boy thought. *Why can't we be friends with these people?* And that thought was still throbbing in his brain when a young Indian suddenly sprang from the willows by the creek and lunged into the water, a rifle in his hand.

For what seemed like an eternity, Kirby watched the young brave, a boy about his own age, leap and thrash through the water. Kirby jacked back the hammer of the

Spencer, sighted in on the brave, and pulled the trigger. The .52-caliber pounded his shoulder, bruising it, for there wasn't much spare meat on Kirby. When the smoke blew away, the young Indian was face-down in the water, his blood staining the stream.

Kirby stared at what he'd done, then fought back waves of sickness that threatened to spill from his stomach.

The boy heard a wild screaming and spun around. His father was locked in hand-to-hand combat with two knife-wielding braves. Too close for the rifle, Kirby clawed his Navy Colt from leather, vowing he would cut that stupid flap from his holster after this was over. He shot one brave through the head just as his father buried the Arkansas Toothpick to the hilt in the chest of the other.

And as abruptly as they came, the Indians were gone, dragging as many of their dead and wounded with them as they could. Two braves lay dead in front of Preacher; two braves lay dead in the shallow ravine with the three men; the boy Kirby had shot lay in the creek, arms outstretched, the waters a deep crimson. The body slowly floated downstream.

Preacher looked at the dead buck in the creek, then at the brave in the wallow with them . . . the one Kirby had shot. He lifted his eyes to the boy.

"Got your baptism this day, boy. Did right well, you did."

"Saved my life, son," Emmett said, dumping the bodies of the Indians out of the wallow. "Can't call you boy no more, I reckon. You be a man, now."*

As his father talked, the dead Indian in the creek jumped to his feet and charged at Kirby's father's back, his knife held high.

"Dad, look out!" Kirby screamed, pointing at the Indian. . . .

* * *

* The Last of the Mountain Man

"Wake up, mister, wake up!" Nate said, shaking the man by his shoulders as he thrashed and called out in his sleep.

The man opened his eyes, staring wildly around the bedroom of Nate's cabin.

"What . . . what happened? Where am I?"

"You're safe, friend. You're in my ranch house. You took a bullet to the head in a little fracas last night."

The stranger's eyes grew puzzled, and he looked at Nate as if he'd never seen him before.

"Who are you?" he asked.

"I'm Nate Champion. We met on the trail yesterday, but you never told me your name."

The man on the bed opened his mouth to speak. Then his eyes went vacant and he said nothing.

"Well," Nate said, smiling to reassure the man he meant no harm. "What's your handle, mister?"

"I don't know," the man said as he looked up at Nate with naked fear in his eyes. "I can't remember!"

12

Nate pursed his lips for a moment, staring at his new friend, then shrugged and bent to examine the wound on his head.

The bleeding where the bullet had been lodged was stopped, and the swelling seemed to be less pronounced.

"How's your head feel?"

The man gingerly explored the swollen tissue with his fingers, his frightened look gradually fading, to be replaced by a slight grin. "How do you think it feels? Like I've been hit in the head with a sledgehammer."

Nate laughed and motioned for the man to follow him. "Get up and come with me. Maybe some cafecito will jog your memory."

"Sounds good to me," the man muttered as he climbed out of bed, wincing as the movement made his head pound again.

In the kitchen of the small ranch house, Nate stirred the coals in the stove and added a couple of sticks of wood. He put a handful of coffee grounds in a pot on the counter, added water, and put it on the stove to cook.

He sat across the table from the stranger and began to make himself a cigarette. When he finished, he handed his cloth pouch of Bull Durham to the man, who did likewise.

When they both had their butts going, Nate asked, "So, you can't remember anything about your past?"

"Not a thing, 'cept I had a dream while I was sleeping earlier. In it, I was a boy about sixteen years old, and the man with me was my dad. He was called Emmett, and he called me Kirby."

"Now we're gettin' somewhere, Kirby. What was the dream about?"

"We were on our way out west, and had got as far as Kansas, when we met up with an old mountain man, called himself Preacher."

When the water on the stove began to boil, Nate got up and crumpled in some egg shells to settle the grounds, then poured them both cups of the steaming, black brew.

While Nate fixed the coffee, Kirby continued to tell him about the Indian attack. "You woke me up just after the Indians had run off."

"You remember dreamin' 'bout your last name?"

"Nope. Kirby is all I can recall."

Nate nodded, taking a drink of his coffee. "Then I guess we'll just have to call you Kirby until the rest comes back to you."

"You think it will?"

Nate shrugged. "Don't rightly know. I had a saddle-partner on a drive once, was kicked in the head by an old, cantankerous mule. He lost his memory for a while, till he got in a bar fight a couple of years later and was slapped upside the head by a .44."

"What happened then?"

Nate grinned. "He remembered everything from before the mule kicked him, but forgot everything in between. Pissed me off, too. I'd loaned him twenty dollars and he said he plumb didn't remember it."

Kirby fingered his head again, a wry look on his face. "So the best I can look forward to is getting my bell rung again, and maybe I'll remember my name?"

Nate laughed. "Oh, I wouldn't go that far. There's a fancy doctor over to Cheyenne, went to some school back East called Harvard. Could be maybe he'll know what to do 'bout all this."

Kirby glanced out the window at the snow that was still falling, but not so heavily as the night before. "Maybe when the storm let's up, I can take a ride over there and let him take a look at me."

"One thing I do know," Nate added, finishing his coffee in a long swallow. "Whoever you are, you are one mean sonofabitch with a Colt in your hand. I ain't never seen nobody clear leather nor shoot as straight as you before."

As Kirby started to reply, the two men heard hoofbeats outside the cabin. They got up and walked to the door, both men taking their belts and holsters off a peg next to the door and putting them on as they peeked out a window.

"Looks like four of 'em," Nate said.

"They don't have their guns out, so maybe they're not hostile," Kirby said.

Nate's lips curled up in a half smile. "Only one way to find out," he said, and opened the door and walked out on his porch.

Without quite knowing why, Kirby reached down and unhooked the hammer thongs from his Colts as he followed Nate outside.

"Howdy, gents," Nate said to the four men sitting on their horses in front of him, a light snowfall drifting down to settle on their hats and shoulders. "What do you boys want?"

The apparent leader of the group—a short, squat man almost as wide as he was tall, and who must have weighed two hundred pounds—spoke up, "My name's Jeremiah Kidder."

As soon as the man spoke, Nate recognized his voice from the night before. He was the same man who'd called out that Nate had killed his partner.

Nate tensed, knowing that now there was certain to be gunplay.

"Oh, is that so?" Nate said. "And just who might you other men be?"

The man sitting to Kidder's left was much better dressed than the other three. He was wearing a suit coat and vest under a thick, rawhide coat with fur lining, highly polished black boots to his knees, and a derby-style hat. He touched the brim of his hat and said, "Mr. Champion, my name's John Clayburg, and I'm head of the stock detectives for the Wyoming Stock Growers Association."

He inclined his head to a man on the far right, who was tall, over six feet, and wore a large handlebar moustache, had suspenders over a white shirt, and carried a long, Sharps .52-caliber rifle in his saddle boot and a Colt in a holster on his right hip.

"That there is Tom Horn, who works for us, and the man next to him is Bobby Burrough."

Nate thought Horn's eyes were the coldest he had ever seen, and right away marked him as the most dangerous of the four men.

"Just what are you gentlemen doing out here on my ranch?"

Clayburg sat back against the cantle of his saddle and pulled a cigar from his coat pocket. After he lighted it, he pointed over his shoulder to the east. "We found one of our men lying dead on the eastern edge of your spread, a man named Zack Renfield."

He stuck the cigar in the corner of his mouth and stared at Nate. "It appears he's been dead since yesterday. You know anything about his death?"

Nate grinned, but his eyes remained serious. "You say you found this gent on my property?"

"That's right, Champion," Kidder growled, his face screwed up in a scowl. "And he was a good friend of mine."

"Just how'd you manage to find this man?"

Clayburg looked puzzled. "What do you mean?"

Nate waved his hand at the ground. "It appears to me there's been almost two feet of snowfall since the storm blew in last night. A person'd have to either be awfully lucky to find a dead man under all that snow, or know exactly where to look."

Out of the corner of his eye, Nate noticed the man named Tom Horn give a slight smile and nod his head approvingly, as if he thought this was a good point.

Clayburg took his cigar out of his mouth and stared at the glowing tip for a moment, as if he were thinking of a suitable reply to Nate's logic. "Be that as it may, we did find him, and I'm asking you if you know anything about it."

"Nope, not a thing," Nate replied. "But"—he inclined his head toward Kidder—"you might ask Mr. Kidder there. Since they was such good friends, maybe he can tell you what this Renfield was doin' on my property in the middle of the night in a snowstorm in the first place."

Tom Horn cleared his throat. "Excuse me, Mr. Champion, but who is your friend there? We haven't been introduced."

Nate looked over his shoulder at Kirby, and decided he didn't want him to get any further involved in his troubles than he already was.

"His name's Kirby, an' he's not exactly a friend. He got lost on the range last night, an' I took him in to give him shelter from the storm. He's just passing through the territory."

"You're a liar, Champion," Kidder snarled, his hand dropping toward his right hip. "You shot my friend down in cold blood, an' I'm gonna make you pay!"

Kidder and Burrough suddenly went for their guns, both men grabbing iron as if on a prearranged signal.

Before they had a chance to clear leather, two shots rang out from next to Nate, who'd barely had time to get his hand on his pistol butt himself.

Kirby stood there, both hands filled with Colts, their barrels smoking, as Kidder and Burrough were blown backwards off their saddles. Kidder had a small black hole in the center of his forehead, with the entire back of his skull blown off, while Burrough had a hole in the left center of his chest and a rapidly spreading stain of blood surrounding it. The two men lay sprawled spread-eagled on their backs in the snow, Kidder dead as a stone, and Burrough dying, moaning and whimpering through bloody froth on his lips.

"God damn!" Clayburg yelled, holding his hands high and staring at Kirby through terrified eyes. "You murdered them in cold blood."

Tom Horn just sat on his horse without moving, his hands crossed on the saddle horn, gazing at Kirby appraisingly. "That's a mighty fast draw for a cowboy, Kirby."

Kirby's eyes, cold as a snake's after striking his prey, turned to Horn. "I never said I was a cowboy, Mr. Horn. But you're a witness. Those men tried to draw down on Nate without any cause."

"That's preposterous!" yelled Clayburg, pointing his finger at Kirby. "You drew first—you had to. Nobody's that fast with a gun. Those men didn't even clear leather."

Horn shook his head. "No, he's right, Mr. Clayburg. Kidder and Burrough made the mistake of going for their guns, without knowing just who they was up against."

Nate nodded at the bodies. "You'd better get your men and hightail it off my property, Clayburg."

Horn and Clayburg got off their horses, picked up Kidder and Burrough, and threw them across their mounts, face-down.

As Horn took the reins and started to ride off, he tipped his hat at Nate and Kirby. "Just want you boys to know, I'm not near as dumb as these two were, and now I know what I'm up against."

Kirby holstered his pistols. "Good-bye, Mr. Horn."

Horn shook his head. "Not good-bye, Kirby, so long. We'll meet again, soon."

After the men rode off, Nate looked at Kirby, shaking his head. "I don't know who you are, Kirby, but one thing's certain. You are the fastest man with a gun I've ever seen." He clapped Kirby on the shoulder. "Come on in, an' let's have some coffee and talk about it."

As they sat drinking coffee and smoking cigarettes,

Nate said, "You still don't remember nothin' 'bout your previous life?"

"Not a thing," Kirby replied. Then he said, "You'd better fill me in on what's going on around here, since it appears I'm in the middle of it now."

The pot of coffee was empty by the time Nate had finished outlining the problems between the large ranchers and small, independent ranchers in Johnson County.

"What about those two who were here?" Kirby asked.

"Clayburg is, as he said, head of the stock detectives hired by the WSGA to kill any men they suspect of being rustlers. Tom Horn is famous all across the country, but this is the first time I've seen him."

"Tell me about him."

Nate settled back and crossed his legs, while building another cigarette. "Horn was a legendary Western scout, Pinkerton detective, and range detective. He started as a scout for the army at age sixteen and worked there for 'bout ten years. It was Horn who, after he was made chief of scouts in the Southwest, tracked Geronimo and his band to their hideout in the Sierra Gordo outside of Sonora, Mexico. Horn rode alone into the Indian camp, talked Geronimo into surrendering, and brought him and his men back to the States, where they gave themselves up to the army."

"The man has some *cojones* to take on Geronimo and his tribe all by himself," Kirby observed.

Nate nodded. "After he quit the army, he became a top cowboy, and once won the world's championship in rodeo steer roping. Then he joined the Pinkertons out of Denver, and chased down bank robbers and train thieves all over Colorado and Wyoming."

Nate lighted his cigarette, and as he exhaled a cloud of smoke, said, "My friend, Flat Nose Curry, who rode with the Wild Bunch and the Hole-in-the-Wall gang, told me a typical story of Horn's bravery. One day, Horn was on the trail of Peg-Leg Watson, a notorious outlaw and killer who had recently robbed a mail train. Horn tracked Watson to a high mountain cabin and called out to him, telling Watson he was coming for him. Watson stepped from the cabin with two six-guns in his hands. He stood there, his mouth hanging open as Horn walked toward him across an open field, his Winchester carried limply at his side. Watson was so unnerved by this display, he gave up without firing a shot. Rumor has it, Horn killed more than seventeen men while working for the Pinkertons."

"So," Kirby asked, "why is a Pinkerton man working for the ranchers here in Wyoming."

"He don't work for the Pinkertons no more," Nate said. "He just recently hired out to the WSGA to hunt down rustlers for them. Word is, they're paying him six hundred dollars for each one he kills."

Kirby nodded. "I noticed he's carrying a Sharps buffalo rifle. That how he does it?"

"Yeah. He spends several days tracking anyone he thinks is a rustler, learnin' the man's habits and watchin' him make camp and such. Finally, when he's good an' ready, Horn ambushes the man with his high-powered, long-distance buffalo gun, that Sharps you seen him carryin'."

"I see," said Kirby. "It seems Mr. Horn has lost his stomach for face-to-face encounters."

Nate nodded. "He shore has gotten strange, too. There's been dozens of men found shot to death on the range. Beneath each man's head was a large rock. Horn says it's his trademark, an' that way he'll get credit for the kill when he comes to collect his blood money from the WSGA."

Kirby stared at Nate for a moment with appraising eyes. "You afraid this Horn fellow is going to come after you next?"

Nate looked down into his coffee cup, as if he might find the answer to Kirby's question there. "Well, now that you mention it, I do know the WSGA is gunnin' for me, but whether they'll use Horn, or some other galoot like Frank Canton, I don't know."

Kirby got up from the table and flipped his cigarette butt out the window. "Why don't you just pack up and leave this area, since you know they're going to kill you if you stay?"

Nate grinned, and Kirby realized he was a man after his own heart. "I dunno, just plain stubbornness, I 'spect."

He took a drink of his coffee and stared out the window over Kirby's shoulder. "The way I figure it, Kirby, once a man starts to runnin' when a little trouble comes his way, 'stead of facin' it and standin' up to it, he might as well keep on runnin, 'cause next time there's more trouble, it's just gonna be that much easier for him to take off again."

He shook his head. "No, this is just somethin' I got to stand up to, or I wouldn't much like the man I see starin' out at me every mornin' from my shavin' mirror."

13

Casper, Wyoming

Major Wolcott, slapping his leg impatiently with his swagger stick, jutted his chin out and tried to straighten his twisted neck as he spoke angrily at Frank Canton.

"God dammit, Canton, these lazy Texicans of yours have rested and sobered up enough! Don't you think two days lying around and eating up our entire budget for this assault is a bit excessive?"

Canton stared back at Wolcott, unintimidated by his ranting. "Major, I've tried to explain to you: It's a hundred-and-fifty-mile ride to Buffalo from Casper, an' for the past two days we've had a heavy winter storm." He looked around at the Texans, most of whom still wore their Texas duds, which were not made for heavy winter riding. "Hell, half these boys would've froze to death had we tried to leave before today."

Unmollified by logic, Wolcott snapped, "Well, be that as it may, could you please get on with it now that the snow has stopped?"

"Why, yes, sir," Canton replied with more than a trace of sarcasm in his voice. "Tom Smith is unloading the horses from the cattle car now. Soon as we get 'em saddled up, we'll be on our way."

Canton grabbed a cup of coffee from the hotel kitchen, using it to keep his hands warm in the barely above-freezing weather, and wandered over to see if Tom was getting the boys set with their horses.

When he arrived, he saw Wolcott was already there, and was raising hell with Smith about something while the country boys from Texas stood around watching.

Just as Canton arrived, Wolcott turned to the Texans and shouted, "For heaven's sake, isn't there a one of you smaller men who will trade with him?"

Canton leaned over to whisper to Smith, "Tom, what the hell's goin' on here?"

Tom grinned and answered back in a low tone, "See that feller over there, the big, fat one with the dumb expression on his face?"

"Yeah."

"His name's Dudley. He can't find a hoss big enough or strong enough to carry his weight, an' none of his friends is willing to trade mounts with him."

Sure enough, Canton could see that the only horse left for Dudley to ride was small-boned through the chest, and was already swaybacked from being broken down in the past. Canton agreed with Wolcott. That horse wouldn't last five miles carrying the big Texan, especially through the ice and snow of the mountains between Casper and Buffalo.

Just as Canton was about to order someone to switch with Dudley, one of the cattlemen's guests, an Englishman named Wallace, offered to trade mounts with Dudley.

Finally, almost an hour after sunup, the expedition, with over fifty riders and three freight wagons full of equipment, supplies, and ammunition and weapons, left Casper and headed up into the hills toward Buffalo.

Within a couple of hours, Canton faced more problems. The heavy freight wagons began to bog down in trails left muddy after the recent snows. The entire first half of the day was spent with men hitching ropes to wagons and practically dragging them the few miles they managed to cover.

It was almost noon, and Canton decided the men had worked hard enough to deserve some warm food, so he ordered camp be made and breakfast cooked. Wolcott, of course, wanted to press on, but Canton and Smith had begun to just ignore his outbursts, further infuriating him.

The Texans, hungry enough after all their work to eat dirt, tied their horses to a small group of sagebrush near the campfires and rushed over to grab tin plates heaping with scrambled hens' eggs, fatback bacon cut thick, and potatoes chopped up and fried with sliced onions and canned tomatoes.

A wolf howled from someplace nearby, spooking the horses, which jerked back on their reins and uprooted the sagebrush, which had much shallower roots than its cousin bushes in Texas had. It was only a few minutes until almost all of the group's horses were running out of sight. The Texans bolted their food and took off on foot after their mounts, taking almost another two hours to round up the frightened beasts.

More than five hours behind schedule now, Canton pushed the men hard to make up for lost time. When they came to a bridge over a shallow dry gulch, he hurried the drivers of the wagons to get across, causing one of the wagons to break through the flimsy boards and go crashing into the gully below. It took another two hours for the men to tie ropes from their saddle horns to the wagon below and drag it up and out of the shallow ravine.

Canton sat on his horse and watched the men dragging the wagon along the ground, shaking his head, thinking things couldn't get much worse. As if he had tempted fate, the dark, black clouds overhead, heavy with snow, opened up and the snow came down. Not just a regular winter snowstorm, but so heavy and thick he could barely see beyond his horse's head, and within minutes, the faint outlines of the trail were obliterated.

The schedule had initially called for the force to spend their first night on the trail at Robert Tilsdale's ranch, located sixty-five miles out of Casper. As it was, it took the beleaguered force almost two full days and nights to reach this place where the riders and their mounts could get out of the weather for a much-needed rest.

Though they arrived there in mid-afternoon, Canton ordered the men to unsaddle their broncs and get inside the ranch house, where some good, hot food was being prepared. Wolcott, for once seeing the necessity of Canton's decision, didn't argue with his plan.

As dusk fell on the ranch, Canton, too dog-tired to undress, threw himself onto a bunk in a room filled with his exhausted men.

I wonder what else can go wrong on this trip, he thought as he fell into a deep, dreamless sleep.

14

KC Ranch
Buffalo, Wyoming

The man who knew himself only as Kirby tossed and turned in his sleep, dreaming of another time and another place. . . .

The man calling himself Buck West looked briefly at the wanted poster with his picture on it. It read:

Wanted
Dead or Alive
The Outlaw and Murderer
$10,000 Reward
Contact the Sheriff at Bury, Idaho Territory

Buck folded the poster and put it in his coat pocket, then looked back over his shoulder. He had yet to catch a glimpse of his pursuers, but he knew someone was tracking him; he knew it by that itchy feeling between his shoulder blades. Twice in as many days he had stopped and spent several hours checking his back trail. But to no avail. Whoever or whatever it was coming along behind him was lying way back, several miles at least, and they were very good at tracking. They would have to be for Buck not to have spotted them, and Preacher had taught the young man well.

Puzzled, Buck rode on, pushing himself and his horses, skirting the fast-growing towns in the eastern part of the state, staying to the north of them. Because of the man, or men, tracking him, Buck changed his plans and his direction. He rode seemingly aimlessly, first heading straight north, then cutting south into the Bridger Wilderness. He crossed into Idaho Territory and made camp on the north end of Grays Lake. He was running very low on supplies, but living off the land was second nature to Buck, and doing without was merely part of staying alive in a wild and untamed land.

The person following him stayed back, seemingly content to have the young man in sight, electing not to make an appearance, yet.

Mid-afternoon of his second day at Grays Lake, Buck watched his horse, Drifter, prick his ears up, his eyes growing cautious as the stallion lifted his head.

Buck knew company was coming.

A voice helloed the camp.

"If you're friendly, come on in," Buck called. "If you want trouble, I'll give you all you can handle."

Buck knew the grizzled old man slowly riding toward his small fire, but could not immediately put a name to him. The man—anywhere between sixty-five and a hundred and five—dismounted and helped himself to coffee and pan bread and venison. He ate slowly, his eyes appraising Buck without expression. Finally, he belched politely and wiped his hands on greasy buckskins. He poured another cup of coffee and settled back on the ground.

"Don't talk none yet," the old man said. "Jist listen. You be the pup Preacher taken under his wing some years back. Knowed it was you. Ante's been upped some on your head, boy. Nearabouts thirty thousand dollars on you now. You must have a hundred men after you. Hard men, boy. Most of 'em. You good, boy, but you ain't that good. Sooner 'er later, you'll slip up, git tired, have to rest, then they'll git you." He paused to gnaw on another piece of pan bread.

"The point of all this is?" Buck said.

"Tole you to hush up and listen. Jawin' makes me hungry. 'Mong other things. Makes my mouth hurt, too. You got anything to help ease the pain?"

"Pint in that pack right over there." Buck jerked his head.

The old mountain man took two huge swallows of the rye, coughed, and returned to the fire. "Gawddamn farmers and such run us old boys toward the west. Trappin's fair, but they ain't no market to speak of. Ten of us got us a camp just south of Castle Peak, in the Sawtooth. Gittin' plumb borin'. We figured on headin' north in about a week." He lifted his old eyes. "Up toward Bury. We gonna take our time. Ain't no point in gettin' in no lather." He got to his feet and walked toward his horses. "Might see you up there, boy. Thanks for the grub."

"What are you called?" Buck asked.

"Tenneysee," the old man said without looking back. He mounted up and slowly rode back in the direction he'd come.

"You're not any better-lookin' than the last time I saw you!" Buck called to the old man's back, grinning as he spoke.

"Ain't supposed to be," Tenneysee called. "Now git et and git gone. You got trouble on your back trail."

"Yeah, I know!" Buck shouted.

"Worser'n Preacher!" Tenneysee called. "Cain't tell neither of you nuttin'!"

Then he was gone into the timber.

Fifteen minutes later, Buck had saddled Drifter, cinched down the packs on his pack animal, and was gone, riding northwest.

He wondered how many men were trailing him. And how good they were.

He figured he would soon find out.

The year 1874 in most of Idaho Territory was no time

for the fainthearted, the lazy, the coward, or the shirker. Idaho Territory was pure frontier, as wild and woolly as the individual wanted to make it. It would be three more long, bloody, and heartbreaking years for the Nez Percé Indians before Chief Joseph would lead his demoralized tribe on the thirteen-hundred-mile retreat to Canada. There, the chief would utter, "I am tired; my heart is sick and sad. From where the sun now stands I will fight no more forever."

But in 1874, the Indians were still fighting all over Idaho Territory, including the Bannocks and Shoshones. It was a time for wary watchfulness.

It had been fourteen years since an expedition led by Captain Elias D. Pierce of California had discovered gold on Orofino Creek, a tributary of the Clearwater River. It wasn't much gold, but it was gold. Thousands had heard the cry and felt the tug of easy riches, and thousands had come. They had poured into the state, expecting to find nuggets lying around everywhere. Many had never been heard from again.

Buck rode through the southern part of the state, heading for the black and barren lava fields called the Craters of the Moon. Even there he was able to see the mute heartbreak of the gold-seekers: the mining equipment lying abandoned and rusting, the dredges in dry creek beds. Now, in early summer, a time when the creeks and rivers were starting to recede, Buck spotted along the banks a miner's boot, a pan. He wondered what stories they could tell.

He rode on, always checking his back trail. He had a vague uneasy feeling that he was still being followed. But he could never spot his follower. And that was cause for alarm, for Buck, even though still a young man, was an expert in surviving in the wilderness.

He skirted south of the still-unnamed village of Idaho Falls, a place that one man claimed "openly wore the worst side out."

Buck rode slowly but steadily, coming up on the south side of the Big Lost, north of the Craters of the Moon.

He stopped at a trading post at what would someday be a resort town called Arco. Inside the dark, dirty place, filled with skins and the smell of rotgut whiskey, Buck bought bacon and beans and coffee from a scar-faced clerk. The clerk smelled as bad as his store.

Buck's eyes flicked over several wanted posters tacked to the wall. There he was.

"Last one of them I seen had ten thousand dollars' reward on it," he said to no one in particular. He noticed several men at a corner table ceased their card playing.

"Ante's been upped," the clerk/bartender said with a grunt.

"Man could do a lot with thirty thousand dollars," Buck said. He walked to the bar and ordered whiskey. He didn't really care for the stuff, but he wanted information, and bartenders seldom talked to a non-drinking loafer. "The good stuff," he told the bartender. The man replaced one bottle and reached under the counter for another bottle.

He grinned, exposing blackened stubs of teeth. "This one ain't got no snake heads in it."

Buck lifted the glass. Smelled like bear piss. Keeping his expression noncommittal, he sipped the whiskey. Tasted even worse.

"Have any trouble coming in from the east?" the bartender asked.

"How'd you know I came in from the east?"

"That's the way you rode in."

"Seen some Blackfoot two-three days ago. But they didn't see me. I didn't hang around long."

"Smart."

"You see four men, riding together?" the voice asked from behind Buck, from the card table.

"Yeah, and so did the Blackfeet."

"Crap! You reckon the Injuns got 'em?"

"I reckon so. I didn't hang around to see."

"You mean you jist rode off without lendin' a hand?"

"One more wouldn't have made any difference," Buck said quietly, knowing what was coming.

"Then I reckon that makes you a coward, don't it?" the cardplayer asked, standing up.

Buck slowly placed the shot glass of bear piss back on the rough bar. He eyeballed the man. Two guns worn low and tied down. The leather hammer thongs off. "Either that or careful."

"You know what I think, Slick? I think it makes you yellow."

"Well, I'll tell you what I think," Buck said. "I think you don't know your bunghole from your mouth."

The man flushed in the dim light of the trading post. His dirty hands hovered over his guns. "I think I'll jist kill you for that."

"Bet or fold," Buck said.

The man's hands dipped down. Buck's right-hand .44 roared. The gunhand was dead before he hit the floor, the slug taking him in the center of the chest, exploding his heart.

"I never even seen the draw," the bartender said, his voice hushed and awe-filled.

"Any of you other boys want to ante up in this game?" Buck asked.

None did.

The dead man broke wind as escaping gas left his cooling body.

"He were my partner," a man still seated at the table said. "But he were wrong this time. I lay claim to his pockets."

"Suits me," Buck said. No one had even seen him holster his .44. "He have a name?"

"Big Jack. From up Montana way. Never spoke no last name. Who you be?"

"Buck West. I been trackin' the man on that wanted poster for the better part of six months."

Big Jack's partner visibly relaxed. "Us, too. I would ask if you wanted some company, but you look like you ride alone."

"That's right."

"Don't reckon you'd give us a hand diggin' the hole for Jack?"

"I don't reckon so."

"Cain't much blame you."

"Bury him out back," the bartender said. "Deep. If he smells any worser dead than alive I'll have to move my place of business."*

Kirby awoke and sat up in bed, the dream so real he was sweating from the closed-in heat of the tavern and could still taste the bitter whiskey and the smell of death on his tongue.

So, he thought, *I was once called Buck West, and there was a reward on my head of thirty thousand dollars.* He grunted as he slipped out of bed, quickly putting his clothes and boots on to ward off the chill of the cabin. *I must've been some bad hombre to warrant that kind of reward money on my head.*

He walked into the kitchen, dipped some water out of the pail on the counter, and put it and a handful of coffee grounds in the pot, stoked the embers in the stove, added a few sticks of wood, and put the pot on the stove to boil.

A dim memory of an old man in dirty buckskins sitting across a campfire from him appeared in his mind. "The trick to makin' good *cafecito* is, it don't take near as much water as you think it do," the man was saying, grinning to show yellow teeth, worn down almost to the gums.

The name Puma Buck came to Kirby, but the memory faded almost as quickly as it came.

Nate walked into the room, buttoning his shirt and yawning prodigiously. "Mornin', Kirby," he said, rubbing his eyes.

Kirby looked back over his shoulder. "Morning, Nate."

"Coffee 'bout ready?"

"I reckon so," Kirby replied, slipping into the accent Buck West had used in his dream.

Nate raised his eyebrows at Kirby, but took the coffeepot

*Return of the Mountain Man

and poured them both steaming cups without remarking on the change in the way Kirby talked. It was amazing. The man sounded like a completely different person.

"You sleep good?" Nate asked, handing a cup to Kirby.

"I had another dream, about my past."

"Oh?"

"Yeah. At one time I went by the name Buck West. Had wanted posters out on me."

Nate stared at Kirby for a moment, then shrugged. "Hell, Kirby. Plenty of men in this part of the country had paper out on them before. That don't mean nothin'."

Kirby smiled and sipped his coffee. The more he was around Nate, the more he liked the man. They had become good friends in the few days Kirby had been staying with him. Somehow, Kirby knew he was used to riding alone, but he thought if he ever had a partner, he would hope it would be a man like Nate. He was a good cowboy, handled steers like he was born to it, but more importantly, he was a *good* man, clear to the bone.

"You feel like doin' some work today?" Nate asked. "I got some beeves need movin' from one pasture to another 'fore the next storm comes through."

"Sure, only I require my wages in advance."

Nate raised his eyebrows.

"You got to feed me some bacon and eggs before we round up any cattle. A man can't work on an empty stomach."

Nate grinned. "Tell you what. I'll cook if you'll go down to the stream in front of the house and fill up that pail of water."

Kirby shook his head and grabbed the pail. "You're not much of a friend, sending a fellow out into the cold this early in the morning."

Nate laughed. "Just be glad we don't have no cows to milk nor chickens to feed."

Kirby smiled as he opened the door, his face stinging from the bitter cold of the predawn in a Wyoming winter.

15

Robert Tilsdale, Frank Canton, Major Wolcott, and Tom Smith were sitting at the kitchen table of Tilsdale's ranch, eating supper and making plans for the attack on Buffalo. They intended to storm the town, kill the sheriff and his deputies, and take over the militia arms stored in the courthouse there. Once they had control of the town, they could proceed to move on to the neighboring Converse and Natrona Counties, eliminating those on their "dead list" as they went.

Canton knew a standing order to militia units to answer only headquarter's orders for assistance and not county officials' calls for help effectively isolated Sheriff Red Angus and his deputies in Buffalo.

Suddenly the door burst open and a man rushed into the room, his shoulders still covered with ice and snow from his evening ride.

"Mr. Tilsdale, I got some news."

"Who is this man, and what does he mean by interrupting our supper?" the testy Wolcott asked.

"He's one of my range foremen," Tilsdale said. "Go on, Johnny, what's your news?" Tilsdale asked the man, who was still standing in the doorway, his hat in his hands.

"I got word there's a band of rustlers holed up at the old KC ranch, runnin' cattle on the ranges there.

Some of the boys an' me want to head on over there and kill 'em."

Several of the Wyoming stockmen from Cheyenne, who were sitting in the other end of the room, shouted out their agreement with this plan.

Canton shook his head. "I don't think that'd be wise, boys. Time is short, and we need to get on over to Buffalo and secure the town 'fore they find out we're comin'."

"Hell," Wolcott said, seizing on any opportunity to disagree with Canton. "With the number of men at our disposal, it'd only take a couple of hours to rid the county of some of these rustling scum."

Canton eyed Tom Smith, who could usually be counted on to agree with him against Wolcott. "What do you think, Tom? I'm worried that the longer we delay getting to Buffalo, the more chance someone there's gonna find out about us comin', an' I don't relish givin' up the element of surprise."

Smith shrugged. "Like the man says, Frank, we got over fifty hands, so it shouldn't take overly long to accomplish the deed." He grinned. "And it means that many less thieves we're gonna have to kill later."

Canton turned to Tilsdale. "Just how far is it to the KC ranch?"

"It's only fifteen miles, about a hour and a half ride is all."

Reluctantly, Canton finally agreed to the assault. He ordered the Texans to saddle up and get ready to ride.

By the time the horses were saddled and the wagons made ready for the trip, it was almost midnight. Finally, after what seemed to be an eternity, Canton and Smith, with Wolcott and his Wyoming stockmen riding along, were ready to leave for the fifteen-mile trip to the KC ranch.

As Canton stepped into his stirrups and swung up into his saddle, the light snowfall of earlier in the evening had turned into a full-fledged winter storm, with driving snow mixed with sleet and temperatures dropping faster than a cowboy's pants in a bawdy house.

Canton leaned over to speak to Smith, and had to

shout to be heard over the roaring wind. "I'm tellin' you, Tom, I got a real bad feelin' 'bout this little jaunt."

Smith pulled his hat down tight against the wind. "I gotta say, Frank, I'm beginnin' to agree with you."

Earlier that same evening, at the KC ranch, Kirby and Nate Champion and a cowboy friend of Nate's named Nick Ray were just sitting down to supper when a shout came from in front of the cabin, "Yo, the ranch house!"

Nate buckled on his belt and holster and pulled his six-shooter out as he went to the door. Cautiously, he opened it a crack and looked out into the gathering darkness.

After a moment, he looked back over his shoulder at Kirby and Nick. "Looks like a single man on a horse."

Nick Ray, who like Nate was on the Cheyenne cattlemen's "death list," pulled his pistol out. "You don't think it's one of those stock detectives of the WSGA been on the prowl for us, do you?"

Nate shook his head. "Naw, this guy looks older'n dirt."

Ray shook his head. "Can't be too careful, Nate. I heard they kilt Bobby Banion the other day. Said they caught him rustlin' cattle." He turned and spat, showing his disgust. "Hell, old Bobby didn't have but fifteen head to his name, and they was all mavericks from the open range."

Nate grunted. "I hadn't heard 'bout Bobby. What's that make, fifteen or twenty they killed in the last year?"

"At least that many," Ray replied, rearing back the hammer on his Colt.

Nate waved his hand at Ray. "Put that away, Nick. This looks like an old mountain man, one of the trappers that live up in the mountains. I don't 'spect he'll be any trouble."

He walked out on the porch, followed by Kirby and Ray, who still had his pistol out but kept it pointing at the ground.

Sitting on a ragged-looking horse was a man who appeared to be in his seventies at least, wearing dirty buckskins covered with a bearskin coat, a Sharps .52-caliber buffalo rifle across his saddle horn.

"Howdy, gents," the old man said, dipping his head in greeting. " 'Pears there's a hell of a storm comin', an' I got caught out here on your range without any suitable cover to make camp. I's wonderin' if'n I might bunk me an' my hoss in your barn for the night, or till the storm blows over."

Nate nodded. "Sure thing, mister—only put the horse in the barn and you can come on into the cabin here. We got plenty of room and hot coffee's on the stove."

The stranger grinned, showing a couple of stubs of yellowed teeth in an otherwise-empty mouth. He touched the front of his wide-brimmed hat and walked his pony toward the barn.

After he joined them in the ranch house, Nate asked the man his name.

"Don't rightly recollect my Christian name, been so many years since I used it, but my friends calls me Bear Claw," he said, reaching up to finger a rawhide necklace around his neck adorned with rows of bear claws hanging from it.

"What are you doin' way out here on the open range?" Nate asked, pouring the man a cup of coffee.

"I been trapping beaver and such up in the mountains, an' ran outta tobaccy. I was on my way into Buff'lo to buy me a couple'a twists of Bull Durham an' some Arbuckle's coffee when my old nose smelt the comin' storm."

He bent his head to drink the coffee, then looked up and smiled in delight. "Boy, that tastes mighty good . . . bit weak, but mighty good nonetheless. I been havin' to make do with acorn coffee, an' it do leave something of a bitter taste on the tongue."

Ray built himself a cigarette and stared at the old man. "I thought all the mountain men were dead by now."

Bear Claw chuckled. "Well, there be fewer of us than

there used to be, but there still be a few of us old beavers alive and kickin' up in the high lonesome."

"I had a dream about a couple of mountain men I used to know the other day," Kirby said, dishing out some beans and fried fatback onto Bear Claw's plate.

As the old man shoveled the mixture into his mouth, he glanced up at Kirby. "Who might that be, boy?"

"They were called Preacher and Puma Buck."

The mountain man's eyes widened in surprise. Then he smiled and his gaze became far away as if he were remembering old friends.

"Gawd, I hadn't heard those names in quite a while."

"Did you know them?" Kirby asked, leaning forward, hoping he might learn something about his past life.

"Hell, boy. Everbody who lived in the mountains knew Preacher. He was one of the first men to come out here, back when there weren't no other white men for a hundred miles."

"Is he still alive?" Kirby asked.

Bear Claw pursed his lips. "Don't rightly know. He'd have to be over ninety years by now." Then he winked. "Course, he was a tough old bird. Had so many bullets and arrowheads in him, he'd sink like a rock if he ever got in the water, which to my certain knowledge he never did."

"How about Puma Buck?"

Bear Claw's eyes looked sad. "Old Puma got kilt a couple of years back, but I heared he took six or seven good men with him 'fore they got him. He was ridin' with a man Preacher raised from a pup, helpin' him out in some trouble he was havin'."

"How'd it happen, old-timer?" Nate asked.

Bear Claw leaned back in his chair. "My mouth's gittin' kind'a dry from all this jawin'. If'n you got somethin' a mite stronger than this coffee, an' some makin's fer a cigarette, I'll tell ya' the tale the way it was tole to me."

After Nate poured some whiskey into his coffee, and Ray gave him a cigarette, Bear Claw's eyes got a faraway look in them and he started to talk. . . .

* * *

Puma Buck walked his horse slowly through underbrush and light forest timber in the foothills surrounding Murdock's spread. His mount was one they'd hired in Pueblo on arriving, and it wasn't as surefooted on the steep slopes as his paint pony back home was, so he was taking it easy and getting the feel of his new ride.

He kept a sharp lookout toward Murdock's ranch house almost a quarter of a mile below. He was going to make damned sure none of those *buscaderos* managed to get the drop on his friends. He rode with his Sharps .52-caliber laid across his saddle horn, loaded and ready for immediate action.

Several times Puma had seen men ride up to the ranch house and enter, only to leave after awhile, riding off toward herds of cattle, which could be seen on the horizon. Puma figured they were most likely the legitimate punchers Murdock had working his cattle, and not the gun hawks he'd hired to take down Puma's friends. A shootist would rather take lead poisoning than lower himself to herd beeves.

Off to the side, Puma could barely make out the riverbed, dry now, that ran through Murdock's place. He could see on the other side of Murdock's ranch house a row of freshly dug graves, some of them his doing, and Smoke's way of depriving the man of water for his horses and cattle.

As Puma pulled his canteen out and uncorked the top, ready to take a swig, he saw a band of fifteen or more riders burning dust toward the ranch house from the direction of Pueblo. Evidently they were additional men Murdock had hired to replace those he and Smoke and Joey Wales had slain in their midnight raid.

"Uh-huh," he muttered. "I'll bet those *bandidos* are fixin' to put on the war paint and make a run over to Smoke's place."

He swung out of his saddle and crouched down behind a fallen tree, propping the big, heavy Sharps across the rough bark. He licked his finger and wiped the front sight with it, to make it stand out more when he needed it. He got himself into a comfortable position and laid out a box full of extra shells next to the gun on the tree within easy reach. He figured he might need to do some quick reloading when the time came.

After about ten minutes the gang of men Puma was observing arrived at the front of the ranch house, and two figures Puma took to be Murdock and Vasquez came out of the door to address them. He couldn't make out their faces at the distance, but they had an unmistakable air of authority about them.

As the rancher began to talk, waving his hands toward Smoke's ranch, Puma took careful aim, remembering he was shooting downhill and needed to lower his sights a bit, the natural tendency being to overshoot a target lower than you are.

He took a deep breath and held it, slowly increasing pressure on the trigger, so when the explosion came it would be a surprise to him and he wouldn't have time to flinch and throw his aim off.

The big gun boomed and shot a sheet of fire two feet out of the barrel, slamming back into Puma's shoulder and almost knocking his skinny frame over. Damn, he had almost forgotten how the big Sharps kicked when it delivered its deadly cargo.

The targets were a little over fifteen hundred yards from Puma, a long range even for the remarkable Sharps. It seemed a long time, but was only a little over five seconds before one of the men on horseback was thrown from his mount to lie sprawled in the dirt. The sound was several seconds slower reaching the men, and by then Puma had jacked another round in the chamber and fired again. By the time the group knew they were being fired upon, two of their number were dead on the ground. Just as they ducked and whirled, looking for the location of their attacker, another was knocked off his bronc, his arm almost blown off by the big .52-caliber slug traveling at over two thousand feet per second.

The outlaws began to scatter, some jumping from their horses and running into the house, while others just bent over their saddle horns and burned trail dust away from the area. A couple of brave souls aimed rifles up the hill and fired, but the range was so far for ordinary rifles that Puma never even saw where the bullets landed.

He fired another couple of rounds into the house, one of which penetrated wooden walls, striking a man inside in the thigh, and then Puma figured he had done enough for the time being. Now he had to get back to Smoke and tell him Murdock was ready to make his play, or would be as soon as he rounded up the men Puma had scattered all over the countryside.

Several of the riders had ridden over toward Smoke's ranch, and were now between Puma and home. "Well, shit, old beaver. Ya knew it was about time for ya to taste some lead," he mumbled to himself. He packed his Sharps in his saddle boot and opened his saddlebags. He withdrew two Colt Army .44's to match the one in his holster and made sure they were all loaded up six and six, then stuffed the two extras in his belt. He tugged his hat down tight and eased up into the saddle, grunting with the effort.

Riding slow and careful, he kept to heavy timber until he came to a group of six men standing next to a drying riverbed, watering their horses in one of the small pools remaining.

There was no way to avoid them, so he put his reins in his teeth and filled both hands with iron. It was time to dance with the devil, and Puma was going to strike up the band. He kicked his mount's flanks and bent low over his saddle horn as he galloped out of the forest toward the gunnies below.

One of the men, wearing an eye patch, looked up in astonishment at the apparition wearing buckskins and war paint charging them, yelling and whooping and hollering as he rode like the wind.

"Goddamn, boys, it's that old mountain man!" One-Eye Jackson yelled as he drew his pistol.

All six men crouched and began firing wildly, frightened by the sheer gall of a lone horseman to charge right at them.

Puma's pistols exploded, spitting fire, smoke, and death ahead of him. Two of the gunslicks went down immediately, .44 slugs in their chests.

Another jumped into the saddle, turned tail, and rode like hell away from this madman who was bent on killing all of them.

One-Eye took careful aim and fired, his bullet tearing through Puma's left shoulder muscle, twisting his body and almost unseating him.

Puma straightened, gritting his teeth on the leather reins while he continued firing with his right-hand gun, his left arm hanging useless at his side. His next two shots hit their targets, taking one gunny in the face and the other in the stomach, doubling him over to leak guts and shit and blood in the dirt as he fell.

One-Eye's sixth and final bullet in his pistol entered Puma's horse's forehead and exited out the back of its skull to plow into Puma's chest. The horse lowered its head and somersaulted as it died, throwing Puma spinning to the ground. He rolled three times, tried to push himself to his knees, then fell face-down in the dirt, his blood pooling around him.

One-Eye Jackson looked around at the three dead men lying next to him and muttered a curse under his breath. "Jesus, that old fool had a lotta hair to charge us like that." He shook his head as he walked over to Puma's body and aimed his pistol at the back of the mountain man's head. He eared back the hammer and let it drop. His gun clicked . . . all chambers empty.

One-Eye leaned down and rolled Puma over to make sure he was dead. Puma's left shoulder was canted at an angle where the bullet had broken it, and on the right side of his chest was a spreading scarlet stain.

Puma moaned and rolled to the side. One-Eye Jackson chuckled. "You're a tough old bird, but soon's I reload, I'll put one in your eye."

Puma's eyes flicked open and he grinned, exposing bloodstained teeth. "Not in this lifetime, sonny," and he swung his right arm out from beneath his body. In it was his buffalo-skinning knife.

One-Eye grunted in shock and surprise as he looked down at the hilt of Puma's long knife sticking out of his chest. "Son of a . . ." he rasped, then died.

Puma lay there for a moment. Then with great effort he pushed himself over so he faced his beloved mountains. "Boys," he whispered to all the mountain men who had gone before him, "git the *cafecito* hot. I'm comin' to meet ya."*

Kirby, with eyes full of tears, felt himself strangely affected by the story Bear Claw was telling. He noticed the mountain man staring at him, a strange look on his face.

Nate, also affected by the courage the story evidenced, nodded. "That's some tale, old-timer. Puma Buck had a set of *cojones* on him, that's for sure."

Bear Claw struggled to his feet, his ancient joints cracking with arthritis, and walked to the stove to pour himself another cup of coffee.

Kirby stood and went to stand next to him, his cup held out for a refill.

Bear Claw glanced at the others and saw they weren't paying attention, so he whispered, "I don't know what's goin' on or why yore callin' yourself Kirby, big fellah, but we need to talk . . . private-like."

Kirby straightened, his heart racing. It sounded like the old mountain man might know something of his past. "Do you know who I am?" Kirby asked, whispering, like Bear Claw.

Bear Claw nodded, winked, and said, "In the mornin'." He drank his coffee down and in a louder voice said, "It's a mite past this old beaver's bedtime, boys. If'n ya don't mind, I'm gonna lay down in that corner over yonder and git me some shut-eye."

Nate and Nick Ray both stood up, Nate muffling a prodigious yawn with his fist. "Me, too, Bear Claw. I'll see you gents in the mornin'."

After the lanterns were extinguished and everyone was bedded down, Kirby lay thinking for a long time about an old mountain man named Puma Buck, whose story had caused an inexplicable ache in his heart.

16

The ride from Casper to the KC ranch was a living hell for the expeditionary force led by Frank Canton. The temperature had dropped into minus figures, and they were riding straight into the face of a howling north wind mixed with snow and ice.

As the men rode, hunched over against the cold and wind, they became coated with ice so thick they could barely move their arms and their hands froze to the reins. Several times horses faltered, falling to their knees, exhausted by the continual battle against the elements.

Finally, after four hours on a trip that was supposed to take only an hour and a half, Canton called a halt. He instructed the men to build several large campfires and try to thaw themselves and their animals out. He knew if he didn't stop and let his men and their horses warm up and eat something, he was going to lose them all.

Sitting so close to the large fire that his clothes were steaming, Canton wrapped blue, bloodless hands around a hot tin cup of coffee and enjoyed warmth for the first time in several hours. Trying to keep his teeth from chattering, he glanced at Major Wolcott next to him. "So, this little jaunt is gonna be like a walk in the park, huh?"

Wolcott, sitting with his back ramrod straight, icicles hanging from his handlebar moustache and mutton-chop sideburns and whiskers, gave Canton a steely look, then dipped his head and went back to drinking his coffee without answering.

Canton leaned toward the man sitting on his other side, Tom Smith, and said, "Tommy, do you think the men will be in any shape for a fight after ridin' through this storm all night and half freezin' to death?"

Smith pursed his lips, head down as he built himself a cigarette and lighted it off a burning branch from the fire.

"Don't rightly know, Frank." He looked around at the men, standing with their hands outstretched toward the fires they had built, most with their horses next to them so they could warm up too. "I guess if we don't get in no hurry and give them plenty of time to eat some hot food and drink lots of coffee, they'll be all right. They's all tough men, hard clear to the bone. That's why we picked 'em, 'member?"

Canton nodded, still unsure. It all depended on how many rustlers were holed up at the KC ranch. At the rate they were going, it was going to be dawn before they got there and were ready to fight, so the surprise of a night attack was lost to them due to the weather. He sure didn't relish trying an assault on a well-fortified ranch filled with dangerous criminals, especially if he and his men were outside exposed to the worst winter storm in his memory.

After an hour spent filling his men's bellies with hot beans and thick slices of fried fatback bacon and gallons of steaming coffee, Canton figured it was time to move on. They were still at least two hours away from the KC ranch, and he knew if there was any chance of their attack succeeding, they had to be in place around the ranch by dawn.

They barely made it, having to stop several times to pull the wagons out of deep snowdrifts with ropes tied to saddle horns. Just as the eastern sky began to lighten, they arrived at the cabin. They were in luck, for with the dawn, the storm began to wane and as the snow slowed to a trickle, the temperature began to rise to bearable levels.

Canton had his men surround the cabin and barn, concealing themselves in a stable, along a creek bed, and in a wooded ravine in back of the house. There were no signs of life in the cabin, and the barn, like most in the high country, was built right next to the house so they couldn't count the horses to see how many men they were facing.

Canton settled down for a cold wait to see what the dawn would bring.

In the ranch house, the men began to stir. Bear Claw, fully dressed, went to the kitchen to start a fire in the stove and make some coffee as the others pulled on their clothes. He lifted the dipper out of the tin bucket on the counter, and noticed there was only a couple of inches of water remaining.

"Boys," Bear Claw said, his voice husky with phlegm and more talking than he was used to in his lonely existence, "I'm gonna go to the crick an' git some water fer *cafecito*."

He walked out the door and disappeared into the early morning fog.

After twenty minutes went by without his return, Kirby could wait no longer. He was desperate to talk to the old man and find out about his past, maybe even his real name. Out of long habit, without remembering why, Kirby buckled on his two pistols, stuck his bowie knife in the scabbard he wore on his belt in the back, and went to find the mountain man.

He struggled through drifts of snow almost to his waist, but had no trouble following the old man's tracks in the fresh snow.

As he entered the wooded area next to the stream running in front of the cabin, two men with drawn pistols slipped from behind trees and eared back the hammers.

"Hold it right there, mister," one of the men said.

Kirby's hand hovered near the butt of his gun, but he realized they had the drop on him. He looked behind them and saw Bear Claw, men on each arm, shake his head, telling him not to resist.

Kirby and Bear Claw were taken deeper into the woods to the leader of the group. A tall man walked up and said, "I'm Frank Canton. Who are you men?"

The mountain man leaned to the side and spat. "My name's Bear Claw, if'n it's any of yore business."

Canton turned to Kirby. "And you?"

"My name's Kirby."

"First or last?"

"I don't rightly know," Kirby answered.

Canton narrowed his eyes. "Well, where are you from and what are you doin' here with this band of rustlers?"

"I don't know that either."

"You don't know much, do you, mister?" Canton said, glaring suspiciously at Kirby.

Kirby shrugged, his jaws tight with anger. "I may not know much, but I'm not the one askin' damn fool questions."

As Canton put his hand on his pistol, Bear Claw spoke up. "We's jest a couple 'a travelers, tooken rufuge in the cabin from the storm. We'uns don't know nothin' 'bout no rustlin' goin' on nor 'bout the men in the cabin."

Kirby looked at him, but the old man just gave a tiny shake of his head, warning Kirby not to speak.

One of the stockmen who came with Major Wolcott spoke up. "He's right, Frank. I lived here all my life an' I never seen neither of these men before. They got to be what they say they are, and neither of their names are on our list."

With a final glare at Kirby, Canton said, "All right. Take 'em out to the stable and tie 'em up good and tight. It won't be long before someone else comes out to see what happened to 'em."

About fifteen minutes later, Nick Ray walked out the door and stood there, looking around, searching for Bear Claw and Kirby.

In the stable loft, Major Wolcott nodded to a redhead called the Texas Kid, who had his rifle trained on the unsuspecting cowboy. He let the hammer down and his rifle exploded, shattering the early morning quiet.

As the rifle shot echoed through the frigid air, his slug staggered Ray, and it was followed by a sudden fusillade from the vigilantes hidden in the creek bed.

Nate Champion ran out the front door, six-shooter in hand. As Ray crawled back toward him, mortally wounded, Champion dragged his friend inside, slammed the door, and began to return fire. He arranged his weapons around the room, next to the windows, and made piles of ammunition next to each one for quick reloading.

After going to each of his windows and firing a couple of shots to keep the attackers back, Nate went to Nick and knelt by his side. The man was semi-conscious and moaning, his blood leaking from several wounds to form a pool around him on the wooden floor of the cabin. *At least there's no spurters,* Nate thought. *He's liable to live a while yet.*

Nate fetched a blanket and pillow from his bed and brought them back to the main room. He gently wrapped the blanket around Nick and put the pillow under his head.

Nick's eyes opened, and for a moment were clear. "Thanks, pardner," he mumbled through dry lips.

"Sure thing, partner," Nate answered. "Soon's I take care of these bastards, I'm gonna get you on into Buffalo and have the doc take a look at you. He'll fix you right up."

Nick groaned as a spasm of pain hit, then managed a small grin. "Don't be blowin' smoke at an old pal, Nate. We been friends too long. I know I'm fixin' to ride the long trail."

Nate, unable to answer, just held his friend's shoulder.

"Now," Nick continued, closing his eyes, "you get back to yore fightin' an' try an' kill a few of those sons of bitches."

Nate crawled toward a back window, falling flat once and covering his head as a number of bullets smacked into the side of the house, several punching through thin areas in the wood to scream through the air and embed themselves in an opposite wall.

He put his Winchester to his shoulder and aimed carefully at the copse of trees down near the creek. When he saw a flash of light from a gun firing, he squeezed the trigger. The rifle slammed back into his shoulder and belched flame and smoke. As the explosion echoed in the room, it was answered by a distant yelp of pain. *Must've winged one of them,* he thought. *Good, maybe it'll keep the bastards from rushing the cabin for a while.*

All morning long Nate held off the attackers. Intending to leave word of what had happened to his friends in Johnson County, whenever there was a lull in the fighting, he pulled a battered notebook from a drawer in the kitchen. During breaks in the fighting, he scribbled in it with the stub of a pencil, keeping a running account of the siege.

"Me and Nick was getting breakfast when the attack took place," Nate began. He described Bear Claw and Kirby's disappearance, and still early in the day he wrote, "Boys, there is bullets coming like hail. They are shooting from the stable and river and back of the house."

Two hours later, Nate looked up from reloading one of his pistols as Nick groaned and tried to sit up, throwing the blanket off. Nate scrambled on hands and knees to his side.

"Partner, you got to be still," Nate said. "You're gonna get those wounds to bleeding again if you keep moving around like this."

Nick stared up at Nate, eyes squinted against the pain. "I think it's 'bout time for me to leave, Nate." As bloody froth oozed from his lips, Nick winked. "I'll see you on the other side of the mountain, kid."

He doubled over, holding his gut as he coughed twice, and then he became limp in Nate's arms.

Nate wrote a terse note. "Nick is dead. He died about nine o'clock. I see smoke down at the stable. I think they have fired it. I don't think they intend to let me get away this time."

He continued to scrabble around the cabin, sometimes crawling, sometimes running bent over at the waist, firing a few shots from one window, then rushing to another to do the same thing. He had little hope of hitting anything—the men were too far away for a good shot—but he wanted them to know he was ready for them if they tried a frontal assault.

Toward noon, he added to his journal. "Boys, I feel pretty lonesome just now. I wish there was someone here with me so we could watch all sides at once."

Wolcott's hammer clicked on an empty chamber, and he backed away from his window in the stable and began to punch out his empties and replace them with fresh cartridges. He ambled over to stand behind Frank Canton, who wasn't shooting at the cabin but just watching the action.

"Canton, why don't you have your men rush the house? Our two prisoners tell us Champion's alone in there, so it ought to be an easy matter to storm the place."

Canton looked back over his shoulder at the major. "I'll tell you what, Major. Me and the Texicans will give you some coverin' fire, an' you can lead the other stockmen from Cheyenne in a rush on the ranch. How's that?"

Wolcott's face reddened. "But that's what we're paying the Texicans for," he snapped, his teeth almost clicking as he bit off the words.

Canton shook his head. "No, you're payin' 'em to come down here and help you kill your competitors, not to get killed in a foolish attack on one lone gunman who's holed up tighter than a tick on a coon hound. He ain't goin' nowheres long as we got him surrounded, so we'll just wait him out for a spell."

"Just how long do you intend to wait, Canton?" the major asked, jamming the last bullet into his pistol and snapping the loading gate shut.

Canton stared out the window, turning his back on Wolcott. "Until 'bout dark. If we haven't gotten him by then, I'll have the boys fire the cabin."

At about three o'clock, Nate noted in his journal, "A man in a buckboard and another on a horse went by the ranch and were fired on. I seen lots of men come out on horses on the other side of the river and take after them."

Nate's last entry was made that evening. "Well, they have just got through shelling the house like hail. I heard them splitting wood. I guess they are going to fire the house tonight. I think I will make a break when night comes, if alive. Good-bye, boys, if I never see you again."

Nate carefully signed the final entry in his journal "Nathan D. Champion," and put the notebook under the boards of the floor where it wouldn't burn if the house was fired.

As the day got later, and burning torches were thrown on the roof, Nate loaded his two pistols, kicked out the door, and made a run for it.

A man stepped from behind a tree and aimed a rifle at Nate, and was hit in the chest by a snap shot from one of Nate's pistols.

The rest of the Regulators opened fire. Two bullets took Nate in the chest, spinning him around, and another took him low in the back. As he sank to his knees, still firing, Nate pulled his triggers on empty chambers, dying the same way he lived, fighting to the end.

From behind the stable, Kirby watched his friend cut down and struggled against his ropes. "Dirty bastards," he mumbled through clenched teeth.

Sitting next to him in the snow, Bear Claw whispered, "Hush, son." His old eyes were damp from watching Nate die with such courage. "We'll git our chance, but now ain't the time. Keep your pie-hole shut an' maybe we'll live to git some revenge for your friend."

After the cabin burned itself out, the Regulators gathered around Nate's body. Canton nudged him with a boot, making sure he was dead.

He turned to Kirby and Bear Claw. "Give these two their guns back and let 'em get on their way. We're done here."

Kirby strapped on his pistols, having to resist with all his might an urge to draw and put a window in Canton's skull for what he'd done.

"You mind if we bury this man?" he asked.

"Why, I thought you said he weren't no friend of yours?"

"Any man who shares his cabin with me durin' a storm is a friend," Bear Claw said, "an' he deserves a proper buryin' no matter what else he's done."

Canton waved a dismissive hand. "I don't care what you do to his carcass." He turned to the Regulators. "Come on, boys, we got business in Buffalo an' we're already a day late 'cause of this outlaw."

As the group of men rode off, Bear Claw pulled a short-handled shovel from one of the packs on his pack-horse.

Kirby stepped over and took the shovel from him. "Why don't you make us some coffee on the campfire, while I dig Nate's grave?"

Bear Claw glanced at Nate's body, took his hat off, and said, "You died real good, son. Yore daddy'd be right proud of you."

17

After Bear Claw and Kirby lowered Nate into the frozen ground, covered his body with dirt, and topped the grave with stones to keep scavengers from it, they began the grisly task of searching through the still-smoldering ruins of the ranch house for Nick Ray's body.

Surprisingly, the fire had burnt itself out before doing too much damage to the floor and lower walls. They found Nick under some roof timbers that had fallen in on him. His corpse wasn't completely burned, and still showed the numerous bullet holes where he'd been gunned down.

As Kirby walked around to the other side of Ray's body to help carry it outside, his foot fell through some floorboards.

When he pulled his boot out of the hole in the floor, Kirby saw Nate's journal lying there. He picked it up and with a glance at Bear Claw, began to read it out loud.

After he was finished, he turned sad eyes on Bear Claw. "Nate left this so the other ranchers around here would know what happened to him."

Bear Claw nodded, glancing back over his shoulder at Nate's grave. "The boy was born with lots of hair on 'im, that's fer sure."

"As soon as we get Nick buried, I'm going to take this

into Buffalo and make sure Nate's friends get a chance to read it."

"You think it'll make any difference?" Bear Claw asked.

"If this notebook doesn't make the other ranchers band together to fight Canton and his men, then they deserve to lose this war," Kirby answered.

At the same time Bear Claw and Kirby were burying Nick Ray at the KC ranch, the two men in the wagon who'd ridden past the ranch were arriving in Buffalo. They'd managed to outrun their Regulator pursuers.

Oscar "Jack" Flagg, the man driving the wagon that had been fired upon, rushed into Sheriff Red Angus's office in Buffalo.

"Sheriff, they's a whole passel of men out at the KC. They got the place surrounded and they're firin' on the house."

"Isn't the KC where Nate Champion's been livin'?" Angus asked.

"Yeah, I believe it is," Flagg answered.

Sheriff Angus grabbed his hat off a post in the wall and shouted at his deputy, "Jim, get a couple of other men and ride out to the nearest ranches an' tell everyone to come on in here to town. We got a bunch of boys headed our way an' I want us to be ready for 'em."

As Angus pulled his hat down tight, he looked at Flagg and his partner. "You boys buyin' into this game?" he asked.

"God damned right," Flagg said, patting his pistol butt with his right hand. "Nate Champion was a good ol' boy, an' if'n they've kilt him, I reckon I'll do my best to see they pay for it."

A few hours later, almost a hundred small ranchers from spreads in the surrounding area, along with their hands, were gathered at the hotel dining room in Buffalo.

Sheriff Angus and Flat Nose Curry were trying to explain to them what Jack Flagg had seen, when two men rode into town at a fast clip. Sentries posted outside the hotel told the men where the meeting was, and Bear Claw and Kirby entered the room.

Everyone stopped talking as Kirby walked to the front of the crowd. He held up Nate's journal. "I've just come from the KC ranch, where Frank Canton and a group of over fifty men have killed Nate Champion and Nick Ray."

A swelling murmur of angry voices began, for both Nate Champion and Nick Ray were popular punchers, and good friends to many of the men in the room.

Kirby handed the notebook to the sheriff. "Why don't you read this to your men, Sheriff? They deserve to know who they're up against, and how one man stood off over fifty for a night and a day."

As Angus read the report of the fight at the KC out loud, many of the men in the room had tears in their eyes, while others' faces turned red with anger at the evil deed.

Flat Nose Curry walked up to stand next to Sheriff Angus as he finished reading. "Boys," Curry said in a harsh voice, roughened by too many whiskeys and cigars, "I think we ought'a ride out and meet those so-called Regulators, an' kill every one of the murderin' sons of bitches!"

A loud shout of approval rose from the crowd, until Angus raised his hands. "All right, boys, here's what we're gonna do," he said as he began to organize the angry mob into a fighting force.

Frank Canton pushed his men as hard as he could. He'd made the difficult decision to leave their wagons behind in order to make better time, for he knew if they lost the element of surprise, it would be very difficult for them to take Buffalo under their control.

After a hard two-hour ride, his men were tired, cold, and hungry. Though there was no raging storm to fight this night, the temperature was still in the low teens and there was plenty of drift snow on the ground to contend with. At two o'clock in the morning, Canton called the vigilantes to a halt at the ranch of one of their Johnson County allies.

Wolcott rode up beside Canton. "Why are we stopping here, Canton?"

"The men are dog-tired, cold, and hungry. I plan on letting 'em get warm for a spell and gettin' some coffee and hot food into 'em."

He stepped from his horse, went to the ranch house door, and pounded on it until a lantern inside was lighted and the door opened.

A sleepy-looking man with tousled hair smiled when he saw Frank Canton standing on his porch.

"Why, howdy, Frank. What in the hell are you doin' out here this time of mornin'?"

Frank glanced back over his shoulder at the group of men sitting on horseback behind him. "Me an' my Regulators are out here after some of those rustlers been killin' your stock, Bob. Trouble is, we're cold and hungry and we got a hell of a fight ahead of us. You think you could have your cook fix us up some coffee and biscuits?"

"Why, hell, yes, Frank. Nothin's too good for you boys, 'specially if you can get those damned rustlers off my back."

"There isn't room for all of us in the house, so I'll just take 'em on out to the barn, an' we'll chow down out there."

It was about an hour and a half later when Canton told his men, "Mount up, boys. We still got some ridin' ahead of us."

As the men began to get their gear together, Jim Dudley walked up to Canton leading a ragged-looking horse by the reins.

"Mr. Canton, I need me 'nother hoss. This one's plumb worn out."

Canton looked down at the huge bear of a man standing before him, weighing 250 pounds at least, and thought, *No wonder the horse is worn out.* He said, "Check with Bob's foreman over there and see if there's not one of his horses he can loan you until this is over. Tell him I'll make good on it if anything happens."

The foreman cast a skeptical eye at Dudley, but took him over to the corral where the ranch's remuda was herded. After trying four or five animals, Dudley still wasn't satisfied.

"None of these animals is big enough for me," whined the Texan.

Wolcott, tired of the antics of the hayseed from Texas, rode over on his horse and snarled, "Cinch up or stay behind!"

With a worried look, Dudley saddled the last horse he tried, a weak-kneed, ugly bronc who turned his head and stared at the man trying to get on his back. The horse immediately tried to buck Dudley off, but soon found itself unable to move that much weight in a hurry.

With Dudley trying his best to keep up, Canton moved the Regulators out, heading toward Buffalo. To ensure against an ambush, Canton sent two outriders ahead to scout the best trails, and to warn of anyone who might be ahead.

They hadn't ridden very long before the outriders came running back to report the presence of a large body of men camped down the road.

Canton halted the men, confused by this turn of events. "Damn," he observed to Tom Smith and Major Wolcott. "I wonder who the hell is out here in the middle of the night. I don't see how anybody could know we're comin', so they can't be waitin' on us."

Wolcott saw his chance to get back at Canton for taking his position away from him. "Hell, Frank, you been leading this group like it was out on a Sunday ride. We spent almost two days on Nate Champion. Then every time the men get a little winded, you stop and feed 'em. I wouldn't be surprised if everyone in Buffalo didn't know we're coming by now!"

He glanced at the men behind Canton and saw an old friend, one of the stockmen from Cheyenne, William

Irvine. "Bill," Wolcott called, "let's you and me walk on up ahead and see what's going on."

Irvine shrugged and climbed down off his horse, following Wolcott up the trail, while Canton and the rest of the men stayed behind.

Wolcott and Irvine walked quite a ways ahead, and were just about to turn around and head back, thinking the outriders had been mistaken, when they heard a pistol discharge around a bend in the trail in front of them.

"Damn," Wolcott whispered to Irvine, "there's someone up ahead."

They quietly walked a little farther and peered around the bend from behind some trees. They could make out several campfires and what looked to be over a hundred dark shapes standing around drinking coffee and resting their horses.

"Come on, Bill. Let's get back and warn the others," Wolcott said.

On the way back, he added, "Bill, you got to back me up and get the men to let me take over. Canton is out of his depth here, and he doesn't know the first thing about how to run this outfit."

Irvine nodded. "I agree, Major. I'll talk to the boys from Cheyenne and see if they won't back your play. It's apparent we need someone with military experience if we're going up against that many men."

When they got back to the Regulators, Wolcott told the men what they had seen. "There's a sizable force up ahead, and it can only be the rustlers and gunfighters, who must know we're on the way. I think it's about time for someone experienced to take over leading this expedition."

Canton, realizing for once the major was probably right, didn't argue, and Wolcott assumed command.

He climbed on his horse and said, "Okay, boys, now it's time for you to act like soldiers, and I'm gonna drill you until I think you're ready to face those gunnies up ahead."

Wolcott lined the men up and began to drill them in the moonlight, making sure they knew how to follow his commands. He did this for several hours, to the astonishment of Canton and Tom Smith.

"I can't believe we're out here riding around in the night while there's a force of men up ahead we need to be goin' after," Canton said to Smith.

"I got a real bad feeling about you lettin' the major take over, Frank. I don't think he knows his ass from his head."

"I didn't have no choice, Tom. The boys from Cheyenne are the ones payin' for all this, and if they want that idiot to take command, then so be it."

Finally, the major was satisfied he'd whipped his men into shape, and he ordered the men to follow him across the range to the right of the trail, explaining he wanted to try and outflank the men up ahead of them.

After riding for another hour, they came to the TA ranch, owned by another rancher friendly to the expedition, located about fourteen miles from Buffalo.

While the major took a few men ahead to see if the other group had moved, Jim Dudley went looking for an easier horse. He convinced the ranch foreman to let him try a big gray that looked fit enough to carry the big man.

As Dudley jumped in the saddle, the gray began to buck, astonishing the foreman, for the horse had never bucked before.

As Dudley went flying through the air, his rifle slipped from the saddle boot and the gun went off when it hit the ground, shooting Dudley through the knee as he fell.

After his wounds were cleaned, the foreman had one of the hands put Dudley in the back of a wagon and sent him to Fort McKinney to see the doctor there.

The rest of the vigilantes mounted up and rode after Wolcott, intending to join him against whatever force was out there waiting for them.

As dawn was breaking in the east, a rider approached them, riding hard, leaning over his saddle horn.

"Turn back! Turn back!" he screamed. "Everybody in town is aroused. The rustlers are massing from every direction. Get to cover as fast as you can if you value your lives!"

Wolcott sat in his saddle, his back ramrod straight, as he considered the warning. Finally, he turned his horse around. "Come on, boys, let's retreat back to the TA ranch. We can set up a defensive perimeter there."

"What the hell do you mean, retreat?" Canton asked.

"Yeah," Tom Smith added. "We came here to do a job, so let's do it. I vote we head on into Buffalo and have it out with the rustlers."

The Texans waited patiently to see which view would prevail. They'd been paid to fight, but it didn't matter much to them whether it was at the TA ranch or in Buffalo.

The members of the Cheyenne Club were of another mind. They spoke out against going into Buffalo, especially since the townspeople were armed and ready for them. They had no stomach for an adversary who wasn't going to be surprised.

Since they were paying the salaries of the fighters, the Cheyenne stockmen had their way and the Regulators retreated back to the TA ranch, to wait for an attack by their intended victims.

On the way, Wolcott rode next to Canton and Smith. "Boys," he said, "I'm going to need your support in the upcoming battle. The men need to trust their leaders, and I can't have you two questioning my every move."

Canton looked at Smith and shrugged. He knew the major was right. It was time to pull together, or they were all liable to be killed.

"All right, Major. We'll keep our mouths shut, at least in front of the men."

Wolcott nodded. "That's all I ask, boys."

18

Kirby and Bear Claw sat on their haunches near the fire, talking with Sheriff Red Angus and Nate's friend, Flat Nose Curry.

"How many men did you say the vigilantes had?" Angus asked Kirby.

"I'd say about fifty or so. Most of them hardened gunfighters, with a few ranchers thrown in."

Angus glanced back over his shoulder at the crowd of people around several other fires nearby. "Well, we got over a hundred people here, but damned few of 'em know which end of a gun the bullet comes out of. They're mostly punchers and townsfolk, and not one in ten have ever fired a pistol in anger, or been fired on."

Flat Nose Curry, his hands wrapped around a tin cup of coffee to keep warm, nodded. "That may be so, Sheriff, but this is the first time since this war started that the people of Buffalo and the small ranchers have stood together against the big-money ranchers. Whatever happens in the upcoming fight, at least we've finally come together. Those bastards from Cheyenne won't be able to ride roughshod over us anymore."

"That's true," Angus said. "One of the merchants in town has even thrown open his store and is giving away blankets, clothing, and ammunition to anyone who is willin' to fight, and the ladies of the town have set up a kitchen and are preparing wagon loads of food for the men at the front."

Bear Claw shook his head. "I jest hope the people know what they're gittin' into." He looked at the group of men gathered nearby, laughing and shouting and swaggering around like they were going to a party. "These men y'all are goin' up against are all gunslicks. This ain't gonna be no cakewalk, that's fer sure."

As he spoke, one of the young punchers was showing off his fast draw and accidently fired his pistol, shooting the toe of his boot off and making everyone nearby duck and fall to the ground.

Kirby could stand it no longer. Though he couldn't remember his past life, he knew somehow he wasn't one to join in and ride with a mob. He felt he needed to be alone, to do things his own way. Nate Champion had been a good friend, even in the short while Kirby had known him, and he planned on wreaking his own brand of vengeance on the men who had shot him down in cold blood.

Kirby stood up, emptied his cup of coffee in the fire, and said, "Sheriff, Flat Nose, I'm going to take off now. I think I'll ride on ahead and see if I can locate the vigilante force. If I find them, I'll get word back to you and your men as soon as I can."

Bear Claw struggled to his feet, grunting as he slowly stood up. "Kirby, if'n ya don't mind overly much, I'll ride along with ya."

Kirby smiled. "Suit yourself, Bear Claw," he said, glad the old mountain man was coming, for he felt sure the man knew more about his past than he had said. Maybe on the ride he could find out more about who he was.

As they rode through the moonlit night, their breaths smoking in the freezing air, Kirby said, "Bear Claw, back at Nate's cabin, just before all hell broke loose, you said you had something to tell me . . . something about my past."

The mountain man nodded, continuing to look straight ahead as he rode. "Ya tole me ya dreamed 'bout a mountain man named Preacher, and a kid and his daddy fightin' some Injuns with him."

"Yes, that was just after I got shot in the head."

"Well, more years ago than I care to 'member, Preacher an' me was holed up durin' a blizzard one winter, an' he got to talkin' 'bout this pilgrim and his son he'd met."

Kirby jerked his head to the side. "Did he tell you their names?"

"Hold your water, son. I'll git to it in good time." He pulled a twist of tobacco out of his pocket, bit off a goodly portion, and began to chew as he talked.

"Well, seems this pilgrim got himself shot, but 'fore he died, he made Preacher promise to raise his young'un, to look after him till he could fend for hisself. Preacher, though by nature a lone wolf, honored his word, an' 'fore long came to look on this pup like his own son. After some years in the high lonesome, teachin' this kid everything he knew, the boy met a woman an' got married an' even had a son of his own."

Kirby, getting more excited by the minute, asked, "You mean I have a son?"

Bear Claw shook his head. "Wasn't too long after that some bad hombres came around whilst the man wasn't to home, an' they kilt his wife an' son, after doin' terrible things to her."

Kirby, faint memories tugging at his mind, felt his stomach go cold with barely remembered fury.

"Well, this man, who Preacher had named Smoke, buried his kin an' then went after the men who done it. . . ."

Long before first light touched the mountains and the valley, creating that morning's panorama of color, Smoke was up and moving. He rode across the valley. Stopping out of range of rifles, by a stand of cottonwoods, he calmly and arrogantly built a cook fire. He put on coffee to boil and sliced bacon into a pan. He speared out the bacon and dropped slices of potatoes into the grease, frying them crisp. With hot coffee and hot food, and a hunk of Nicole's fresh-baked bread, Smoke settled down for a leisurely breakfast. He knew the outlaws were watching him; he'd seen the sun glint off glass yesterday afternoon.

"That bastard!" Canning said, cussing him from the outlaws' vantage point.

But Felter again had to chuckle. "Relax. He's just tryin' to make us do something stupid. Stay put."

"I'd like to go down there and call him out," the Kid said. His bravado had returned from his sucking on the laudanum bottle all night.

Felter almost told him to go ahead, get the rest of his butt shot off.

"You just stay put," he told Kid Austin. "We got time. They's just one of him, four of us."

"They was twice that yesterday," Sam reminded him. Felter said nothing in rebuttal.

The valley upon which the outlaws gazed, and in which Smoke was eating his quiet breakfast, as Seven, his horse, munched on young spring grass, was wild in its grandeur. It was several miles wide, many miles long, with rugged peaks on the north end, far in the distance, covered with snow most of the time, with thick forests. And, Smoke thought with a grim smile, many dead-end canyons. One of which was only a few miles from this spot. And he felt sure the bounty hunters did not know it was a box, for it looked very deceiving.

Clark had told Smoke, in the hope that he would only get a bullet in the head, not ants in the brain, that it was Canning who'd scalped his wife, Canning who'd first raped her, Canning who'd skinned her breast to make a tobacco pouch with the tanned hide.

Smoke cleaned up his skillet and plate and then set about checking out the two Remington .44's he had chosen from the pile of guns. Preacher had been after him for several years to switch, and Smoke had fired and handled Preacher's Remington .44 many times, liking the feel of the weapon, the balance. And he was just as fast with the slightly heavier weapon.

He spent an hour or more rigging holsters for his new guns, then spent a few minutes drawing and firing them.

To his surprise, he found the weapon, with its sleeker form and more laid-back hammer, increased his speed.

His smile was not pleasant. For he had plans for Canning.

Mounting up, he rode slowly to the northeast, always keeping out of rifle range, and very wary of any ambush. When Smoke disappeared into the timber, Felter made his move.

"Let's ride," he said. "Let's get the hell out of here."

But after several hours, Felter realized they were being pushed toward the northwest. Every time they tried to veer off, a shot from the big Sharps would keep them going.

On the second day, Canning brought his horse up sharply, hurting the animal's mouth with the bit. "I 'bout had it," he said.

They were tired and hungry, for Smoke had harassed them with the Sharps every hour.

Felter looked around him, at the high walls of the canyon, sloping upward, green and brown with timber. He smiled ruefully. They were now the hunted.

A dozen times in the past two days they had tried to bushwhack Smoke. But he was as elusive as his name.

"Somebody better do something," Felter said. " 'Cause we're in a box canyon."

"I'll take him!" Canning snarled. "Rest of you ride on up 'bout a mile or two. Get set in case I miss." He grinned. "But I ain't gonna do that, boys."

Felter nodded. "See you in a couple of hours."

Smoke had dismounted just inside the box canyon, ground-reining Seven. Smoke removed his boots and slipped on moccasins. Then he went on the prowl, as silent as death. He held a skinning knife in his left hand.

"No shots," Kid Austin said. "And it's been three hours."

Sam sat quietly. Everything about this job had turned sour.

"Horse comin'," Felter said.

"There he is!" Austin said. "And it's Canning. By God, he said he'd get him and he did."

But Felter wasn't sure about that. He'd smelled wood smoke about an hour back. That didn't fit any pattern. And Canning wasn't sitting his horse right. Then the screaming drifted to them. Canning was hollering in agony.

"What's he hollerin' for?" Kid asked. "I hurt a lot more'un anything he could have wrong with him."

"Don't bet on that," Felter told him. He scrambled down the gravel and bush-covered slope to halt Canning's frightened horse.

Felter recoiled in horror at the sight of Canning's blood-soaked crotch.

"My privates!" Canning squalled. "Smoke waylaid me and gelded me! He cauterized me with a runnin' iron." Canning passed out, tumbling from the saddle.

Felter and Sam dragged the man into the brush and looked at the awful wound. Smoke had heated a running iron and seared the wound, stopping most of the bleeding. Felter thought Canning would live, but his raping days were over.

And Felter knew, with a sudden realization, that he wanted no more of the man called Smoke. Not without about twenty men backing him up, that is.

Using a spare shirt from his saddlebags, Felter made a crude bandage for Canning. But it was going to be hell on the man sitting a saddle. Felter looked around him. That fool Kid Austin was walking down the floor of the canyon, his hands poised over his twin Colts. An empty laudanum bottle lay on the ground.

"Get back here, you fool!" Felter shouted.

Austin ignored him. "Come on, Smoke!" he yelled. "I'm going to kill you."

"Hell with you, Kid," Sam muttered.

He tied Canning in the saddle and they rode off, up the slope of the canyon wall, high up, near the crest. There they found a hole that just might get them free. Raking their sides, the animals fought for footing, digging and sliding in loose rock. The horses realized they had to make it—or die. With one final lunge, the horses cleared the crest and stood on firm ground, trembling from fear and exhaustion.

As they rested their animals, they looked for the Kid. Austin was lost from sight.

They rode off to the north, toward a mining camp where Richards had said he would leave word, or send more men should this crew fail.

Well, Felter reflected bitterly, we damn sure failed.

Austin, his horse forgotten, his mind numbed by over-doses of laudanum, stumbled down the rocky floor of the canyon, screaming and cursing Smoke. He pulled up short when he spotted his quarry.

Smoke sat calmly on a huge rock, munching on a cold biscuit.

"Get up!" the Kid shouted. "Get on your feet and face me like a man oughtta."

Smoke finished his meager meal, then rose to his feet. He was smiling.

Kid Austin walked on, narrowing the distance, finally stopping about thirty feet from Smoke. "I'll be known as the man who killed Smoke," he said. "Me! Kid Austin."

Smoke laughed at him.

The Kid flushed. "I done it to your wife, too, Jensen. She liked it so much she asked me to do it to 'er some more. So I obliged 'er. I took your woman—now I'm gonna take you." He dipped his right hand downward.

Smoke drew his right-hand .44 with blinding speed, drawing, cocking, firing, before Austin could realize what was taking place in front of his eyes. The would-be gunfighter felt two lead fists of pain strike him in the belly, one below his belt buckle, the other just above the ornate silver buckle. The hammerlike blows dropped him to his knees. Hurt began creeping into his groin and stomach. He tried to pull his guns from leather, but his hands would not respond to the commands from his brain.

"I'm Kid Austin," he managed to say. "You can't do this to me."

"Looks like I did, though," Smoke said. He turned away from the dying man and walked back to Seven, swinging into the saddle. He rode off without looking back.*

"Smoke Jensen," Kirby mumbled into the wind as he rode alongside Bear Claw. The name, though unfamiliar, felt easy on his lips, like old boots that have been worn long enough to become soft and comfortable. He glanced to the side. "So, you think I'm this man named Smoke?"

Bear Claw nodded. "Cain't hardly be two men like that ridin' round the country. Preacher said his boy grew to be a hand over six feet tall, shoulders broad as an ax handle, and was so fast with a short-gun it was plumb scary."

He leaned to the side and spat brown tobacco juice onto the ground. "I seen you handle that six-killer, son. You be Smoke Jensen all right."

Kirby shook his head. "I believe you, Bear Claw, but knowing my name hasn't brought back any memories of just who I am."

Bear Claw shrugged. "Could be ya won't ever 'member what went before, son, or ya could wake up in the mornin' an' it'd all be jest like it was. The haid is a funny thing. Sometimes I can 'member thangs happened forty years ago like they was jest yesterday, an' then again I cain't 'member what I ate fer breakfast."

Kirby was about to reply when out of the corner of his eye he glimpsed moonlight reflecting off metal, off to his left.

He stared off that way for a moment, and he noticed he could make out a force of men riding on the horizon, silhouetted against the night sky.

The Last Mountain Man

Kirby reached out his hand and grabbed Bear Claw's shoulder, pulling him to a halt. "Look over there. It looks like a bunch of men riding off to the south."

Bear Claw shaded his eyes against the moonlight and looked, then nodded. "That must be the vigilantes, all right. Appears to be close to fifty men, just like at Nate's ranch."

Kirby pulled his Winchester rifle from its saddle boot and worked the lever, jacking a shell into the chamber.

Bear Claw cocked an eyebrow at him. "You ain't meanin' to go after them boys by youself, is ya?"

Kirby glared at Bear Claw, and the old man could see why the Smoke Jensen he'd heard of had such a fearsome reputation. There was death lurking in those eyes for anybody who crossed the big man.

"Yes."

Bear Claw shook his head and pulled his Sharps .52-caliber from its saddle boot. "Boy, you gonna git us killed 'fore this is over."

"You don't have to join this dance, Bear Claw."

"I ain't never ducked a good fight yet, son, an' I don't intend to start now at this late age. What's yore plan?"

"There's too many for us to just ride up and start shooting, so I'm going to ride on ahead and set up an ambush. If we can fire down on them from both sides, knock a few out of their saddles, then ride like hell around them, shooting into the crowd, they'll never know what hit them."

Half an hour later, Wolcott and Canton and Smith rode along at the head of the vigilante group they called Regulators. They were in no hurry, and were discussing how they planned to combat the force of townspeople from Buffalo.

Suddenly something buzzed by Canton's head and he heard a flat slapping sound behind him, followed a few seconds later by the sound of gunfire ahead. He glanced over his shoulder in time to see a man riding behind him grab his chest and fall out of the saddle.

Before he could say anything, there was another

whistling buzz and the slap of a bullet hitting home, accompanied by a grunt of pain as another man was blown from his saddle.

The booming sound of a big Sharps firing was unmistakable ahead of them, and Canton knew they were under attack.

He started to yell a warning when he felt a sharp stinging in his head as a piece of his left ear was neatly cut off by a passing bullet.

"God damn!" he screamed, grabbing the side of his head. "Look out, men!" he yelled. "We're under fire!"

As a bank of clouds began to cover the moon and the night became dark, whoops and yells could be heard from in front of the group, followed by flashes of fire as more men were shot out of their saddles.

The Regulators began to ride in all directions at once, shooting at shadows and sometimes each other, as they couldn't tell who or where their attackers were.

One of the Texans, hearing the fearsome yells of the men riding down on them, hollered, "Injuns! We's bein' attacked by Injuns!"

Canton began yelling orders, trying to get his men to form up in some semblance of order. "Line up, men!" he hollered. "Over here, make a line and stand and fight!"

Without warning, a man riding bent low over his saddle horn, his reins in his teeth and both hands filled with iron, barreled through the milling, confused group of vigilantes.

Three more men went down, and only one man managed to snap off a shot at the specter as he weaved his horse through the crowd, guiding the animal with his knees as both hands fired into the Regulators.

Two more of the vigilantes were knocked from their saddles by large-caliber Sharps bullets, and three men went down from shots fired by their comrades, who were shooting at every shadow that moved.

Finally, Wolcott and Canton were able to get the men to follow them and they rode hell-bent for leather for the

TA ranch, trying their best to get away from whoever was attacking them.

The attack had only lasted five minutes, but the Regulators had lost at least ten men. Kirby sat on his horse, reloading his Colts, as Bear Claw rode up.

The old mountain man glanced at the bodies lying on the frozen ground and the horses milling about without riders.

"Gawd almighty, son! I ain't never seen nothin' like that since the time I fought some Comanch' over on the plains."

Kirby grinned, but his eyes were flat and cold, still filled with hate. "You think we got their attention?"

Bear Claw nodded. "Where'd you learn to ride like that, boy?"

Kirby shrugged. "I don't know. It just seemed like the thing to do at the time."

"I 'spect it was Preacher showed you them moves. He always was more Injun than white man anyhow."

After a few minutes, the men from Buffalo came riding up, having heard the shots.

Sheriff Angus and Flat Nose Curry rode slowly, looking at the carnage around them, the dead bodies lying sprawled in the bloody snow.

"Jesus," Angus whispered, taking his hat off and sleeving sweat from his forehead. "Did you two do this by yourselves?"

"Ya see anybody else round here, Sheriff?" Bear Claw answered, pushing cartridges into his Sharps.

Flat Nose Curry said, "Who did you say you were, mister?"

Kirby stared at him. "I didn't say. But the men we're after rode off in that direction," he said, pointing off to the south.

Angus nodded. "Looks like they're headed for the TA ranch."

"That figures," Curry said. "It won't be easy to get them out of there. That damn place is set up like a fort."

Angus turned to the side, speaking to a young boy in his teens. "Billy, you ride on into Buffalo and tell everybody we're gonna be out at the TA. They can send us some supplies out that way, 'cause we may be there a spell."

Angus twisted around in his saddle and hollered at the men grouped up behind him. "Come on, boys. They're up ahead of us, but be careful and watch out for ambushes."

Kirby watched Angus as the lawman turned back around and put the spurs to his horse, leaning over the neck as if he hoped they could catch up to the Regulators before they had time to set up in the TA ranch.

Kirby kicked his horse into a gallop following the sheriff. He knew most of the sheriff's riders were cowboys, and not professional gunfighters, and he was still uncertain of how they'd react when put up against men who made their living with a gun. *Well, hell,* Kirby thought as he charged through the frigid night on his horse, *I guess it's about time we find out.*

19

Sugarloaf Ranch
Big Rock, Colorado

Pearlie and Cal jumped from their horses and rushed into the cabin, hollering, "Miss Sally, Miss Sally."

Sally walked out of the kitchen, drying her hands on her apron. As always, when she was under stress or worried about Smoke, she tried to keep her mind busy by baking. So far today, she had baked two apple pies, a peach cobbler, and a huge batch of bear sign. She was doing all she could to try and avoid thinking of all the reasons why Smoke hadn't contacted her when he reached Buffalo.

"Yes, boys. Any word at the telegraph office?"

Pearlie, his hat in his hand, said with a serious expression, "No, ma'am. The telegraph operator said he's been tryin' to raise someone at Buffalo, Smoke's last stop on the train, for two days now, like you told him."

"And?" Sally asked, worry wrinkling her forehead.

"Nothin'," Cal answered. "He says he got through to Casper, an' the man on the wire there said there was a big shootout between some rustlers and a vigilante force."

"They're callin' it the Powder River War," Pearlie

added. "The man at the telegraph says all the lines into Johnson County have been cut."

"That settles it," Sally said, and she began to walk back toward her bedroom.

"What're you plannin' on doin', Miss Sally?" Pearlie asked.

"I'm going to pack and go to Buffalo and see what's happened to Smoke. He said he would wire me when he got to Buffalo, before he headed up into the mountains." She shook her head. "Smoke wouldn't forget a promise like that. If he didn't send me a message, then something terrible has happened to him."

Pearlie glanced at Cal, who shook his head. "You can't do that, Miss Sally," Pearlie said. "That country is no place for a woman this time of year, 'specially if'n there's a range war goin' on."

"Pearlie's right, Miss Sally," Cal added. "Why don't you let me an' Pearlie head on up there? We'll find out what's goin' on with Smoke, an' why he hasn't gotten in touch, an' if he's in some sort of trouble, we'll make sure he gets out of it."

Sally stared at the boys. She knew they were right. Someone needed to stay at the Sugarloaf and keep the hands on their winter chores, and the trip would be much more difficult for a woman than for two men traveling together. Damn, but sometimes it rankled her to be a female.

She walked up to them and put her hands on their shoulders. "Men, go on up there and bring my Smoke back to me, you hear?"

They both nodded. "Yes, ma'am," Pearlie said, and they headed out to the bunkhouse to pack for the trip.

As they walked across the yard, Cal asked in a low voice, "Pearlie, what if Smoke's dead?"

Pearlie shook his head. "Can't none of those Wyoming men kill Smoke Jensen." He stared at Cal. "Can't nobody kill Smoke Jensen." He patted the Colt revolver on his hip. "But if perchance they've managed to get the drop on Smoke, they're gonna have a couple of Colorado boys to deal with."

20

At the TA ranch, Wolcott began to organize his frightened Regulators back into a fighting force. The night attack had demoralized them, making them realize they were facing a formidable force of fighting men who weren't going to be easily defeated.

"Goddamn that Nate Champion," he muttered. He knew now that the time they had spent killing the cowboy had given their opponents the opportunity to get ready for them. If they ended up losing this war, he thought, it was all because of the bravery of one lone cowboy, who had fought them to a standstill for almost two days.

He took Canton and Smith and rode around the perimeter of the TA ranch, planning on how best to defend it.

The ranch seemed well situated for defense. Its main buildings, nestled in a bend of Crazy Woman Creek, were surrounded by a log fence seven feet high, with a barbed-wire fence beyond it. The ranch house stood in a windbreak of trees, surrounded by outbuildings, a stable, an icehouse, a small henhouse, and a dugout for storing potatoes. Within this compound there was also a stack of thick timbers, recently purchased for the construction of a new building. Beyond the barbed-wire fence, the terrain stretched away in rolling hills dotted with crevices and ravines, making an approach in force difficult.

As dawn approached, Major Wolcott barked out orders for the fortification of the ranch. On a knoll about fifty yards from the stable, he had his men build a log fort measuring twelve by fourteen feet, with openings through which sharpshooters could cover the approaches to the ranch. Trenches were dug inside the fort and breastworks were raised around the ranch house. By mid-morning the next day, the ranch was ready, and the stockmen and Texans were dug in, awaiting the appearance of the citizens from Buffalo.

As the morning fog and light snow cleared, the vigilantes could see their attackers in the distance, digging rifle pits and throwing up breastworks on every hill and hogback around the ranch. Wolcott counted fifty men who had dug in during the night, and he could see Sheriff Angus riding up with another forty or so men from the direction of Buffalo.

"Damn," he said to Canton and Smith. "It looks like the whole blamed town is coming out to fight."

Shooting started early in the morning, with sharpshooters from the town leaning their rifles over their breastworks and taking careful aim at the men dug in below at the TA ranch.

The attackers' first target was the corral. Their rifles began to pick off the vigilantes' horses. As the large-caliber bullets slapped into the animals, they screamed and began to run around the enclosure, trying to escape the slaughter.

"God almighty, Major," Canton hollered, pointing at the fallen animals. "They're shootin' our mounts. We got to do somethin'!"

Wolcott stomped around the ranch house, peering out the window as another horse went down as though he'd been poleaxed. "Frank, go send one of the Texicans out there to see if he can get what's left of the horses into the stable and under cover."

Canton watched as the deadly accurate firing knocked

another horse to the ground. He shook his head. "Not me! If I remember correctly, Major, you took command of this expedition, so it's your job to give the orders . . . 'specially when it means sendin' a man out into that hail of bullets."

"How about you, Smith?" the major asked Tom Smith.

Smith looked up from making a cigarette and gave a small smile, shaking his head.

With an angry snort, Wolcott walked over and stood behind two of the Texans who were peering over the top of a pile of timbers, watching the men from Buffalo picking off the horses.

Wolcott tapped the men on the shoulder. "Okay, boys, I need two men who aren't cowards to run on over there and get those broncs into the stable."

One of the men, the one who called himself the Texas Kid, glanced back at the major. "Are you crazy? We'd get our butts blown off if we stepped out there into that fire."

Wolcott cocked an eyebrow. "So, you're awfully brave when it comes to shooting a man down from cover, like you did with Champion, but you don't have the guts to face someone who's firing back at you, huh?"

The Texas Kid shrugged. "I ain't no coward, Major, but I ain't stupid neither."

He turned back to watch the battle.

Wolcott drew his Army .44, cocked it, and placed the barrel against the back of the Kid's head. "Well, son, I'm giving you a direct order. You can obey it and maybe get shot, or you can ignore it, and I'll kill you right where you sit. You got that, soldier?"

The Kid gulped, and looked walleyed at the big pistol stuck against the back of his head. "Yes, sir," he mumbled as he got to his feet. "Come on, Jimmy," he said to the young man next to him. "Let's go get them hosses."

Bending low and running in a zigzag pattern, the two boys made a run for the corral. With bullets pocking the ground around them, they finally managed to bring the panicked, jostling surviving horses into the stable.

As they made a run back toward the ranch house, the

boy named Jimmy was hit in the shoulder and spun
around to land sprawled on his face in the snow and mud.
The Texas Kid stopped long enough to grab him by the
shirt, jerk him to his feet, and half drag him into the
house, just as a fusillade of bullets splintered the doorway.

Wolcott smiled as the two men scrambled into the
room. "Now, that wasn't so bad, was it?"

"No worse'n hell," the Texas Kid mumbled as he
wrapped his bandanna around his friend's bleeding
shoulder.

With no horses left to shoot at, the attackers soon
turned their attention to the cattle, and after that anything that moved.

They soon found the range of the doors to the ranch
house and began to pour lead into the building, forcing
those inside to crawl when they needed to move about
within the rooms.

A boy of about sixteen, who had been at the ranch
when the vigilantes arrived, was pestering all of the men
to give him a gun so he could join in the battle. He finally managed to find an old shotgun in the loft, and was
sitting in a corner cleaning it, telling all around him how
he was going to blow hell out of those rustlers.

A bullet smashed though the wooden wall next to him
and creased his neck, burning a shallow furrow in the
skin and causing a considerable amount of blood to flow,
though the wound wasn't at all serious. After that, the
boy shut his mouth, put the shotgun down, and lay on a
blanket in the corner, pressing a cloth to his neck, his
eyes wide with fear.

On a hill overlooking the TA ranch, Smoke sat next to
a campfire, drinking coffee and talking with Bear Claw.
Though his memory hadn't fully returned, he was beginning to have flashes of his old life. A pretty, brown-haired
woman featured prominently in most of these—
a woman Bear Claw said could only be Smoke's wife,
Sally.

Sheriff Angus had ridden off some hours earlier to return to Buffalo, to further organize the efforts there to repel any additional firepower he was sure the cattlemen from Cheyenne would eventually send to reinforce the vigilantes.

Shortly after he left, a burly, unkempt figure arrived on the scene, and began to give orders. It was a man named Arapahoe Brown, who had twice previously been defeated for county sheriff.

Smoke didn't like the man from the first moment he laid eyes on him. To Smoke, he seemed the typical bully, a man who tried to foist his ideas on others by force rather than by logic.

By now the attackers from Buffalo had over three hundred men surrounding the TA ranch. Smoke and Bear Claw watched as Arapahoe Brown gathered the crowd in a large circle around him.

As he talked, he strutted around with his hands in his coat like a peacock, filled with self-importance. "Here's my plan, men. We'll close in on the TA by short dashes, using covering fire from above; then we'll burn the bastards out by firing the ranch."

Smoke glanced at Bear Claw, and saw the mountain man's expression was as disgusted as his own was. Smoke got to his feet and approached Brown.

"Have you given any thought to giving the men down there a chance to surrender?" he asked.

Brown glared at him through narrowed eyes. "And just who are you, mister, to be givin' orders around here?"

Smoke shrugged, his eyes flat and burrowing into Brown's. "I'm a friend of Nate Champion's, and I was there when those men burned him out, and then shot him down in cold blood. I didn't much like it when they did it, and I don't much like it now that you're advocating doing the same thing."

Brown, who was several inches shorter than Smoke but outweighed him by fifty pounds, stepped up close, his face next to Smoke's. "I'm tellin' you to butt out of this affair, stranger, an' mind your own business!"

As he finished talking, he put a hand on Smoke's chest and gave a shove, trying to push Smoke back. He might as well have tried to move a boulder.

Smoke looked down at the hand and spoke low. "Take your hand off me, Brown, before I break it."

Brown looked around at the crowd, his face burning red, and curled his hand into a fist and drew it back.

Before he could move, Smoke threw a short right jab, his broad, work-hardened knuckles smashing Brown's nose almost flat. As blood and mucus splattered and Brown blinked at the sudden pain, Smoke followed up with a left cross to the jaw, knocking the big man out cold and sprawling him in the snow on his back.

"Anyone else want to try and push me?" he asked.

When there were no takers, he nodded. "Now, I'm going to ride down to the ranch and see if those men will surrender. Any objections?"

There were none, but quite a few men nodded, as if they agreed with Smoke's plan.

He fixed a white shirt to the barrel of his Winchester and, holding it aloft, rode slowly down toward the ranch house.

As he approached, Major Wolcott, Frank Canton, and Tom Smith appeared at the front door, all with pistols drawn and aimed at Smoke's chest.

"What do you want?" Wolcott asked, his head cocked to the side from his neck injury.

"I hear you're a military man," Smoke said.

Wolcott nodded. "Yes. So what?"

"Then you must know you're in an untenable situation. Your men are surrounded by a superior force and you have no hope of escape." Smoke pointed over his shoulder. "Sheriff Angus has over three hundred men on those hills up there, and they're planning on burning you out and killing you to the last man."

Canton and Smith looked at each other. They evidently had no idea their situation was so desperate.

"What of it?" the major asked. "We're dug in here

pretty good, and they'll lose plenty of men if they try to rush us."

Smoke wagged his head. "Why should they do that? You've got nowhere to go, and you can't have many supplies stored up. All they have to do is wait until dark, sneak up on the ranch like you did to Nate Champion, and pick you off when you come out."

"So, just what are you proposing, mister?" Canton asked.

"If you and your men surrender, I will promise you a fair trial."

Wolcott shook his head. "There is no way we could get a fair trial if we surrendered to that mob. They'd shoot us down like dogs."

"They're going to shoot you down like dogs anyway, Major. At least this way some of your men might live through this."

Wolcott considered his options for a moment, then shook his head. "No, I won't chance it. We're expecting reinforcements from Cheyenne, and we've sent a runner out last night to the U.S. troops at Fort McKinney and to Governor Amos Barber, asking them for help."

Smoke gave a small smile. "Well, Major, for the sake of your men, I hope they respond soon, or you'll all be dead before they get here." Smoke looked back over his shoulder, then back at Wolcott. "I'll try to hold those men up there off until the authorities arrive, if I can."

"Why should you help us after we killed your friend Champion?" Canton asked, recognizing Smoke as the man they had taken from Champion's cabin.

Smoke shrugged. "Strange as it may seem to a man heading up a bunch of vigilantes, I believe in the rule of law, when it's available. If it was up to me, I'd shoot you down like the murdering cowards you are, but then I'd be no better than you are. No, if it's possible, I'll let the law decide what to do with you."

With that final word, he reined his horse around and trotted back up the hill toward the attackers from Buffalo.

21

When Smoke got back to the top of the hill, Sheriff Angus was waiting for him.

"What did they say?" he asked Smoke.

"They're considering the offer to surrender," Smoke said, electing not to mention what Wolcott had said about possible reinforcements on the way.

Angus glanced at Arapahoe Brown, standing on the edge of the crowd of men, his hand holding a bandanna to his still bleeding nose, a look of pure hatred in his eyes as he glared at Smoke.

"Well," Sheriff Angus said, "I'll give them until tomorrow. Then we'll attack and burn them out if they're still undecided."

"Good," Smoke said. "That sounds fair to me."

"Fair has nothing to do with it," Angus answered, his voice rough. "As long as I'm wearin' this badge, I'll do my best to work within the law, and that don't include shootin' men like they was fish in a barrel."

Smoke inclined his head toward Arapahoe Brown. "Maybe you ought to tell that to Brown over there."

Sheriff Angus fixed Brown with a baleful stare. "Brown ain't runnin' this operation. I am." He paused and then spoke louder, playing to the crowd. "All of you get that?"

There was murmuring among the crowd of onlookers, but none questioned Angus's authority.

Smoke, satisfied that he had at least bought the vigilantes some time and the possibility of a trial instead of a slaughter, walked back to his campfire, where Bear Claw sat watching him with a slight smile on his wrinkled face.

Smoke stood in front of the fire, taking the cup of coffee Bear Claw offered, and enjoyed the smell of the fire, the cold, crisp mountain air with a touch of pine scent to it, and the view of the snowcapped mountains in the distance.

He took a deep draft of his coffee and knelt on his haunches, facing Bear Claw. "You know, partner, I'm getting mighty tired of all this," Smoke said. He looked around at the men behind the breastworks, some still firing occasionally down into the ranch house as if they were afraid they might not get a chance to kill someone before the vigilantes surrendered.

Bear Claw nodded, a look of distaste on his face. "I know what you mean, son. Hell, I ain't been around this many people since the last gatherin' of mountain men four year ago." He shook his head, staring down into his coffee cup. "Mankind ain't all that bad when you take 'em one at a time, but when you git more'n a couple together . . ." He paused, then spat into the fire, making it hiss.

Smoke stood up and dumped the rest of his coffee onto the ground. "I think I'll take a little ride over to Fort McKinney."

Bear Claw stared at him, a questioning look on his face. "Oh?"

"Yeah. Major Wolcott told me he sent a courier through the lines last night to see if he could get the commanding officer there to send some soldiers to try and bring an end to this mess. I want to make sure his man made it, and see if there are some soldiers on the way."

"Why are you so all-fired determined to help those men down there out, 'specially after they killed Nate Champion?"

"It's like I said to the sheriff, I don't much cater to mob rule, or to killing fifty men when they're pinned down and helpless." Smoke paused, thinking of the man named Jim Dudley he'd met on the train. "Some of 'em sure as hell deserve what they get for the murder of Nate, but most of those boys down there are just up here to try and earn some money by tracking down rustlers, and have just been doing what their leaders tell them to do." He shook his head. "To me, that doesn't necessarily mean they ought to die for following orders."

Bear Claw used his Sharps to lever himself to a standing position. "You hankerin' for some company on this little jaunt?"

Smoke grinned. "Sure. On the way, maybe you can tell me some more about this Smoke Jensen that I'm supposed to be."

As they mounted up and rode out of camp, neither man saw Arapahoe Brown gather several cowboys around him and stare after them, his pig-eyes glittering hate.

Several hours later, as they rode at an easy trot down the trail, Bear Claw cleared his throat and pulled his Sharps out of its saddle boot.

"Don't look now, Smoke, but I just saw a reflection off somethin' up on the side of that hill over yonder." He cut his eyes to the right without turning his head.

Smoke glanced ahead to an area where the trail narrowed and passed between two hillocks on either side.

He pursed his lips, thinking. "That'd be a right dandy place for an ambush, wouldn't it?"

"My feelin's exactly. How do you want to handle it?"

Smoke looked around, noticing there was no cover between them and the narrow pass, and saw that the snow was piled too high off the trail for any fast horseback riding.

"There's no place for us to go, so I figure if we just pull up here and wait, they'll eventually have to come to us."

Bear Claw nodded. "An' right now we're outta rifle range, 'less they have a Sharps like I do."

The two men reined their mounts to a stop and sat there, Bear Claw with his Sharps across his saddle horn, and Smoke with his Winchester resting on his thigh.

As they waited, Smoke built himself a cigarette and Bear Claw cut a long piece of tobacco off a twist he pulled from a pocket and stuck it in his mouth.

After a wait of twenty minutes, four men rode out of cover and began to ride up the trail toward them.

Smoke gave a low laugh. "It looks like Arapahoe Brown and some of his cronies. He must think we have some unfinished business between us."

Bear Claw leaned to the side and spat a brown stream into the snow as he eared back the hammer on his Sharps. "It don't never pay to humiliate a bully, Smoke. They's all cowards at heart."

When the men riding toward them got within pistol range, Smoke booted his Winchester and slipped the rawhide hammer thongs off his Colts.

Brown reined his men to a halt twenty yards from Smoke and Bear Claw. "Where do you gents think you're goin'?" he asked with a belligerent tone to his voice.

Smoke raised his eyebrows, a slight grin turning up the corners of his mouth. "Why do you ask, Mr. Brown, not that it's any of your business?"

Brown snorted. "I figure you're on your way to try an' get help for those bastards that kilt our friends, Nate Champion and Nick Ray."

Smoke laughed out loud. "You know, Arapahoe, I only knew Nate and Nick for a few days, but I doubt very seriously if either one of them would have ever called a scurrilous son of a bitch like you a friend."

Smoke's jibe must have struck home, for one of the men with Brown gave a short laugh, as if it were true. Brown's face reddened and he leaned forward in the saddle. "Never mind your smart-ass comments, stranger—just answer my question."

Bear Claw cocked his head to the side, "By the way, just where did you get the name Arapahoe anyhow? It cain't be 'cause you a half-breed out of some Arapahoe squaw, 'cause I know for a fact the Arapahoe never bred with no donkeys."

Brown became so furious he began to sputter, spittle

forming at the sides of his mouth as he and his men went for their guns.

In the blink of an eye, Bear Claw swiveled his Sharps around and let the hammer down, the big .52-caliber rifle exploding and blowing a fist-sized hole in the chest of the man on Brown's left.

As he flung his arms out and flew backward out of his saddle, Smoke's right-hand Colt blasted smoke and fire from its barrel, sending a .44-caliber slug into Brown's neck, dead center, blowing a hole in his spine and dropping him like a sack of potatoes to slump forward over his saddle horn.

The second bullet from Smoke's pistol took the third man in the center of his forehead, shredding his skull and tearing a chunk of his scalp off.

The fourth man, his gun still in leather, shouted, "God damn!" and quickly raised his hands as Smoke's Colt turned toward him.

"Jesus," he whispered, "I ain't never seen nothin' like it! I never even saw your hand move."

"If'n you know which way the stick floats, lil' beaver," Bear Claw said, his voice husky with rage, "you'll head on back down the trail the way you came, an' maybe you'll live to tell your kids you tried to draw on Smoke Jensen an' survived."

He chuckled at the expression on the man's face as it blanched white at the mention of the name Smoke Jensen. "Not many hombres can say that!" Bear Claw added.

"Yes . . . yes, sir!" the cowboy said as he jerked his horse's head around and spurred it into a gallop. He leaned low over the saddle horn, glancing back as if he expected Smoke or Bear Claw to shoot him in the back as he rode away.

Smoke watched him ride away, a thoughtful expression on his face. "I can see by that puncher's reaction that the name Smoke Jensen carries some weight around here."

Bear Claw laughed out loud. "Son, you got that right!

You're only the most famous gunfighter in the country, bar none."

Smoke holstered his pistol and said, "Come on, Bear Claw, we got some miles to ride yet and we're burning daylight."

"What about these bodies?" Bear Claw asked.

Smoke looked down at the bloody remains for a minute, then leaned to the side and spat. "Let the wolves have them—it's only fitting."

22

The giant steam engine pulled into Buffalo with a screech of breaks and a hiss of steam.

Cal and Pearlie climbed down out of the passenger car, stretching to get the kinks out after their long ride. As they walked up the boardwalk toward the small station, five men with rifles and shotguns at the ready blocked their way.

"Howdy, gents," one of the men said, levering a shell into his rifle.

Pearlie looked at Cal, a puzzled expression on his face. "Howdy," he replied to the man with the rifle.

"Where you boys comin' from?" the man asked.

"We're from Colorado," Pearlie answered, "but just what business is it of yours?"

The man shifted a chaw of tobacco from one cheek to the other, then spat a stream of tobacco juice onto the ground.

"We're deputy sheriffs, an' we been havin' a spot of trouble with some vigilantes from Cheyenne. We're here to make sure no more of the dirty scum try to come up here an' cause more trouble."

"We don't know nothin' 'bout that," Cal said, scowling. "We're here to look for a friend of ours that arrived last week. He was supposed to wire us back home that he made it all right, only we ain't heard nothin' from him."

One of the other men asked, "What be your friend's name?"

"Smoke Jensen," Pearlie replied.

"Smoke Jensen, the famous gunfighter?" the first man asked, a surprised expression on his face.

"One and the same," Cal replied.

The man shook his head. "Nobody like that's been through here."

The second man added, "We have been havin' some trouble with the telegraph, though. Mayhap the lines were down when he came through and he just kept on goin'."

"What's he look like?" the first man asked.

Cal smiled. "I don't think you could've missed him. He's a hand over six feet tall, shoulders wider'n an ax handle, clean-shaven, and has light-colored hair, cut short."

The man raised his eyebrows and looked at the others. "There was a man like that, only he called hisself Kirby. Got into a little fracas with the vigilantes, only he left town yesterday, travelin' with an old mountain man name of Bear Claw."

Pearlie, recognizing the name Kirby as Smoke's given name, decided to keep his mouth shut until he figured out the lay of the land and just what had been going on up here.

"Naw, that don't sound like Smoke." He paused, then said, "I 'spect we'll just head on up into the mountains an' look for him there. You got anyplace that serves food around here? We're a mite hungry after three days on the train."

"Sure, there's Mary Sue's place, on over to the hotel. She serves a mean breakfast."

Pearlie nodded. "Then that's for us. Thank you kindly."

The deputies shouldered their weapons and walked on down the train, checking to make sure there were no reinforcements for the vigilantes in the other cars.

As they sat down to eat, Cal asked, "Why didn't you tell 'em Kirby was Smoke's Christian name?"

Pearlie shook his head. "No need to tip our hand just yet, Cal. If'n Smoke was usin' another name, he must've had good reason. We'll nose around here for a day or so and see what's been goin' on. Then if we don't find nothin' out, we'll hire a coupl'a broncs and head on up toward where the Nez Percé are camped an' see if Smoke's up there."

Smoke and Bear Claw were shown into the commanding officer's office at Fort McKinney.

"My name is Colonel Cartwright," the man behind the desk said, without rising or offering to shake hands. "What can I do for you gentlemen?"

"There's a range war going on over at Buffalo, in Johnson County, Colonel. The townspeople have about fifty or sixty men trapped in a ranch there and plan on killing them all for murdering some cattlemen friends of theirs. I was hoping you might be able to send some troops to restore order, and save those men's lives."

Cartwright studied Smoke for a moment, then picked up a telegram from his desk. "It's funny you should be here, Mr. Jensen. I just got this wire from President Benjamin Harrison. It seems Governor Amos Barber wired some senator friends of his and they got the President out of bed to send me this wire you see here. The President requests I send troops to Buffalo immediately to 'quell an insurrection' by the citizens there."

He looked up at Smoke and Bear Claw. "That doesn't exactly square with what you're telling me, now does it?"

"Colonel," Smoke said, an expression on his face as if he'd tasted bad meat, "there are two things I never put much stock in. One is anything a lawyer says; the other is anything a politician tells me." He shrugged. "I don't much care why you send troops to Buffalo, as long as you do something to help keep those men from being slaughtered."

"Just what's your stake in all this, Mr. Jensen?"

"Those men killed a couple of friends of mine in cold blood, and I'd like nothing better than to see the ones responsible for it punished. Trouble is, a lot of those men up there are just boys from Texas who didn't do nothing they deserve to die for."

Colonel Cartwright sat thinking, curling the ends of his moustache as he considered what to do.

Finally, after a few moments, he said, "Well, I sure as hell can't disobey a direct order from the President of the United States, so I'll send three troops of cavalry to Buffalo, with orders to stop the fighting and bring those men in for trial."

He looked up at Smoke. "That suit you, Mr. Jensen?"

"Sure does, Colonel."

After they left Colonel Cartwright's office, Bear Claw asked, "What're you gonna do now, young beaver?"

Smoke yawned and stretched. "I think I'm going to get some shut-eye. It's been a busy few days. Then I'm going back to Buffalo and make sure things get settled there. They may need my testimony about the killing of Nate Champion and Nick Ray. Then I'm going to get my supplies and head on up into the mountains and see if I can't get some Palouse studs for my ranch down in Colorado. What about you?"

The old man shook his head. "I've had 'bout all of humanity I can stand for a while. I'm goin' up into the high lonesome and see if there's any beaver left up there to trap." He smiled, showing yellow stubs of teeth. "It's time I got my camp ready for the winter."

Smoke took his hand. "It's been a pleasure meeting you, Bear Claw. I thank you for telling me about my past."

The mountain man stared into Smoke's eyes. "Maybe, if'n you give it some time, you'll recollect the rest, Smoke."

"Maybe," Smoke said as he turned and went looking for a hotel to get some sleep.

He waved as Bear Claw climbed on his pony and rode

off toward snow-covered peaks in the distance, wondering if the man named Preacher was still up there, trapping his own beaver.

Soon after he fell asleep, images began to appear in Smoke's mind. He was sitting in a cafe eating, and one table over from him was a beautiful young lady with brown hair. In his dream, he knew her name was Sally Reynolds and she was a schoolteacher. He was going by the name Buck West at the time, and they were the only customers in the cafe.

Buck ordered the lunch special and coffee. He felt eyes on him, and looked up into her hazel eyes. He smiled at her.

"Pleasant day," Buck said.

"Very," Sally replied. "Now that school is out for the summer, it's especially so."

"I regret that I don't have more formal education," Buck said. "The War Between the States put a halt to that."

"It's never too late to learn, sir."

"You're a schoolteacher?"

"Yes, I am. And you?"

"Drifter, ma'am."

"I . . . don't think so," the young woman said, meeting his gaze.

Buck smiled. "Oh? And why do you say that?"

"Just a guess."

"What grades do you teach?"

"Sixth, seventh, and eighth. Why do you wear two guns?"

"Habit."

"Most of the men I've seen out here have difficulty mastering one gun," Sally said. "My first day out here I saw a man shoot his big toe off trying to quick-draw. I tried very hard not to laugh, but he looked so foolish."

Buck again smiled. "I would imagine so. But I should imagine the man minus the toe failed to find the humor in it."

"I'm sure."

Conversation waned as the waitress brought their lunches. Buck just couldn't think of a way to get the talk going again.

Deputy Rogers entered the cafe, sat down at the counter, and ordered coffee.

Rogers glared at Sally as she said to Buck, "Will you be in Bury long?"

"All depends, ma'am."

"Lady of your quality shouldn't oughtta be talkin' to no bounty hunter, Miz Reynolds," Rogers said. "Ain't fittin'."

Buck slowly chewed a bite of beef.

"Mr. Rogers," Sally said. "The gentleman and I are merely exchanging pleasantries over lunch. I was addressing the gentleman, not you."

Rogers flushed, placed his coffee mug on the counter, and abruptly left the cafe.

"Deputy Rogers doesn't like me very much," Buck said.

"Why?" Sally asked bluntly.

"Because . . . I probably make him feel somewhat insecure."

"A very interesting statement from a man who professes to have little formal education, Mr. . . . ?"

"West, ma'am. Buck West."

"Are you a bounty hunter, Mr. West?"

"Bounty hunter, cowhand, gunhand, trapper. Whatever I can make a living at. You're from east of the Mississippi River, ma'am?"

"New Hampshire. I came out here last year after replying to an advertisement in a local paper. The pay is much better out here than back home."

"I . . . sort of know where New Hampshire is. I would imagine living is much more civilized back there."

"To say the least, Mr. West. And also much duller."

Hang around a little longer, Sally, Buck thought. *You haven't seen lively yet.* "Would you walk with me, Miss

Reynolds?" Buck blurted out. "And please don't think I'm being too forward."

"I would love to walk with you, Mr. West."

The sun was high in the afternoon sky, and Sally opened her parasol.

"Do you ride, Miss Reynolds?" Buck asked.

"Oh, yes. But I have yet to see a sidesaddle in Bury."

"They ain't too common a sight out here."

"Ain't is completely unacceptable in formal writing and speech, Mr. West. But I think you know that."

"Yes, ma'am. Sorry."

She tilted her head, smiling, looking at him, a twinkle in her eyes. As they walked, Buck's spurs jingled. "Which line of employment are you currently pursuing, Mr. West?"

"Beg pardon, ma'am?"

"Bounty hunter, cowhand, gunhand, or trapper?"

"I'm lookin' for a killer named Smoke Jensen. Thirty-thousand-dollar reward for him."

"Quite a sum of money. I've seen the wanted posters around town. What exactly did this Jensen do?"

"Killed a lot of people, ma'am. He's a fast gun for hire, so I'm told."

"Faster than you, Mr. West?"

"I hope not."

She laughed at that.

A group of hard-riding cowboys took that time to burst into town, whooping and hollering and kicking up clouds of dust as they spurred their horses, sliding to a stop in front of one of the saloons.

Buck pulled Sally into a doorway and shielded her from the dust and flying clods.

As they stepped out on the boardwalk again, a grand carriage passed, driven by a coachman all gussied up in a military-looking outfit. Four tough-looking riders accompanied the carriage. Two to the front, two to the back.

As the carriage passed, Buck removed his hat and bowed gallantly.

Even from the boardwalk, Sally could see the woman

in the carriage flush with anger and jerk her head to the front. Sally suppressed a giggle.

"Oh, you made her mad, Buck."

"She'll get over it, I reckon."

He took her elbow and they began to walk toward the edge of town. They had not gone half a block before the sounds of hooves drumming on the hard-packed dirt came to them. Two of the bodyguards that had been with the woman in the carriage reined up in the street, turning their horses to face Buck and Sally.

Buck gently but firmly pushed Sally to one side.

"Stand clear," he said in a low voice. "Trouble ahead."

"What . . . ?" she managed to say before one of the gunhands cut her off.

"You run on home now, schoolmarm. This here might git messy."

Sally stuck her chin out. "I will stand right here on this boardwalk until the soles of my shoes grow roots before I'll take orders from you, you misbegotten cretin!"

Buck grinned at her. Now this lady had some sand to her.

"Whut the hell did she call me?" the cowboy said to his friend.

"Durned if I know."

The cowboy swung his eyes back to Buck. "You insulted Miss Janey, boy. She's madder than a tree full of hornets. You got fifteen minutes to git your gear and git gone."

"I think I'll stay," Buck said. He had thumbed the thongs off his .44's after pushing Sally to one side.

"Boy," the older and uglier of the bodyguards said, "do you know who I am?"

"Can't say I've had the pleasure," Buck replied.

"Name's Dickerson, from over Colorado way. That ring a bell in your head?"

It did, but Buck didn't let it show. Dickerson was a top gun. No doubt about that. Not only was he mean, he was cat-quick with a pistol. "Nope. Sorry."

"And this here"—Dickerson jerked a thumb—"is Russell."

Buck hadn't heard of Russell, but he figured if the fella rode with Dickerson, he'd be good. "Pleased to meet you," Buck said politely.

Dickerson gave Buck an exasperated look. "Boy, are you stupid or tryin' to be smart-mouthed?"

"Neither one. Now if you gentlemen will excuse me, I'd like to continue my stroll with Miss Reynolds."

Both Dickerson and Russell dismounted, ground-reining their ponies. "Only place you goin' is carried to Boot Hill, boy."

Several citizens had gathered around to watch the fun, including one young cowhand with a weather-beaten face and a twinkle in his eyes.

"Stand clear," Buck told the crowd.

The gathering crowd backed up and out of the line of impending fire. They hoped.

"I've bothered no one," Buck said to the crowd, without taking his eyes from the two gunhands facing him. "And I'm not looking for a fight. But if I'm pushed, I'll fight. I just wanted to make that public."

"Git on your hoss and ride, boy!" Russell said. "And do it right now."

"I'm staying."

"You a damn fool, boy!" Dickerson said. "But if you want a lead supper, that's up to you."

"Lead might fly in both directions," Buck said calmly. "Were I you, I'd think about that."

Some odd light flickered quickly through Dickerson's eyes. He wasn't used to being sassed or disobeyed. But damn this boy's eyes, he didn't seem to be worried at all. Who in the devil were they up against?

"That's Buck West, Dickerson," the young cowboy with the beat-up face said.

"That don't spell road apples to me," Russell said. He glared at Buck. "Move, tinhorn, or the undertaker's gonna be divvyin' up your pocket money."

"I like it here," Buck said.

"Then draw, damn you!" Dickerson shouted. He went for his gun. Out of the corner of his eye, he saw Russell grab for his .45.

Buck's hands swept down and up with the speed of an angry striking snake. His matched .44's roared and belched smoke and flame. The ground-reined horses snorted and reared at the noise. Dickerson and Russell lay on the dusty street. Both were badly wounded. The guns of the two men lay beside them in the dirt. Neither had had time to cock and fire.

"Jumpin' jackrabbits!" the young lady said. "I never seen nothin' like that in my life."

Buck calmly punched out the spent brass and dropped the empties to the dirt. He reloaded and holstered his .44's, leaving the hammer thongs off.

Sheriff Dan Reese and Deputy Rogers came at a run up the wide street. Many townspeople had gathered on the boardwalks to crane their necks.

"Drop those damn guns, West!" Reese yelled before arriving at the scene. "You're under arrest."

"I'd like to know why," Sally said, stepping up to stand beside Buck. Her face was very pale. She pointed to Dickerson and Russell. "Those hooligans started it. They ordered Mr. West to leave town. When he refused, they threatened to kill him. They drew first. And I'll swear to that in a court of law."

"She's right, Sheriff," the young cowhand said.

Reese gave the cowboy an ugly look. "Which side are you on son?"

"The side of right, Sheriff."

Dickerson cried out in pain. The front of his shirt was covered with blood. The .44 slug had hit him squarely in the chest, ricocheted off the breastbone, and exited out the top of his shoulder, tearing a great jagged hole as it spun away.

Russell was the hardest hit. Buck's .44 had struck him in the stomach and torn out his lower back. The gunhand was not long for this world, and everybody looking at him knew it.

"Any charges, Sheriff?" Buck asked, his voice steady and low.

There was open dislike in Reese's eyes as he glared at Buck. He stepped closer. "You're trouble, West. And you and me both know it. I hope you crowd me, gunfighter. 'cause when you do, I'll kill you!"

"You'll try," Buck replied in the same low tone.

Reese flushed. He stepped back. "No charges, West. It was a fair fight."

Buck turned and took Sally's arm. "Shall we continue?"*

Smoke smiled in his sleep, his mind picturing the woman who would later come to be his wife.

Just before dawn, the beautiful woman in his dream faced him with her hands on his shoulders and looked him straight in the eye. "Smoke Jensen," she said, "you ride with your guns loose, and you be sure and come back to me, because I love you."

At those words, something clicked in Smoke's brain, connections were made, and suddenly he was Smoke Jensen again, with all his memories intact.

He sat upright in bed, looked around as if he wasn't sure how he got to be here, then grinned in the darkness.

"Sally," he whispered, "once again you saved me. Don't fret, darling, I'll be home soon."

With that, he climbed out of bed and began to get dressed. He had some business in Buffalo.

*Return of the Mountain Man

23

Back at the TA ranch, the cattlemen had just about given up hope that their friends back in Cheyenne were going to send help. As they became more discouraged, there began to be friction between the cattlemen from Cheyenne and the Texas gunfighters.

As bullets continued to strike the building, occasionally penetrating the wall to scream across the room and slap into the opposite wall, tempers became short.

At noon, Frederic deBillier stretched and yawned, then, crouched over, calmly walked toward a back room, blandly announcing he always took a nap at noon and requesting that no one disturb his sleep.

The Texas Kid snorted, looking over his shoulder as deBillier, still dressed in expensive city clothes, disappeared into the other room. "I tell you, boys," he said, speaking to the other Texans lying in front of windows, occasionally returning fire just to show the attackers they were still alive, "I cain't believe we come all the way up here to try an' help these men, an' then find out they nothin' but a bunch of candy-assed dandies."

Frank Canton and Tom Smith looked at each other, worry in their eyes. They both knew if they lost the Texans, or the gunfighters elected to give themselves up, there was nothing to keep the men from Buffalo from riding in and killing all of them.

"Now, Kid, take it easy," Canton said, trying to make peace. "He don't mean nothing by it. You got to remember, he ain't as young as you boys are."

Another Texan, who went by the name Bronco, laughed. "Yeah, Kid. It's jest that he needs his beauty sleep a lot more'n we do, ain't that right, boys?"

This last was greeted with catcalls and hoots, relieving Canton's mind. As long as the Texans were laughing at the Cheyenne cattlemen, they wouldn't be leaving them to die.

A while later, Wolcott, oblivious to the mounting tension between the two groups, stood up and pointed at one of the Cheyenne cattlemen. "Hey, Carl."

"Yes, sir, Major. What do you want?" answered Carl Robinson, who owned a large ranch just outside Cheyenne.

"Pick out some of the gunmen from Texas to go with you and run up the hill behind the house and relieve the men stationed at the outlying fort we built."

"Yes, sir." Robinson moved in a crouch around the room, tapping men on the shoulder until he had seven men getting ready to go with him. He looked over at Bronco and said, "You, Bronco, you're coming too."

Bronco glanced back over his shoulder at Robinson and laughed. "Like hell I am. It's too damn light out there. We'll be killed for sure if'n we try an' run up that hill now."

Wolcott exploded, forgetting where he was and standing up in the middle of the room. He pulled the big Army .44 from his holster and cocked the hammer, pointing the gun at Bronco's back.

"Which do you prefer, being killed going up the hill or being killed right here? You white-livered son of a bitch, you will either do as ordered, or I'll kill you myself!"

The other Texans all turned and aimed their guns at Wolcott, cocking the hammers with a multitude of metallic clicks.

Bronco smirked. "Oh, I don't think you gone be killin' anybody today, Major. Not unless you want about a pound of lead in your belly."

Wolcott's face turned fiery red, and he was about to fire and be damned, when Robinson called out, "That's all right, Major. I got enough men as it is."

He gestured at the others, and they followed him out the door and up the hill, without sustaining a single casualty.

Less than an hour later, Canton yelled out, "Look what's happening now, Major!"

Major Wolcott looked out the window and saw an immense ark of heavy timbers and bales of hay slowly moving toward the ranch compound.

"Damn," the major exclaimed, "the bastards are using our very own wagons against us."

Canton shook his head, calling from his post across the room, "I told you not to leave those wagons and supplies behind, Major."

"It couldn't be helped. They were slowing us down."

"You fool," Canton said, "do you remember what is in those wagons?"

Wolcott nodded. He remembered very well the amount of extra ammunition, weapons, provisions, and worst of all, dynamite that was now in possession of the Buffalo attackers.

He was about to call for the men in the compound to lay down a heavy fire, when he saw a man ride up from the north to halt his horse in front of the ark. He seemed to be trying to stop the attackers. . . .

Smoke reined his horse to a halt directly in front of the large, rolling fortress, forcing the men pushing it to stop.

Sheriff Red Angus stepped from behind the ark and yelled, "Kirby, what the hell do you think you're doin' out there? Get out of the way and let us do our job. We're gonna dynamite those bastards to hell and back."

"I can't let you do that, Sheriff."

Angus cocked his head to the side, an incredulous look on his face. "You can't *let* us do that? Boy, look around you. We got almost three hundred men here, primed and ready for some killin', an' you think you can stop us?"

"Sheriff, my name's not Kirby—it's Smoke Jensen."

The sheriff stopped, his mouth hanging open for a moment. Then he asked, *"The* Smoke Jensen?"

Smoke grinned. "I'm the only one I know about, Sheriff. But the main reason you can't go ahead with your plan is the United States Cavalry troops that are about five minutes behind me. They're coming up here to maintain law and order, and to arrest those men responsible for Nate Champion's and Nick Ray's deaths."

"You young fool," Angus called. "Once the soldiers take over, those men will never go to trial. They've got all the politicians bought and paid for."

As he finished speaking, from a short distance across the range there came a loud bugle call, and as the men from Buffalo turned at the sound, they could see dust and waving cavalry flags in the near distance.

All the shooting stopped as the soldiers arrived, circling their horses around the attacking force, with Sheriff Angus in the center.

Colonel J.J. Van Horn, the commander of the cavalry detachment, stepped off his horse to confer with Sheriff Angus.

"Sir," the colonel said, bowing formally, "I have an order from President Harrison to assist in quelling this disturbance. Will you cooperate and have your men stand down?"

Angus chewed on his moustache as he thought. After a moment, he answered, "Yes, sir, I will. On one condition."

"What is that, sir?"

"Your troops can have all the men we have trapped, but the vigilantes must later be turned over to civilian authorities for trial."

Colonel Van Horn didn't hesitate. "That is acceptable, Sheriff."

He made an about-face and marched down to stand just in front of the compound. "Gentlemen," he called, "are you willing to surrender quietly?"

Major Wolcott, holding a rifle with a soiled white rag on it, walked out of the building. "We are," he answered, "but only to the military, not to that man over there." He pointed at Sheriff Angus.

The colonel said, "Then by order of President Harrison, I hereby place you under military arrest."

In less than thirty minutes, the Cheyenne cattlemen along with the Texas gunfighters were stripped of their weapons and led away under military escort toward Fort McKinney.

As they began to ride away, Smoke walked over to stand next to Sheriff Angus. He stuck out his hand. "No hard feelings, Sheriff."

Angus glared hate at Smoke. "These people came in here with murder and destruction in their hearts and hands. They have murdered and burned and defied the law, and it was my duty to arrest them. They were mine. I had them in my grasp and you took them away from me."

Smoke looked down at his empty hand and lowered it, then glanced up at Angus, speaking in a low, firm voice. "You had no intention of arresting those men, Sheriff. You were going to dynamite them out of the building and then shoot them down in cold blood."

As Angus's eyes dropped and he stared at the ground, Smoke continued. "In my mind, that don't make you a whole lot different from the men you were planning to kill."

When Sheriff Angus refused to meet his gaze, Smoke turned and walked to his horse, stepping into the saddle. He looked up and found two young cowboys sitting on horses, watching him with small grins on their faces.

"Miss Sally was right, Smoke," Pearlie said in his soft drawl, "you just can't manage to stay out of trouble without Cal and me to watch out for you."

Smoke threw back his head and laughed. "Boys," he said, riding toward them, "you don't know how good it is to see familiar faces."

24

Smoke reached across his horse's neck and shook hands with Cal and Pearlie, a smile of real welcome on his face.

"Smoke," Cal said, "would you mind tellin' us just what the heck's been goin' on up here?"

Smoke nodded. "Later, boys. Give me a few minutes. I want to say something to those men being taken away."

He wheeled his horse and rode off after the cavalry detachment. When he caught up to Colonel Van Horn, he said, "Colonel, do you mind if I have a word with your prisoners before you leave?"

Van Horn eyed the Colts on Smoke's hips. "You aren't gonna try anything foolish are you, Mr. Jensen?"

"No, sir."

"Well, go ahead then."

Smoke spurred his horse until he was riding next to Major Wolcott and Frank Canton and Tom Smith, who rode at the head of the procession of prisoners.

Wolcott glanced over at him. "Mr. Jensen, the colonel tells me we have you to thank for getting the army here to rescue us."

"Major, let me make this clear. I apprised the troops of your situation in order to make sure that you received a fair trial for the killing of my friends, Champion and Ray." He jerked his head at the group of Texas gunfighters riding behind them. "And I didn't want some of those young men back there to be killed for something that was your responsibility, and yours alone."

"Well, be that as it may, I want to thank you for saving our lives, all of our lives."

Smoke nodded, his eyes flat and dangerous as he stared at Wolcott, Canton, and Smith. "The colonel has assured me that you will stand trial for what you've done, and I believe him to be a man of his word. But if I find out that you somehow manage to buy your freedom from the politicians your rich friends have in their pockets, I'll consider it a personal affront."

Wolcott grinned, his lips curling in a nasty smirk. "So?"

"If that happens, and we ever cross trails again, I will shoot you down like the mad dogs you are." He tipped his hat, his own lips curling in a similar grin. "You have the word of Smoke Jensen on it, sir."

Wolcott found himself looking into eyes as cold and dangerous as a rattler's about to strike. His face drained of color, and he quickly looked around to make sure Colonel Van Horn was nearby.

"I'll be following your trial with a great deal of interest, Major. You can count on it."

He glanced at Canton and Smith to make sure they understood what he was saying, then jerked his horse's reins around and rode off back toward where Cal and Pearlie were waiting for him.

Wolcott took his hat off and sleeved sweat off his forehead, watching Smoke's back as he rode off. "Damn fool," he muttered.

Canton chewed on the end of his moustache. "I don't know about you, Major, but I almost hope we do stand trial. I don't relish spendin' the rest of my days lookin' back over my shoulder to see if Smoke Jensen's there."

Back in Buffalo, Smoke took Cal and Pearlie to the hotel dining room and ordered them all a big meal.

Pearlie rubbed his stomach. "Boy howdy, Smoke, but

I been lookin' forward to this. I'm so hungry, my stomach thinks my throat's been cut."

Cal shook his head. "Yeah, Smoke, ol' Pearlie there only ate enough for two men this mornin' 'fore we headed out to see if we could find you."

As Smoke chuckled, Cal added, "For him, that's like bein' on half rations."

"It's sure good to see you boys," Smoke said. "How's Sally, and the Sugarloaf?"

Pearlie looked up from cutting his steak. "Sally and the ranch are doin' fine, Smoke. Only she was awful worried when she didn't hear from you when you got to Buffalo."

Smoke nodded. "When I first arrived, the telegraph lines had been cut by the Cheyenne ranchers. They were hoping to catch the town by surprise and take over the county, then follow up by killing all the men on their 'death list' of cowboys who were trying to start their own spreads."

Cal shook his head. "How did they ever hope to get away with somethin' like that, Smoke?"

Smoke shrugged. "They damn near did, Cal. In this country, at this time of year, the only connection with the outside world is through the telegraph line. They figured if that was cut, they and their hired guns from Texas could do just about anything they wanted, and by the time anyone found out about it, it would be all over."

Pearlie grinned. "They just neglected to figure on Smoke Jensen gettin' involved, huh, Smoke?"

Smoke shook his head. "Don't give me the credit, Pearlie. They failed because of the bravery of one man, Nate Champion."

As they ate, Smoke told them about how Champion held off fifty gunmen for two days, long enough for word to get to Buffalo and the populace to arm themselves and set up a defense.

Cal's forehead wrinkled in puzzlement. "I still don't understand why you went to all the trouble to get the

Army to rescue those men, after they took you and Bear Claw hostage, and killed your friends."

Smoke took the last bite of his steak, leaned back in his chair, and pulled a long, black cigar from his pocket. "Cal, I always think the law ought to be given a chance to work, if it's possible. This country's growing fast, and the more it grows, the more the rule of law has to take over from the rule of the gun."

Pearlie belched, rubbed his stomach, and leaned forward, his elbows on the table. "But Smoke, what if that Sheriff Angus is right? What if those boys get their politician friends to buy their way outta trouble?"

Smoke took a deep drag of his cigar and tilted smoke from his nostrils, watching as the ceiling fans blew it away. "Then the rule of law has failed, and it's back to the rule of the gun. I made those men a promise as they rode off, that they were going to be judged for what they did, one way or the other, either by the law or by me."

Cal asked, "Now that the war is over, what are your plans?"

Smoke stubbed out his cigar and took a final drink of his coffee. "I'm going to get some provisions and a couple of packhorses, and head on up into the mountains to see if I can find that tribe of Nez Percé. I still need to get some good Palouse stock to breed into our remuda back at the Sugarloaf."

Pearlie rubbed his lips, glancing back over his shoulder. "Just when are you plannin' on doin' that, Smoke?"

"Right away. Why?"

"Oh, I's just wonderin' if we have time for some of that apple pie I smell back in the kitchen." He rubbed his stomach. "Now that I've taken the edge off my appetite, I figure I can relax and enjoy a piece or two."

Smoke shook his head and waved at their waitress. "Hell, might as well get the whole pie. We don't want Pearlie going off half-starved, do we, Cal?"

"No, sir," the young man said, a grin on his face. "But I might oughta eat a piece or two also, 'cause I wouldn't want Pearlie to eat it all and get stomach cramps on our trip."

25

By the time they had finished filling Pearlie's belly, it was getting late, and another winter storm had blown in. With visibility down to twenty feet and the temperature in minus figures, Smoke decided to take a couple of rooms at the hotel and start their journey in the morning.

Dawn found the snowfall down to manageable levels, and they bought supplies and packhorses and got ready to leave. They stopped at the hotel for what Pearlie said was to be their last "civilized" meal before taking to the trail.

As they ate heaping plates of scrambled hens' eggs, thick slices of smoked bacon, and sliced potatoes fried with slabs of sweet onions, some men at a nearby table glared at them, hatred in their eyes.

Cal glanced nervously over his shoulder at the men, then leaned forward and asked Smoke, "What do you think them men are starin' at, Smoke?"

Smoke continued to eat, seemingly unconcerned. "Don't pay them no mind, Cal. They're just pissed-off that they didn't get to kill the vigilantes from Cheyenne. They'll get over it."

Jack Curry, one of the cowboys at the table, finally called in a loud voice, "Hey, Jensen. How does it feel to set the men free who killed Nate Champion?"

When Smoke ignored him and continued to eat, Curry stood up and headed toward Smoke's table.

"Are you deaf, as well as a coward, Jensen?" he called, strutting across the room, his hands near the butts of his pistols.

Smoke sighed and pushed his plate away, leaning back in his chair to look for the first time at Curry.

"I heard you, cowboy. I just didn't think it necessary to answer a damn-fool question. By the way, what is your name anyway?"

Curry glanced over his shoulder to make sure his friends were all watching as he backed down the famous gunfighter Smoke Jensen. "My name's Jack Curry. Why?"

Smoke shrugged. "I just wanted to know what name you wanted carved in the cross over your grave."

Curry's face flamed red and he squared his shoulders. "You think you got the sand to take me on, gunslick?" He gave a short laugh. "Folks around here say you're a famous gunman, but I ain't never heard of you afore."

Smoke pushed back his chair and got slowly to his feet. He walked over to stand a few feet from Curry. He glanced over the man's shoulders at his friends, still sitting at their table. "Any of you gents want to ante up in this game, or is this fool playing a lone hand?"

Curry grinned and looked back over his shoulder. Then his smile faded when the other men shook their heads and looked down at the table, clearly wanting no part in the upcoming fight.

Curry stared at Smoke, licking his lips, his hands trembling as they hovered over his weapons when he realized he might have bitten off more than he could chew.

"I hate killing a man before lunch, Curry. You want to reconsider your play?" Smoke's voice was low and almost bored, as if he had played this game too many times in the past.

"I'm gonna drill you, Jensen, and then I'm gonna spit on your body," Curry said with false bravado.

"Then let's dance, hombre," Smoke said, his eyes flat

and dangerous, no longer bored, but glittering with anger.

Curry took a deep breath and went for his pistol, his hand grabbing iron.

Before he could clear leather, Smoke's .44 appeared in his hand as if by magic, leveled and cocked and pointing at Curry's face, two inches from his nose. Curry's gun was still in its holster, and his eyes were wide, sweat beginning to bead on his forehead.

"You really want me to let the hammer down and scatter your brains all over your friends, or are you gonna go back over there and finish your breakfast?" Smoke asked.

"Gawd damn!" one of the men at the table whispered, awe in his voice. "I never even seen him draw."

Before Curry could answer, Sheriff Red Angus stalked into the room, a shotgun leveled in his hand.

As he eared back the hammers, he glanced over at Smoke's table and saw two pistols aimed at his head, Cal and Pearlie grinning over the barrels. "Take it easy there, Sheriff," Pearlie said, his voice hard. "That gent drew first."

Angus lowered his shotgun, easing the hammers down. "It don't appear that way from here. Curry's gun's still in leather."

"That's 'cause he's slower'n molasses in January, Sheriff," Cal said.

"He's right, Sheriff," one of the men at the other table said, holding his hands out in plain sight. "Jack forced the play. Jensen didn't have no choice in the matter."

Curry released his pistol and slowly raised his hands, sweat running off his face to drip on his vest. "I . . . I guess I was wrong in what I said, Jensen," he mumbled, his shoulders slumped and his head hanging down.

Smoke spun his pistol and dropped it in his holster, still staring at Curry. "I'll take that as an apology, Mr. Curry."

He spun on his heels, dropped a gold double-eagle on the table, and said, "Come on, boys. Let's hit the trail."

As Smoke and Cal and Pearlie walked from the room, Curry stumbled over to his table on legs made of rubber, flopping in his chair and sleeving sweat off his face. "Damn! That Jensen's faster'n a rattlesnake with that short-gun."

The sheriff walked over to stand staring down at Jack Curry. "You're a lucky man, Jack . . . stupid, but lucky!"

Smoke and his friends got on their horses and slowly walked them out of town through a light snowfall toward the Yellowstone Mountains.

They didn't look back, and so they didn't see four men mount up and ride out of town, leaning over on their horses to follow their tracks in the snow.

After a five-hour ride, Pearlie removed his hat and brushed accumulated snow off the brim as he glanced around at the magnificent scenery along their journey. "I can see why you love the high lonesome, Smoke," he said. "It's pretty as a picture up here."

Smoke nodded. "It's something I've never tired of seeing, Pearlie, and I've been living up in the mountains off and on for more than twenty years."

"It's so quiet up here," Cal said. "The only sound is the wind whistlin' through the pines."

Smoke gave a short laugh. "It's anything but peaceful, Cal. You're looking but not seeing. You've got to learn to open your eyes and see everything going on around you."

He paused and pointed off to the side. "See those tracks there—the small ones with larger ones alongside? That's a rabbit, being trailed by a fox, and if you follow the tracks, you can see a little batch of red-colored snow where the fox made his kill."

After a moment, Smoke halted his pony and pointed to a tall pine tree next to the trail. It was easy to see where the bark had been rubbed off to a height of eight feet. "And there's where a bear, probably a grizzly from the size of him, has been scratching his back on that tree." He looked at Cal. "It is anything but peaceful up here, Cal boy. In the winter, there's a constant battle going on, a battle for survival, and only the strongest, or the smartest, will survive."

"Speakin' of survival, Smoke," Pearlie said, glancing back down the trail the way they had come. "I think somebody's back there on our back trail."

Smoke smiled and nodded. "Good, Pearlie. I've been wondering when you'd notice. They've been back there since we left town."

Cal looked nervously back over his shoulder. "You think they mean to attack us?"

Smoke pursed his lips. "I can't see no other reason they'd be following us, Cal. Weather's too bad to be doing any cattle driving today, and if they were friendly, they'd of let their presence be known by now."

"What do you plan to do about it, Smoke?" Pearlie asked as he took his pistol out of his holster and opened the loading gate to check his loads.

Smoke glanced up at the sky, watching the gathering darkness. "It's getting on toward dusk. I think we'll make us a camp up there near that grove of poplar trees," he said, pointing ahead to a small group of trees near the trail. "We'll make us a nice, warm fire, and put some beans and bacon on to cook."

Cal looked surprised. "That's all?"

"Yeah. They won't be able to build much of a fire without giving themselves away. When the temperature starts to drop, I figure that's when they'll make their move."

"But we'll be easy targets near that fire," Cal protested.

Smoke grinned. "No, we won't. I'm gonna show you something Preacher taught me when I was just about your age, Cal."

They spurred their horses and rode into the grove of trees. "While Pearlie and I gather some wood for the fire, I want you to strip some branches off those trees, ones with plenty of leaves still on 'em," Smoke told Cal.

As darkness fell and their fire caught and began to burn brightly, Smoke made a trestle, hung a pot of beans with thick chunks of bacon in it over the fire to cook, and placed a pot of coffee on coals near the edge of the campfire.

He took a handful of the branches Cal had gathered, walked over about thirty feet from the fire, and scooped a shallow depression in a snowbank there. "Lie down in there, Cal, with your Winchester cocked and ready."

Cal gave him a disbelieving look, but climbed down in the hole in the snow, and Smoke covered him with the branches, then sprinkled snow on top of the limbs until Cal was completely hidden, with only a short section of the barrel of his rifle sticking out.

Keeping out of the light shed by the fire, he walked to the other side of their camp and did the same thing, covering Pearlie up until he couldn't be seen. He leaned over and whispered, "Don't worry, Pearlie. The branches and snow will keep you warm as toast."

After he had Cal and Pearlie situated to his satisfaction, Smoke slung his double-barreled ten-gauge Greener shotgun over his shoulders on its rawhide strap and climbed up one of the poplar trees until he was ten feet off the ground, hidden among the leaves there. Then he settled down, his back against the trunk of the tree. He didn't figure he had long to wait, for the smell of food and coffee and the inviting warmth of the fire would bring their attackers out soon.

Smoke was right. In less than thirty minutes several shadowy figures could be seen slipping through the darkness up to the edge of the light from the campfire.

Smoke had laid out their ground covers and sleeping bags, stuffing them with leaves and branches and putting their hats on their saddles as if they were lying in them near the fire.

Smoke heard a hoarse whisper almost directly under his tree. "Jack, are you ready?"

A low voice answered, "Yeah. Let 'em have it, boys."

The darkness exploded as four men opened fire on the sleeping bags, shooting into them without warning, then running into the light for closer shots.

After a moment, one of the men bent over and threw the covers back, aiming his pistol to fire again.

He looked up, his eyes wide, and muttered, "Oh, shit!"

Smoke leveled his Greener and let both hammers down, making sure he was braced against the tree trunk so the recoil wouldn't throw him out of the tree.

The shotgun exploded, sending fire and smoke and molten lead pellets into the man next to the sleeping bag, blowing him almost in two, and the slugs shredded his head and shoulders, spinning him around to land half in the fire.

Cal aimed his rifle at another figure standing off to the side and slowly squeezed the trigger, as Smoke had taught him. The rifle fired, kicking back and rolling Cal slightly to the side as the man in his sights grabbed his chest and doubled over to sprawl face-down in the snow.

The other two men, seeing their ambush fail, turned and tried to run away. As one was stomping through knee-deep snow, trying to run, Pearlie rose up out of the ground in front of him, his rifle at his hip, a grin on his face, his teeth gleaming in reflected firelight like some demon from hell.

The gunman, seeing this apparition arise from the earth, screamed in fright and held his hands out in front of him, as if they could somehow protect him from evil.

Pearlie's bullet passed through the man's palm and entered his chest, exploding his heart and ending his fear and his life simultaneously, blowing him backwards in a crumpled heap in the snow. He lay there, his eyes staring upward sightlessly, filling slowly with melting snow flakes.

The fourth man threw his gun to the ground and held up his hands, screaming, "I give up! Don't shoot me! Please, Mother of God, have mercy!"

Smoke jumped from his tree, landing on cat-feet directly in front of the hollering man, almost scaring him to death.

"Jack Curry, if I'm not mistaken," Smoke said, his voice hoarse with fury.

"Jensen . . . I'm sorry. I didn't mean. . . ." the man cried, tears running down his face, terrified.

As Cal and Pearlie walked up, Smoke said, "Cal, pull that galoot out of the fire. He's stinking up our camp."

After the bodies had been piled in a heap, away from the camp, Smoke threw Curry a shovel. "Here, asshole, bury your friends."

Curry looked at Smoke in disbelief. "I can't dig in this ground. It's frozen solid."

"You'll bury 'em, or I'll kill you where you stand," Smoke growled.

Curry took the shovel and began to hack at the ice-covered ground, slowly making a shallow hole.

While he worked, Smoke and Cal and Pearlie went over next to the fire and began to eat the beans and bacon, washing it down with steaming-hot coffee from the pot.

Cal glanced over at Curry, digging furiously as if that might somehow save his life.

"What are you gonna do with him, Smoke?"

"I haven't decided yet. What do you propose?"

Cal stared into the fire. "I don't rightly know." He cut his eyes up at Smoke and said, "Can I sleep on it and decide in the morning?"

Smoke nodded. "I'll leave it up to you, Cal. It'll be another lesson in life in the high lonesome."

After Curry finished burying what remained of his friends, Smoke invited him over to the fire and gave him food and coffee.

As he ate, Curry glanced around at the men watching him. "What are you gonna do with me, Jensen?"

Smoke yawned, finished his cup of coffee, and threw the dregs in the fire, making it hiss and crackle. "We'll decide in the morning. For now, we're all gonna get some shut-eye."

He took a rope from his packhorse and tied Curry's hands and feet, covered him with a blanket, and patted him on the cheek. "But if I were you, Curry, I'd spend what time I have left making your peace with God, 'cause I have a feeling you're gonna see Him before too long."

* * *

In the morning, they restarted the fire and cooked a breakfast of scrambled eggs, bacon, and coffee. Cal remained quiet, thinking on what they should do with the killer they'd captured. Though he was still in his teens, Cal was trail-hardened from his life on the frontier and had killed men before, but it had always been in the heat of battle, never in cold blood.

After they broke camp and gathered the ambushers' horses from where they'd been picketed, Smoke stood in front of Cal.

"Well, Cal, it's time to decide."

Curry, white-faced, looked from one of the trio to the other. "You mean you're gonna let that boy decide what happens to me?"

"You got a better idea?" Smoke asked.

Curry nodded vigorously. "Yeah, let me go and I promise not to ever bother you again." He jerked his head at the fresh graves nearby. "You've already killed three of my friends. Isn't that enough?"

"Cal?" Smoke asked, looking at his young friend.

"I think he's right, Smoke. I don't think I can kill a man in cold blood." He paused. "And I don't think you or Pearlie can neither."

Smoke nodded, his eyebrow cocked, wondering what Cal was leading up to.

"I thought about what you told him last night, about making his peace with God, so I'm gonna let God decide if he lives or dies."

"What?" Curry asked, his mouth hanging open.

Cal walked to his horse, took a long bowie knife out of his saddlebags, and flipped it end-over-end to land sticking in the snow in front of Curry's feet.

"Take the knife—you're free to go."

"You mean you're lettin' me go free?" Curry asked, a grin starting to form on his lips.

"That's right," Cal answered, his expression serious.

Curry grabbed the knife and started to get on his horse.

"Uh-uh," Cal said, shaking his head. "No horse. You're gonna have to walk back to town."

Curry stared at him. "That's a three-day walk, an' the temperature's below freezing!"

Cal nodded. "We're gonna let God an' the high lonesome decide if you're worth savin'."

"But I'll freeze to death!"

Cal shrugged. "Maybe. But this way you have a chance, which is more'n you gave us when you thought we were sleepin' an' you fired on our sleepin' bags."

Curry looked at Smoke. "Jensen, try an' talk some sense into that boy. This is crazy!"

Smoke grinned. "No, I agree with Cal. It's only fitting we give you a chance to survive. I've done it with less, so if you're man enough, you can too. You're starting off with a full belly and a weapon, which is more than fair. Now, get moving!"

Curry stuck the knife in his belt and pulled his coat tight around his shoulders. He looked into their eyes, but saw no mercy, so he turned and began to walk back toward the direction of town, his shoulders hunched against the freezing wind.

Cal glanced at Smoke. "Them horses of theirs will make a good present for the Nez Percé when we go to tradin' for the Palouse you're lookin' for."

Smoke grinned. "Damn if I don't believe you've got some mountain man in you, Cal."

Pearlie clapped Cal on the back. "That's 'cause he's learned from the best mountain man around, Smoke. Now, let's get movin' 'fore my feet freeze to the ground."

26

When they stopped for a nooning later that day, Smoke pulled out his maps of the region and took some sightings off nearby peaks to ascertain which direction to go to find the Nez Percé camping area.

"What's that X marked there on the map?" Cal asked, pointing with his finger.

"That's where the Kiowa brave I told you about, Walking Bear, said he thought the Nez Percé might be," Smoke answered.

He looked up, found his landmark, a ridge on the side of one of the mountains that looked like a bear's head and snout, and pointed up to a notch cut in the mountains.

"He said they usually head for a small valley near that notch this time of year. According to him, it's got a stream that runs fast enough not to freeze over and plenty of nearby beaver and deer and elk for the Indians to hunt to keep them eating throughout the winter months."

Cal pulled his fur-lined coat tight around him and moved a little closer to the fire, shivering in the frigid wind. "I guess if you intend to spend the winter in the high lonesome, you got to plan ahead."

Smoke nodded. "That's right, Cal. There's plenty of bones bleaching up in the mountains from men who neglected something as simple as pitching their camp near a stream, or where there was plenty of wildlife to feed off of." He looked around at the snow-covered land stretching as far as the eye could see. "It's mighty hard, when the temperature is twenty below and the snow is chest high, to travel very far looking for water or food."

Pearlie followed Smoke's gaze, feeling the cold eat right into him down to his bones. "Any other tricks we ought'a know about, Smoke?"

Smoke grinned. "You planning on becoming a mountain man, Pearlie?"

Pearlie's face remained serious. "Well, the more I'm around people like that Jack Curry and his friends, the more I like my horse."

Cal laughed. "Come on, Pearlie. The way you put the chow away, if you spent the winter up here there wouldn't be no animals left at all come spring."

"And it'd be a long time between bear sign and apple pies, my friend," Smoke added.

Pearlie nodded. "Yeah, there is that to consider." He glanced at Smoke. "Guess I'd have to try and find me somebody like Miss Sally to winter with."

"No chance, Pearlie," Smoke said, his eyes far away.

Smoke's mind drifted back to the woman he had left in Colorado. Of all the things he'd seen and done in his entire life, there were only three people he thought unforgettable. *No wonder it was so easy for you to lose your memory, old hoss,* he thought to himself. *There wasn't all that much you wanted to remember.* He thought about his dreams while his mind was confused. It was significant that the three people in his nighttime memories were his father, his substitute father Preacher, and the love of his life, Sally Reynolds Jensen. He mused on this for a few minutes, thinking it extraordinary that a man could live as long as he had and go through as much and still, when push came to shove, have only three people who meant everything to him.

He forced himself to return to the present, and glanced over at Pearlie. "There isn't but one Sally Jensen, and they broke the mold when they made her," he said.

He leaned over, picked up the coffeepot, and poured them all another cup, finishing off the pot. "Better drink up, boys. It's gonna be a while 'fore we get anything else warm in our bellies."

When they finished their coffee, they broke camp and climbed onto their horses, Pearlie holding the dally rope to the two packhorses, while Cal took charge of the rope attached to the four horses Curry's men had donated to their expedition.

Smoke pointed his horse's nose directly north, into the wind coming over the mountains from Canada, and pulled his bandanna up to cover his face and prevent frostbite. He spurred his mount, and they began the long climb toward the notch in the mountain range up ahead.

When it became too dark to see where they were heading, he set up another camp in a small grove of trees to protect them from the worst of the wind and snow. He pulled the horses together, tied them to a tree so their bodies were against each other for added warmth, and fed them plenty of oats to help keep their body temperatures up against the frigid air.

After the men ate, he had Pearlie wrap their food up in a blanket and hang it from the branch of a birch tree, so it was six feet or so off the ground.

"Why are you doin' that, Smoke?" Cal asked.

"This time of year, most of the bears are trying to put on weight for their winter hibernation. They can smell food for miles, and anything they can smell they think is theirs." He grinned. "Nothing worse than having a hungry bear waking you up trying to get your food, or even worse, trying to make you his dinner."

Cal's eyes got wide, and he looked back and forth in the gathering darkness. "You think there's any chance of that happenin' tonight?"

"Always a chance up here," Smoke said. "That's why we're gonna take turns keeping that fire going strong until the morning. Bears have a natural aversion to fire." He hesitated, and before he lay down he pulled his Winchester from its saddle boot, jacked a slug into the firing chamber, and laid the rifle next to his bedroll. "Course sometimes, if he's hungry enough, a bear'll come right into camp, fire or no fire, so sleep with one eye open, boys."

Cal's face paled. "Thanks for tellin' us that, Smoke. Now I probably won't get any sleep at all."

In spite of his professed fear, two minutes after his head hit his saddle, which he was using for a pillow, Cal's snoring could be heard for twenty yards.

Pearlie raised his head and smirked. "Hell, if the fire don't keep them bars away, Cal's snoring surely will."

Two days later, they came upon the entrance to the valley below the notch in the mountains. For the first time since they left Buffalo, the ground was level, and the temperature seemed less extreme.

"Why's it gettin' warmer, Smoke?" Pearlie asked, looking around.

Smoke pointed to either side of them. "Look up there, Pearlie. We're protected on three sides by the mountains as they rise around the valley. I suspect that's another reason the Nez Percé pick this place to winter every year."

The farther they traveled into the valley, the shallower the snowdrifts became, until there were hardly any on the ground at all.

Suddenly, Cal pulled his rifle out of its boot and aimed off to the side, cocking the hammer back.

"What are you doing?" Smoke asked, reaching over to push the barrel down.

Cal pointed off toward a large buck deer, standing in the shallow snow seventy-five yards away, its head down as it pawed snow off tender green shoots of grass and grazed.

"I thought I'd shoot that buck over there and we'd have some venison for dinner tonight."

Smoke shook his head. "You see those small piles of stones every fifty yards or so along the trail, piled up to a point?"

Cal shook his head. "No, I hadn't noticed."

"Those are Nez Percé signal rocks. They show this is their territory, and I doubt they'd take kindly to us killing game on land they've claimed as their own."

"But I haven't seen an Indian yet, Smoke."

"Oh, they're there. They've been trailing us for the past six hours, keeping just out of sight on the mountainsides on either side of us."

"Damn," Cal said in frustration. "I don't think I'll ever git the hang of this mountaineering."

Smoke patted him on the shoulder. "Don't feel bad, Cal. I lived up here for several years with Preacher when I was about your age, and a day didn't go by that he didn't teach me something new about being a mountain man. There's a hell of a lot to learn, and if you don't have a good teacher, the mountain'll jump up and kill you 'fore you have a chance to learn it all."

Pearlie chuckled. "Seems like the more Cal and I learn, the more we don't know 'bout life up here."

Smoke got down off his horse and undid one of the ties to the packhorse. He pulled a bag of Arbuckle's coffee out of the pack along with the coffeepot. "Help me make a fire, boys. I think it's time we introduced ourselves before we get any closer to the Nez Percé camp. It ain't polite to go calling until we've been invited."

After they had the fire going and a large pot of coffee brewing, Smoke instructed Cal and Pearlie to sit next to the fire, hands in plain sight and away from their weapons. As they sat drinking the coffee, he set several more cups around the fire, off to the side by themselves. "That's just to let them know they're expected, and welcome," Smoke said when Cal and Pearlie looked at him with puzzled expressions on their faces.

Within fifteen minutes, two braves who appeared to be in their early twenties, accompanied by a younger brave about twelve years old, walked their ponies into Smoke's camp.

Without getting up, Smoke waved them toward the

campfire. "Coffee's brewing, and you're welcome to join us," he said in a slow voice.

Cal whispered, "You think they speak English?"

Smoke nodded. "Most of the younger braves do by now. There's been so many trappers up here, they've managed to learn enough to get by. If they don't, we'll have to use sign language, but I'm a mite rusty, so I hope these men know our lingo."

As the braves dismounted, Smoke noticed one was carrying an old muzzle-loaded rifle, while the other two had bows and arrows, one with a stone tomahawk stuck in his breeches within easy reach.

As they approached, Smoke said in a low voice, "Most of the Indians I've met have a real taste for coffee, and they don't get to partake of it very often."

The eldest of the three walked up to stand next to the fire, staring down at Smoke. He patted his chest with an open palm. "I am called Spotted Elk," he said in a deep voice.

Smoke stood up and placed his hand on his chest. "I am known as Man Who Walks on Mountain."

The brave's eyes widened and he grinned, turning to talk rapidly in his own language to his companions.

"Would you care for some coffee?" Smoke asked, pointing at the coffeepot resting on coals next to the fire.

"*Cafecito?*" the brave asked, making Smoke smile when he used the slang term for coffee favored by most of the mountain men Smoke had known.

As they gathered close to the fire and Smoke poured them full cups, he said over his shoulder to Pearlie, "Get the bag of sugar out of the pack. Indians have a real hankering for sugar with their coffee."

When the young brave tasted his coffee, and made a face at its bitterness, Smoke reached over and poured a generous helping of sugar into the strong, black brew.

The brave took another tentative sip, and broke into a wide grin, smacking his lips and drinking down the entire cup in one long swallow.

The two older braves laughed, along with Smoke and Cal and Pearlie.

Spotted Elk leaned over and said to Smoke, "Running Deer's first time with the black water called *cafecito*."

"It does take some getting used to," Smoke observed, grinning as the young boy held his cup out for a refill.

Spotted Elk held out his hand to stop Running Deer, trying to impart some manners to the kid, but Smoke shook his head. "That's all right—we have plenty more." He refilled the boy's cup, and watched him drink it slower this time, savoring the sweetness of the coffee.

As they drank, with the Indians sitting on their haunches around the fire, Smoke said, "We're looking for Gray Wolf." He pointed over his shoulder at the four horses tied nearby. "We have presents for your tribe, and come in peace to make a trade."

Spotted Elk finished his coffee and handed the cup back to Smoke, then walked over to run his hands down the flanks of the horses, stopping to pry open their mouths and glance at their teeth as he examined them. He looked back over his shoulder and said something in the Nez Percé language to his friends, who immediately got up and ran to their ponies. They jumped up on them and rode off with a couple of whoop and hollers, evidently on their way to let the chief know they had visitors on the way.

As Spotted Elk got on his pony, Smoke handed him the dally rope to the horses, letting him lead the animals into the village so he would get credit for the trade. In this way, Smoke knew they had at least one ally among the Nez Percé who would help break the ice in the upcoming bargaining for the Palouse ponies they were after.

27

Smoke and Cal and Pearlie followed Spotted Elk into the main part of the Nez Percé camp. In addition to the numerous hide huts and deerskin tepees, there were several log structures and elaborate lean-tos, showing the semi-permanent nature of this camp.

Smoke pointed out the wooden structures to Cal and Pearlie. "Evidently, the Nez Percé return to this same location every winter. Some of those cabins look like they're several years old, at least."

"I always thought Injuns roamed around, making camps wherever they happened to stop," Pearlie observed.

"That used to be true," Smoke said, "but lately, since they've become more peaceful and less warlike, and more used to the white man's presence, they seem to've become more settled in their ways."

He shook his head. "Just another part of the life up here that's passed on due to interference by white men, and will never be the same."

A brave stepped from one of the largest of the wooden cabins, holding up his spread hands in welcome. Smoke was surprised at his young age. "That must be Gray Wolf," he said in a low voice to his companions. "I would've thought he'd be older to be chief."

The Indian appeared to be in his late thirties or early forties, very young for a full chief of the Nez Percé, who, like most Indian tribes, equated age with wisdom in choosing their leaders.

"Welcome," Gray Wolf said, his face showing neither happiness nor dismay to see them.

"Indians would make great poker players," Smoke whispered. "They don't tend to show their emotions much."

He stepped off his horse and walked up to the chief. "Hello. I am Man Who Walks on Mountain," Smoke said, lowering his head a mite showing deference to the chief's position as leader of his tribe.

"We have heard your song many times," Gray Wolf said. "One of our Kiowa brothers, Walking Bear, sent word of what you did for his people in the white-eyes camp called Denver. He said your are known as an honorable man, and a friend to all our peoples."

Smoke nodded, not saying anything, waiting to see what would happen next. He knew Indians could be very unpredictable, welcoming one minute, dangerous the next.

"Come inside. We will smoke and eat, as friends should," the chief said, turning and leading the way into his cabin.

When they entered, Smoke and Cal and Pearlie found the floor to be dirt, covered with elaborate hides of deerskin and bearskin. In the middle of the room, underneath a hole in the roof, was a small fire.

Gray Wolf waved them to be seated next to the fire, and he joined them, sitting cross-legged on the ground. Spotted Elk and the younger brave who had been with him at Smoke's camp joined them around the fire.

Gray Wolf pointed at the young brave. "This my son, Running Deer." Gray Wolf looked at the boy with undisguised pride. "He be next chief of Nez Percé someday."

Smoke nodded. "He is a fine-looking young brave. He will bring much honor to your house."

Gray Wolf picked up a wooden pipe and put it in his mouth, lighting it with a burning branch from the fire. After several puffs, he handed it across to Smoke, who also took a couple of puffs, his tongue burning from the bitter taste of the uncured tobacco, then passed it over to Cal and Pearlie.

After everyone around the fire had a taste of the pipe, Smoke took a handful of cigars from his pocket and passed them out. The chief quickly put the pipe down and lighted one of the cigars, showing he didn't much care for the taste of his tobacco either.

After a few minutes, the chief signaled a woman kneeling behind him, and she ladled liquid from a pot on the edge of the fire into small bowls and gave each of the visitors one.

Pearlie looked into his bowl with some distaste. "What do you suppose this is?" he asked Smoke in a low voice.

Smoke plucked a chunk of meat out of the stew and popped it in his mouth, chewing and smiling at the same time. "Elk stew," he said to Pearlie. "Eat it, and try to look like you enjoy it, or you'll insult our host."

Eating with their fingers, since Indians didn't use spoons and forks, they soon finished their stew, Pearlie smacking his lips as if it was the best thing he'd ever eaten.

As Gray Wolf relighted his cigar and leaned back on an elbow, he said, "Spotted Elk has shown me your gifts to the Nez Percé. What do you ask in trade?"

"I would like to take with me some of your spotted ponies, two males and two females."

"Why do you wish our spotted ponies? Your horses seem adequate for your needs."

"I have a ranch in Colorado, and I know the spotted ponies of the Nez Percé can run like the wind from sunup to sundown without tiring. I have need of such animals in my herd. They will add much to my stature among the white-eyes of my tribe."

"You have traveled far to get these ponies. You must wish them very bad, no?"

Smoke smiled and spoke out of the side of his mouth to Cal and Pearlie. "The old bastard is starting to negotiate now, making the point that I came to him, so I must give up the most in the trade."

To Gray Wolf, he said, "That is true. In addition to the horses I have already offered, I have brought white man's wampum—greenback dollars, or gold if you prefer."

Smoke opened his buckskin shirt and pulled out his money belt. He took a handful of hundred-dollar bills along with a handful of gold double-eagle pieces, and spread them on the rug in front of him.

Gray Wolf smiled and spread his hands. "Your dollars are of no use to us here on the mountain," he said, his eyebrows raised.

Smoke leaned forward. "In the spring, when you and your people travel to the south to graze your ponies and hunt the elk and deer to fill your cooking pots, these dollars can be traded for whatever you need in the white man's camps . . . tools, knives, food or grain for your ponies, beads, mirrors, blankets for your squaws."

Smoke held up a hundred-dollar bill. "Just one of these bought Walking Bear enough food to feed all his people for the entire winter."

Spotted Elk leaned over and spoke softly and rapidly to Gray Wolf in the language of the Nez Percé.

After a moment, Gray Wolf turned back to Smoke. "Spotted Elk tells me the knives of the white-eyes are much superior to ours, and that your gold can buy many knives."

Smoke nodded. "Spotted Elk speaks with much wisdom."

He took the bowie knife from his belt and held out his hand to Spotted Elk, who, after a moment, passed over his handmade knife to Smoke.

Smoke swung the bowie knife, and it cut through the blade of Spotted Elk's knife as if it were made of wood.

As Gray Wolf's eyes widened, Smoke handed the bowie knife across to him. "For you, a blade as strong as the Nez Percé's chief is."

The chief sat a little straighter at Smoke's words, a slight smile tugging at the corner of his lips.

Smoke got to his feet. "We have more on our pack-horse."

He walked outside, followed by the chief and Spotted Elk and Running Deer. He stepped to the packhorse and untied the ropes holding a large canvas bag to the back of the mount, letting it fall to the ground.

When the pack hit the ground, it opened, spilling out piles of metal pots and pans, knives, woven woolen blankets in bright colors, and several packages of candies, coffee, tobacco, and flour.

Smoke bent and took a package of peppermint sticks, handing them to Running Deer, who quickly put one in his mouth, his eyes wide with delight.

Gray Wolf nodded. "Let us go to our ponies to find some suitable for your fine gifts."

They walked over toward where the Palouse herd was confined in a large corral of bushes set in a large semi-circle, leaving the tribe's squaws to paw through the pots and pans and blankets, chattering like small children at the treasure.

One of the studs immediately caught Smoke's eye. He was taller than the others, and heavily muscled for a Palouse, which tended to be slimmer than white man's horses.

The chief saw where Smoke was looking, and nodded. "Man Who Walks on Mountain has a good eye for ponies. That is one of my best, stronger and faster than others."

He turned to Spotted Elk and spoke a few words in their language. Spotted Elk quickly jumped over the bushes and walked into the herd of horses, grabbing several by the rope halters the Indians used instead of the leather ones used by white men.

Soon they had two magnificent studs, one gray with dark black spots on its rump, and another one with reddish-colored spots over a white coat. Both had the blue eyes with a circle around the iris showing the true full-blooded Palouse genes.

The mares were only slightly smaller, and both had

good lines, with strong legs and sleek muscles, showing they had been very well cared for.

Gray Wolf held out his hand. "Are these what you wish?"

Smoke walked over to run his hands over the big stud's neck and back. "These are just what I've been looking for."

Gray Wolf nodded. "Then may they carry you past your enemies in time of need, Man Who Walks on Mountain."

Smoke looked over his shoulder at Pearlie and Cal. "Throw a rope over these horses, boys, before he changes his mind."

Pearlie took the rope halters in his hand while Cal tied dally ropes to the animals. "Smoke, these are some of the finest Palouse I've ever seen," Pearlie said.

"These boys'll make old Seven a mite jealous when they're put out to breed alongside of him," Cal added.

"If they turn out to be half the horse old Seven was, they'll do just fine," Smoke said. "Excuse me for a minute, boys. There's something I want to ask Gray Wolf before we leave."

Smoke took Gray Wolf by the arm, led him off to a spot a few yards away, and began to talk to him in a low tone that Cal and Pearlie couldn't quite make out. As they talked, the chief looked over at the two young cowboys occasionally, a smile on his face as he nodded his head. After talking earnestly with the chief for about five minutes, Smoke grinned and shook the brave's hand, then returned to where Cal and Pearlie were holding the Palouse horses.

Soon, the trio had said their good-byes to Gray Wolf and Spotted Elk, and were on their way back down the mountain toward Buffalo. They made good time, since the weather had cleared and they were going with the north wind instead of against it.

"Smoke, when we breed these Palouse with those Morgans you got from John Chisum, we're gonna have the best remuda in the territory," Pearlie said.

Smoke nodded. "If we can manage to get the speed and intelligence from the Morgans mixed with the bottom and toughness of the Palouse into one animal, it'll be a tough horse to beat."

As they made their way down the mountain, Pearlie looked over at Cal, a satisfied smile on his face. "Well, Cal, I guess Miss Sally won't have to skin us alive after all."

"What do you mean?" Smoke asked.

Cal grinned. "When she sent us up here after you, Miss Sally as much as said if'n we let anything happen to you, she'd never let us forget it."

"And now that we've cleared up that little fracas down in Johnson County, an' you've got the Palouse you came after, it shouldn't be too hard to get you home with your hide in one piece," Pearlie added to Smoke.

Smoke glanced over at Pearlie. "Who said we're heading home right away?"

Cal said, "I don't like the sound of that, Pearlie."

"Well, ain't we?" Pearlie asked, a fearful expression on his face, not really wanting to hear Smoke's answer.

"Not just yet we aren't," Smoke said. "There are some things I want to do before we head back to Colorado."

"Such as?" Pearlie asked.

"When I got the cavalry involved, I was promised those boys that killed my friends Nate and Nick were going to be tried for their crimes. Once I make sure that's gonna happen, then the Johnson County War is over, and not before."

Pearlie cut his eyes heavenward. "Please God, let things go the way they're supposed to, just once."

"Smoke," Cal said, pleading, "if someone ends up shootin' a hole in you, Miss Sally'll never bake us no bear sign nor pies again."

Smoke grinned. "Well, boys, knowing how much you like Sally's cooking, I'll do my best not to let that happen."

"Besides," Pearlie added, trying to convince Cal as well as himself that everything was going to be all right, "that Colonel Van Horn looked like a right honorable man.

I'm sure he was tellin' the truth when he told Smoke those boys were goin' to be tried for the killin's."

"It's not Van Horn I'm worried about," Smoke said. "It's those lily-livered politicians in Cheyenne that control things that are liable to muck things up. I never met a politician, or a lawyer for that matter, that didn't know which hand held the money. Most of 'em don't give a damn about justice, just where their next payoff is coming from."

"Smoke," Cal said, a questioning look on his face, "you said there were a couple of things you wanted to do. If one of 'em is makin' sure those Regulators get what's comin' to 'em, what's the other?"

Smoke looked over at Cal and Pearlie, a slight smile on his lips. "Well, it occurred to me when we were up there with the Nez Percé, that the only thing you boys know about the mountain men are what you've heard sitting around a campfire."

Pearlie nodded. "So?"

"I think it's about time I broadened your education a mite. What do you say to staying up here in the mountains and doing a little hunting and camping for a couple of weeks?"

Cal glanced back at their pack animal and its bare back. "But Smoke, we ain't hardly got no supplies left at all."

"That's the point, boys. You need to learn how to live up here like the mountain men did, hunting and killing your food, living off the land without relying on store-bought supplies for your life."

Cal and Pearlie stared at each other for a moment. "Does that mean eatin' bark an' such?" Pearlie asked, a worried expression on his face.

Smoke laughed. "Hell, no, Pearlie." He waved his hands at the scenery around them. "The high lonesome is God's own general store. He's put everything you need to live right here for the taking. All you got to do is learn how to take it, before it takes you."

"But Smoke," Pearlie said, giving it one last try, "you

said the Indians done marked this land as theirs, an' they'd be mighty pissed off if'n we hunted it."

"That's right, Pearlie. That's why I had that little palaver with Chief Gray Wolf before we left. I told him you boys were pilgrims who needed some lessons only the high lonesome could teach. He agreed on how important that was for young men to learn, so he gave me his permission to camp up here a while and teach you what I could about living on the mountain."

Cal broke out in a wide grin and nodded his head gleefully. "Gee willikers, Smoke, I think it'd be a great adventure!"

Pearlie agreed, albeit reluctantly. "I guess so. After all, that elk stew wasn't so bad."

"Good, then it's decided," Smoke said, jerking his horse's head around and heading off in a wide sweep back up the mountain, toward areas remote from the Indians' camp.

"Wait a minute," Cal said. "What about Miss Sally? Won't she be worried?"

"No. Before we left Buffalo, I wired Sheriff Monte Carson in Big Rock, telling him to let her know we were all right and we'd be home when we got there and not to worry—you boys had the situation well in hand."

28

When it came time to leave the trail and head up into untraveled territory, through snowdrifts two and three feet deep, Smoke hung back. "I'm gonna let you boys take the lead and see if you remember what I told you about picking a place to make our base camp."

"No problem," Cal said, with the exuberance and cockiness of youth. "Come on, Pearlie, let's see if we can find a stream that ain't iced over, with plenty of beaver on it."

"Yeah," Pearlie said, entering into the situation with good humor, "an' we need to find someplace sheltered from the wind and snow, near a cliff or overhang or in some heavy timber so we won't freeze our *cojones* off when the next blizzard hits."

Smoke smiled to himself, thinking how much he was going to enjoy imparting some of the knowledge Preacher had given to him during his early days in the mountains.

It was getting close to dusk before they found a suitable campsite. It was situated next to the sheer stone face of a mountain wall, facing south so the north wind would be blocked during snowstorms. A gurgling, rushing stream was within twenty yards of the camp, and there was evidence of several beaver dams within easy reach, indicating an abundance of wildlife.

The site was below the timberline, so there was plenty of woodfall for making fires, and the trees had many low-hanging limbs that would be useful for forming sides and roofs on the lean-to Smoke would show them how to build to keep the worst of the weather off.

As they gathered wood for their first fire, Smoke stood in the small clearing with his hands on his hips, satisfied the boys would be apt pupils for what he had to teach them.

He helped them pick out fist-sized stones to place in a circle around the fire, explaining how the rocks were called gravel, and had been deposited by giant glaciers that had moved through the area millions of years before.

He showed them how to build a pit for their waste away from the camp, and told them it had to be covered over so it wouldn't bring predators like bears and mountain lions to their camp.

That first night, before they had their lean-tos built, they were lucky and the skies were clear, with little snowfall. They sat around the fire and made a meal of hot coffee, strong enough to float a horseshoe, and dried, jerked beef, hard enough to break a tooth if they weren't careful.

Sitting there with a roof of stars over their heads, warmed by the golden flames of a wood fire, he told them stories of the mountain men he had known and camped with, men who were legends in the lore of the early frontier.

Men with names like Preacher, Puma Buck, Huggy Charles, Dupre, Grizzly Jones, and others. Men who had lived their entire lives forsaking the company of other men to be alone in the high lonesome.

His stories were punctuated with the cries of wolves, singing to their mates in the moonlight, the occasional guttural growl of a night-hunting grizzly, and the wild scream of a mountain lion, celebrating its night-kill.

Finally, Cal and Pearlie fell asleep, with visions of buck-skin-clad men, fighting bears, lions, and Indians, forging lives of happy solitude in the highest reaches of frozen mountain ranges.

When dawn came, cold and clear, Smoke began his lessons. He instructed the boys on which trees to cut to form the walls of their lean-to, how to strip the smaller branches, leaving the topmost ones for forming the roof, placing the poles at an angle against the side of the mountain cliff so as to shed the snow that was sure to come with the next winter storm.

Once they had their shelter completed, he led them on a hunting expedition, both for food and for furs to help ward off the freezing temperatures he expected in the coming days.

Cal was the first to shoot, picking out a large doe deer, after Smoke told him to ignore the buck standing nearby, since the doe's meat would be much more tender and less gamy to the taste.

Once they had skinned the deer, hanging the skin away from the camp to cure, he had them hang the meat from a tree, suspended out of the reach of hungry bears or mountain lions.

Next, they went hunting for bear, to get skins to line the walls of the lean-to and to sleep under for warmth. He showed them how to track the big animals, following spoor of bear droppings as well as tracks in the fresh snow. They passed up several shots at females, who had small cubs in tow, Smoke telling them not to kill the mothers as the cubs couldn't survive on their own.

As they were walking through dense undergrowth, suddenly a giant grizzly reared up, spreading his arms and growling in anger at their intrusion onto his hunting grounds.

Pearlie, standing firm and unafraid, raised his rifle and planted his feet.

"Through the heart, Pearlie," Smoke advised, ready-ing his own rifle in case Pearlie missed. "You want to drop him with one shot. Can't afford to waste ammunition up here."

As the animal charged, Pearlie stood his ground and placed his shot directly in the bear's chest, dropping him like a stone only yards from where they were standing.

"Damn," Cal exclaimed, wiping fear-sweat from his brow, "that was a fine shot, Pearlie."

Pearlie, white-faced and with trembling hands now that the danger was past, grinned. "Whew, that was close. Those bears can move faster'n I thought."

"They can outrun the fastest horse for short distances, especially through deep snow," Smoke told them as he pulled out his skinning knife. He glanced up at them. "That's something it'll pay you to remember if you ever jump one on horseback."

He handed the knife to Pearlie. "Here, son, it's your kill, so you get to do the honors."

As Pearlie approached the dead bear, he drew back, making a face. "Gawd almighty! He stinks to high heaven."

Smoke grinned. "Bears aren't partial to baths, Pearlie." He hesitated, thinking of his old friends. "And neither are mountain men, 'cept maybe once a year in the spring. A couple of weeks up here, and you won't smell much different."

As the days on the mountain passed, Cal and Pearlie soaked up the knowledge Smoke taught them like sponges. Before long they were skinning and cutting wild game as if they were born to it. Smoke was amazed at how rapidly they assimilated the lessons of living in the high lonesome, thinking they would have made admirable mountain men had they been born thirty years sooner.

The boys, for their part, mostly looked forward to the nights spent around the campfire, listening to the tales of mountain men Smoke told them each night.

When their store-bought supplies ran out, Smoke taught them to make coffee from ground up acorns and piñon nuts, how to pick grapevines to smoke instead of tobacco, and how to make a passable flour out of roots of certain trees. He taught them to hunt for and find wild onions and yams, which berries could be safely eaten and which would cause debilitating stomach cramps, and how to build traps for beaver and birds and squirrels, saving their precious ammunition, which was beginning to run low.

On this diet, the baby fat the boys had accumulated melted off, and they became lean and their muscles began to strengthen and grow wiry from the hard physical labor of surviving in the wilderness.

Smoke taught them to make needles from birds' bones and rawhide string from deer hides so they could mend and take up their clothes that were hanging loosely on their now-thin bodies.

Soon, they were all wearing homemade buckskins, much like the mountain men they had seen. Cal was even sporting a wispy, thin beard, since shaving with the frigid mountain stream water didn't much appeal to him.

Toward the end of their sojourn, Smoke took to staying in camp, getting the Palouse horses used to having saddles on their backs instead of Indian blankets, while Cal and Pearlie ran their traps and hunted for food and fresh vegetables in the woods.

Finally, Smoke decided they were ready to leave the mountain, the boys having learned enough about being mountain men to be able to survive on their own if need be.

On their last night around the campfire, Smoke took out his knife and lightly touched Cal on the shoulder. "I'm giving you a mountain man name, Cal. I'm gonna call you Deerstalker Woods, for your ability to sneak up on a deer close enough to spit in his eye without him ever hearing you," Smoke said.

As Cal beamed, Smoke looked over at Pearlie. "Your mountain name will be Hawkeye, 'cause you've become one of the best trackers I've ever known. I think you could track a field mouse through a blizzard if you had to," Smoke said, pride in his voice.

"Do we have to leave?" Cal asked.

Smoke's eyes got a faraway look in them. "Yeah. It's time we head back down the mountain and see what became of the men who killed Nate Champion and Nick Ray. I have a feeling we have some unfinished business with those boys."

29

When Smoke and Cal and Pearlie rode into Buffalo, they got some strange looks. They were still in their buckskins, Cal's and Pearlie's only partially cured, and all three had heavy beards and long, unkempt hair.

They took their horses to the livery stable and instructed the man there to rub them down and feed them plenty of grain. Then they headed toward the hotel. As they approached the door to the hotel, Sheriff Red Angus was walking along the boardwalk toward them from the opposite direction. When he saw them, he stopped and stared at Smoke with his head cocked to the side.

"Smoke Jensen? Is that you?"

Smoke stopped and said, "Yes, Sheriff, it is. What can I do for you?"

Angus stepped closer, put his hand on Smoke's shoulder as if to say something, then wrinkled up his nose and took a step back. "Jesus, you boys are a mite gamy."

"Three weeks in the mountains will do that to you," Smoke said.

"Well, I just wanted to warn you. Things aren't goin' so good here in Johnson County since the Army came and took the Regulators away."

"Oh? What do you mean?"

Angus looked nervously around to see if anyone was

watching, then put his hand on Smoke's arm and ush-ered him off the street and into the hotel lobby. "It's too complicated to go into right now. Why don't you boys get cleaned up and then meet me over at my office?"

"Sheriff, I don't know what's got you so riled up, but we intend to take a hot bath, then go to the dining room for a good meal. We've been eating out of a pan for three weeks and we all want a good meal. If you need to talk to us, you can meet us here in . . . oh, about an hour."

"All right," Angus said, "only, watch your backs till I get to talk to you. You ain't exactly the most popular gent in town right now."

Smoke pursed his lips as he watched Angus walk away, wondering what was going on.

After a moment, Pearlie touched his arm. "Smoke, I think we'd better go get those baths 'fore the manager has to open all the windows in this place."

They walked up to the front desk. Smoke said, "I need three rooms and three baths, with plenty of hot water."

The desk man peered down his nose at the three men standing before him, the expression on his face showing he didn't like the way they smelled and looked.

"We don't rent to . . . men such as you. I'd suggest you take your business down the street to a . . . less expensive establishment."

Smoke opened his shirt and unbuttoned his money belt, letting the clerk see the wads of greenbacks in it. He pulled a hundred-dollar bill out of the stack and handed it to the man. "Partner, how about getting those baths ready, and you just let me know when you've gone through this one and we'll give you another one just like it, all right?"

The clerk smiled as if it hurt his face, and rang the bell on the counter. "Front!" he called, then instructed the bellboy to take their bags up to the third floor and show them where the bathroom was.

Upstairs, Smoke and the boys stripped their buckskins off and threw them in a pile. "Take these out and burn them, if you don't mind," he said to the boy in his teens working the bathroom.

As the boy bent to pick the rancid clothes up, he turned his face away, saying, "No, sir, I don't mind at all. Matter of fact, it'll be a pleasure to git 'em out of here."

Smoke laughed, and settled slowly into a tub filled with steaming-hot water. "And young man, put more water on to heat. I have a feeling we may be here a spell."

Pearlie took a long-handled brush, rubbed soap on it, and began to scrub his back, an expression of near-ecstasy on his face. "You know, Smoke, I ain't never been one to be 'specially fond of baths, but I gotta tell you, after three weeks in the high lonesome freezin' my butt off, this ranks right up there with Miss Sally's bear sign."

Cal, who was sunk down in steaming water until nothing showed but his bearded head, gave a contented sigh. "I don't know 'bout *that*, Pearlie, but this do feel right nice."

Smoke laughed. "I love the mountains, boys, but there is something to be said for civilization, too."

The attendant came back into the room after taking their stinking buckskins out to burn, and stared at the men with wide eyes. "Are you mountain men?" he said, as if he'd never seen anyone like them up close.

Smoke glanced at Cal and Pearlie, then answered, "We sure are, young fellow. Those two over there are two of the roughest, toughest mountain men I've ever had the pleasure to make camp with."

Cal and Pearlie beamed at the compliment, sitting a little straighter in their baths.

"What's it like livin' up in the mountains?" the boy asked.

"Well," Pearlie said, as if he were an expert, "other than the bears an' mountain lions an' wolves tryin' to make you their dinner, an' the Injuns wanting to take your scalp an' hang it on their lodge pole, it ain't so bad."

Cal nodded. "An' if'n the temperature don't get much under thirty below an' the snow stays less then five feet deep, it ain't bad a'tall."

Smoke grinned, thinking how much both Cal and

Pearlie had been changed by their experience in the high lonesome. Cal was no longer just a cowboy in his teens. He seemed to have matured from having to face death on a daily basis, with only his skill and brains to keep him alive. *There's nothing like knowing you're only one mistake away from being killed to make a man grow up fast and give him confidence,* Smoke thought.

Smoke climbed out of the tub and dried off, the attendant's eyes widening again at the sight of his massive body, covered with knife and bullet scars from all the scrapes he'd been in.

As Smoke stepped in front of a mirror hung on a pole and began to shave his beard off, Pearlie asked, "You plannin' on shavin', Cal?"

Cal rubbed his hands over his beard. "I ain't decided yet. You think this growth makes me look older?"

Pearlie laughed. "Uglier, if'n that's possible, not particularly older."

"You'd better shave it off, Cal," Smoke said, glancing at him in the mirror. "If I take you home looking like that, Sally's liable to shoot you, thinking you're a *bandido* or rustler come to steal our stock."

Pearlie looked at Cal's hair, hanging down over his eyes. "A little time in a barber's chair wouldn't do any of us any harm neither," he said.

Finally, when they had soaked and scrubbed until their skin was red and shining, and after they'd shaved their beards, Cal electing to leave his wispy moustache in place, they climbed into fresh clothes and headed down the stairs toward the dining room.

"I can already taste that beefsteak," Pearlie said, licking his lips.

"Smoke," Cal said, "I ain't sayin' you ain't a right good cook, but it'll sure be nice to eat some meat you don't have to cut with an ax 'fore you put it in your mouth."

Just as the waiter placed their food in front of them, along with steaming cups of real coffee, Sheriff Angus walked up and took a seat at their table.

Smoke gestured at the plates of food. "Would you like something to eat, Sheriff?"

Angus shook his head. "No. To tell you the truth, I ain't had much of an appetite lately, Jensen."

Smoke cut a piece of his steak off and stuck it in his mouth. "Why don't you tell us what's going on around here that has you all riled up, Sheriff."

Angus looked around over his shoulder to make sure no one else was listening, then leaned forward, speaking in a low tone of voice. "Jensen, since that fracas with the Regulators, this county has gone to hell. Before they came, it was a nice place to live." He shrugged. "Oh, sure, we had a little rustlin' and a little stealin', but it was on a minor scale, and was mainly directed against the large ranchers that could afford to lose a few head of stock."

"Things have changed?"

"You're damn right they have, and not for the better. I've lost all control of the county. The men around here have gone from being minor outlaws to full-fledged desperados. They're goin' around shootin' and killin' everybody they think may have helped out the Regulators."

"Well, you got to expect that."

"Yeah, but they're not stoppin' there. There's a lot of men takin' advantage of this, an' they consider anybody who has somethin' they want to be fair game." He paused long enough to build himself a cigarette, sticking it in the corner of his mouth, where it bobbed up and down as he talked. "Hell, just the other day the foreman of the Hoe Ranch, George Wellman, was gunned down in cold blood, all for about ten head of beef."

"You know who did it?"

"Sure, but there ain't no way I could get a jury in this county to convict 'em. I tell you, Jensen, it's become every man for himself around here."

"Sounds like you got yourself a problem, Sheriff."

"That's for sure, an' to make matters worse, Tom Horn and the other so-called stock detectives are still out there, shootin' up anybody they think is rustlin' the big ranchers' cattle."

Smoke's eyes narrowed. "I thought all that would stop when the Regulators and the men who led them were put on trial for the killing of Nate Champion and Nick Ray."

Angus smirked. "I guess you ain't heard 'bout that little fiasco either."

"No. Tell me."

"Soon after Wolcott and Canton and Smith and their men were taken to Fort McKinney, a sympathetic judge said they couldn't get a fair trial in Johnson County, so they were taken by train to Cheyenne."

Smoke shook his head. "As if the trial there would be fair."

"Exactly. Hell, they were transported in a private Pullman car stocked with champagne and all the whiskey they could drink."

Smoke's face clouded. "Sounds like the fix was in."

"You got that right. They were set up in a bowling alley at Fort Russell and given anything they wanted, including visits from their wives and other . . . female friends."

"What about the trial?"

"The only charges brought were for the killings of Nate Champion and Nick Ray. And since the only witnesses were you and that mountain man, and nobody made any effort to get you to testify, the prisoners were turned loose without any bond. Well, hell, by then we knew we'd never win any case against them in Cheyenne, so the charges were all dropped."

"What about the gunmen from Texas?"

"They've all gone on their way, some back to Texas, others to God only knows where."

Smoke nodded, thinking over his options.

"So, no one is going to be made to pay for killing Nate and Nick, huh?"

"Not by the law, they ain't."

Smoke leaned back and took a cigar out of his pocket. He struck a lucifer on his boot and lighted the stogie. He peered through clouds of blue smoke at the sheriff. "Well, then, maybe it's time someone other than the law took a hand in the matter."

Sheriff Angus shook his head. "I got to warn you, Jensen, to watch your back. There ain't any men on either side you can count as your friends."

"That's the way I like it, Sheriff. Then I don't have to worry about who gets in my way." Smoke took the cigar out of his mouth and stared at the glowing red end for a moment. When he spoke, it was as if he were talking to himself more than to the sheriff. "You know, Sheriff, a man's got to have a creed to live by, a set of standards that he just won't violate. Me, I'm an Old Testament kind of person, and I still believe in the old adage, an eye for an eye and a tooth for a tooth."

Angus leaned forward. "Jensen, I hope to hell you ain't plannin' on tryin' to get vengeance on your own for Champion and Ray. You won't stand a chance in Cheyenne, 'cause them boys got the law in the palm of their hands."

Smoke's lips curled up in a grin that made the hair on the back of Angus's neck stir in fear. "That may be so, Sheriff, but it doesn't matter a whole lot. By the time they know I'm coming after them, it'll be too late to do anything about it." His eyes turned flat and cold as ice. "Did you ever see a rattlesnake warn the rabbit before it strikes?"

The sheriff shook his head, not really sure he understood what this very dangerous man sitting across from him meant, but he was sure thankful he didn't have him on his back trail.

Smoke poured another cup of coffee and leaned back in his chair, crossing his legs and folding his arms across his chest as if they were old friends discussing the price of beef.

"Now, Sheriff Angus, I want you to tell me all you know about the men behind the Regulators, the men who were really responsible for what happened here in Johnson County."

30

Smoke and Cal and Pearlie got off the train in Cheyenne and made arrangements for their horses to be boarded in the livery stable for a few days until they were ready to leave again.

They found a hotel in the seedier part of town, a place so low on the economic scale that Smoke was sure none of the wealthy men he was going after would find out they were there.

After eating a meal that even Pearlie wasn't too happy about, they met in Smoke's room to plan their attack.

"I wish you boys would reconsider and go on back to Colorado and let me do this on my own," Smoke said.

Pearlie shook his head. "Not a chance, Smoke. Miss Sally would cut us off at the knees if she found out we didn't back your play in this."

"Besides," Cal added, "men don't take off and turn tail when their partner's up against the kind'a odds you're facin' here. From what Sheriff Angus said, there are over a hundred members of the Cheyenne Club."

Smoke smiled, grateful for the support even though he was worried that he might be getting them all into something they wouldn't be able to get out of.

"Well, we're not going after all hundred members, just those directly responsible for the killings in Johnson County."

He leaned back on his bed on his elbow. "There's a book Sally got me to read a while back. It's called the *Art of War*, by some Japanese man whose name I don't recollect right now. Anyway, one of the things he emphasizes if you're going to war with someone, is to learn all you can about your enemy before you try to take him on."

"Is that the book you told us about with those men who dressed all in black, the ones called ninjas?" Cal asked.

"Yes, it is. Now, what we have to do is hang around the Cheyenne Club for a day or two and find out all we can about how it operates, how to get in and out in a hurry, and then ask around and see if we can find some time when the men we're after are all going to be there together."

"Why don't we just take them out one at a time?" Pearlie asked.

Smoke shook his head. "Because after the first one or two, they'd know we were coming and would be ready for us. No, we're only going to get one chance at this, and we'd better do it right the first time. Remember, these are powerful men who have the entire law enforcement system on their side."

After talking some more about their plans, the three walked over to the more exclusive part of town where the Cheyenne Club was located.

They spent two days watching men come and go from the place, making sure no one noticed them hanging around. By spreading some money around the local saloons and stores, Smoke was able to learn all about the men he was interested in: Major Wolcott, Frank Canton, and the two men who'd planned the whole expedition, Hubert Teschemacher and Frederic deBillier.

Smoke and his band were in luck. They learned that Teschemacher, deBillier, Wolcott, and several others played poker in a weekly high-stakes game, and that on those nights the club was otherwise almost deserted since it was in the middle of the week.

Cal managed to hire on with a local whiskey merchant, and did some deliveries to the club, managing to learn about the interior layout and how best to get in and then out again without getting trapped inside. He also found out there were only two guards, one in front and one in back, the patrons evidently feeling they were secure in this high-class part of town.

When the night of the poker game arrived, Smoke took all of their baggage and their horses and loaded them on the train that was overnighting in the station. It was supposed to leave for Denver the next day at eight o'clock in the morning, and he planned that they would be on it and headed out of town before the law could be mobilized to come after them.

Smoke and the boys ate a large dinner and took their time. They wanted the poker game to be well under way and the men in it heavy into their whiskey and wine before they struck, and the later they made it, the less time the sheriff in Cheyenne would have to track them down.

It was two in the morning when Smoke walked up to the guard at the rear entrance to the Cheyenne Club.

The big man put his hand on Smoke's chest and snarled, "This is a private club. Get away from here!"

Smoke grabbed the man's hand and with a sudden downward motion, twisted and turned it back, breaking the guard's wrist with a snap and driving him to his knees. Smoke threw a short right cross that snapped the man's face to the side and put him out for the rest of the night.

Cal and Pearlie appeared out of the shadows, their arms full of weapons. Cal handed Smoke his Greener ten-gauge short-barreled express gun, while keeping a sawed-off twelve-gauge of his own. Pearlie had two pistols stuck in his belt along with the one in his holster.

Smoke opened the door and let Cal lead them into the building and up the stairs to the third-floor meeting room where the poker game was being played.

They stepped into the room, but stayed back in the shadows, wanting to get a feel for the place before they made their move.

Teschemacher and deBillier were sitting next to each other, with Wolcott on their left, and four other men arranged around the table. Smoke recognized some of them from Angus's descriptions, and knew that all of these men bore responsibility for the Johnson County massacre of his friends.

Fred Hesse, the Englishman who managed a large ranching system for distant owners, was directly across from Wolcott, and next to him was William Irving, director of the Cheyenne and Northern Railroad. The other two men were unknown to Smoke.

As Smoke and his friends watched, Wolcott dealt the cards. They were playing five-card stud. After looking at his hole card for a few seconds, deBillier said, "Ace bets one hundred."

Teschemacher grunted. "That little bitsy old ace isn't going to win this hand, Freddy." He shoved a pile of chips out into the pot. "I'll call the hundred and raise another two hundred."

"Damn," Wolcott said, "you boys must be drunk to be betting like that after only two cards. I fold."

Smoke walked out into the light, his shotgun cradled in his arms. "Howdy, gents, mind if I ante up in this game?"

The men's faces blanched and their eyes widened at the sight of the three cowboys, loaded for bear, walking into the room.

"How did you get in here?" Teschemacher asked indignantly. "This is a private club!"

"Why, we just walked right in," Smoke answered. "We heard there was a big game up here and thought we'd join in the fun."

"Bullshit!" Wolcott growled. "You're here to rob us."

"Well," deBillier said, stifling a yawn with the back of his hand, "you're out of luck, gentlemen. We play with chips and IOUs here. There isn't any cash." He acted entirely bored with the entire matter.

Smoke stepped over to the table and in a lightning-fast movement, slapped deBillier across the face with the back of his hand, snapping the man's head around and knocking him out of his chair to land sprawled on his back on the floor.

"No, I think you're out of luck, deBillier."

"Who *are* you men, and why are you here?" Hesse said, his hand slowly moving inside his coat. Cal leaned over, put the barrel of his shotgun against Hesse's forehead, and eared back the hammers. "That better be a cigar you're reachin' for, mister. Otherwise, even your best friend won't recognize you after I let these hammers down."

Hesse brought out a derringer two-shot pistol, holding it delicately with two fingers by the barrel. "Here, take it. I wasn't going to use it anyway."

Smoke glared at Hesse, his eyes as hard as flint. "We're friends of Nate Champion and Nick Ray, the men you paid to have slaughtered in Johnson County."

DeBillier whined from the floor, "But we've already been tried for that and we were acquitted."

"In a court your cattle money bought and by a judge in your pay," Smoke said. "That don't count a whole lot with us. You see, I was there that night, and I know what you did."

Wolcott snapped his fingers, looking at Smoke with narrowed eyes. "You! You're the man who called himself Kirby that was in the cabin with Champion . . . but I don't understand. Aren't you also the one who went to Fort McKinney and got the troops that saved our lives up in Buffalo?"

Smoke nodded as he turned his attention to Wolcott. "Just one of the mistakes I've made in my life. Wasn't the first, won't be the last."

Wolcott jumped to his feet, and Smoke noticed he was wearing a side arm, a big Colt Army .44 pistol.

"I won't stand for this intimidation," Wolcott snapped, his voice trying for the force of a commanding officer in the Army. "You men are trespassing here and I demand that you leave at once!"

Smoke slowly turned and placed the shotgun on the floor butt first, leaning it against a post. He squared his shoulders and faced Wolcott, his hands hanging at his side next to his pistols. "I see you're armed, Major. Why don't you make us leave? All it takes is for you to go for that hogleg on your hip."

Wolcott licked suddenly dry lips, his eyes darting around the room to glance at Cal and Pearlie. "And have your hooligan friends shoot me down?"

Smoke wagged his head. "They won't interfere—you have my word on it. You and your friends here called the dance up in Johnson County. Now it's time someone paid the band. Fill your hand, you dirtbag."

Sweat beaded Wolcott's face and his hand was trembling where it hung by his pistol. "I've seen you draw, Kirby," he said, still calling Smoke by the only name he knew him by. "You're a professional gunfighter. I wouldn't stand a chance."

"I figure about the same chance Nate and Nick had when they were ambushed in their own home without warning," Smoke said. "Now, are you going to show some courage and draw, or not?"

Wolcott shook his head, pulling his hand out from his body and away from his gun. "I don't think so. I'll not give you the satisfaction of killing me."

Smoke walked up to the terrified man. "You are a coward, aren't you? Pretty tough when you're leading a hundred men against two lone men, but when it comes down to standing up for your honor when the odds are one to one, you don't have the sand."

Wolcott hung his head, looking at the floor.

Smoke slapped his face with an open palm, the crack of it sounding like a pistol shot, then backhanded him the same way, snapping his head back and forth.

Infuriated, his face blazing red with humiliation, Wolcott growled and charged at Smoke, his hands out as if to choke the mountain man.

Smoke leaned to the side and threw a short left jab, smashing Wolcott's nose, sending blood and mucus flying and stopping the man in his tracks. Smoke then followed with a roundhouse right cross that caught Wolcott flush on the chin, standing him up on his tiptoes and crossing his eyes. He stood balanced there on his toes for a moment, like a bloodied ballerina, then toppled face-first down onto the hardwood floors, unconscious.

With a horrified expression on his face, Hubert Teschemacher screamed out, "Guards, help! Help, come quick!"

Cal quickly stepped over and smashed the butt of his shotgun into Teschemacher's face, shattering his front teeth and splitting his lip from top to bottom. As Teschemacher shook his head, sending blood and teeth flying across the table, the door at the end of the room burst open and three men with drawn pistols charged into the room.

Smoke whirled and drew, his hand moving so fast it was almost a blur.

Cal eared back the hammers on his sawed-off shotgun and leveled it at the men, bracing the butt against his right hip.

Pearlie filled his hand with iron, drawing and cocking only a second behind Smoke.

All three friends fired at the same time, their pistols and shotguns exploding with a noise that echoed off the walls of the enclosed room like canon blasts, filling the room with billowing clouds of gunsmoke.

The three guards did the dance of death. One, almost shredded by the molten lead 00–buckshot pellets from Cal's shotgun, spun halfway around and was blown back against the wall, hanging there for a moment like some terrible painting by a deranged artist before sliding down the wall to the floor.

Pearlie's shot took his man in the chest, blowing a hole over the heart and stopping it in mid-beat. The man managed to get off one shot before he died, which went wide to the side and creased Cal's left cheek, burning a small furrow that oozed blood.

Smoke's bullet hit his target in the forehead, creating a third eye, snapping the man's head back and blowing out the back of his skull, sending hair and bone and brain splatting against the wall behind him.

As the smoke slowly cleared, and the men at the poker table could see what had happened, Frederic deBillier leaned over to the side and vomited on his two-hundred-dollar boots, retching and coughing in the sudden silence.

William Irving, himself no stranger to violence, screwed up his face and looked away from the carnage, certain that in a few moments the same thing would happen to him.

Hubert Teschemacher stared at the bloody mess of his guards with wide eyes, his ruined mouth and lips so swollen he couldn't speak, bloodstains covering the front of his expensive suit.

Tears ran down Fred Hesse's cheeks, and he could be heard quietly sobbing as he contemplated his own death, his eyes fixed on the table in front of him, as if by not looking at his attackers he could forestall their wrath.

Wolcott remained unconscious on the floor, and was spared the spectacle of the guards' deaths.

Smoke looked at the men at the table and shook his head in disgust. "Would you look at these men, boys? The most powerful men in the territory and not one of them willing or able to stand up and fight for their lives. I guess they have to have others do that for them, since they haven't got the guts to do it for themselves."

Cal and Pearlie nodded, glaring at the men as though they were something that would crawl out from under a rock, while Cal held a bandanna against his cheek to stop the bleeding from his bullet wound.

Smoke picked up his shotgun and eared back the hammers. "Well, it's clear these men aren't worth killing, but maybe we can leave them a message anyway."

He turned and aimed his Greener at the long mirror behind the fifty-foot mahogany bar that had been imported from France. He let the hammers down, shattering the mirror and twenty thousand dollars worth of wine and whiskey and brandy on the shelves underneath it.

Cal calmly reloaded his shotgun, snapped the barrel

into place, and blew the billiard table, imparted from Germany, into so much kindling.

Pearlie filled both hands with pistols and one by one, placed bullets through some of the most expensive portraits and paintings in the country that were hanging on the walls around them.

DeBillier held up his hands. "Not the Monet!" he yelled at Pearlie.

"Mo . . . who?" Pearlie said as he put one right in the center of the painting that had cost more than Smoke's entire ranch.

William Irving, unable to stand it any longer and certain he was going to be killed anyway, jumped to his feet and clawed at his pistol.

Smoke dropped his right hand, drew his Colt, and fired from the hip without taking the time to aim. His bullet hit Irving in the right elbow, shattering the joint and almost amputating the lower arm.

Irving screamed and grabbed his arm as he fell to the ground, trying to stop the spurting blood.

Smoke looked at Pearlie and nodded, and the young man quickly stepped to Irving's side and took his bandanna off. He wrapped it around the upper arm and tied it so that it cut the bleeding off.

"There you go, mister," he said to a pale-faced, sweating Irving. "That'll save your hide, but you'll never use that arm to draw a piece again."

Smoke glanced around at the shattered and ruined Cheyenne Club, then back at the men at the table. "Gents, I hope this teaches you a lesson. If it doesn't, or if I ever see any of you, or men sent by you, again, then I'll make you this promise. I will personally hunt each and every one of you down and shoot you like a dog, without warning and without mercy. You got my word on it."

He hesitated, then added, "And you can give a message from me to Tom Horn. Tell him, if he ever comes down to Colorado, he'd better ride with his guns loose, because if I see him, I'll kill him on sight."

He spun on his heels and walked out the door, followed

by Cal and Pearlie, who were, incredibly, whistling as they exited. The men at the table could hear Pearlie teasing Cal about being a magnet for lead, since he seemed to get shot on a regular basis.

After their attackers were out of the building, deBillier straightened up, adjusted his vomit-stained clothes, and said grandly, "Those thugs will be sorry they did this. As soon as it's daylight, I'll have the sheriff and a posse on their trail."

Teschemacher, his eyes wide with fright, shook his head violently from side to side, though his mouth was so swollen he couldn't speak.

Hesse looked up through reddened and tear-stained eyes. "Are you crazy, Freddy? Did you see the look in that madman's eyes when he said he'd kill us if we sent anyone after him? I don't want any part of that. I vote we cut our losses and forget this ever happened."

Teschemacher and Irving, from his place on the floor, both nodded their agreement.

"Now get me a doctor, before I bleed to death," Irving said, grimacing in pain.

31

It was almost a week later that the train carrying Smoke and Cal and Pearlie and the Palouse horses pulled into Big Rock, Colorado, just after dawn.

It was almost noon by the time they made their way on horseback to the Sugarloaf Ranch. As they rounded the final turn in the trail to the ranch, Pearlie smacked his lips loudly. "You know, fellahs, I can almost smell those bear sign of Miss Sally's already."

"Count on you, Pearlie, that the first thing you think of when you're gettin' home is food," Cal said.

Pearlie raised his eyebrows, looking surprised. "What else is more important?"

Smoke gave a small smile. "Seeing the woman you love and missed like hell, for one thing," he said to himself.

When they were almost there, Sally appeared in the yard of the log cabin she and Smoke shared, her head cocked to the side as if she had somehow sensed the presence of her man.

Smoke broke into a gallop and reined up just in front of her, jumping off his horse and sweeping her up in his arms.

Neither of them spoke for a moment, just clung together in a tight embrace, both smiling as if they were now complete.

Sally finally broke the embrace and stepped back, her

hands on her hips. "I need to have a few words with you, Mr. Jensen. Something about a promise to wire me when you got to Buffalo," she said with arched eyebrows.

Smoke held out both hands. "Now wait a minute, Sally. There's a good explanation, and I'll tell you later. Right now, I want to get these Palouse into the pasture."

She turned, noticing the horses for the first time. She walked over and ran her hands down the flanks of one of the mares. "Oh, Smoke, they're beautiful. They're going to make a great addition to our remuda."

Smoke nodded. "Let's put 'em in with Seven, and see how the old man likes the company."

Pearlie opened the gate to the nearby pasture where Seven, the Palouse that Preacher had given to him, resided. He was standing in a far corner, eating the sweet, green winter grass on the high mountain plateau.

The two young studs and the two mares shook their heads and took off at a run when they were freed from their halters.

Smoke, Cal, Pearlie, and Sally leaned on the wooden fence, watching to see how the old stud would take to the new additions to his pasture.

As the newer animals ran into the open meadow, Seven perked up his ears and stood erect, sniffing the air. After a moment, he whinnied a loud challenge and raced toward the two young stallions.

The larger and more dominant of the two reared back on his hind legs and then galloped toward Seven, intending to meet his challenge. The two large Palouse ran almost into each other, then danced around for a minute, each trumpeting and screaming threats at each other. Then, in a lightning movement, Seven closed the distance between them and bent his head, biting at the jowls under the neck of the younger stud. They bumped and jostled each other briefly; then Seven spun around and gave the youngster a heavy kick in his flanks with his hind legs, almost knocking the horse off his feet.

He stumbled back, whinnied a couple of times, then

turned tail and ran as Seven followed, nipping at his backside.

After Seven had shown the newcomer who was boss, he trotted over toward the two mares, who were prancing around, their tails in the air, in obvious invitation.

"Look at those hussies," Sally said, mock indignation in her voice. "They are too stupid to play hard to get when a male comes around."

Smoke grinned. "Looks like the old stud still has the stuff in him to get them excited."

Sally put her arm around Smoke's waist and laid her head on his shoulders. "I'm kind'a partial to old studs myself," she said with a wicked grin.

As she and Smoke walked slowly off toward their cabin arm in arm, Pearlie glanced at Cal. "I guess right now might not be a particularly good time to ask Miss Sally to bake us some bear sign, would it?"

AUTHOR'S NOTE

Creed of the Mountain Man is a work of fiction, but the events portrayed in the Johnson County War are for the most part true. The characters were true heroes and villains of the war, and while some of their actions were modified for creative reasons, the essence of what they did was preserved. After the war was over, the real-life characters continued with their lives.

Frank Canton, who became the chief detective in the vigilante war on alleged rustlers, had a past none of his employers knew about. His real name was Joseph Horner, born in 1849 the son of a Virginia doctor who moved to Texas after the Civil War. At the age of twenty-six, he was wanted for rustling, bank robbery, and assault with intent to kill. In 1874, in a barroom brawl with some soldiers, he shot his way out of town, killing one of the soldiers, and resurfaced in Wyoming under the assumed name Frank Canton. After the Johnson County War was over, Canton moved to Oklahoma Territory and resumed his career as a lawman, working for a while under "Hanging Judge" Isaac Charles Parker of Fort Smith, Arkansas. During this time, Canton helped wipe out Bill Doolin's gang, and in a stand-up gun duel reminiscent of the movies, outdrew and killed the sharpshooting outlaw Bill Dunn. Later, he followed the gold rush to the Klondike, and served for some years as a deputy U.S. marshal in Alaska. Years later, he returned to Texas and asked for and received a pardon for his earlier crimes from the governor.

Jim Dudley, the overweight Texan who shot himself in the knee when he fell off his horse, was taken to nearby Fort McKinney for medical treatment. Unfortunately, gangrene set in and he later died in agony, screaming in pain.

When the Texans were turned loose without bond by the judge in Cheyenne, they had a farewell party given by their Cheyenne employers, and then scattered out to all parts of the country. Some went back to Paris, Texas, where Tom Smith had first recruited them; others headed for Indian Territory or the wide-open towns of Oklahoma. Two of the Regulators from Texas—G.R. Tucker, nineteen years old, and Buck Garrett, twenty-two years old—moved to Ardmore, Oklahoma, where Tucker served as deputy U.S. marshal and Garrett as sheriff.

Tom Smith returned to serve again as a deputy U.S. marshal in Texas, and was killed a few months later in a shoot-out with an outlaw.

The Texas Kid, who fired the first shot at Nick Ray at the KC ranch, returned home to Texas. Soon thereafter, he quarreled with his girlfriend when she refused to marry him because he had gone off to Wyoming and left her at home. He shot her to death, and then said, just before he was hanged, he wished he'd never gone to Wyoming.

In one of the last fights of the Johnson County War, Mike Shonsey shot and killed Dudley Champion, Nate's twin brother. Though many witnesses claimed otherwise, Shonsey was released after he claimed self-defense in the shooting.

Though the war was now officially over, stock "detectives" such as Tom Horn continued killing men they claimed were rustlers for years, until Horn killed a fourteen-year-old boy by mistake, thinking the boy was his father. After bragging about the killing in a saloon, with the sheriff and others listening through a thin wall, Horn was convicted of murder and hanged.

GUNS OF THE
MOUNTAIN MAN

1

Calvin Woods was talking to himself as he rode out to the northern section of the Sugarloaf Ranch. He and Pearlie, the foreman, had been stringing fence earlier, and Cal had forgotten to load up the extra wire and tools when it came time to head back to the ranch house. Now he was having to ride all the way back out there to pick up the tools, and was giving Pearlie first shot at the bear sign donuts Miss Sally was sure to have cooling in the kitchen.

"Darn it all, by the time I get back Pearlie'll have 'bout near all them bear sign eaten up, Dusty," Cal said bitterly to the back of his horse's head. "I'll be lucky if'n I get more'n one or two."

Cal's horse was the offspring of a cross between Joey Wells's big strawberry roan named Red and one of the Palouse mares Sally had given to him and his wife a couple of years ago. The horse, called a quicksilver gray, was actually almost pure white, differing from a true white albino by having blue eyes instead of pink. The bronc was a pale gray in front with snow-white hips, without the typical Palouse spots on its hindquarters. Cal had named him Dusty, and had formed a deep bond with the animal the first time he'd ridden him.

He found the tools where he'd left them and loaded them in a burlap sack, which he tied to the back of his saddle. As he stood next to his horse, he built himself a cigarette. He figured he'd smoke it out here, since Smoke Jensen's wife, Sally, didn't much care for him smoking. She said he was too young, and he'd have plenty of time to smoke and drink all he wanted when he got older.

Heck, he thought, *I'm old enough to smoke or drink if'n I want to. I'm dang sure old enough to string ten miles of fence 'round this here pasture an' work 'til I'm sore all over.*

As he puffed, he looked out over the herd of Hereford and shorthorn mixes. *Smoke was really smart to get those Herefords from Mr. Chisum an' breed 'em with the shorthorns last year,* he thought. *They sure do throw off some good lookin' calves.*

He remembered what Miss Sally had said when she proposed the crossbreeding—that the crosses would be more hardy, give more and better tasting meat, and be more resistant to disease than either of the parent breeds.

Just as he stubbed out his cigarette, he heard the sound of horses, lots of them, coming from just over a nearby ridge.

Wonder who that could be? he thought. *This pasture is smack in the middle of the Sugarloaf, and there shouldn't be nobody riding across it unless they're up to no good.*

He swung into the saddle and loosened the rawhide hammer thong on his Colt as he rode toward the ridge. Lately, he'd taken to imitating his hero, Smoke Jensen, and carried both a Winchester in his left saddle boot and a Greener 10-gauge double-barreled express gun in his right boot.

Cresting the ridge, he pulled the shotgun from its scabbard and eared back the hammers as he reined his horse to a halt.

Down the hill, he saw a group of about fifteen or twenty men on horseback. Several of the riders were cutting a fat steer out of the herd while the others sat in their saddles, watching.

Cal was trying to decide whether he should ride down and brace the men alone or hightail it back to the ranch house and get some help. He didn't particularly like the odds of twenty to one, but he knew if he took the time to go for backup the men might be gone by the time they got back here.

His decision was made for him when one of the rustlers looked up and saw him sitting on the ridge. He leaned over and spoke to a tall man wearing a black frock coat, who turned to stare at Cal.

"Heck," Cal mumbled to his horse, "in for a penny, in for a pound, as they say."

He spurred his bronc down the hill and rode up to the group.

"Howdy, gents," he said, speaking to the tall man who appeared to be in charge.

Up close, the galoot was even stranger looking than he had been from a distance. He appeared to be over six and a half feet tall, was skinny to the point of being gaunt, and had a scraggly goatee covering his lips and chin. His eyes had a wild, haunted look as if there was nothing behind them, and he was dressed all in black, from his coat and vest to his pants and boots. His boiled shirt was the only spot of lightness about him. As he turned in the saddle, Cal could see he wore a Colt on each hip, and a Henry Yellow Boy rifle was resting across his thighs.

All in all, he reminded Cal of the man named Ichabod Crane in the story "The Legend of Sleepy Hollow" Miss Sally had read to him when he was taking his schooling.

"You men are aware you're trespassin' on private property, aren't you?" Cal asked when he got no response to his greeting.

"What is your name, boy?" the man in black asked.

"My name's Cal. What's yours?"

"Lazarus. Lazarus Cain," the man answered, acting as if the name should mean something to Cal.

It didn't.

"Have you been saved, Cal?" Lazarus asked.

Cal snorted. The man's eyes didn't lie. He was crazy.

"Saved from what?" Cal asked, his eyebrows raised.

"Why, from hell and damnation, of course."

"What's all this got to do with the fact you men are stealin' my boss's cattle?"

"I don't like this young pup calling me a thief, boss," a young Mexican said, kicking his horse to ride up in front of Cal. He put his hand on his pistol butt and added, "Why don't I just kill him?"

Lazarus turned his head to look at Cal, his eyebrows raised, as if waiting to see how Cal would handle the challenge.

"Anytime you think you're ready, *cabrón*," Cal said, easing the barrel of the express gun toward the Mexican.

Cabrón being about the worst thing a Mexican could be called, the man went for his pistol.

Cal let the hammer down on his shotgun, firing from the hip, and splattered the Mexican all over the men behind him, blowing him out of the saddle to land in several pieces on the ground.

As the explosion echoed across the hilly landscape and the horses jumped and crow-hopped at the noise, Cal pulled the barrel around until it pointed at Lazarus.

"We got you outnumbered twenty to one, boy," Lazarus said, staring at Cal with an appraising stare.

Cal inclined his head toward the body on the ground. "Nineteen to one now, Mr. Cain, an' if'n any more of your men get itchy trigger fingers, you'll be the next one I kill."

"You're pretty brave sitting behind that shotgun, boy."

Cal showed his teeth, but he wasn't smiling. "Like Mr. Colt said, God created all men equal, only this here express gun makes some more equal than others." He inclined his head. "Now, I'd suggest you gentlemen ride on outta here, leavin' the beeves you've cut outta the herd behind."

As he finished speaking, Cal saw out of the corner of his eye a man start to raise a pistol.

He swiveled in his saddle and fired the second barrel of the Greener, blowing the man's right arm off at the shoulder and slamming him out of the saddle.

Before he could turn back, Lazarus drew his pistol and fired twice, one slug taking Cal in the left shoulder and the other in the right chest, shattering a rib and imbedding itself deep within his chest.

Cal was catapulted off his horse to land flat on his back, staring at a cloudless, blue sky.

Lazarus got off his mount and walked over to stand looking down at Cal.

"You got a lot of sand—I'll say that for you boy."

Cal's vision blurred, then focused in time to see Lazarus do the strangest thing . . . He pulled out a Bible and held it up, spreading his hands wide toward heaven. Then he began to pray for Cal's soul in a loud, harsh voice.

As the crazy man prayed, Cal noticed blackness creeping across the sky until it became a large, dark hole which swallowed him up.

After Cal lapsed into unconsciousness, Lazarus continued to pray for a few moments. He had started to walk back toward his horse when he noticed Dusty standing a short distance away from Cal.

He pursed his lips, thinking. Then his eyes widened and a joyful expression came over his face. He walked over and picked up Dusty's reins, calming the horse with a low, soothing voice when he tried to shy away from the stranger.

Lazarus pulled the reins and led Dusty over to the group of men waiting to see what he would do next.

He grinned and pointed at the white horse with one hand, held up his Bible, and began to speak in low, sonorous tones, "So I looked, and behold, a pale horse. And the name of him who sat on it was Death, and Hades followed with him. And power was given to them over a fourth of the earth, to kill with sword, with hunger, with death, and by the beasts of the earth."

"What the hell is that supposed to mean, Lazarus?"

asked Blackie Jackson, who sat leaning forward in his saddle with his arms crossed over his saddle horn.

Lazarus cut his eyes toward Blackie. "That, Blackie, for your information, is from the Bible, the Book of Revelation, chapter six, verse eight."

"Yeah, boss, but what's it mean?" asked Curly Joe Ventrillo as he upended a small bottle of whiskey and drained it dry.

"Coming upon this young man, with his pale horse, is another sign from God that I . . . that is *we*, are on the correct path. That we are indeed doing his bidding and will be rewarded with his blessings."

"So, you intend to take that white hoss, or what?" asked another of Lazarus's gang members—Tom "Behind the Deuces" Cartwright.

Lazarus bent and released the belly cinch on Cal's saddle and let it drop to the ground. "Yes, I intend to ride this pale horse, as the Bible said, and I will ride across a fourth of the country, like Death followed by Hades, killing and doing God's work until he calls us home."

Blackie Jackson covered a prodigious yawn with a ham-like hand. "Well, whatever the hell you're gonna do, you better hurry up and do it. Them shots are liable to bring some more punchers on the run."

"If anyone else comes, we will deal with them the same way we did this young man," Lazarus said, as he tightened down his saddle on Cal's bronc.

"I for one do not mind fighting, old chap," said Jeremy Brett, the Englishman, "but personally, I would rather save my energies for when there might be a possibility of profit in the matter."

Lazarus climbed into the saddle. "Well said, Jeremy." He put the spurs to Dusty's flanks and called out, "Let's ride!"

2

Smoke Jensen, legendary gunfighter, leaned against the wall of his cabin with his arms folded and watched his ranch foreman, Pearlie, devour Sally's bear sign donuts as if he hadn't eaten for months. Sally, standing next to the kitchen table, wiped flour off her nose and shook her head. As many times as she'd seen Pearlie eat, it still amazed her how much food the cowboy could put away.

Standing just under six feet tall, Pearlie weighed no more than a hundred and fifty pounds and hadn't an ounce of fat on his body. His face was brown as mahogany and wrinkled from twenty years riding in the sun, and one could usually tell what he'd had for his last meal from the crumbs that accumulated in his handlebar mustache. He was a good foreman, and his hands were intensely loyal in spite of the many practical jokes he played on them.

"Pearlie," Smoke asked, "didn't you just have breakfast a few hours ago?"

Pearlie mumbled something, but his mouth was so full Smoke couldn't understand him.

"Come again?"

Pearlie swallowed with an audible gulp, then washed the donuts down with a tall glass of fresh cow's milk. "I said, I was runnin' late this mornin' an' I only got to eat three or four hen's eggs and a handful of bacon and three or four biscuits. Wasn't hardly enough to keep a body alive 'til noontime."

"Oh, I see what you mean," Smoke said. "I guess I'm going to have to talk to Cookie about keeping you men on starvation rations."

Pearlie nodded, then took the platter of bearsign and put them in the cabinet, out of sight. He broke off a small piece of one and placed it in the middle of the table on a plate.

"Pearlie, what are you doing?" Sally asked.

Pearlie grinned. "When Cal gets back here, all he's gonna see is that little bitty piece of bearsign, an' he's gonna think I ate 'em all up." He laughed. "Boy, he gonna be mad."

Pearlie, like most of the Sugarloaf hired hands, thought of Cal as a little brother, and was continually teasing him about one thing or another. Cal had even complained that he was getting calluses on his back from Pearlie riding him so much.

Smoke walked out on the porch to light a cigar and finish his coffee, as Sally didn't allow smoking in the cabin. He smiled to himself, thinking back on how Pearlie had come to work for him and the changes in the young man since that day.

Pearlie had come to work for Smoke in a rather round-about way. He was hiring his gun out to Tilden Franklin in Fontana when Franklin went crazy and tried to take over Sugarloaf, Smoke and Sally's spread. After Franklin's men raped and killed a young girl in the fracas, Pearlie had sided with Smoke and the aging gunfighters he had called in to help put an end to Franklin's reign of terror.*

Pearlie was now honorary foreman of Smoke's ranch, though he was only a shade over twenty years old himself— boys grew to be men early in the mountains of Colorado.

*Trail of the Mountain Man

As Smoke emptied his coffee cup, he heard a distant booming, followed by two sharp cracks which echoed off nearby mountain peaks. He jerked his head around to look toward the area the sounds came from.

"Pearlie!" he called, stepping off the porch to get a better look.

Pearlie, recognizing the urgency in Smoke's voice, came running out the door.

"Yes sir?"

"I just heard what sounded like shots from the direction you and Cal were working in this morning. Is anybody else out in that section?"

"No sir," Pearlie answered, a worried look on his face. "The rest of the hands were over to the west, worming the new calves."

"What's wrong, Smoke?" Sally asked, wiping her hands on her apron as she followed Pearlie out the door.

"I don't know, but I'm afraid Cal is in some trouble. Gunshots from the pasture where he's working."

Smoke hesitated just a moment, then said to Sally, "You get a buckboard and head on out to the north pasture, where we have the Hereford crosses. Pearlie and I'll ride on ahead to see what's happening."

"All right," she said, jerking her apron off.

"And Sally, bring your medical kit and your pistol."

Smoke ran to the hitching post in front of the cabin where he and Pearlie had their horses tied. He was riding a new two-year-old stud Joey Wells had sent over from Pueblo, Colorado. Joey and his wife had bought the old Rocking C Ranch after killing Murdock, the man who owned it, and Smoke and Sally gave them some Palouse mares to breed with Joey's big roan, which he called Red.*

Smoke's stud was a blanket-hipped Palouse, roan-colored in the front with hips of snow white, without the usual spots of a Palouse. He'd named him Joker because of his odd coloring.

*Honor of the Mountain Man

Pearlie also had one of the offspring of Red, a gray-and-white Palouse he'd named Cold. When Smoke asked him why he'd named him that, Pearlie said it was because the sucker was cold-backed in the morning and bucked for the first ten minutes every day when Pearlie saddled him up.

In spite of this, both studs were beautiful animals and had inherited their father's big size and extreme strength and endurance, along with the Palouse's legendary quickness and intelligence.

Smoke and Pearlie leaned over the necks of their mounts and rode hell-bent-for-leather toward the pasture where Cal was.

A short time later, Smoke was leaning over Cal's still body, holding a bandanna soaked in water from his canteen pressed tight against the boy's chest wound when Sally arrived in the buckboard. Pearlie's bandanna was tied as a tourniquet around Cal's arm just below the shoulder, and had slowed the bleeding there to a trickle.

Sally grabbed her medical bag from the seat next to her and jumped to the ground. After ripping Cal's shirt open to get a better look at his wound, she took a deep breath and glanced at Smoke with a worried frown on her face.

"It's a lung wound. See how the blood on his lips is frothy, and bright red?"

Smoke nodded. No stranger to gunshot wounds himself, he'd come to the same conclusion. "Do you think there's any chance?"

Sally frowned. "If we can stop the air from his lungs from coming out of the wound, it might allow his lung to re-expand and keep him alive until Doc Spalding can operate on him."

She glanced over her shoulder at the wagon she'd ridden in on. Pulling a clean, white cloth from her medical kit, she handed it to Smoke. "Here, take this rag over to the wagon and smear axle grease from around the wheel bearings all over it. Put on a thick coat."

Smoke did what she said, then handed her the grease-covered cloth.

Sally opened it up and slapped it over Cal's sucking chest wound, plugging the hole and stopping air from hissing in and out every time he tried to breathe.

The grease had the added effect of slowing the blood from the wound, but even so, Cal was the color of flour.

"He's lost a lot of blood," Sally said.

"Do you think he's able to make the trip into Big Rock?" Pearlie asked.

"We don't have any choice. If he's going to have any chance of survival at all, Doc's going to have to operate as soon as possible."

"Smoke, looky here," Pearlie called.

Smoke walked over and saw Pearlie standing over Cal's saddle, lying on the ground. Nearby were two large pools of blood, soaking into the soil.

"It appears Cal put lead into at least two of 'em," Pearlie said, pointing to the bloodstains.

"Yeah, and the bastards stole Dusty after they shot Cal," Smoke added, his face as dark as clouds fronting a thunderstorm.

As soon as Cal was breathing more normally, Smoke and Pearlie lifted him up and put him in the back of the wagon.

Pearlie grabbed the reins and drove while Sally and Smoke sat in the back, trying to keep Cal from rolling around too much as they traveled over rough terrain.

Once, Cal's eyes flicked open for a second. They were vacant, as if he really wasn't fully conscious.

Smoke leaned close to his ear. "Cal, it's Smoke. Who did this to you?"

"Ichabod . . . Ichabod Crane," Cal croaked through dry, blood-covered lips.

Smoke sat back, wondering what the hell he meant. As he watched the young man fight for his life in the back of a bouncing wagon, Smoke thought back to the day the boy had come to work for him. . . .

Calvin Woods, going on nineteen years old now, had been just fourteen when Smoke and Sally had taken him in as a hired hand. It was during the spring branding, and Sally was on her way back from Big Rock to the Sugarloaf. The buckboard was piled high with supplies, because branding hundreds of calves made for hungry punchers.

As Sally slowed the team to make a bend in the trail, a rail-thin young man stepped from the bushes at the side of the road with a pistol in his hand.

"Hold it right there, miss."

Applying the brake with her right foot, Sally slipped her hand under a pile of gingham cloth on the seat. She grasped the handle of her short-barreled Colt .44 and eared back the hammer, letting the sound of the horses' hooves and the squealing of the brake pad on the wheel mask the sound. "What can I do for you, young man?" she asked, her voice firm and without fear. She knew she could draw and drill the young highwayman before he could raise his pistol to fire.

"Well, uh, you can throw some of those beans and a cut of that fatback over here, and maybe a portion of that Arbuckle's coffee, too."

Sally's eyebrows raised. "Don't you want my money?"

The boy frowned and shook his head. "Why, no ma'am. I ain't no thief. I'm just hungry."

"And if I don't give you my food, are you going to shoot me with that big Navy Colt?"

He hesitated a moment, then grinned ruefully. "No ma'am, I guess not." He twirled the pistol around his finger and slipped it into his belt, turned, and began to walk down the road toward Big Rock.

Sally watched the youngster amble off, noting his tattered shirt, dirty pants with holes in the knees and torn pockets, and boots that looked as if they had been salvaged from a garbage dump. "Young man," she called, "come back here, please."

He turned, a smirk on his face, spreading his hands, "Look lady, you don't have to worry. I don't even have any bullets." With a lightning-fast move he drew the gun from his pants, aimed away from Sally and pulled the trigger. There was a click but no explosion as the hammer fell on an empty cylinder.

Sally smiled. "Oh, I'm not worried." In a movement every bit as fast as his she whipped her .44 out and fired, clipping a pine cone from a branch, causing it to fall and bounce off his head.

The boy's knees buckled and he ducked, saying, "Jiminy Christmas!"

Mimicking him, Sally twirled her Colt and stuck it in the waistband of her britches. "What's your name, boy?"

The boy blushed and looked down at his feet. "Calvin, ma'am. Calvin Woods."

She leaned forward, elbows on knees, and stared into the boy's eyes. "Calvin, no one has to go hungry in this country, not if they're willing to work."

He looked up at her through narrowed eyes, as if he'd found life a little different than she described it.

"If you're willing to put in an honest day's work, I'll see that you get an honest day's pay, and all the food you can eat."

Calvin stood a little straighter, shoulders back and head held high. "Ma'am, I've got to be straight with you. I ain't no experienced cowhand. I come from a hard-scrabble farm, and we only had us one milk cow and a couple of goats and chickens, and lots of dirt that weren't worth nothing for growin' things. My Ma and Pa and me never had nothin', but we never begged and we never stooped to takin' handouts."

Sally thought, *I like this boy. Proud, and not willing to take charity if he can help it.* "Calvin, if you're willing to work, and don't mind getting your hands dirty and your muscles sore, I've got some hands that'll have you punching beeves like you were born to it in no time at all."

A smile lit up his face, making him seem even younger than his years. "Even if I don't have no saddle, nor a horse to put it on?"

She laughed out loud. "Yes. We've got plenty of ponies and saddles." She glanced down at his raggedy boots.

"We can probably even round up some boots and spurs that'll fit you."

He walked over and jumped in the back of the buckboard. "Ma'am, I don't know who you are, but you just hired you the hardest workin' hand you've ever seen."

Back at the Sugarloaf, she sent him in to Cookie and told him to eat his fill. When Smoke and the other punchers rode into the cabin yard at the end of the day, she introduced Calvin around. As Cal was shaking hands with the men, Smoke looked over at her and winked. He knew she could never resist a stray dog or cat, that her heart was as large as the Big Lonesome itself.

Smoke walked up to Cal and cleared his throat. "Son, I hear you drew down on my wife."

Cal gulped. "Yes sir, Mr. Jensen. I did." He squared his shoulders and looked Smoke in the eye, not flinching though he was obviously frightened of the tall man with the incredibly wide shoulders standing before him.

Smoke smiled and clapped the boy on the back. "Just wanted you to know you stared death in the eye, boy. Not many galoots are still walking upright who ever pulled a gun on Sally. She's a better shot than any man I've ever seen except me, and sometimes I wonder about me."

The boy laughed with relief as Smoke turned and called out, "Pearlie, get your lazy butt over here."

A tall, lanky cowboy ambled over to Smoke and Cal, munching on a biscuit stuffed with roast beef. His face was lined with wrinkles and tanned a dark brown from hours under the sun, and his eyes were sky-blue and twinkled with good-natured humor.

"Yes sir, boss," he mumbled around a mouthful of food.

Smoke put his hand on Pearlie's shoulder. "Cal, this here chow hound is Pearlie. He eats more'n any two hands, and he's never been known to do a lick of work he could get out of, but he knows beeves and horses as well as any puncher I have. I want you to follow him around and let him teach you what you need to know."

Cal nodded, "Yes sir, Mr. Smoke."

"Now let me see that iron you have in your pants."

Cal pulled the ancient Navy Colt and handed it to Smoke. When Smoke opened the loading gate, the rusted cylinder fell to the ground, causing Pearlie and Smoke to laugh and Cal's face to flame red. "This is the piece you pulled on Sally?"

The boy nodded, looking at the ground.

Pearlie shook his head. "Cal, you're one lucky pup. Hell, if'n you'd tried to fire that thing it'd of blown your hand clean off."

Smoke inclined his head toward the bunkhouse. "Pearlie, take Cal and get him fixed up with what he needs, including a gun belt and a Colt that won't fall apart the first time he pulls it. You might also help pick him out a shavetail to ride. I'll expect him to start earning his keep tomorrow."

"Yes sir, Smoke." Pearlie put his arm around Cal's shoulders and led him off toward the bunkhouse. "Now, the first thing you gotta learn, Cal, is how to get on Cookie's good side. A puncher rides on his belly, and it 'pears to me that you need some fattin' up 'fore you can begin to punch cows."

Smoke glanced up from his reverie to see Sally staring at Cal, too, tears in her eyes. He figured she was remembering the same things he was.

He reached across and took her hand in his, squeezing it to show he was as worried about Cal—a young man they'd both come to look upon as a son—as she was.

"We can't let him die, Smoke," she said, her voice husky with worry.

"Cal's too tough to die, Sally. He'll make it through this, I promise."

As the buckboard bounced and rocked over the uneven road toward Big Rock, Colorado, both Sally and Smoke prayed silently for their friend.

Pearlie, on the hurricane deck fighting the reins, was too busy to pray, but not too busy to cuss the men who'd had the gall to shoot his best friend, a man he considered closer than a brother.

In between hollering at the horse team pulling the wagon to run faster, Pearlie pledged he'd repay those who had done this to Cal if it was the last thing he ever did.

3

As he rode, Lazarus enjoyed the feel of the pale horse underneath him. The animal was long through the croup, and thus had an easy, rocking chair gait. It was truly another sign from God that he was a chosen one, picked out of all the men on earth to spread God's word, and more importantly, to punish those evildoers who didn't obey His commandants.

The easy motion of the bronc lulled Lazarus into a dreamlike state, and his mind roamed back to the day the Lord took him under His wing. . . .

It was just one of thousands of dirty little battles in the War Between the States, not even important enough to have a name. The Sixth Confederate Brigade from Arkansas was pinned down in a copse of woods—live oaks, maples, and birch mainly. It was the tail end of winter, and there were ragged patches of snow still on the ground in areas shadowed by trees or rocks.

The young boy from Lizard Lick, Arkansas, was more frightened than he'd ever been in his life. Laz, as he was called by his friends, lay on his stomach in the soggy, frigid mud and prayed that God would let him live through this terrible day. Over half the men in his troop had been killed or wounded, and the fire from the Yanks on the hills above them was devastating and showed no signs of stopping.

Another kid from his neck of the woods, Johnny Slater, was lying next to him in the muck, mumbling over and over how he wanted his mom and how he didn't want to die. Laz, whose father was a lay preacher in the Blood of the Sacred Lamb Pentecostal church back home, planned to follow his father into the preacherhood. He scrabbled over to Johnny on his hands and knees, pulling out his Bible.

"Johnny, pray with me for a minute, an' God will get us through this," Laz said, holding up the palm-sized Bible his dad had given him when he marched off to do battle for the Confederacy.

Johnny had raised wide, bulging eyes to stare at Laz. Then he'd broken out in maniacal laughter, his voice rising to levels that would have made a choirmaster proud. "Git away from me, Laz. Yore gonna draw their fire, you crazy bastard!" he screeched, waving Laz back with his hand.

"But, Johnny, you've got to take the Lord by the hand or we'll never survive this battle," Laz pleaded.

Just as he finished talking, a ball from a Yankee musket sang as it passed over their heads, making an evil-sounding thump as it buried itself in a tree trunk next to them.

"See, see?" Johnny screamed, rolling over to get farther away from Laz. "I tole you ya' was gonna bring their fire down on us with yore damn yappin' an' Bible-thumpin'."

"But—" Laz started to say.

"But nothin'," Johnny yelled, scrambling to his feet and lifting his musket out of the mud. He eared back the hammer and held the long rifle in front of him as he started running, low and bent over, toward a thicker group of trees fifty yards away.

"Johnny," Laz called, holding up his Bible, "trust in the Lord!"

Johnny paused and stood up to look back over his shoulder at Laz, and his eyes widened and his mouth opened in surprise as a bullet passed into his back and erupted out of his chest, taking a good part of his ragged gray tunic with it.

The boy stood there a moment, looking down at the hole in his chest as if he couldn't believe it. Then he glanced up reproachfully at Laz, just before he tumbled to lie facedown in the soggy grass of the field.

At the sight of the death of his friend from home something snapped in Laz, and he jumped to his feet. He jammed his Bible into his breast pocket, where his dad had told him to wear it over his heart, and picked up his rifle. He began to yell and scream, urging his friends and fellow troops to get off their bellies and attack the Yankee dogs.

Unmindful of the withering fire from the slopes and hillocks around them, Laz walked out of the woods and began to fire and reload, fire and reload, all the while remaining miraculously unhit by musket balls and pistol bullets that flew around his head like angry bees.

Both shamed and inspired by this act of bravery, the men in Laz's troop jumped up and began to run at the Yankee troops dug in on the hills around them. As they ran they gave rebel yells and screams, terrifyingly loud and eerie in the foggy, misty morning air, ghostly tendrils of fog coming from their mouths.

Men around Laz began to fall from the fire above, but he remained unhit, firing his musket until the barrel glowed a ruddy red and steam poured off it. The sight of the rebel troops—advancing into hellish fire, screaming and yelling like madmen—unnerved the Yanks, and one by one they began to leave their positions and run away, looking back over their shoulders to see if those crazy rebs were still coming.

One of the last to leave took aim on the man leading the charge and fired. His ball took Laz in the chest and slammed him backward to land spread-eagled on his back in a patch of snow.

Some of the men nearby walked over to stare down at Laz, and almost fainted when he shook his head and sat up, a look of wonder on his face.

"Laz, boy, you awright?" Billy Manright asked around a plug of tobacco in his cheek.

Laz put his hand to his chest and pulled his father's Bible out of his pocket. Imbedded in it was the bullet meant to take Laz's life. At that moment, surrounded by dead and dying men, inhaling the stink of cordite and sulphur and blood and excrement, Lazarus Cain knew he'd been chosen by God for some important purpose.

"God saved me, boys!" Laz shouted. "He wants me to kill some more Yanks 'fore I die!"

The men gathered around him shouted and yelled, and they all turned to finish their attack, completely routing the superior Yankee forces that had them pinned down.

After the battle, Lazarus Cain received a promotion and a commendation. Before the war was to end, he would make colonel and lead his own troops into battle, always carrying his Bible with the bullet in it.

After that traitor to the cause, Robert E. Lee, surrendered, Lazarus and his band of men continued to fight, raiding towns sympathetic to the Yankees, killing and pillaging, looting and burning, until there was no place in the country they could go without being hunted. They were wanted in virtually every state and yet they continued to fight, even after forgetting what they were fighting for and who their enemy was. It became a way of life for them, and as his men got killed or captured Lazarus replaced them with men equally bloodthirsty and dangerous. . . .

This thought brought him fully awake, and he looked around him at the men riding with him. On his right hand was his second in command, Blackie Jackson. Five feet ten inches in height and weighing over two hundred and fifty pounds of solid muscle, Blackie had hands like hams and arms thicker than most men's necks. He was an ex-blacksmith from a small town in Texas. He had come to ride with Lazarus after catching his wife with another man. He'd worked on the man's head like it was a

horseshoe, and when he finished with him had turned
to his wife, sticking her head in his coal pit until it had
burned to ashes. He was a man who liked to fight with
his hands, and had never in his life been beaten.

On Lazarus's left rode Tom "Behind the Deuces"
Cartwright. An ex-gambler, Tom got his nickname from
his habit of betting heavily at faro whenever he was dealt
two deuces. Physically, he was a small man with a rat-like
face and a pencil mustache, skinny of frame with greasy,
black hair that was thinning on top. Sensitive about his
balding head, thinking he was a ladies' man, he rarely
took his hat off. His favorite weapons were a derringer
two-shot .44 he carried in his vest and a knife hidden in
his boot. Though for long range he used a Winchester
rifle, he much preferred the derringer, stating he liked
to see the look in a man's eyes when life left him.

Behind Cartwright rode Curly Joe Ventrillo. Of Italian
descent with dark, curly hair, he was twenty years old and
a favorite with girls and women of all ages, having a baby
face that was very handsome. His good looks hid his
propensity for heavy drinking and violence toward women.
This began on the owlhoot trail after cutting up a prosti-
tute's face when he couldn't perform one night after
getting drunk. He soon discovered he liked rough sex and
hurting females, and repeated the act every chance he got.

On the other side of the group was Pig Iron Carlton,
ex-professional fisticuffs champion. He had been running from the law since beating two men to death in a
barroom brawl. Tall, muscular, he had hands and knuckles covered with scar tissue from his many bare-knuckled
fights, so he couldn't hold a pistol very well. He favored
a Winchester .44/.40 rifle and a sawed-off 10-gauge shotgun for close-in work. He wasn't particularly mean, and
only killed when forced to by circumstances. His cauli-
flower ears and the scar tissue around his eyes and his
oft-broken nose made him look frightful—and no man
dared laugh at his appearance.

Riding next to Carlton was Jeremy Brett, an Englishman relatively new to America. Jeremy talked with a

heavy British accent, and his dress was very dapper—a bowler hat and dark suit covered with a black duster while on the trail. Soft-spoken, he used a shoulder holster with a Smith and Wesson American sheriff's model .44 caliber pistol. No one knew why he'd chosen to ride the owlhoot trail, as he wouldn't speak of it and became extremely violent if pushed on the matter.

The last of Lazarus's lieutenants was King Johannson. A big, fair-haired, blue-eyed Swede farmer from up in Minnesota, he was borderline mentally retarded. Though his mind was slow he was very quick with his guns and could be very mean when he was upset, going into violent rages if crossed. At other times he was like a small child, sweet and mild-tempered. He carried a shotgun on a sling around his shoulders and a long, machete-type knife in a scabbard on his belt, the blade of which was rusty from the blood of his victims. He never wiped the sword-like instrument off after using it.

There were another fifteen or so men at any one time riding with Lazarus, each and every one as mean and dangerous as the next. They had no real plan and no real destination. The gang rode wherever they wanted and took whatever they needed. So far there hadn't been anyone brave enough, or good enough, to stand against them.

Lazarus had no compunction about killing anyone who crossed him. In his mind he could do no wrong, since he'd been personally chosen by God. If by chance he happened to kill an innocent man or woman, he felt they would be rewarded by God and taken to heaven. He didn't have to feel guilt since he was sending them to a better place. On the other hand, if someone deserved to die God would send them to hell, and Lazarus was just doing God's work for Him.

"Hey, boss, looks like there's a town up ahead," Blackie said, interrupting Lazarus's reverie.

Lazarus glanced down at the weather-beaten sign next to the road. "Fontana?" he said. "I don't remember a town by that name on the map."

"Me neither, Lazarus," said Tom "Behind the Deuces."

Lazarus shrugged. "Well, boys, let's ride on in and see what this Fontana's like."

As they rode down the center of the town's main street, they were greeted by broken-down, rotting buildings and boardwalks that'd seen better days.

"Damn, looks like a ghost town," said Curly Joe.

"Nope," answered Pig Iron Carlton. He pointed up ahead. "There's some hosses outside that saloon."

Sure enough, there were three horses reined to a post in front of a saloon with a faded, hand-lettered sign hanging askew over the door—DOG HOLE.

"Sounds like my kind of place," said Tom "Behind the Deuces." "Wonder if they got a faro game."

"Hell, I wonder if they got any whiskey," said Blackie. "Place looks pretty rundown."

The gang dismounted and walked into the saloon. A man behind the counter had a silver star on his chest and a dark top hat on his head.

Lazarus, upon seeing the badge, placed his hand on his pistol butt. "Are you the local sheriff?" he asked the man.

The man laughed, pointing at his badge. "Hell, yes. I'm the sheriff, the mayor, the dogcatcher, and the bartender. In fact, I'm just about the whole damn town."

Lazarus relaxed, seeing the man was no real lawman. "What's your name?"

"I'm Bob Blanchard. You men come on in and have a seat. There's plenty of whiskey and beer, though not much food."

"You got any women?" asked Curly Joe, a lecherous gleam in his eyes.

Blanchard smiled. "Oh yes. I've got a couple." He looked over his shoulder and then leaned forward and whispered, "They ain't much to look at, but they'll get the job done, if you know what I mean."

As he spoke, a woman walked out of a room upstairs and leaned over the railing, smiling a gap-toothed smile. She weighed at least two hundred pounds, and her hair looked as if someone had pulled part of it out of her scalp.

"They'll get the job done, all right," Tom "Behind the Deuces" said, "after about a quart of whiskey, maybe."

Curly Joe grinned. "I don't need no whiskey, at least not first . . . maybe later." He started up the stairs.

"Curly Joe," Lazarus said, his voice hard.

"Yeah, boss?"

"I don't want any trouble, not until we're ready to leave. You understand me?"

Curly Joe, a disappointed look on his face, shrugged. "All right."

Lazarus turned to Blanchard. "Set up whiskey for all my men. Then you can tell me what happened to this town."

After Blanchard had set out bottles of whiskey on each of the tables he leaned on the bar, absentmindedly wiping it with a dirty rag as he talked.

"Town was founded by a man named Tilden Franklin a number of years ago after gold was discovered here. He named it after a Mexican girl he once knowed."

Lazarus's interest was piqued. "Gold? They discovered gold here?"

"Yeah, only most of this valley belonged to a man named Jensen, Smoke Jensen. And he didn't particularly care to have a bunch of miners running around on his land lookin' for gold."

"So what happened?"

Blanchard shrugged. "Franklin brought in a gang of toughs. Some of the meanest men in several states came here to help him take the valley away from Jensen."

"And did they?"

Blanchard shook his head. "Naw. Jensen called in a bunch of old gunfighters, men most people thought were long dead, an' they had one of the biggest gunfights in history right here in Fontana. Streets ran red with blood, I'm told."

"Must have been something to see."

"I guess. I weren't here myself, but those who survived either left town, or were carried out on boards."*

Trail of the Mountain Man

"Where did the ones who left go?"

Blanchard pointed south. "On down the road a ways, to a town Jensen started, called Big Rock, Colorado."

"And the gold?"

Blanchard leaned forward, speaking in a hoarse whisper. "Still here, I reckon. Since then, no one's had the courage to try and dig it outta the ground, 'cause they know Jensen'd be on 'em like ticks on a hound dog if'n they did."

Lazarus turned and leaned back, his elbows on the bar. "You don't say? Mr. Blanchard, do you have a telegraph in this town?"

"Yes sir. I forgot to mention, I'm also the chief telegraph operator."

4

Sally felt Cal's pulse, a worried look on her face.

"I don't like the way Cal looks, Smoke. I have a feeling you'd better ride on ahead and have Doc Spalding ready to operate as soon as we get there."

Smoke didn't question Sally's expertise. She'd treated more bullet wounds than most doctors, a good many of them on him.

He grabbed Joker's reins, which were tied to the rear of the wagon, and pulled the animal alongside. He didn't dare take the time to stop their progress toward Big Rock, so he jumped into the saddle from the rear of the buckboard. He gave Sally a smile for encouragement, then leaned over Joker's head and spurred him into a full gallop toward town.

Smoke rode into Big Rock as fast as his horse could run. As he passed the sheriff's office, Monte Carson stepped out the door and pushed his hat back on his head, watching Smoke race by, a quizzical look on his face.

When Smoke reined up in front of Dr. Cotton Spalding's office, Monte came running, knowing something bad had happened.

Smoke jerked the door open, startling several women and two children who were waiting to see the doctor.

He touched his hat, mumbled a quick apology, then stepped to the consulting room door. Restraining his first impulse to burst through the door, Smoke tapped lightly instead.

After a moment, Cotton opened the door, his sleeves rolled up and a frown on his face.

"What is it?" he asked, then noticed it was Smoke knocking on the door, and the anxious look on his face.

"Oh, I'm sorry, Smoke. Didn't know it was you."

"That's all right, Doc. But Cal's been hurt real bad, took a bullet in the chest and the shoulder."

"Oh!"

"Sally says to tell you it's in his lung, an' he's lost a lot of blood. She says you need to operate as soon as they get here."

"Well, if Sally says it, then it must be serious."

He stepped into the waiting room and said, "I'm sorry, ladies. I have an emergency coming in that's going to need surgery. There's no need for you to wait here. Why don't you come back in a couple of hours?"

As the women and children left, he turned back into his consulting room. Smoke looked over his shoulder and saw a man bent over the table, his buttocks exposed and showing a bright red lump on one cheek.

"Earl, I'm afraid I'm going to have to lance that boil later. I've got an emergency coming in."

Earl straightened up, looking angry. "Look here, Doc. I'm in pain, and I want this boil cut now! The other can wait his turn."

Cotton put his hand in front of Smoke, who'd started through the door with his fists clenched.

"Earl, I've got a young boy with two bullets in him, one in his chest," Cotton said in a low, even tone, not a trace of anger or annoyance in it. "He's gonna die if I don't operate right away. Do you really want me to make him wait his turn?"

Shamefaced, Earl lowered his gaze, his expression

softening. "No, of course not, Doc. It's just that this damned carbuncle is driving me crazy."

Cotton walked to the medicine cabinet and took out a small bottle. "Here, Earl. Take this laudanum. Two sips every hour or so and you won't feel the pain. Come back in a couple of hours and I'll fix you up permanently."

Earl pulled up his pants and took the bottle. "Thanks, Doc, and I'm awful sorry 'bout your friend, mister. I didn't mean nothing by what I said before."

Smoke nodded, tempted to smile in spite of the circumstances.

Just then, Sheriff Monte Carson came into the office. "Hey, Smoke. What's going on?" he asked, a concerned look on his face.

Smoke and Monte Carson had become very good friends over the past few years. Carson had once been a well-known gunfighter, though he had never ridden the owlhoot trail.

When Tilden Franklin hatched his plan to take over the county and dig up most of the gold that had recently been discovered for himself, he'd hired Carson to be the sheriff of Fontana, a town just down the road from Smoke's Sugarloaf spread. Carson went along with the man's plans for a while, 'til he couldn't stomach the rapings and killings any longer. Then he'd put his foot down and let it be known that Fontana was going to be run in a law-abiding manner from then on.

Franklin sent a bunch of riders in to teach the upstart sheriff a lesson. The men killed Carson's two deputies and seriously wounded him, taking over the town. In retaliation, Smoke had founded the town of Big Rock, and he and his band of aging gunfighters cleaned house in Fontana.

When the fracas was over, Smoke offered the job of sheriff of Big Rock to Monte Carson. Monte married a grass widow and settled into the job as if born to it. Neither Smoke nor the citizens of Big Rock ever had cause to regret his taking the job.

"Cal's been shot, Monte."

"Is it bad?"

"About as bad as it can be and him still be alive."

"Any idea who did it?"

Smoke shook his head. "He woke up long enough to say it was Ichabod Crane, but I don't know what he meant by that."

"Ichabod Crane?"

"A character in a story by Washington Irving," Cotton called from the next room. "Tall, skinny, with a prominent Adam's apple, as I recall."

Monte pursed his lips. "You think that's what he meant, Smoke? Tryin' to describe the fellow for us?"

"Possibly, but I'm more concerned with saving his life right now. I'll get to the man who did this after it's over, one way or another."

Monte nodded. He knew Smoke didn't let anyone harm a friend of his, not without making them pay dearly for it.

"Come on, Smoke," Cotton called from his consulting room. "You can help me set up for the surgery."

"I'll talk to you later, Monte."

"Sure, come on by the office. Meanwhile, I'll be goin' through some posters, see if I can find the galoot who did this."

Smoke walked into the consulting room, and Cotton led him through a rear door into his operating room— surgery, as he called it.

There were windows on every side of the room to let as much light in as possible, and two large lanterns in sconces on each wall. In the middle of the room was a long table with a pad on it. There were straps for arms and legs, for those occasions when it wasn't possible to give an anesthetic.

"Smoke, fill that basin with carbolic acid and dump that tray of instruments into it, will you?"

"Carbolic acid? What's that for?"

"There's this man in Austria, named Semmelweis, who says the reason wounds get infected is due to contamination with small organisms, called bacteria."

Smoke didn't look up as he filled the basin from a large bottle of liquid, turning up his nose at the strong astringent smell. "Uh huh. I've never seen any small animals in wounds with pus, unless you're talking about maggots."

"No, these organisms are too small to be seen with the naked eye. You need a microscope. Anyway, Semmelweis says if doctors would wash their hands and instruments in carbolic acid, and wash wounds with soap and water, it would cut down on the number of infections and save a lot of lives."

"And you believe him?"

Cotton shrugged as he laid out dressings and sutures in preparation for the operation.

"I don't know. Some of the other doctors in Austria say the man is crazy. But my feeling is it can't hurt, so why not give it a try? I do know that since I've been doing it I haven't had a single wound suppuration following surgery."

Smoke heard the buckboard pulling up outside the office. "Better get your hands washed, Doc. Here they are."

Smoke and Pearlie carried the unconscious Cal into the surgery and laid him on the table. Sally began stripping his clothes off. "You men go on outside. I'll stay and help Cotton with Cal."

"Put the closed sign on the door, will you, Smoke? That way we won't be interrupted."

"All right. We'll get Monte and go on over to Longmont's for some coffee. You can reach us there if . . . if anything happens or you need us," Smoke said, his voice breaking as he realized it might be the last time he saw Cal alive.

As soon as they left, Cotton washed his hands in the weak solution of carbolic acid and had Sally do the same. Then he laid out his instruments on a side table next to where Cal lay unconscious, his breathing labored, bloody froth on his lips.

Sally had stripped him to his waist and positioned herself next to the instruments, ready to assist in the surgery.

"Scalpel, please," Cotton said, holding out his hand.

After Sally placed the razor-sharp knife in his hand, Cotton bent low over the table and made an incision horizontally over the entrance wound of the bullet in his chest.

"I'll work on the chest wound first," he said, "since that's the most dangerous."

After opening the incision wider, he took a long, blunt-tipped probe and used it to follow the path of the slug, being gentle so as not to cause any more bleeding than was necessary.

Cal was so deeply asleep that he didn't move when the probe was inserted.

After a few moments of this, Cotton looked up. "It's as I feared when I saw the froth on his lips. The slug is imbedded in his right lung. Luckily, from the depth the probe went in, it doesn't appear to be deep in the lung but just on the edge. I suspect hitting the rib slowed the bullet up enough so it couldn't penetrate any farther."

Taking the scalpel again, he lengthened the incision even more and used a clawlike tool to spread Cal's ribs apart. Using blunt dissection, he followed the path of the bullet to where it lay against the lining of the right lung. After about an hour of painstaking dissection, he felt the metal object with the tip of his scissors, doing most of his work by touch since he couldn't see the bottom of the wound.

Sally handed him some long, narrow-tipped forceps and he plucked the bullet out, placing it in a metal basin with a clank.

Using gauze he first dipped in the carbolic acid, he stuffed the wound full and used bandages to hold it tight and compress it so as to stop the bleeding and close the hole in the lung, allowing it to re-expand.

Next, he gave his attention to the shoulder wound and was happy to find the bullet had passed cleanly through flesh, missing Cal's arm bone. Cleansing the wound as best he could, he packed it with gauze and wrapped a tight bandage around the entire arm.

Finally, exhausted and dripping with perspiration, he stepped back from the table and sleeved sweat off his face and forehead.

"Now it's in God's hands. I've done all I can."

Sally slumped against the table, as tired as Cotton was.

"You did a great job, Cotton. No one could have done more," she said.

Louis Longmont was sitting at his usual table, playing solitaire, when he saw Smoke and Pearlie and Monte walk through the batwings. Noticing the serious expressions on their faces, he signaled a waiter.

"Johnny, bring a pot of coffee and three more cups to the table."

"Yes sir, Mr. Longmont," the young black man answered.

Louis got to his feet and held out his hand to Smoke. They'd been friends for a long time.

Louis was a lean, hawk-faced man with strong, slender hands and long fingers, the nails carefully manicured and hands clean. He had jet-black hair and a black, pencil-thin mustache. He was, as usual, dressed in a black suit with a white shirt and dark ascot—something he'd picked up on a trip to England some years back. He wore low-heeled boots, and a pistol hung in tied-down leather on his right side. It was not for show, for Louis was snake-quick with a short gun and was a feared, deadly gunhand when pushed.

Louis was not an evil man. He had never hired his gun out for money, and while he could make a deck of cards do almost anything, he did not cheat at poker. He did not have to cheat. He was possessed of a phenomenal memory, could tell the odds of filling any type of poker hand, and was one of the first to use the new method of card counting.

He was just past forty years of age. He had come to the West as a very small boy, with his parents, arriving from

Louisiana. His parents had died in a shantytown fire, leaving the boy to cope as best he could.

He had coped quite well, parlaying his innate intelligence and willingness to take a chance into a fortune. He owned a large ranch up in Wyoming Territory, several businesses in San Francisco, and a hefty chunk of a railroad.

Though it was a mystery to many why Longmont stayed with the hard life he had chosen, Smoke thought he understood. Once Louis had said to him, "Smoke, I would miss my life every bit as much as you would miss the dry-mouthed moment before the draw, the challenge of facing and besting those miscreants who would kill you or others, and the so-called loneliness of the owlhoot trail."

Sometimes Louis joked that he would like to draw against Smoke someday, just to see who was faster. Smoke allowed as how it would be close, but that he would win. "You see, Louis, you're just too civilized," he had told him on many occasions. "Your mind is distracted by visions of operas, fine foods and wines, and the odds of your winning the match. Also, your fatal flaw is that you can almost always see the good in the lowest creatures God ever made, and you refuse to believe that anyone is pure evil and without hope of redemption."

When Louis laughed at this description of himself, Smoke would continue. "Me, on the other hand, when some snake-scum draws down on me and wants to dance, the only thing I have on my mind is teaching him that when you dance, someone has to pay the band. My mind is clear and focused on only one problem, how to put that stump-sucker across his horse, toes down."

Smoke took Louis's hand.

"You look worried, my friend," Louis said.

"Cal's been shot, Louis. Bad shot."

"Is he—"

"No. Doc and Sally are working on him right now."

Louis sat them at his table and poured coffee all around while Pearlie and Smoke built cigarettes and

Monte fired up his pipe. Louis took a long, black cigar from his vest pocket and joined them in smoking.

"I offered Smoke and Pearlie some coffee at my office," Monte said, "but for some reason they wanted to come over here."

"Has that pot in your office ever been cleaned, Monsieur Monte?" Louis asked, trying to lighten the mood of their two friends, like Monte.

Monte nodded. "Of course. Two year ago, I believe it was."

"Did you find any papers on the man Cal described?" Smoke asked, not in the mood for their usual banter.

"Well, there were several it could have been, but none have been reported in this neck of the woods. 'Bout the nearest one I saw was a man name of Lazarus Cain. He and his gang did some raiding down in Arkansas recently, but there was no mention of his heading this way."

"Well, if this Cain has decided to pay us a visit and did this to Cal, he's gonna wish he'd never left Arkansas," Smoke said through gritted teeth.

5

It was over two hours before the solemn group gathered in Longmont's saloon heard any news from the doctor. Longmont had tried cheering them up by ordering a special meal from his French chef, Andre, but in spite of the wonderful food they all just picked at their plates with no real enthusiasm. Even Pearlie, who could normally eat his weight in foodstuffs, barely tasted the roasted duck with orange sauce and fried potatoes with sliced tomatoes and peach halves.

When Sally walked through the batwings they were all on their feet asking questions at the same time. Exhausted, and looking as if she hadn't slept for days, she flopped down at the table and requested coffee, and lots of it.

After drinking half her first cup in one long swallow, she leaned back and pushed stray wisps of hair out of her face. "Cal made it through the surgery, though it was scary going for a while. Dr. Spalding says it's in God's hands, but that Cal is young and healthy and has a lot going for him."

"He's gonna make it!" Pearlie said with conviction, his eyes wet with unshed tears. "That boy's had plenty of experience with gittin' shot, an' he's tough as an old boot. He'll be all right, I just know it."

"Did he wake up at all, Sally? Was he able to say any more about who shot him?" asked Monte.

She shook her head. "No, he didn't even move when Doc made his incision. Doc says he's in a coma from shock and loss of blood."

Seeing she was on the verge of breaking down, Smoke put his hand over hers on the table. "Come on, Sally. Let's go home. Doc'll let us know how he does."

Pearlie stood up. "If it's all right with you, Smoke, I'll just hang around here for a while. Make sure Doc don't need nothin'. I can watch Cal while he tends to his other patients."

"Sure thing, Pearlie. That'd be very nice, and I know that when Cal wakes up he'll be glad to see a friendly face by his side."

"Friendly, hell! I'm gonna box his ears for lettin' hisself get shot up without me there to take care of him," Pearlie said with mock ferocity. "If I've said it once, I've said it a dozen times—that boy's a magnet for lead."

As Pearlie left to go over to Doc's, Monte said, "I'm going to wire the surrounding sheriffs and see if anyone's had any trouble lately with any tall, skinny galoots, or if they've heard of this Cain feller. I'll get in touch with you at the Sugarloaf if I hear anything."

"Don't bother, Monte," Sally said. "As soon as we get the ranch house shut up, Smoke and I'll be back to town to sit with Cal until he's better."

"Yes, we'll take a room at the hotel," Smoke added.

"Nonsense, I won't hear of it," Louis said with some heat. "You and Sally will stay at my place on the edge of town. I have a spare bedroom, and the food is guaranteed to be better than the hotel's."

A year or so back, tired of living in hotels, Louis had bought a widow's house on the outskirts of town. It was bigger than he needed, but he said he was tired of looking at the same four walls all the time. He wanted some room to roam around in when he wasn't at the saloon. Since then, he'd fixed it up really nicely, with an extra bedroom for guests and a place in the back where his cook lived.

* * *

Smoke showed up at Louis's house around nine that night. "Sally's going to sit with Cal for a while. I'm supposed to pick her up at ten o'clock," he told Louis when he opened the door.

"Come in and make yourself at home, Smoke. Would you like some coffee?"

"Sure. It's been a hell of a long day."

As they drank coffee and smoked, Louis one of his ever-present black cigars and Smoke a handmade cigarette, Smoke asked, "Did Monte hear anything back on his wires?"

Louis wagged his head. "Not as far as I've heard. He said he probably wouldn't hear anything for a day or two."

Noticing the worry in Smoke's eyes, Louis asked, "How are you doing, pal?"

Smoke looked up. "Not too well, Louis. Since our children have been over in Europe for the past two years with Sally's father, Cal and Pearlie have been like sons to us. Now, with the prospect of maybe losing one, Sally and I are really worried."

"Like the doc said, Cal's young and tough. I'm sure he'll pull through."

"But I keep blaming myself for letting him go out there alone. Someone should have been with him."

"Nonsense, Smoke. Cal is a grown man, and this is a tough country. Like you always say, a man's got to saddle his own horse and kill his own snakes."

"You're right, of course. Whatever Cal got into out there on the Sugarloaf, he was ready and willing to do it. I figure the first shots I heard were his."

"Did you find any bodies?"

"No, but there was a hell of a lot of blood, and it was scattered over too large an area to be all Cal's. I think he got at least one, maybe two, before they took him down."

"So there must have been several men he was facing, if there were enough left after losing two for the others to cart off the bodies."

"That's the way I figure it."

Louis shook his head, admiration in his eyes. "If that's

true, then Cal must've drawn on them knowing the odds were heavily against him."

Smoke nodded. "There never was any back up in Cal. That boy would bow his back and face down the devil himself if it ever came to that."

"Kind of like someone else I know," Louis added with a smile at his friend.

6

Lazarus Cain was sitting at the table he'd appropriated as his own in the Dog Hole Saloon. His chair was in a corner, so he had walls on both sides at his back and an unobstructed view of the batwings that served as the entrance to the bar.

It had been two weeks since he and his gang had settled in Fontana, and he was now the acknowledged leader of the town that was only a few citizens away from being a ghost town. Bob Blanchard, the man who'd been top dog here until Lazarus arrived, had accepted his new role as servant to Lazarus and his men without complaint, figuring it was the smart thing to do, and necessary if he were to go on breathing.

"Bob," Lazarus called, "bring me and the boys another round over here."

As Bob brought another bottle of whiskey to the table, he stopped for a moment.

"Mr. Cain, one thing I can't figure out."

"What's that, Bob?" Lazarus asked as he filled his glass to the brim with the amber-colored liquid.

"Well, the boys all say you're a holy man of sorts, having been called by the Lord to do his work."

"Yes?"

"Well, how is it you drink so much whiskey and beer? Doesn't the Good Book speak out against such things?"

Blackie Jackson cast a worried glance at his boss, wondering just how he would take this question. Lazarus's moods were hard to predict. One time he'd laugh and throw his arm around someone. The next, he was as likely to draw his Colt and put a bullet in the offending man's head.

This time, Blanchard was lucky. Lazarus was in a forgiving mood.

"Bob, I refer you to the Good Book, First Timothy, chapter five, verse twenty-three."

Bob pursed his lips. "Uh . . . Mr. Cain, I ain't exactly on speakin' terms with the Bible. I'm not familiar with that particular verse."

"It says, 'No longer drink only water, but use a little wine for your stomach's sake and your frequent infirmities'," Lazarus quoted with a benign smile.

"Oh," Blanchard said, "wine."

"Yes, and since they didn't have Kentucky bourbon in those days, I'm sure the Lord would have included it if there'd been any around to drink. The point is, the Lord recognized a man sometimes needs a little alcohol to soothe him when life begins to get too much to handle."

"Thanks for clearing that up," Blanchard said, grinning. "I'll have to remember that particular verse so's I can quote it if'n someone ever tries to make me quit drinkin'."

Lazarus took a deep swallow of his whiskey and wiped his mouth with the back of his sleeve. "Perish the thought, Bob, perish the thought."

After Blanchard walked off to stand behind the bar and await further orders, Blackie leaned back in his chair and gave Lazarus an appraising glance. Since he seemed to be in one of his good moods today, he figured he'd ask him again about what the rest of the boys had been wondering.

"Say, Lazarus, when are you gonna tell us what you got planned, an' why we been stuck here in this two-bit excuse for a town for the past two weeks?"

Lazarus pursed his lips as if thinking it over, then nodded and leaned forward on his elbows.

"I've decided to stay around here and do a little gold mining."

"Gold mining?"

Lazarus nodded. "From what I hear, that Jensen fellow's land is absolutely brimming with gold. Word is it's so thick over there you don't even have to dig in some places. It's just lying around on the ground waiting to be picked up."

"But boss, we ain't miners. What made you decide to do this?"

Lazarus leaned back, a look of smug self-satisfaction on his face. "Spreading the Lord's word is expensive, Blackie. That's why we've been having to spend too much of our time raising money by rustling and robbing the occasional bank. If I can make one big score, get me enough money to last the rest of my life, then I can devote all my energies to doing the Lord's work. I might even open me up a church somewhere, one like my pappy used to preach at."

Blackie nodded, knowing it would do no good to try to talk Lazarus out of his scheme once his mind was made up. But there were other things to worry about.

"What about this Jensen fellow? Blanchard said the last guy that tried to take that gold had twenty or thirty men and got plumb wiped out."

Lazarus grinned, as if he had a secret. "I know. It won't be easy, especially since Jensen's built that town of Big Rock and has all the citizens in it behind him."

"So, you think the twenty of us can pull it off, tree the town, and get the gold before the U.S. Marshals or the army finds out about it and sends in the troops?"

"No, twenty of us can't, so I've wired for some help."

"Oh?"

"Yes. I've sent for some . . . special men who once rode for the Yellow and Gray, men who didn't quit when that traitor General Lee surrendered. Men who kept fighting the good fight."

"Who's that, boss?"

"Men who rode with Bloody Bill Anderson and Quantrill's Raiders and Merrill's Marauders."

"I heard Bloody Bill an' his men got pretty well shot up a year or so back. Word is that Bloody Bill was shot in the head by Marshal Wyatt Earp and some other galoots over in Dodge City."

Lazarus grinned again. "Yes, and do you know who was mixed up right in the middle of that little fracas?"

"No."

"It was this same Jensen, Smoke Jensen, that practically wiped out Bloody Bill and his men. The ones that survived are thirsty for revenge."

"But I heared they was all put in jail in Dodge, and due to be hanged," Blackie said, his chubby cheeks screwed up in an expression of puzzlement.

Lazarus gave a slow grin. "They were, 'til one of their other gang members snuck into town one night while Wyatt was busy dealing faro over at the Oriental Saloon and broke 'em out."

"Oh."

"Yeah. They hightailed it up into a little town a couple of hundred miles from here, called Sweetwater, Colorado."

"How'd you know all this?"

"I heard it from a man at that last tradin' post where we took on supplies. He was run out of town by some of the outlaws, and was pretty mad about it. Said he was going to tell the first marshal he ran across where they were hidin' out."

"So, them're the ones you sent the wires to?"

"Yes, and a few others scattered around the territory who might be interested in some gold that's just lyin' around for the takin'."

"When do you think they'll be gettin' here?"

Lazarus peered over Blackie's shoulder, and then drained the last of his whiskey in one long swallow.

He pointed out the window. "Right about now, I suspect."

Blackie looked over his shoulder and saw a group of

four men riding up. They were wearing dusters and hats that were covered with trail dust.

Lazarus stood up and stretched. "Time to meet our new partners, boys."

Four men walked through the batwings, hands on pistol butts as they surveyed the room.

One of the men, a youngster who looked no older than seventeen or so, walked with a pronounced limp. His face lit up with a smile when he saw Lazarus, and he hobbled over to shake his hand.

"Howdy, Lazarus."

"Hello, Floyd. How's the leg?"

"Stiff, an' it hurts like hell when the northers come through."

Lazarus shook his head in sympathy, then shook hands with the other men.

"It's sure good to see you boys," he said. "It's been a long time since we all rode with Quantrill."

He turned to his men, seated at several tables in the corner of the room. "Men, let me introduce you to some boys that know how to fight."

He pointed to the young one with the limp. "This here is Floyd Devers. He's still carrying a bullet Smoke Jensen put in his right leg. The others are Walter Blackwell, Tad Younger—Cole's cousin—and Johnny Sampson. These are the last of Bloody Bill's gang."

Lazarus's men crowded close and shook hands all around with the outlaws.

"Mr. Blanchard, more whiskey for these men. They need something to wash the trail dust outta their throats," Lazarus called to the bartender.

7

After Floyd and the others all had bottles and glasses full in front of them, Lazarus sat at their table.

"Floyd, tell me about what happened that day Bloody Bill got killed."

Floyd took a long drink of his whiskey and wiped his mouth with the back of his sleeve, then began to talk in a low tone, as if he didn't particularly like to relive those hours. . . .

Bill stood on a rock ledge just before dusk, watching their backtrail with his field glasses. He and Buster Young talked as Bill studied the horizon from the highest point they could find while the men waited in a draw, resting and drinking whiskey to pass time or dress a few minor flesh wounds that three of his gang had taken during the robbery. It had been a hard push to cover so much ground—hard on horses as well as men. And there was a problem of another sort—a man, or several men, who kept following them, who had killed Dewey and Sammy with a knife in a spot where they should have been able to see someone stalking them. Bill had watched closely for dust sign to the rear, and he'd seen nothing all day—not so much as a wisp of trail dust. What was happening didn't make a hell of a lot of sense. He'd been running from lawmen and Union cavalry for so many years that he'd been sure he knew all the tricks of the game—until then. For reasons he couldn't explain, he felt it was the work of just one man, and that was even more puzzling. Who would go alone after a gang the size of his? Only a madman, or one crazy son of a bitch.

"Joe an' Shorty ain't comin'," Buster said. "The guy who got Dewey an' Sammy got them, too."

"Not Joe Lucas," Bill answered. "He's too damn careful to get bushwhacked. It's just takin' 'em more time than they figgered."

"This gent's slippery," Buster argued. "He could even be the feller who got Scar Face. Maybe he's got some others with him . . . a posse. That'd explain why it's takin' Joe and Shorty so long to git back. They coulda run into a whole bunch of guns back yonder."

"We'd've seen some dust if it was a posse," Bill said, passing his glasses along the crests of hills, then along the low places between them. "It's that sumbitch who flung Homer off the roof who's responsible. I've got this feelin' about it, about how it's him."

"It can't be no good feelin', if it's just one man," Buster told him, frowning. "It just don't figger why some tough son of a bitch would be in Dodge this time of year. The gent who got Homer wasn't no lawman. Big feller . . . real tall, from what I seen of him. I remember one more thing. He yelled real loud when he throwed Homer's body, like he wanted us to know it was him an' that he was up there. Damn near like he was darin' somebody to shoot at him. Could be he's crazy."

"Crazy like a fox," Bill replied angrily, still reading the horizon through his lenses. "A genuine crazy man woulda showed hisself by now. I seen a few crazies durin' the war, when they seen too much blood, too much dyin'. They'd come runnin' at our lines like they was bulletproof, screamin' their damn fool heads off 'til a bullet shot 'em down. Some of 'em would get right back up an' come chargin' at us again whilst they was dyin'. It was a helluva sight to see. This bastard who's followin' us ain't that kind of crazy. Somehow, he's able to sneak up on us without showin' hisself . . . which is damn hard to do in this open country. But I still don't figger he got Joe. Shorty, maybe, but not Joe Lucas."

"Ain't no man bulletproof, not even Joe," Buster said after a pause.

Bill's glasses found movement on a distant hill. A pair of horses came trotting into view. Bill let out a sigh. "Yonder they come, both of 'em," he told Buster. "I can see both their horses—a sorrel an' Joe's big buckskin."

"Let's hope they killed the sumbitch," Buster remarked. "If they did, we can quit worryin'."

Bill watched the horses a little longer, because something about them seemed wrong, yet he couldn't put a finger on just what it was. Dusky darkness made it hard to see detail. Long black shadows fell away from the hills in places, preventing him from seeing Joe and Shorty clearly.

He waited while the horses came closer, holding a slow trot along a trail of horse droppings and hoofprints his gang had left in their wake. Bill was in too much of a hurry to make the alabaster caves west of old Fort Supply, where they could hide out, and there hadn't been time to be careful about leaving a trail to follow until they crossed over the Kansas line at the Cimarron River. In the river, they could ride downstream in the shallows and lose any possemen or cavalry when the current washed out their horse tracks.

"I can see 'em now," Buster said, squinting. "Two horses, only they sure as hell are comin' real slow. Looks like they'd be in a hurry to bring good news. Maybe they couldn't find the sneaky son of a bitch."

The pair of horses rounded a low hill, and Bill could now see them plainly enough. His jaw muscles went taut when his teeth were gritted in anger. "Damn!" he said, taking one last look before he lowered his field glasses, hands gripping them so tightly his knuckles were white.

"What the hell's wrong, Bill?" Buster asked, unable to see all of what Bill had seen, without magnification.

"He got 'em," Bill snapped.

"What the hell're you talkin' about?" Buster wanted to

know, glancing back to the horses that were approaching the ledge where they stood. "Yonder they come. That's Joe's yeller dun, an' that's Shorty's sorrel, ain't it?"

Bill's rage almost prevented him from answering Buster. A moment passed before he could control himself. "It's the horses," he growled. "Shorty an' Joe are tied across their saddles. Means they're dead."

"Dead? Why would the bastard take the time to tie Shorty an' Joe to their saddles?"

"He's sendin' us a warnin'," was all Bill could say right then, fuming.

Buster frowned at the horses a third time. "Son of a bitch," he said softly, unconsciously touching the butt of his pistol when he said it. "They *are* dead. I can see their arms danglin' loose." He turned to Bill. "What kind of crazy son of a bitch would do that?"

Bill tried to cool his anger long enough to think. "A man who don't give up easy. He aims to dog our trail all the way to the Nations. Can't figure why, only it's real clear he ain't in no mood to give up."

"I ain't so sure it's one man, Bill. One man couldn't have handled Joe and Shorty so quick. I say there's a bunch of 'em back yonder. Damn near has to be."

"I've got this feelin' you're wrong," Bill said, swinging off the ledge, taking long, purposeful strides down to the spot where his men rested. "But there's eleven of us left, an' we'll be more careful from here on," he added.

"We've lost some of our best shooters," Buster reminded him when he saw the men waiting for them in the draw.

Bill was in the wrong humor to discuss it. "Send a couple of men out to fetch Joe an' Shorty back here. Their horses're comin' too slow, followin' the scent of these others. I'll have everybody get mounted. Maybe we can lose that bastard when we come to the river."

Pete Woods and Stormy Sommers led the horses, with bodies lashed to saddles, over to Bill. Stormy's face wasn't the right color.

"Joe's got a hole blowed plumb through his neck," Pete said while jerking a thumb in Joe Lucas's direction. "Shorty caught one in the chest right near his heart."

Bill paid no attention to the swarm of blowflies that were clinging to both bodies, wondering how anyone could have taken Joe Lucas by surprise. "Cut 'em down an' leave 'em here. We'll use their horses for fresh mounts. See if there's any money in their pants pockets. Don't leave nothin' valuable behind."

"Whew, but they sure do stink!" Pete said, climbing down to cut pieces of rope that were holding the corpses in place. Shorty's body fell limply to the dirt. Joe slid out of his blood-soaked saddle to the ground with a sickening thump. "Goddamn flies been eatin' on 'em, on the blood."

Bill didn't care to hear about the smell. "Search their pockets like I told you," he said. "Time we cleared outta here quick. Been here too long. We oughta hit the river close to midnight."

"Who you reckon done this?" Charlie Walker asked, fingering his rifle in a nervous way.

"A crazy man," Buster answered when Bill said nothing. "He has to be outta his goddamn mind."

Bill wheeled his horse, heading south onto a darkening prairie, leading ten men and four pack animals loaded with bags of money toward the Cimarron.

In the back of his mind he wondered what kind of man was following them. Unlike Buster, Bill wasn't quite so sure the stalker was crazy. Deadly might be a better word.

And to make matters worse, the man on their trail seemed to be enjoying himself, in a way. Why else would he have sent the bodies back, unless he wanted fear to cause Bill and his gang to make another careless mistake?

The clatter of horseshoes on rock announced their arrival at the Cimarron River. Beyond the sluggish, late fall current, trees grew in abundance, which suited Bill Anderson just fine—more places to hide in the all-but-total darkness of a night without a moon.

Buster rode up next to him while they halted on the riverbank to look things over.

"Seems quiet enough," Buster observed.

Bill wasn't satisfied. He gave the far bank a close look, listening.

"Yore actin' real edgy, Bill," Buster said. "That bastard can't get ahead of us, hard as we been pushin' these horses. I say we get across quick."

Bill had been thinking about what had happened to Joe, Shorty, Dewey, and Sammy for the last few hours. "I've done give up on tryin' to predict what he'll do. But once we get in the river, we're gonna ride down it maybe a mile or two. It'll make it harder for him to find out where we came out. We'll look for a stretch of rock north of them alabaster caves to ride out. Can't no man track a horse on them hard rocks."

"This ain't like you, Bill, to act worried 'bout one or two men, however many there is. We used to ride off like we was in a damn parade every time we pulled a job. Seems like we're runnin' with our tails tucked between our legs now, an' all on account of one or two gents chasin' us."

Bill scowled at the forests beyond the Cimarron. "Things have started to change, Buster. This land ain't empty like it was before. An' the sumbitch behind us— maybe it is two or three—has proved to be pretty damn good."

"That ol' fort is abandoned. We could ride for it hard an' be there by daylight. No matter who's behind us, we can stand 'em off there real easy."

"It's gettin' across this river that's got me playin' things safe. Send a couple of men down to the water ahead of us. If nobody shoots at 'em, we'll bring the money down."

Buster turned back in the saddle, picking out men newer to the gang. "Floyd, you an' Chuck ride down to the river, an' keep your rifles handy."

Two younger members of the gang spurred their trail-weary horses past the others to ride down a rocky embankment to the water's edge. Both men approached cautiously, slowing their mounts to a walk.

Bill waited until no shots were fired at his men. "Let's go," he said, sending his horse downslope.

Floyd Devers turned to Chuck Mabry. Beads of sweat glistened on Floyd's face. "Looks safe enough," he said to his cousin from Fort Smith.

As Chuck was about to speak, a rifle cracked from the opposite bank, accompanied by a blossom of white light from a muzzle flash.

Mabry, the newest member of Bill Anderson's gang at the tender age of nineteen, fell off his horse as if he'd been poleaxed. Floyd's horse bolted away from the shallows when it was spooked by the explosion.

Floyd was clinging to his saddle horn when a bullet struck him in the right hip. "Yee-oow!" he cried, letting his rifle slip from his fingers. Pain like nothing he'd ever known raced down his leg, causing him to let go of the saddle and to slide slowly off to one side.

Floyd landed in the water with a splash, thrashing about, making a terrible racket, yelling his head off about the pain.

From Bill Anderson's men, half-a-dozen guns opened up on the muzzle flash. The banging of guns rattled on for several seconds more, until the shooting slowed, then stopped.

Bill turned his horse quickly to ride back behind the bank of the river, out of the line of fire.

"Goddamn!" Buster yelled, trying to calm his plunging, rearing horse. "How'd that bastard get across ahead of us?" he wondered at the top of his voice.

Bill was furious. He knew he should have sent an advance scouting party ahead to get the lay of things at the river, but with fatigue tugging at his eyelids he'd forgotten to do it until it was too late.

He could hear Floyd thrashing about in the water, making all manner of noise. The kid, Chuck, fell down like he was dead the moment the bullet hit him.

"This don't make no sense," Bill said when Buster got his horse stilled. "We've been ridin' as hard as these damn horses could carry us an' he still beat us to the river."

"Give me two men," Buster said, "an' I'll ride upstream an' cross over so we can get behind him. He won't be expectin' that from us."

Bill knew men as well as he knew anything on earth. "This son of a bitch, whoever he is, has got us outguessed with every move we make."

"We can't just sit here all night, Bill."

"Wasn't aimin' to," Bill replied. "We'll swing to the east and ride as hard as we can. Let's test his horse, see if he can stay up."

"He sure as hell ain't had no trouble so far," Buster said before he reined his mount around.

"Make sure you stay close to the money," Bill added in a quiet voice. "If one of our own decides to get rich while all this is goin' on, shoot him."

"I'll stand by you, Bill. Always have. But this gent we got shootin' us a few at a time is smart. You'll have to hand him that. We need to stay together. It's when we split up that he cuts some of us down."

"Numbers don't appear to make no difference to this son of a bitch," Bill answered. "Just do like I say. Stay close to the packhorses. We'll ride the riverbank for a ways an' see what he does next."

"We need to make it over to them trees, Bill," Buster told him. "Out here in the open, he's got a clear shot at us damn near every time. We'll be a helluva lot safer on the other side. We keep on this way, he's gonna bushwhack us all."

"I've got eyes, Buster, an' I don't need no help countin' the men he's killed. Start ridin'."

"Hold on a minute, Bill!" Pete Woods cried, pointing down the river. "Listen to Floyd yonder. He's hurt real bad, an' he needs somebody to go an' fetch him outta that water."

Bill aimed a hard-eyed look at Pete. "You go fetch him out, if you want," he said. "I ain't gonna make no target out of myself. Floyd can figure his own way out."

"He's just shot in the leg!" Pete protested.

Bill had grown tired of the useless banter. "You could

get shot in the head if you run down there, Pete. This was a chance every one of us took when we decided to rob them banks. Men get bullet holes in 'em sometimes when they take what ain't theirs. But if you're so damn soft-hearted, you ride right on down to that river an' lend Floyd a hand."

"Sure seems hard," Pete said, quieter.

"Robbin' folks of their money ain't no church picnic," Bill said.

Pete lowered his head, unwilling to challenge Bill over it any longer.

Bill rode off in the lead, and beyond the lip of the riverbank he could hear Floyd crying out for help. It reminded him of the war, when no one had been there to save all the brave soldiers from Missouri or Tennessee when they begged for assistance.

Someone near the loaded pack animals began to gag, and Bill knew it was the kid, Stormy Sommers. He ignored the sound, and spoke to Buster. "High time some of the little boys learned a thing or two about robbery. If it was easy, every son of a bitch who owned a gun would take up the profession."

Buster sounded a touch worried. "Don't leave us with but nine men, Bill."

"Nine?" Bill asked, his voice rising. "You don't think nine men stack up right?"

"Whoever's doin' the shootin' at us has been real good, or real lucky, today," Buster answered.

"Luck is all it is," Bill said.

Another rifle shot boomed from across the river, and Bill pulled his horse to a stop, turning his head to listen. He heard another painful cry coming from the Cimarron.

"Damn! Damn!"

It was Pete Woods's voice.

"Pete was dumb to ride down there so soon," Buster said with his head turned toward the sound. "He shoulda waited for a spell to see if things was clear."

"We don't need no careless men," Bill announced to

the men around him. "Pete wasn't thinkin' straight, or he'd've knowed to wait, like Buster said."

Stormy continued to gag, gripping his sides. Bill's nerves were on edge, and he had to do something to calm them. "Shut the hell up, Stormy, or I'll kill you myself. If you ain't got the stomach for robbin' banks, then ride the hell away from here—an' do it now!" Bill's right hand was on the grips of one revolver when he said it.

"We're all gonna die," Stormy whimpered. "That feller who's followin' us ain't no ordinary man."

Bill didn't want Stormy's fear to infect the others. He took out his Colt .44, cocked it, and fired directly at Stormy's head.

Stormy's horse bolted away from the banging noise as he went off one side of it. He landed with a grunt, falling on his back, staring up at the stars.

"Anybody else don't like the way I'm runnin' things?" Bill asked defiantly.

When not another word was said, he reined his horse to ride east, spurring his horse to a trot. He hadn't wanted to kill any more of his own men, like he'd had to do when Lee Wollard pulled that damn fool stunt inside the bank, hitting the banker so hard it knocked him out. But there were important things for men to learn if they aimed to stay outside the law, and one was when to take orders and follow them to the letter. A leader couldn't run a military outfit any other way.

Keeping his men and their precious cargo well out of rifle range from the far side of the Cimarron, Bill led his men east at a gallop, determined to make a crossing into the Nations as soon as he felt it was safe. . . .*

"What happened next, Floyd?" Lazarus asked.

"Well, when I saw Pete Woods hit whilst tryin' to get me outta the water, an' then Bill an' the others ride off

*Pride of the Mountain Man

into the darkness, I knew I was done for. I managed to crawl an' swim to the bank, and put my leg up on a rock so's the bleedin' would slow down."

He paused to refill his whiskey glass, his voice hoarse from all the talking.

"After about ten minutes or so, this real tall galoot ridin' with another, younger man, 'bout my age, comes crossin' the Cimarron as cool an' unconcerned as if he were out for a ride to enjoy the evenin' air. He says his name's Smoke Jensen, an' he proceeds to take his bandanna off and wrap it around my leg, tyin' it down real tight."

"Why didn't he just finish you off right then?" Blackie Jackson asked, his head cocked to the side.

Floyd shrugged. "Don't rightly know. It's sure what Bill woulda done. Anyways, he tells me to get on over to Dodge City and give myself up to Marshal Wyatt Earp, 'cause he's gonna go on after Bill an' the others."

"And he expected you to do that?" Lazarus asked.

Floyd nodded. "Yep. He said if'n he got back to Dodge an' I wasn't there, he'd hunt me down an' kill me."

"Did you believe him?"

"Damn straight! That's why I agreed to join this little party of yours. I've been lookin' over my back ever since I broke outta jail, just knowin' he was gonna be standin' there some day, lookin' down at me over the sights of his Colt."

Floyd shook his head. "I gotta finish this with Jensen, one way or another, so I can quit watchin' my backtail.

"I can't believe you just waltzed on back to Dodge City and asked Marshal Earp to put you in jail 'cause you was afraid of Jensen," Blackie said

Floyd gave the big man a look. "Just wait, big mouth. Soon you'll be facing Jensen, with those eyes that look like they're made of ice, an' we'll see how big you talk then."

8

When Smoke walked into the hotel room where Cal was being nursed back to health, he found Pearlie standing next to the bed with his hands on his hips, arguing.

"Dammit, Cal! Doc says you got to eat or you ain't gonna make up for all that blood you lost. Now I'm tellin' you for the last time, either eat that stew or I'm gonna get a tube and stick it down your gullet and pour it in there myself."

Cal cast worried eyes over Pearlie's shoulder to stare at Smoke, as if asking for some help dealing with this mother hen he was facing.

"Take it easy, Pearlie," Smoke said as he walked over to the bed. "Just because Cal can't shovel grub in like you do doesn't mean he's not eating enough. Doc says he's doing just fine."

"Well, he needs to eat more. That boy don't eat enough to keep a bird alive."

Cal grimaced with pain as he pushed himself up to a sitting position against a pile of pillows. "Now, if Miz Sally would cook up some bearsign, then I'd probably feel a whole lot better about eatin'. Might perk up my flaggin' spirits a mite, too."

Smoke laughed. "Cal, I can see you're learning real fast how to take full advantage of being wounded."

"Trouble is, if Miz Sally did make those bearsign," Cal

said mournfully, glancing at Pearlie out of the corner of his eye, "I have a feelin' somebody else'd eat 'em up 'fore they got here."

Pearlie's eyes got big and he looked astonished that Cal would say such a thing. "Well that's a fine howdy do. I sit up here day an' night for two weeks spoonfeedin' this young'un so he can get well, an' he accuses me of eatin' his bearsign."

"Seems to me Sally did bring a platter of donuts up here last week. Didn't Cal get any of those?" Smoke asked.

Pearlie blushed a bright red. "Uh . . . not exactly. At the time Miz Sally brought those, Doc still had Cal on liquids only, so naturally—"

"See! I tole you he'd eat 'em up 'fore I got any," Cal said, pointing his finger at Pearlie. He turned his head to look at Smoke. "From now on, if you don't mind, Smoke, would you ask Miz Sally if'n she'd bring me those bearsign personally? That's the only way I'm ever gonna get any."

"All right, Cal, I'll tell her myself to cook up a fresh batch for tomorrow. Now, we need to talk about what happened out there the day you got shot. Doc said you're feeling up to discussing it now."

"Yes sir."

Pearlie walked to the corner of the room and pulled two chairs over for him and Smoke to sit on while Cal told his story.

After Cal finished telling them about Lazarus Cain and about the two men he'd shot before they got him, Smoke nodded his head.

"That's about how we had it figured, only we didn't know how many men you were facing that day. You say there were about fifteen or twenty?"

"Yes sir, minus the two I shot."

"And this man told you his name was Lazarus Cain?"

"Yes sir."

"Sheriff Carson has some paper on him, but it didn't say anything about him being headed this way."

"Smoke, that man is plumb crazy," Cal said, his face paling a little as he thought back on the shooting incident.

"What do you mean, Cal?"

"Well, I seem to remember, after he shot me an' I was lyin' there, feelin' my life sorta ebbin' away, he stood over me and began to pray for my soul."

"Pray? Like to Jesus an' everthing?" Pearlie asked, astonishment on his face.

"Yeah. He even had this old raggedy Bible with a bullet stuck right in the middle of it."

Smoke nodded but didn't say anything, seeing that thinking about it was making Cal feel bad.

"Has anybody reported any problems or seein' these galoots since they shot Cal, Smoke?" Pearlie asked.

Smoke wagged his head. "No, and that's the strange thing. You'd think with a group that big someone would have run into them, or they'd have robbed or shot someone else by now. They don't exactly seem the kind of men to move quietly through an area without attracting any notice."

"Maybe some of the outlying ranchers have seen 'em an' just haven't been to town to tell anybody yet," Cal said.

"That's a good thought, Cal." Smoke stood up and grabbed his hat off the dresser. "I think I'll ride on a little circuit around the area and see if anyone's heard or seen anything. It might be good to warn them to stay away from this gang if they can, so no one else will get hurt," Smoke said.

"I think I'll come with you, Smoke, if it's all right. I'm gettin' cabin fever cooped up here with this ungrateful pup," Pearlie said, casting a hurt look at Cal.

Cal laughed. "You know I'm grateful to you, Pearlie. You're about the best friend a man could ever have, long as they ain't no bearsign to come betwixt us."

Pearlie smiled. "Since you put it that way, I'll make sure to bring those bearsign out to you myself, first thing in the mornin'."

"Try an' leave at least one or two out of the whole bunch, Pearlie," Cal said, a grin on his face.

* * *

Smoke and Pearlie began to ride a wide circuit around Big Rock. The first ranch they came to belonged to Johnny and Belle North. Johnny North was an ex-gunfighter who'd come to town a few years back to settle an old score with Monte Carson. Seems they'd both loved the same woman for a time. Instead of fighting, the two men had sat down and eaten a meal together, and found neither one could much remember what they were supposed to be mad at each other about.

Later on, Johnny decided to settle down when Belle Colby's husband got himself shot to death in a gunfight with the men who'd raped their daughter and killed their son. Johnny moved in to help her with their ranch and teenage daughter, and before long they were married. He'd hung up his guns for good that day.

As Smoke and Pearlie approached the North ranch, Belle appeared on the porch, cradling a shotgun in her arms.

Smoke raised his hands as he walked Joker closer to the cabin. "Don't shoot, Belle. It's me, Smoke Jensen."

"I know who you are, Smoke. I'm not so old I can't see. At least, not yet. How are you doing, boys?"

Smoke crossed his arms on his saddle horn and leaned forward. "We're doing fine, Belle. Where's Johnny?"

She inclined her head. "He's off with the hands, brandin' some of the new calves. By the way, thanks for those Hereford bulls. They sure do make a good cross with our shorthorns."

Smoke nodded. "They sure do. By the way, Belle, where is George Hampton? Doesn't he work for you anymore?"

Belle smiled. "Not exactly. Johnny and I gave him a hundred acres up to the north. He and my daughter Velvet are plannin' to get hitched this spring, so we figgered we'd make him a rancher 'stead of a hired hand."

Smoke and Pearlie both smiled. "Congratulations, Belle. And give Velvet my best wishes. George is a good man."

Belle pointed to the east. "Johnny's just over that rise there, 'bout four or five miles, if you need to see him."

Smoke and Pearlie tipped their hats and reined their horses around and headed east.

"I can't hardly believe Velvet's gettin' married," Pearlie said.

Smoke glanced at him out of the corner of his eye. "That's right. Didn't I see you dancing with her quite a bit at the last Fourth of July picnic?"

Pearlie blushed a bright red. "Well, maybe one or two dances, is all. She is a right smart lookin' woman, though."

"About your age, I believe?"

Pearlie looked at Smoke. "Now, don't you go gettin' no ideas. I ain't near old enough to be thinkin' 'bout gettin' hitched."

"You aren't getting any younger, Pearlie, and there aren't that many eligible women around."

"Smoke, you heard Miss Belle. Velvet's engaged to George Hampton, an' he's a good man."

"Yes, he is," Smoke said with a grin, thinking back to the day he'd first met George Hampton. He and Pearlie and Cal had been out in the forest cutting wood for the upcoming winter. Smoke had gone to take a nap while the younger men finished loading the buckboard with their morning's work. . . .

The sound of a gunshot brought Smoke instantly awake and alert. Years in the mountains with the first mountain man, Preacher, had taught Smoke many things. Two of the most important were how to sleep with one ear listening, and never to be without one of his big Colt .44s nearby. The gun was in his hand with the hammer drawn back before echoes from the shot had died.

"Sh-h-h, Horse," he whispered, not wanting the big Appaloosa to nicker and give away his position. He buckled his gun belt on, holstered his .44, and slipped a sawed-off 10-gauge American Arms shotgun out of his saddle scabbard. Glancing at the sun, he figured he had been asleep about two hours. Cal and Pearlie were nowhere in sight.

Raising his nose, Smoke sniffed the breeze. The faint smell of gunpowder came from upwind. He turned and began to trot through the dense undergrowth of the mountain woods, not making a sound.

Smoke peered around a pine tree and saw Cal bending over Pearlie, trying to stanch the blood running down his left arm. Four men on horseback were arrayed in front of them, one still holding a smoking pistol in his right hand. "Okay, now I'm not gonna ask you boys again. Where is Smoke Jensen's spread? We know it's up in these hills somewheres."

Cal looked up, and if looks could kill the men would have been blown out of their saddles. "You didn't have to shoot him. We're not even armed."

"You going to talk, boy? Or do you want the same as your friend there?" The man pointed the gun at Cal, scowling in anger.

Cal squared his shoulders and faced the man full on, fists balled at his sides. "Get off that horse, mister, and I'll show you who's a boy!"

The man's scowl turned to a grin. His lips pulled back from crooked teeth as he cocked the hammer of his weapon. "Say good-bye, banty rooster."

Smoke stepped into the clearing and fired one barrel of the shotgun, blowing the man's hand and forearm off up to the elbow, to the accompaniment of a deafening roar.

The men's horses reared and shied as the big gun boomed, while the riders clawed at their guns. Smoke flipped Cal one of his Colts with his left hand as he drew the other with his right.

Cal cocked, aimed, and fired the .44 almost simultaneously with Smoke. Smoke's bullet hit one rider in the middle of his chest, blowing a fist-sized hole clear through to his back. Cal's shot took the top of another man's head off down to his ears. The remaining gunman dropped his weapon and held his hands high, sweating and cursing as his horse whirled and stomped and crow-hopped in fear.

Smoke nodded at Cal, indicating he should keep the man covered. Then he walked over to Pearlie. He bent down and examined the wound, which had stopped bleeding. "You okay, cowboy?"

Pearlie smiled a lopsided grin. "Yeah, boss. No problem." He reached in his back pocket and pulled out a plug of Bull Durham, biting off a large chunk. "I'll just wet me some of this here tabaccy and stuff it in the hole. That'll take care of it until I can get Doc Spalding to look at it."

Smoke nodded. He remembered Preacher had used tobacco in one form or another to treat almost all of the many injuries he endured living in the mountains. And Preacher had to be in his eighties, if he was still alive, that is.

With Pearlie's wound seen to, Smoke turned his attention to the man Cal held at bay. He walked over to stand before him. "Get off that horse, scum."

The man dismounted, casting an eye toward his friend writhing on the ground and trying to stop the bleeding from his stump.

"Ain't ya gonna hep Larry? He's might near bled to death over there."

Smoke walked over to the moaning man, stood over him, and casually spat in his face as he took his last breath and died, open eyes staring at eternity. With eyes that had turned ice-gray, Smoke turned to look at the only one of the men still alive. "What's your name, skunk-breath?"

"George. George Hampton."

"Who are you, and what're you doin' here looking for me?"

"Why, uh, we was lookin' fer Smoke Jensen."

Smoke sighed, shaking his head. "I *am* Smoke Jensen, you fool. Now you found me, what do you want?"

Hampton's eyes shifted rapidly back and forth from Cal to Smoke. "You can't hardly be Smoke Jensen.

You're too danged young. Jensen's been out here in the mountains killing people for nigh on ten, fifteen years."

"I started young." He drew his .44 and eared the hammer back, the sear notches making a loud click. "And I'm not used to asking questions more than once."

Hampton held up his hands. "Uh, look Mr. Jensen, it was all Larry's idea. He said some gunhawk gave him two hundred dollars to come up here and kill you." He started speaking faster at the look on Smoke's face. "He said he'd share it with we'uns if we'd back his play."

"What was this gunhawk's name?"

Hampton shook his head. "I don't know. Larry never told us."

Smoke looked at Hampton over the sights of his .44. "You sold your life cheap, mister."

Cal cried out, "Smoke! No!"

Smoke lowered his gun, sighing. "Cal's right. I've gone this long without ever killing an unarmed man. No need to change now, even though you sorely need it." He stopped talking, an odd expression on his face. He sniffed a couple of times, then looked at Hampton through narrowed eyes. "That smell coming from you, mister?"

Hampton's face flared red and he looked down. "Uh, yes sir. My bowels kinda let loose when you cocked that big pistol of yours."

Pearlie let out a guffaw. "Hell, Smoke. You don't want to kill this 'un. Let him go, and if he's any kind of man he'll die of shame 'fore the day's over."

Smoke holstered his gun and turned to walk away. Cal nodded at Hampton. "Get out of here while the gettin's good."

As Hampton stepped in his saddle and took off looking for a hole, Pearlie called out, "And you can tell your kids you once looked over the barrel of a gun at Smoke Jensen and lived to tell about it. Damn few men can say that!"

Later that afternoon, Smoke was halfway to Big Rock when Horse began to act up. First the horse snorted, pricked his ears and looked back toward Smoke with eyes wide. Smoke had been lost in thought about who might be gunning for him, letting Horse find his own way to town. He came fully awake and alert when the animal began to nicker softly.

Leaning forward in the saddle, he patted Horse's neck and whispered, "Thanks, old friend. I hear you." Mountain-bred ponies were better than guard dogs when it came to sensing danger. Smoke shook his head, thinking Preacher would be disgusted with him. If there was one thing the old mountain man had stressed it was that the mountains were a dangerous world, and not to be taken lightly. Riding around with your head in the clouds, especially when you knew someone was trying to nail your hide to the wall, was downright stupid, if not suicidal.

Smoke slipped the hammer thongs from his Colts, then put his hand on the butt of the Henry rifle in the scabbard next to his saddle and shook it a little to make sure it was loose and ready to be pulled.

He tugged gently on the reins to slow Horse from a trot to a walk and settled back in the saddle, hands hanging next to his pistols.

Even with his precautions, he was surprised when a man jumped out of the brush into the middle of the trail in front of him. It was George Hampton, and he was pointing a Colt Navy pistol at Smoke.

"Get down off that horse, you bastard."

Smoke spread his hands wide and swung his leg over the cantle and dropped, cat-like, to the ground. "Hampton, I thought you'd be halfway home by now."

"I ain't gonna go home 'til I've put a bullet between the eyes of the famous Smoke Jensen."

Smoke glanced at the revolver Hampton was holding, smiled, and shook his head. "Hampton, I really don't want to kill you. Why don't you just put that gun down and head on home?" He spread his hands wider, stepping closer to him. "And just where is your home, anyway? You never got around to telling me yesterday."

Hampton licked his lips, the gun trembling a little in his hand. "Just keep yore distance, Jensen. I'll admit I ain't no expert with the six-gun like you are, but I can't hardly miss at this distance."

Smoke kept his hands in front of him. "Okay, okay, don't get nervous. I'll stay back. But it seems to me a man ought'a know just why he's bein' killed."

Hampton nodded. "Well, yore right. I can see the justice in that, 'cept I don't rightly know. Larry, the man you kilt, he made me and the other boys the offer down on the Rio Bravo in Texas. Seems that gunhawk met him in a saloon in Laredo, and told him he wanted you dead in the worst way . . . somethin' about how you had humiliated him a while back, and he wanted you in the ground because of it."

Smoke's eyes narrowed and turned slate gray. "So you and the other boys decided to pick up some easy money on the owlhoot trail, huh?"

Sweat was beading on Hampton's forehead in spite of the cool mountain air. "Naw, it wasn't like that. We're just cowboys, not gunslicks. There's an outbreak of Mexican fever in the cattle down Texas way, and there ain't much work for wranglers, leastways not unless you're hooked up with one of the big spreads." He shook his head, gun barrel dropping a little. "Hell, it was this or learn to eat dirt."

Smoke relaxed, his muscles loosening. "I'll tell you what, Hampton. There's always work for an honest cowboy in the high country. If you're willing to give an honest day's labor, you'll get an honest day's pay."

The pistol came back up and Hampton scowled. "Yore just sayin' that cause I got the drop on you."

Smoke smiled. Then, quick as a rattlesnake's strike he reached out and grabbed Hampton's gun while drawing his own Colt .44 and sticking the barrel under Hampton's nose. "No, George, you're wrong. You never had the drop on me." He nodded at Hampton's pistol. "That there is a Colt Navy model, a single action revolver. You have to cock the hammer 'fore it'll shoot, and I can draw and fire twice before you can cock that pistol."

Hampton's shoulders slumped and he let go of his gun and raised his hands. "Okay, Jensen, it's yore play."

Smoke holstered his Colt and handed the other one back to Hampton. "I told you, George, you got two choices. You can get on that pony there and head on back to Texas, or I can give you a note and send you up to one of the spreads hereabouts and you can start working and feeling like a man again. It's all up to you."

Hampton looked down at his worn and shabby boots and britches, then back to Smoke. "That's no choice, Mr. Jensen. You give me that note and I promise I'll not make you sorry you trusted me."

Smoke walked to Horse and took a scrap of paper and a pencil stub out of his saddlebags. After a moment, he handed the paper to Hampton. "Take this note to the next place you see up to the north of mine. It belongs to the Norths. They can always use an extra hand, and Johnny pays fair wages."

Hampton held out his hand. "I don't know how to thank you, Mr. Jensen, but . . . thanks."

Smoke grinned, knowing Hampton was a friend for life. In the rough-hewn country of the West, favors, or slights, were not soon forgotten. Help a man who was down on his luck, and he was honor-bound to repay you, even at the cost of his life if it came to that . . .*

Vengeance of the Mountain Man

9

Smoke and Pearlie found Johnny North just where Belle said he would be. He was bending over a tied-down calf with a branding iron in his hand while two of his men held the struggling animal down.

After the red-hot iron seared the North brand into the calf, sending smoke smelling of burned flesh into the air, Johnny stepped back and sleeved sweat off his forehead.

One of his men pointed over his shoulder and he looked, smiling widely when he saw Smoke and Pearlie approaching.

"You boys keep on workin'. I'm gonna take a short break an' talk to Smoke," he said, handing the still smoking iron to his foreman.

He walked over to the campfire nearby and squatted, pouring three mugs of coffee as Smoke and Pearlie got down off their horses.

"You men look like you could use some *cafécito*," Johnny said.

"Thanks, Johnny," Smoke said, taking a cup.

"Much obliged," Pearlie said, nodding his hello.

Johnny took a sack of Bull Durham out of his shirt pocket and began to build a cigarette. "What brings you boys way out here on a workday?"

"Cal was shot a couple of weeks back while working on the Sugarloaf," Smoke said.

"Damn!" Johnny exclaimed. "Is he gonna be all right?"

"Looks like he's going to make it."

"Who did it? Somebody local?"

Smoke shook his head. "No. Cal says there were about twenty men, give or take. He shot two before they got him. I was wondering if you or any of your hands had seen anything of a bunch like that lately."

Johnny stuck the cigarette in his mouth and lighted it, shaking his head. "Not that I've heard of. I'll ask around to make sure, but I'm certain they'd've mentioned it if they'd seen a group of men that big."

Smoke finished his coffee and put the cup next to the fire. "Well, ride with your guns loose, partner. These are bad men, and they're up to no good if they're still around. Tell Belle to be careful too, all right?"

"Sure thing, Smoke. I'll keep an eye out. Thanks for the warning."

"Oh, and congratulations on George and Velvet's engagement. We're all mighty proud of her around here."

"Thanks, Smoke. I'll tell her and George both you said hi."

Smoke and Pearlie got on their horses and rode toward the next ranch, hoping to find some sign Cain and his men had been spotted. . . .

Back in Fontana, Lazarus turned to Walter Blackwell. "Walt, tell us what happened out there after Floyd was shot and you and Bloody Bill and the others rode off."

Walter nodded and leaned forward, his elbows on the table as he started to talk. . . .

Four men sat huddled around a small fire, deep within a rock cavern with curious, glistening walls of solid alabaster. Bloody Bill Anderson was chewing a mouthful of jerky, washing it down with whiskey. Deeper into the cave, their horses and pack animals were hobbled and fed what little grain the gang had left in towsacks. Bags of money lay near the fire, and piles of currency, along with gleaming gold and silver coins, were stacked in neat rows. Bill watched Walter Blackwell count the money.

"More'n forty thousand so far, Bill," said Walter, a quiet, retiring man who was a remarkably good shot with a pistol.

"We're rich," Bill said, cocking an ear toward the entrance where Buster, Billy Riley, and Cletus Miller were standing guard. "Best of all, we gave that sneaky bastard the slip, so our troubles're over. He'll never find us here. Hell, the cavalry an' dozens of U.S. Marshals from Fort Smith've been ridin' past these caves for years. Hardly nobody knows they're here. We lay low for a little while, maybe five or six weeks, an' then we ride out free as birds." He gave Walter a stare. "Keep on countin'. You ain't hardly more'n half done. There's gonna be sixty thousand dollars, way I figure."

Tad Younger, the cousin of Cole and his famous outlaw bunch, was frowning. "Sure do hope whoever's been behind us don't show up. He's made a habit out of showin' up when he ain't supposed to."

Bill wagged his head. "We lost him. Can't no Indian or white man find a horse's tracks where we just rode. Slabs of rock don't leave no horse sign."

"Here's ten thousand more," Walter said, adding a stack of banknotes to the counted money.

Bill grinned. "Maybe there's gonna be seventy thousand, after all—" He abruptly ended his remark when a series of loud explosions came from the mouth of the cave.

Bill leapt to his feet, clawing both six-guns out of his holsters, shattering the bottle of whiskey he'd been holding.

A scream of agony came from the tunnel, followed by a much louder bellowing string of cusswords in Buster Young's voice.

Bill took off in a run for the entrance, leveling his pistols in front of him, almost tripping in the dark. Then two more heavy gun blasts sounded, and he recognized Cletus Miller's cry of pain.

Racing up to the opening, caught in a wild fury beyond his control when he knew the man who'd been tracking them had showed up at the cave in spite of all his precautions, he stopped when he saw three dark shapes lying behind a pile of boulders where his guards had been hiding. Big Buster Young was writhing and rocking back and forth, holding his belly, gasping for air, his face twisted in a grimace.

Billy Riley lay facedown on the rocks in a pool of blood and he wasn't moving. Cletus sat against a big stone, a shotgun resting on his lap, arms dangling limply at his sides while his mouth hung open, drooling blood on his shirt.

And when Bill saw this—all three of his men dead or dying from three, well-placed shots—he tasted fear for the first time in his life. Gazing out at the darkness, where only dim light from the stars showed any detail of his surroundings, something inside him stirred—a knot of terror forming in his chest that had never been there before. And he noticed that the hands holding his pistols were shaking so much he knew his aim would be way off target . . . if he could find anything to shoot at.

"Come on out, Anderson!" a deep voice shouted. "Got you cornered! There ain't gonna be no escape!"

Bill crouched down. In spite of the night chill, sweat poured from his hatband into his eyes. "You're gonna have to kill us!" he yelled back. "You ain't takin' none of us alive!"

"Suits the hell outta me!" the voice answered.

Bill heard soft footsteps coming up behind him. He didn't bother to turn around to see who it was. "Get your rifles," he said in a whisper. "We'll gather up the money an' shoot our way out of here."

"He'll kill us!" Walter Blackwell said.

"Like hell he will," Bill snapped. "Just do like I say, an' get rifles ready. Tell the others to saddle our horses an' put the money on them packsaddles."

Walter, always soft-spoken, said, "I've never disobeyed an order from you, Bill, but this is different. It'll be like we killed ourselves if we try to ride out. Whoever that feller is, he don't miss."

Bill's fear turned to anger. "Shut the hell up, Walter, an' do what I ordered!"

"I won't do it," Walter said very quietly.

Bill turned an angry glance over his shoulder, staring up at Walter's dark shape standing right behind him. "You what?" he demanded.

Bill heard a soft click while Walter spoke. "I won't let you get the rest of us killed," he whispered.

The sudden realization of what Walter meant to do struck Bill Anderson a split second before the hammer fell on a Mason Colt .44/.40 conversion. A roar filled the cave mouth, and then Bill's ears, when it felt as if a sledgehammer had hit him squarely in the middle of his forehead.

He was slammed against a cavern wall, with his ears ringing, until the noise made by the gunshot died away. He stood there, leaning against the wall with blood streaming down his face and into his eyes for a moment. Then he slumped limply to the ground. . . .*

Lazarus leaned back in his chair, his eyes hard. "So, you shot Bill, huh?"

"That's right. He didn't leave me no choice in the matter," Walter said quietly.

"What happened next?"

Walter shrugged. "We gave ourselves up. Smoke Jensen took us and the money back to Dodge City and turned us over to Marshal Earp."

Lazarus looked skeptical. "You mean Jensen had the drop on you men, and there was over seventy thousand dollars on those packhorses?"

"That's right."

"A man'd have to be crazy to pass up a fortune like that when all he had to do was finish you boys off and no one

Pride of the Mountain Man

would ever know he'd taken it," Lazarus said, staring at Walter.

Walter shook his head, a small smile on his face. "Jensen ain't like no ordinary man. Money don't seem to mean nothin' to him."

"I need to find out more about this man if we're gonna go up against him," Lazarus said.

He glanced at the table where some of his men were sitting, drinking whiskey and playing poker.

"Pig Iron, you and Curly Joe come on over here. I got a job for you to do."

When they got to his table, Lazarus said, "I want you two to ride on over to Big Rock an' get the lay of the land. See what the people are sayin' 'bout that runt we killed, and see if you can size up Smoke Jensen. I want to know if he's got as much sand as Walter and Floyd here say he does."

10

As they rode into Big Rock, Curly Joe gave a low whistle. "Damn, Pig Iron, we been holed up in that ghost town so long I've almost forgot what a real town looks like."

Pig Iron nodded. "Yes. It's kind'a nice to see people on the street instead of tumbleweeds."

When they came to a buckboard parked in front of the general store with a man loading sacks of flour in it, Curly Joe reined his horse to a halt.

"Say, mister, you happen to know Smoke Jensen?"

The man looked up with a smile. "Sure, everybody in Big Rock knows Smoke. Why?"

"You know where he might be found?"

"Well, if he's in town he's usually over at the sheriff's office or at Longmont's saloon."

"Thank you kindly," Curly Joe said, tipping his hat as they rode on down the street.

As they passed the sheriff's office a man in the doorway, leaning against the wall drinking a cup of coffee, gave them a long look.

"Appears the sheriff don't much cotton to havin' a pair of strangers ridin' into town," Curly Joe said with a grin, as if to show he didn't much care what any hick town sheriff thought.

Pig Iron nodded, but he wasn't as carefree about it as

Curly Joe. He realized from what the citizen back there had said that the sheriff and Jensen were good friends, and that was going to make it that much harder to try to take Jensen out—now or later.

At the Longmont Saloon they dismounted and tied their mounts to the hitching rail in front. Curly Joe, as usual, swaggered through the batwings first, trying to impress Pig Iron with his bravado.

Pig Iron shook his head, knowing better. He'd always figured Curly Joe was a coward deep inside, like all braggarts and showoffs, and he didn't intend to count on him for any backup.

They walked to the bar and ordered whiskey, and were glad to see that the bottle the bartender placed in front of them actually had a label on it.

"This has got to be better than that rotgut we been drinkin' over at—" Curly Joe started to say. Pig Iron interrupted him with a sharp jab in the shoulder with his elbow.

"Sh-h-h," Pig Iron whispered. "There ain't no need in advertising where we been stayin', you fool."

Curly Joe assumed a hurt look, as if he wouldn't have been that stupid. "I know that," he said. "I was just gonna say that *other place.*"

Pig Iron turned around and leaned back, his elbows on the bar, and surveyed the room. It was a nice saloon, furnished much better than most such places he'd been in. Almost all the tables were full, indicating it was a popular place to eat and drink. He noticed most of the people at tables were eating, not just sitting around drinking.

"Food must be pretty good here, too," he said.

"Huh?" Curly Joe asked, pouring himself another glass of whiskey.

"Never mind," Pig Iron said, realizing he'd been right—Curly Joe wasn't going to be much help to him today. The man was dumber than a post.

Pig Iron turned back around and asked the bartender, "Say, is Smoke Jensen around today?"

The barman glanced around the crowded room for a

moment, then shrugged his shoulders. "Nope. Don't see 'im."

"A friend told us to look him up and say howdy, but he didn't tell us what the man looked like."

"You can't miss Smoke Jensen. He's 'bout the biggest man in town, couple'a inches over six feet, with shoulders wide as an ax handle, sandy-colored hair, an' he's usually wearin' buckskins."

"Thanks," Pig Iron said with a smile. "We'll keep an eye out."

Smoke and Pearlie eased out of their saddles in front of Longmont's.

"Damn, I'm stiff as leather been sittin' in the sun fer too long," Pearlie said, putting his hands in the small of his back and leaning back, trying to stretch muscles grown sore from too long in the saddle.

Smoke rubbed his butt cheeks with a sigh. "I can see we've both been having it much too soft lately. I can remember the time when I could sit a saddle from dawn to dusk and not feel this sore."

Pearlie chuckled. "Yeah, but that was back when you was a lot younger, Smoke. You got to realize yore gettin' older now, got to take it a mite easier than you used to."

"Old?" Smoke said as they pushed through the batwings. "What do you mean by that, you young whippersnapper?"

They saw Louis Longmont sitting at his table drinking coffee and walked over to join him.

"I mean it, Smoke. It's 'bout time for you to get a rockin' chair and sit on the porch all day an' let young'uns like me an' Cal do the hard work."

Louis arched an eyebrow. "What is this I hear? The redoubtable Smoke Jensen, mountain man extraordinaire, being told to seek early retirement?"

Smoke flopped in a chair, glaring at Pearlie with mock anger. "Can you believe it, Louis? This young pup thinks I'm getting old just because I got a little saddle-sore after riding around the mountains all day."

Pearlie grinned. "Say, Louis. Have you got in your shipment of sarsaparilla yet?"

"Yes, Pearlie. It arrived yesterday. Would you like some?"

"Sure, an' some food too, if'n you don't mind."

"What is the house special today, Louis?" Smoke asked. "I'm hungry enough to eat raw bear meat."

"I'm sorry, Smoke. We are fresh out of bear meat. Today's special is Steak *Louie*. That is a tender fillet of young beef, cut thin and marinated in white wine for twelve hours, then cooked over a low flame until it is barely seared on the outside, but still red and moist on the inside. It is served with asparagus spears, fresh corn on the cob, and a salad of assorted greens."

"I'll take an order of that," Pearlie said, licking his lips, "'cept you can leave off that asparagus. It makes my pee turn green an' smell funny."

"And that bothers you, *mon ami?*" Louis asked, smiling.

"Naw, it don't bother me, but it does kind'a give me a start the next mornin' to look down and see a green stream comin' out."

"How about you, Smoke?"

"I'll have the lunch special also, Louis, and you can give me Pearlie's asparagus. I'm so hungry my stomach thinks my throat's been cut."

As Louis turned to call out the order to the waiter, he saw two men approaching the table. Their expressions were hard, and so were their eyes.

He turned back to face Smoke, reaching down and unhooking the rawhide hammer thong on the Colt at his side. "Looks like trouble approaching, Smoke."

"I see 'em, Louis," Smoke said, his hand at his side undoing his hammer thong at the same time.

As the two men approached the table, Smoke examined them closely with an appraising eye. One was tall, over six feet, and looked to be built well, all muscle and no fat. From the scar tissue on his cheeks and his flattened, misshapen ears and gnarled knuckles, Smoke knew he'd been a professional fighter. His eyes were intelligent, and Smoke could see the man was sizing him up at the same time.

The other man was shorter, about five feet eleven, with dark, curly hair and a face that was handsome in a weak sort of way. His eyes were cold and vacant, and it was plain he was a man who wouldn't hesitate to kill—but only if he had an edge. He had the look of a coward about him.

When they stopped in front of the table Smoke leaned back in his chair, extending his right leg a bit to make it easier to reach for his Colt should the need arise.

"Good afternoon, gentlemen," Smoke said, since they were both staring at him.

"Are you Smoke Jensen?" the tall one asked, his voice firm, with no animosity in it.

"Yes, I am."

"My name is Carlton, Pig Iron Carlton. I ran into an old acquaintance of yours the other day, and he said to look you up and say hello."

"And who was that?" Smoke asked.

"Floyd Devers."

"Devers, huh? Last I heard he was in jail, waiting to be hanged for robbery and murder over in Dodge City."

"Not anymore. He's out now, and he says he can't wait to see you. He says you're a lying, cheating, back-shooting bastard."

Smoke's eyes narrowed, and the room grew quiet at the sound of those words, which in the West were almost always followed by gunfire.

"Oh, so that's what he says? What do you say, Mr. Carlton?"

"I say I believe him. You look like a coward to me, Jensen. Like a man with a yellow streak down his back a mile wide."

Smoke sighed and stood up, knowing there was no way to avoid a confrontation now. The man had come looking to pick a fight, and that was what he was going to get.

Smoke walked toward the door, pulling a pair of thick,

black leather gloves from his waistband and putting them on.

"Are you running away, Jensen?" the shorter, curly-haired man called out, a smirky grin on his face.

"Nope. Just taking it outside so your friend doesn't bleed all over Mr. Longmont's furniture."

"You're the one that's going to bleed, Jensen," Pig Iron said, following Smoke through the batwings.

Smoke stopped in the street and turned to face Pig Iron. "Oh, I suspect we're both going to bleed, Mr. Carlton, but I've been bloody before, and I've always been the last one standing when it was over."

Pig Iron stripped his shirt off, revealing rows of well-sculpted muscles.

"Jesus," Pearlie whispered from the boardwalk, where he and Louis and the rest of the patrons of Longmont's had gathered to watch the fight. "He looks hard as a rock."

"Where do you think he got the name Pig Iron?" Louis asked. "He was the fisticuffs champion of the United States for a few years."

"What happened? Did someone beat him?" Pearlie asked.

"Not that I know of. He got in some trouble with the law and just disappeared."

"Do you think Smoke knows that?"

Louis shrugged. "Wouldn't make any difference to Smoke. He knew the man wanted to pick a fight, so there was no way out other than to oblige him."

In the street, the two men circled each other, Pig Iron's hands up in the classic pugilist's stance.

"I see you used to be a professional fighter," Smoke said, moving his head around and swinging his arms to loosen his neck and shoulder muscles.

"That's right," Pig Iron said. "Over a hundred professional fights, and never lost one."

"Well, out here, we don't go by the Marquis of Queensberry's rules of fisticuffs. There's only one rule in the West."

"What's that?" asked Pig Iron.

"There aren't any rules," Smoke said, leaning to the side and lashing out with his right foot.

The toe of his boot caught Pig Iron in the solar plexus, doubling him over as his breath escaped with a whoosh.

Smoke stepped in and swung a short left jab to Pig Iron's head, flattening his right ear and tearing it partially off.

Pig Iron, after two blows that would have knocked a lesser man out, stood up and danced toward Smoke, his hands in the air.

Pig Iron's eyes were watering, but they remained clear and focused, showing the punches hadn't addled his brain any. It was evident he'd been hit before, and was used to taking punishment. Smoke realized he needed to end the fight as soon as possible or he was going to be in trouble.

As Pig Iron swung a sharp, right jab, Smoke leaned back, using his momentum to soften the blow to his cheek, then hunched his right shoulder as Pig Iron swung a roundhouse left hook into him.

The force of the blow staggered Smoke and almost knocked him off his feet. He thought again that he couldn't afford to mess around with this man. He was much too dangerous an adversary. He had to end the fight quickly, in any way he could.

Pig Iron danced in, trying to follow up his advantage while Smoke was still off-balance, but Smoke stepped nimbly to the left and kicked out with his right foot into the side of Pig Iron's knee.

There was a loud crack as the cartilage in the knee snapped and gave way. Pig Iron yelped in pain and went down on one knee, while Smoke stepped in and swung a right upper cut to his chin. The blow lifted Pig Iron up onto both feet again, snapping his head back.

Smoke quickly stepped in close and, almost faster than the eye could follow, peppered Pig Iron's stomach with rapid-fire blow after blow.

Pig Iron doubled over, blood streaming from his smashed lips and torn ear, both hands holding his abdomen. He was completely defenseless, and looked up out of the corner of his eye with his head tilted, waiting for Smoke to finish it.

Instead, Smoke took off his bandanna and dipped it in a nearby horse trough. He handed it to Pig Iron, saying, "Better put some pressure on your mouth 'fore you bleed to death."

On the boardwalk, Curly Joe, seeing Pig Iron was beaten, put his hand on the butt of his pistol.

He froze when he felt a gun barrel pressed against his temple and heard the hammer eared back. A soft voice said in his ear, "Unless you want your brains spread all over the street, you'd better unhand that pistol."

He glanced around and saw the gambler, Louis Longmont, smiling over the sights of his Colt. "I would dearly love for you to give me a reason to fire this. I haven't had to kill a man for over a month now, and I am getting out of practice," Louis said, the hardness in his eyes belying the grin on his lips.

Curly Joe pulled his hand away from his pistol and crossed his arms over his chest, fear-sweat springing out on his forehead while a fine tremor made his hands shake.

Monte Carson walked up to Smoke, where he stood breathing hard next to Pig Iron.

"What's goin' on here, Smoke?"

"A small difference of opinion, Monte. Nothing to get excited about."

"All right," Monte called, waving his hands. "All you people, break it up. The fight's over, so go on about your business."

Curly Joe wasted no time and rushed over and grabbed Pig Iron by the shoulder, having to help him walk on his ruined knee toward their horses. After he helped him get in the saddle, he jerked his horse's head around and pointed at Smoke.

"You haven't heard the last of this, Jensen," Curly Joe snarled with mock bravado.

Smoke gave him a lazy smile. "I suspect not, mister. But you can tell Devers something for me."

"What's that?"

"The last time I saw him, I told him if I ever laid eyes on him again I was going to kill him. That still stands."

As the two gunmen galloped out of town, Smoke looked at Louis. "You think our food's ready yet, Louis? I'm still mighty hungry."

Pearlie pointed to Smoke's cheek, which was cut and leaking a fine trail of blood down his face. "Maybe you ought'a have Doc take a look at that, Smoke."

Smoke sleeved the blood off. "It'll heal, Pearlie. I've bled before, and I'll probably bleed again. Let's go eat."

11

In the hotel room where Cal was recuperating, Sally looked up as Smoke and Pearlie walked in. Her eyebrows raised, she stared at Smoke's cheek for a moment before getting up and crossing to him.

She gave him a kiss on the other cheek and gazed into his eyes. "What's that I see on your face, Smoke Jensen?"

Smoke reached up and fingered the cut, which was already scabbing over. "Nothing, dear."

She put her hands on her hips. "Have you been fighting again?"

Smoke grinned sheepishly, like a small boy caught stealing cookies. "Well, maybe a little."

Sally turned to Pearlie, who was standing nearby trying to look innocent. "Pearlie, I'm ashamed of you! You're supposed to keep Smoke out of trouble when I'm not around."

"I'm sorry, Miz Sally, but there weren't nothin' I could do 'bout it. The man was spoilin' fer a fight, an' he didn't give Smoke no chance to avoid it at all."

Cal moved as if to get out of bed, but Sally rushed over to push him back against the pillows.

"Just where do you think you're going, young man?" she asked.

He grinned at her as he cut his eyes to Smoke and Pearlie. "It's clear to me, Miss Sally, that those two can't manage to stay out of trouble without me around. I need to get out of this bed and get back to work."

"Oh no, you don't, Calvin Woods," Sally said firmly. "Dr. Spalding says you have to stay in bed at least another week, and it's going to be at least three weeks before you can sit a horse, so no arguments."

Smoke approached the bed. "Cal, I was braced by a couple of men today who said they'd been in touch with Floyd Devers. Do you remember him?"

Cal nodded. "Sure, he was the one you shot in the leg durin' that fracas with Bloody Bill Anderson a while back. I was there with you."

"Did you happen to notice if Devers was with that bunch that shot you?"

Cal wagged his head. "No, sir. He weren't there, I'm sure of that. I'd've noticed him for sure."

"How about a big, tall man with scars on his face and funny lookin' ears?" Pearlie asked.

Cal shrugged. "Nope, can't say for sure 'bout him. There were so many of 'em that I only really noticed the two I shot an' the leader—the tall, skinny galoot dressed all in black."

"Smoke, did you have any luck with the surrounding ranchers?" Sally asked.

"No. Either the gang has left the area or they're holed up somewhere where nobody can see them. Not one person we spoke to had even seen them riding by."

"That's strange."

He shrugged. "Not really, not if they want to stay out of sight. There's thousands of acres around here where a group of that size could make a camp without being seen."

"But why would they want to stay out of sight, Smoke?" Pearlie asked. "Fer all they know, they kilt Cal deader'n yesterday's news, so if'n the only person who could tell anybody they done it wasn't around no more, why hide out?"

"You're right, Pearlie, it doesn't make sense." He shrugged, puzzled by it.

"Maybe they just rode on out of the county on their way somewhere else," Pearlie offered.

Sally looked worried. "Smoke, I have a bad feeling about all this. I don't think those men have left the area."

"I agree, Sally. I think they're up to something, but I'm hanged if I know what it is."

"You think they might be after the bank in Big Rock?"

He shook his head. "If they were, they would have already hit it. There wouldn't be any reason for them to hang around cooling their heels for two weeks after shooting Cal."

"Well, I just know they're up to something no good."

"You can bet on it, dear, but I'm afraid we're just going to have to wait and see what it is. If they have gone somewhere else, we'll find out about it. Monte Carson has wired all the neighboring towns to be on the lookout and let us know if they're spotted."

"And if they are?" she asked, although she knew the answer already. She'd lived with Smoke too many years not to know what he had in mind.

"Then I'm going to ride to wherever they are and teach them a lesson about minding their manners when they're on my property," he answered, his face serious.

In Fontana, more men were arriving every day, in groups of two, three, and four so as not to attract too much attention from the surrounding towns and ranches.

There were already over forty hard men, most wanted one place or another, who had come seeking easy money. Just the mention of the word gold could make normal men do strange things, and these men were by no stretch of the imagination normal to begin with.

Things were getting so hectic with all the new residents that Bob Blanchard had to send for supplies and reopen the general store, as well as the hotel. Lazarus had also ordered a large amount of ammunition and extra weapons, including two small cannons. He figured if he was going to try to tree a town, he needed all the help he could get.

Mickey O'Donnel, a man small in stature and mean as

a snake, had arrived two days ago and was busy trying to drink up the entire supply of whiskey in Fontana all by himself. The more he drank, the meaner he got. Even the other hard cases in town moved across the room when he was in one of his dark moods.

"Hey, Lazarus," he shouted just after noon, while most of the men were in the saloon eating lunch.

"Yes, Mickey. What is it you want?" Lazarus asked, looking up from his beans and enchiladas—about the only things the Mexican cook Blanchard had hired could cook that were worth eating.

"Tell me again why it is that you're plannin' to go up against this entire town when it's just the one man who's stoppin' us from gettin' our hands on all that gold."

Lazarus used the tip of his knife to pick a piece of stringy beef from between his teeth, then looked across the room at Mickey. He noticed the shanty Irishman hadn't eaten, but had drunk his lunch, as usual.

"Well, Mickey me boy, it's like this. First of all, Jensen has quite a reputation as a gunfighter, so he won't be all that easy to kill. Second, word is he is quite popular in the town, and anyone who does manage to kill him certainly won't be allowed to hang around mining for gold on his property."

"What if several of us could manage to catch him alone someplace? Then, we could hide his body so it'd be some time 'fore anybody even knew he was dead. That ranch of his is a big place, an' we could be gettin' the gold off the more isolated parts while his hands were lookin' for him."

Lazarus stroked his goatee and mustache. The man's idea did make some sense, assuming of course any of the riffraff in this town was good enough to take Jensen, even if they outnumbered him four to one. Still, it was worth a try, and he had nothing to lose except men who were easily replaced should Jensen manage to kill them.

Lazarus stood up and addressed the room. "Men, Mickey O'Donnel has come up with an idea. While we're waiting for the rest of our supplies to get here, he thinks a team of four men should try and kill Smoke Jensen. I've got five gold twenty dollar pieces for anyone willing to give it a try. That's more'n a year's wages for most cowboys."

Mickey stepped away from the bar, a pugnacious sneer on his face. "It were my idea, so I'm goin'."

Lazarus nodded. "All right, that's one. I need three more men who're good with a gun."

Two men at a corner table stood up. They were obviously brothers, for they looked alike, both tall, with dark, curly hair and prominent noses on narrow faces. "Tom and me'll go, Mr. Cain," said Joe Blakely.

"Ah, the Blakely brothers," Lazarus said. "Anyone else?"

A very young-looking boy of about eighteen years stood up. He was dressed like the gunfighters in the dime novels—with black pants tucked into knee-high, black leather boots, a black leather vest over a white shirt with a black bow tie—and carried Colts on both hips, tied down low on his leg. "How about if one man could get the job done by himself, Cain? Would he get all the money?"

Lazarus recognized the boy. He called himself the Arizona Kid, and claimed to have bested eleven men in gunfights so far. Lazarus had seen him practicing his draw, and he was cat-quick with a handgun, but was he quick enough to beat Smoke Jensen?

"No, Arizona. This is too important to risk it that way. The plan is for four men to go."

"What if I don't like your plan, Cain? You fast enough to make me do it your way?" the Kid said, loosening the rawhide hammer thongs on his Colts and squaring off to face Lazarus from across the room.

Lazarus's lips curled in a half-smile. He'd known this would happen sooner or later—one of the miscreants he'd summoned would challenge him for leadership of the group. Might as well get this over with.

Lazarus pulled his coat open and tucked the tail in the back of his pants out of the way, letting his hand hang next to the Colt on his right hip.

As he squared to face the Arizona Kid, Blackie Jackson and King Johannson stood up, ready to back his play. "Hold on, boys," Lazarus said. "I'll handle this young pup alone."

"All right, boss," Blackie said, and he and King sat down.

"Arizona, have you been saved?" Lazarus asked, his voice low, his eyes hard and black as flint.

The Kid laughed. "Saved? You mean like in church an' all?"

"That's right. Have you given your soul to God, son?"

"No, old man. Why?"

"'Cause in the final reckoning, your soul belongs to God, but your butt belongs to me," Lazarus said as his hand flashed toward his gun.

The boy was quick, and he managed to get his pistol out of his holster and cocked before Lazarus's first shot hit him in the breastbone, shattering it and driving him back against the wall.

He leaned there, an astonished look on his face, as blood ran down the wall behind him to pool at his feet. "But . . . but . . . I'm the Arizona Kid," he mumbled, still trying to raise his pistol.

As he managed to get it waist high, Lazarus casually aimed and let the hammer down on his Colt, putting his slug directly between the Kid's eyes, blowing brains and bits of scalp and skull all over the wall.

The Kid hit the floor about the same time Lazarus returned to his meal. "Let me know if anyone else wants to try and take command of this operation," he said, as he shoveled some beans into his mouth.

When no one spoke up, he glanced at Mickey O'Donnel. "Mickey, I'm going to let you pick your fourth man. Meet with me later this afternoon and we'll go over the plan."

"What do you want us to do with Arizona, boss?" Blackie Jackson asked.

Lazarus said around an enchilada he was chewing, "Drag his carcass out back and let the coyotes take care of it."

"But it's gonna stink somethin' fierce," said Curly Joe.

"Good," Lazarus said. "Every time the men smell it, they'll be reminded of the consequences of going up against me."

12

Smoke Jensen stood next to the buckboard and tucked in the edges of the quilt covering Cal in the back. "Looks like they got you pretty well set up, Cal," Smoke said.

"Yes sir. Pearlie piled enough hay in here to feed half the horses on the Sugarloaf, and then Miz Sally fixed up all these quilts so I feel snug as a bug in a rug."

"I may need to add another couple of hosses to this rig, Smoke," Pearlie said from the driver's seat of the buckboard. "Cal's fattened up so much from all this babyin' we been doin' to him that I don't know if only two animals can handle the load."

"You think maybe we need a couple of Percheron draft horses?" Smoke asked.

"Two could probably handle it if'n we was goin' downhill all the way."

"Perhaps we should stop off at the general store and get him some new pants to wear," Smoke said, grinning.

Cal raised his head, an indignant look on his face. "Hey, fellows, I ain't gained all that much weight."

"Oh, it must be table muscle then," Pearlie said sarcastically.

Just then, Sally appeared from the doctor's office, carrying a brown bottle in her hands. "Doc Spalding sent this laudanum in case the pain gets too bad on the trip back, Cal."

Pearlie rolled his eyes and shook his head. "I swear to goodness, Miz Sally, you're gonna plumb ruin that boy by spoilin' him like that. I ain't never gonna get no work outta him in the future."

Cal winked at Smoke and called out, "Yeah, Pearlie, you're right. The doc told me not to do any heavy liftin' for at least six months."

"What?" Pearlie said, half turning in his seat, until he saw Smoke and Cal laughing at him.

"Huh! I'm gonna take pains to remind that boy just who the ramrod is on the Sugarloaf, an' he won't never forget again."

Smoke helped Sally up onto the seat next to Pearlie.

"Are you coming with us, Smoke?" she asked.

"Not just yet. I'm going to go meet with Monte and see if he's heard anything on the whereabouts of the gang that shot Cal. Then I'll be coming home."

"All right, dear. We'll see you later," Sally said.

After the buckboard was out of sight, Smoke walked along the boardwalk toward Monte Carson's office. Out of a habit that had been with him so long he no longer noticed it, his eyes flicked back and forth as he walked, analyzing and checking everything he saw for possible danger. Having been a gunfighter and sometimes wanted man for most of his adult life, Smoke had learned the hard way that life was dangerous and the only way to survive it was to be ever vigilant.

More than once his life had been saved because he'd noticed a shadow where it shouldn't have been, a furtive movement in an alleyway, or someone's eyes hastily averted when he looked at them.

On the way to the sheriff's office, his habit of watchfulness paid off. He noticed several things that weren't quite right.

Down the street, a man was standing next to a pair of horses, and he was wearing a long duster. That struck Smoke as odd because the day was mild and the temperatures were in the low eighties, much too warm for standing around in a duster doing nothing. If the man had been standing in front of the bank, Smoke would have worried about a robbery about to take place. There was a feeling about the scene of the man waiting for something to happen.

Just as he was about to tell himself he was being foolish and overly suspicious, Smoke noticed something else out of kilter.

Two other men whose faces he didn't recognize were climbing up on their horses fifty yards ahead. Both had long guns in their hands, one a short-barreled shotgun and the other a Winchester Yellow Boy, the brass-plated rifle that'd been made a few years before. The funny thing was, Smoke could see empty saddle boots on both animals, so there wasn't any need for the men to be carrying the long guns unless they expected to be using them shortly.

When Smoke came to Monte's office, he went in the door without looking back over his shoulder at the three strangers who were acting suspiciously.

"Hey, Smoke. What's up?" Monte asked from his usual position—sitting in his chair with his boots up on the desk and a coffee cup in his hand.

Smoke walked over to the stove in the corner and took a cup off a peg on the wall. He poured himself a cup of coffee from the pot that had been cooking there as long as he could remember. The thick black liquid looked to be the consistency of syrup as it flowed slowly into Smoke's cup.

"Damn, Monte. This stuff'd float a horseshoe," Smoke said.

"Remember what your old mountain man friend Puma Buck used to say about makin' good coffee? It don't take near as much water as you think it do," Monte said, raising the pitch of his voice to do a credible imitation of Smoke's old friend.

"Well I can tell you didn't make too many trips to the well for this pot," Smoke said, grimacing as he took a tentative sip.

"You come all this way just to gripe about my coffee?"

"No. I was just wondering if you'd had any answers to your wires asking about Lazarus Cain and his men."

"Some. I heard from Earp over at Dodge City. He said Floyd Devers, Walter Blackwell, Tad Younger, and Johnny Sampson all broke jail while he was out of town serving a warrant. He also said to tell you hello, and to let him know if we spotted 'em."

Smoke nodded. "Anything else?"

"Yeah, now that you mention it. Several sheriffs and marshals in surrounding towns wired back that they hadn't seen anything of Cain, but that some other hard cases had passed through their towns over the past couple of weeks."

Smoke shrugged. "What's so strange about that? There are a lot of hard men in this territory, and they often have to move around 'cause no one wants them in their counties."

"The strange thing is, they all seemed to be headed in this direction. The sheriffs to the south said the men were headed north, and the ones to the north said the gunslicks were headed south."

Smoke looked at Monte over the rim of his cup. "I see what you mean. You think it's connected somehow with Lazarus Cain?"

Monte wagged his head. "I don't know what to think, but I don't much like the idea that a bunch of men on the edge of the law are on their way in our direction. This is a good town, an' I don't want it to change. Hell, I ain't even had to draw my gun in nigh on two weeks."

Smoke edged over to glance out of the window on the front wall of the office, standing to the side so he couldn't be seen from outside.

"Well, dust the cobwebs off your Colt, Monte. I have a feeling you're gonna get to use it before long."

"What do you mean?" Monte asked as his feet hit the floor and he came out of his chair in a quick, clean movement, his hand already on the butt of his pistol.

"Stand off to one side and peek out the window."

As Monte looked, Smoke pointed out the three men

he'd noticed on his way into the office. "At first I just thought I was being overly suspicious, but they still haven't moved or changed position. And see how every few minutes they glance over here? I think they're waiting to ambush someone, either you or me, when we come out of the door."

"I know the two men on the horses," Monte said. "I remember them from my days when I used to hire out my gun."

"Who are they?"

"Tom and Joe Blakely. Tom ain't so bad, but Joe is mean as a snake, an' twice as slippery. Tom's pretty good in a fight, but Joe plumb enjoys killin', an' he's done plenty of it to my certain knowledge."

"You know the other galoot, the short man over there with the duster on?"

"No, I don't think I've ever seen that one before."

"Any reason the Blakelys would be after you?"

"No, not that I know of. We parted on good terms last time I worked with 'em."

Smoke glanced at Monte out of the corner of his eye. His friend had been a noted gunman years ago, though he'd never been wanted by the law as far as Smoke knew.

"I won't ask about that," Smoke said, grinning.

Monte gave a half-smile. "That's a story for some winter sittin' around your fireplace up on the Sugarloaf."

"How do you want to handle this?" Monte asked, stepping over to the gunrack on the wall and pulling down a double-barreled 10-gauge express gun. He broke open the barrel and shoved two shells in and snapped it shut, adding a handful of shells to his vest pockets.

"Give me about five minutes to get in position, then come out the front door," Smoke said. "While their attention is on you, I'll brace 'em from behind."

It was a long five minutes, and by the time the hand on the wall clock had ticked five times Monte was sweating. As brave as Monte was, and as experienced at gunplay, he knew that luck played a big part in who lived and who died when lead started flying. It'd been a lot of years since he'd made his living holding a pistol. He hoped when push came to shove, as he knew it would, he wouldn't be so rusty that he got himself or his friend Smoke killed.

Finally, it was time. Monte hitched up his pants, eared back the hammers on the shotgun, and ambled out the door, looking a lot more calm than he was.

He stepped out on the boardwalk and stretched and yawned, looking around as if he had nothing more on his mind than a stroll through town.

He glanced across the street and acted as if he'd just noticed Tom and Joe Blakely sitting on their horses.

He walked casually toward them, the shotgun over his shoulder. "Hey boys, long time no see," Monte called, a fake grin on his face.

Tom looked at Joe and spoke in a low tone. "Did you know Monte Carson was involved in this?"

"Naw, but it don't make no difference, does it?"

Tom glanced at Monte ambling toward them as if he hadn't a care in the world. "Yeah, it does. Monte was always good to us, an' he never did us no hurt."

"Well, if he keeps his nose outta it he'll be all right. We're here to put lead in Smoke Jensen, not Monte."

"Hey, Monte," Tom called, his voice a little shaky with nerves. "What're you doin' here?"

Monte pointed to his left chest, where he had a star pinned to his vest. "I'm the sheriff of Big Rock, boys," he said, stopping about twenty feet from the two men.

"That's a hoot," Joe Blakely said with a smirk. "The famous Monte Carson a sheriff."

Monte smiled a lazy, half-smile. "Yeah, I can see where you'd think that. But boys, I want you to know I take my job very seriously. I don't allow nobody, even old friends, any slack when it comes to this town."

Tom shifted nervously in his saddle, while Joe glared at Monte through narrowed eyes. "Monte, this ain't no concern of your'n. Why don't you just go on back in that nice, safe office and tell Jensen he's got to come out sometime, an' we're waitin' here 'til he does."

Monte nodded, his face set, his eyes serious. "Oh, you men waitin' on Smoke Jensen?"

"That's right. We got some business with him," Joe replied, holding up the rifle in his hand.

"Well, here I am," Smoke called from fifteen feet behind the men. He was standing partially hidden in shadows in the alley behind the two men, just off the street.

As the Blakelys whirled around—Tom trying to bring his shotgun up and Joe thumbing back the hammer on his Winchester as he pointed it—Smoke made a move.

Both hands suddenly appeared in front of him filled with iron. His Colt .44s fired almost simultaneously, exploding with a deafening roar and belching flame and smoke from the barrels.

A slug from his right-hand gun took Tom Blakely in the neck, punching a hole through his Adam's apple, ripping out his windpipe. He dropped his shotgun and grabbed for his neck, as if he could somehow hold in the blood and air that was pumping out in a scarlet, frothy stream.

The slug from Smoke's left gun hit Joe high in the chest, spinning him halfway around in his saddle, his horse jumping and crow-hopping at the sudden noise. As the animal bucked, Joe, a bloody grin on his face exposing teeth stained red, raised the rifle again.

At the same time, the short man in the duster ran a few steps out into the street, drawing his pistol.

As Smoke fired both his Colts again, two holes appeared in Joe's head, one under each eye, shattering his cheekbones and blowing the back of his head off.

He and his brother hit the dirt at about the same time, both dead as stones.

Mickey O'Donnel got off two quick shots, one passing over Smoke's head, the other burning a grove in his right thigh.

Monte dove onto his stomach, his shotgun out in front of him. He fired both barrels, hoping to distract Mickey from shooting at Smoke.

One barrel missed, but the other load of .00-buckshot

hit Mickey just above his right knee, tearing his leg completely off and spinning him around to fall in a heap, screaming in pain.

Smoke jerked his bandanna off and held it against his leg as he hobbled over toward the fallen men. He knew at a glance Tom and Joe were done for, so he continued over to Mickey.

He and Monte arrived at the same time. Monte knelt and put his hands on Mickey's shoulders, trying to hold him still as he writhed on the ground, moaning and crying in pain.

"Dear Lord, save me! Help me, Jesus!" the man cried, using the holy names for probably the first time in his adult life.

Blood was spurting from his leg in a thick, crimson stream as if from a pump, and Smoke knew he had only moments to live.

"Who sent you?" he hollered, trying to get the man's attention.

After a couple of seconds, the man quieted, futilely holding his leg as if he could hold in the blood that was leaving his body and taking his life with it.

His eyes cleared momentarily, and he looked up at Smoke. "Count your days, Jensen. Cain is coming. . . ."

Then his eyes clouded and there was no life behind them as the man went limp and the blood coming from his leg slowed to a trickle, stopping completely as he died.

Another man, hidden in an alley across the street, quietly holstered his pistol. *Damn,* he thought, *I never even saw Jensen draw his pistols 'fore he was blowin' Tom an' Joe to hell an' gone.*

He watched as Smoke and Monte stood over Mickey while he bled to death. *It's too late fer them,* he thought. *I'd do better to ride on back to Fontana and tell Cain what happened.*

He slipped back through the alley to where he had his horse tied up and jumped into the saddle, spurring the animal toward Fontana as fast as he could ride.

When he got there, he wasted no time in rushing into the saloon.

Cain was at his usual table, and he looked up as the man burst through the batwings.

"Ah, Jimmy," he said, calling to the man. "How did it go in Big Rock?"

Jimmy, sweating profusely from both his ride and from having to face Cain and tell him they failed, walked to his table.

"You ain't gonna believe this, Mr. Cain, but Jensen got Mickey an' Tom and Joe. They's all deader'n stones."

"What? How did that happen?" Cain asked, his face turning beet red.

"It was somethin' to see. There Tom an' Joe was, they rifles and shotguns in they hands, pointin' 'em at Jensen, when suddenly his hands were full of six-guns an' he blasted 'em outta they saddles 'fore they could pull the triggers."

"You're tellin' me they had the drop on Jensen an' he was still able to draw an' fire before they could shoot?"

"Yes sir! That Jensen's quicker'n a rattlesnake, an' twice as mean."

"What about Mickey?"

"He was able to get off a couple'a shots—one of 'em hit Jensen in the leg—'fore the sheriff blowed his leg clean off with a shotgun. He bled to death right there in the street with Jensen and the sheriff watchin' him die."

Cain shook his head. "And you, what did you do to help?"

Jimmy's face flushed scarlet. "There weren't nothin' I could do, boss. It all happened so fast, it was over 'fore I could draw an' fire."

In a lightning motion, Cain reached out and slapped Jimmy across the face, almost knocking the man off his feet.

"Get your gear and clear out of here, Jimmy. I don't allow no cowards to ride with me!"

"But Mr. Cain . . ."

Cain let his hand fall onto the butt of his pistol. "One more word, an' I'll shoot you down right where you stand."

13

George Hampton glanced over at Johnny North riding next to him as they approached the outskirts of Fontana. "I don't know as how this is such a great idea, Johnny," he said, sleeving fear-sweat off his forehead.

Johnny returned his stare, "Don't worry about it, George. We're just a couple'a cowboys ridin' through town. They don't need to know why we're here."

"What if your idea is right, and this Lazarus Cain Smoke was askin' 'bout and his gang are holed up here?"

Johnny shrugged. "Then we'll have a sociable drink an' be on our way. They won't know we're gonna tell Smoke where they're hidin'."

The first thing both men noted as they entered the city limits was the amount of horse droppings in the street and their apparent freshness. This didn't look like the virtual ghost town it had become after the Tilden Franklin affair of a few years back.

"Uh oh, Johnny, looky there," George said as they rode past the rundown livery stable barn. It was full of horses, with not a single stall unoccupied. "Looks like there's quite a few men here."

Johnny's eyes narrowed as he looked around the town, seeing a number of men lounging on the boardwalks or pitching horseshoes in the alleyways. "Smoke said he thought Lazarus was ridin' with about fifteen or twenty men. Seems to me to be more like forty or fifty hanging around here from the number of hosses I can count."

At the saloon there wasn't room to tie up their horses, the double hitching rail in front already being full, so they walked down a few yards and tied up in front of the general store.

"Look in there," George said. "Them shelves is plumb full'a goods an' things."

"Don't exactly appear as if these gents're passin' through, does it?" Johnny remarked. "Matter of fact, it looks like they is plannin' on settin' up home here."

Johnny led the way through the batwings of the saloon, trying not to show any surprise at the number of men sitting around at the tables drinking and playing cards. About the only thing the place lacked was a piano player in the corner to bang away on the yellowed, stained keys.

When Johnny got to the bar, he ordered beer for himself and Hampton.

As the bartender placed foaming glasses in front of them he stared at Johnny for a moment, a puzzled expression on his face.

"You look a mite familiar, friend," Bob Blanchard said. "Do I know you?"

Johnny snorted and took a deep swig of his beer. "Partner, I don't know who in the hell you are, or who you know," Johnny said in a harsh voice. Then he leaned forward and added, "And you know what else, mister? I don't really give a damn, either."

Blanchard's face paled at the implied threat, and he took a step back, his hands held out in front of him. In the West, it was sometimes a fatal mistake to show too much interest in who a man might be or where he hailed from, and it was certainly considered impolite to ask unless the information was volunteered.

"I'm sorry, mister. Didn't mean no disrespect," Blanchard stammered, sweat forming on his brow.

"None taken," Johnny muttered, and he turned to lean his back against the bar and survey the other patrons.

He immediately saw the man Cal said had shot him. He was sitting at a corner table that was full of hard-looking men who were drinking whiskey like there was no tomorrow.

The tall, skinny, mean-looking man glanced up and his eyes met Johnny's for a second before Johnny looked away.

Out of the corner of his eye he noticed the man Smoke said was named Cain get to his feet and amble toward him at the bar.

Cain took a position next to Johnny and held out his hand to Blanchard, who quickly put a glass of whiskey in it.

"Howdy, stranger," Cain said, leaning on the bar as he stared at Johnny.

Johnny gave him a look, his face blank. "Howdy."

"What brings you and your friend to Fontana?" Cain asked casually, as if the answer didn't really matter all that much to him.

Johnny turned until he was facing Cain. "What's it to you, mister?"

Cain shrugged. "Well, I'm kind'a the head man around here, an' we don't particularly cotton to strangers hangin' around."

Johnny gave him a cold half-smile. "We're not exactly hangin' around. My friend and I are on our way north, and stopped off to water our mounts an' wash the trail dust outta our mouths. Is there any law agin that in these parts?"

Cain wagged his head. "Not if that's all you're plan-nin' on doin'."

"Good," Johnny said and turned back to the bar, ig-noring Cain.

"I didn't catch your name, mister," Cain said, his voice harder, as if he wasn't used to being ignored.

Johnny emptied his glass and held it out to the bar-tender for a refill. "That's 'cause I didn't throw it," he replied, forcing boredom into his tone.

Cain made a slight motion with his head and a man with a heavy growth of whiskers stepped from a nearby table and squared off facing Johnny, his hands hanging next to his pistols.

"Mr. Cain asked you what your name is, mister. You'd better be tellin' him or I'm gonna have to make you."

Johnny looked back over his shoulder at the gunny. "First of all, I don't take orders from nobody, not even your Mr. Cain," Johnny growled as he turned to face the man. "And second, if you even twitch toward that hogleg on your hip, you'll be dead before you clear leather."

"You talk awful big, stranger," the man answered.

"If you think it's only talk, jerk that smokewagon and go to work, sonny boy," Johnny said in a hoarse whisper, unhooking the leather hammerthong on his Colt.

The man's face turned red, and he grabbed for his gun.

In a flash, Johnny's hand appeared before him filled with iron, the pistol making a harsh click as he eared back the hammer, the barrel inches from the astonished gunman's face.

"Now, this can go one of two ways," Johnny snarled. "You can unhand that gun and go sit back down to your card game, or I can scatter what little brains you have all over the saloon floor." He gave a tiny shrug with his shoulders. "Your call, sonny boy."

Cain quickly stepped between the two men, smiling, his hands out as if to make peace.

"Whoa, mister. I can see you're pretty handy with that sixkiller. My name's Lazarus Cain, an' I'm askin' you nicely what yours is."

Johnny holstered his Colt. "Johnny North."

Cain frowned. "Johnny North? I thought you were dead."

Johnny smirked. "Not likely."

Cain turned to the crowd in the saloon who were watching the action intently. "Men," he said in a loud voice. "This here is Johnny North, one of the most famous gunfighters of a few years back."

He put his hand out and Johnny took it. "Pleased to meet you, Johnny. I've heard a great deal about you, though not in recent times," Cain said in a friendly tone.

Johnny picked up his beer and took a deep swallow. That had been a close call, but he was glad to see he hadn't lost any of his quickness. It had been some time since he'd drawn on anyone.

"Times have been slow. I worked the Lincoln County war a few months back, but there hasn't been much call for my services since then," he said, referring to when he and Smoke had intervened with John Chisum in New Mexico.

Cain nodded. "I heard about that little fracas. Unfortunately, I was busy elsewhere an' didn't get to see it."

Johnny gave a half-smile. "It was interestin' for a while, then it just got boring. Chisum didn't have the stomach to really clear out the opposition, and he made peace a little too soon for my taste."

Cain laughed. "Well, Chisum is a businessman, and they often have goals that are different from men like us."

Johnny didn't answer, but continued to stare at Cain, waiting for him to get to the point.

Cain pursed his lips, as if considering what to say next. After a moment, he said, "I've got a little operation goin' on here that you might be interested in, Johnny."

"Yeah? What's that?" Johnny asked.

"Before I say any more, why don't you introduce me to your companion?"

"This here is George Hampton, from down Texas way," Johnny said.

George nodded at Cain, then turned back to his beer as if ignoring their conversation.

"Is he . . . in the business?" Cain asked.

Johnny smirked. "In a small way, but it's just a sideline for him. He's got a small spread down near Del Rio, an' he's just makin' some spare cash to buy a herd. His got wiped out by tick fever from some stock he . . . appropriated across the border."

Cain laughed. "Appropriated stock will sometimes do that, especially Mexican steers."

Hampton nodded without looking up. "Yeah, an' there ain't no one to go to for a refund, neither."

Cain laughed again.

"Well, if you boys are lookin' for work I may be able to oblige you. Like I say, I've got a deal workin' here that may pay off handsomely."

Johnny shook his head. "Maybe in a couple of weeks. We're on our way over to Pueblo to see a man about something else. If you're still around here when we finish up with that job, we'll stop by on our way back south."

A suspicious look crossed Cain's face. "And just who are you goin' to see in Pueblo?"

"A man name of Wells, Joey Wells," Johnny answered. "He's an old friend of George's, an' he asked us to help him with a little problem he's having with some U.S. Marshals up that way."

"Joey Wells is in Pueblo?" Cain asked.

"Yeah."

"I heard he killed more'n a hundred men durin' the big war."

"More like two hundred, I reckon," George said.

"I rode for a while with Bill Quantrill's raiders, an' we would've given a lot to have him with us," Cain said.

Johnny smiled. "Joey had retired across the border, 'til a bunch of *bandidos* shot his wife an' son. That's what brought him up here, to make 'em pay for that."

Cain nodded. "I wouldn't want Wells on my backtrail."

"Neither would I," Johnny said. "That's why I don't aim to disappoint him after sayin' I'd help out."

"I can see your point," Cain said. "Well, tell Joey that there's some work waitin' for him here if he's so inclined. Meanwhile, enjoy your journey and stop back by on your way south. We may still have need of your services."

"Thanks, we'll do that," Johnny said, flipping a gold coin on the bar for their drinks. Cain reached over and picked up the coin and handed it back to Johnny. "Your money's no good here, Johnny. The drinks are on me."

"Thanks," Johnny said.

Cain grinned. "No problem. It's not every day I get to meet a legend like Johnny North."

14

After Johnny and George left the saloon, Cain held his glass out for a refill.

"Bob," he said, as he took a sip of the alcohol, "you don't see many like that anymore. The old gunfighters had class, something sorely lackin' in these new young punks that seem so prevalent nowadays."

"Yes sir," Bob said, wiping down the bar with a rag that looked as if it'd seen better days. "Only—"

Catching the hesitation in his voice, Cain looked up at him. "Only what, Bob?"

"It's just that I seem to remember somethin' 'bout Johnny North, somethin' 'bout him hangin' up his guns a while back."

Cain's eyes narrowed. "Oh? Well if that were true, why wouldn't he've just said so?"

"I don't know, Mr. Cain. Maybe he found he didn't much care for retirement an' went back to gunnin' fer a livin'."

"Yeah, maybe . . . only, if North lied about one thing, maybe he lied about other things, too. If he comes back, we'll have to keep a special eye on Mr. Johnny North."

Smoke was on his front porch having a cup of coffee and a cigarette when Johnny North and George Hampton rode up.

"Light and set, boys," Smoke said, giving the old mountain man greeting to his friends.

While they dismounted, Smoke stuck his head in the cabin door and asked Sally if she'd make some more coffee for their company.

Within ten minutes, they were all sitting on the porch, coffee in one hand and some of Sally's pastries in the other.

"Smoke," Johnny said, "we rode out to Fontana and found that Lazarus Cain you been lookin' for camped out there with all his men."

"What made you think to look in Fontana?" Smoke asked. "I thought it wasn't much more than a ghost town."

"It were Johnny's idea, Mr. Jensen," George said around a mouthful of *pan dulce*.

"Yeah. I got to thinkin' after your visit when you tole me Cain'd disappeared without nobody havin' laid eyes on him," Johnny said. "There was only one place I knowed where that many men could hunker down an' not be noticed."

Smoke nodded. "It was a good thought, Johnny. No one would see them there because no one around here ever goes to Fontana anymore."

"Did you talk to him?" asked Sally, who was standing behind Smoke's chair with her hands on his shoulders.

"Tell 'em, Johnny," George said, reaching for another piece of Mexican sweet bread. "Tell 'em how you walked right into that den of rattlesnakes and chatted 'em up as pretty as you please."

"Well, I noticed on the way into town that there were quite a few more men than Smoke had thought. First off, there were at least fifty to sixty hosses on the street and in the livery, an' I could count more'n twenty men sittin' around the boardwalks an' gabbin'."

Smoke frowned. "You mean to tell me Cain has over fifty men with him in Fontana?"

Both George and Johnny nodded.

"At least that many," Johnny continued. "Anyway, we went into the saloon, that bein' the best place I know to pick up any gossip or to see what's happenin' in a town."

"You were very brave to do that, Johnny," Sally said.

"Dumb is more like it," George said, his eyes wide. "I never been more scared in my entire life."

"It wasn't all that bad, Miss Sally," Johnny said. "The saloon was filled to the brim with hard-lookin' men. Smoke, you know the kind I'm talkin' 'bout."

Smoke gave a half-grin. "Yeah, Johnny. Men who look like us. Men whose eyes tell you they're on the prod, looking for trouble, and not afraid of it when it comes."

Johnny nodded. "Right. Well, as I'm havin' my drink I notice this tall, skinny dude over in the corner who looks like the man you described as the one shot Cal. Sure enough, after a minute or two, he saunters over an' starts askin' me questions—"

"You should'a seen it, Mr. Smoke," George interrupted. "Johnny changed, right 'fore my eyes, into another man. He got this look on his face . . . like he was meaner'n a snake with a sore tail."

Johnny cut his eyes toward Sally. "That's my gunfighter face, Miss Sally."

Sally smiled. "Yes, I know the one. Every now and then, when something happens, like to Cal, I see Smoke change the same way. All the softness and gentleness leaves, and a shell comes down that's hard as the granite in those mountain peaks."

"Yes, ma'am," Johnny said. "Anyhow, one thing leads to another an' he offers me a job, a gunhand type of job. Says he's got somethin' in the works that's gonna make 'em all rich, only he needs all the guns he can find."

"He say what it was?" Smoke asked.

"No, but I made up some story 'bout goin' over to Pueblo to see Joey Wells, just to get us outta there, an' he 'bout wet his pants. He said he'd heard of Wells, an' shore wished he'd come to ride with his gang. I tole him it'd be a couple of weeks or more 'fore we could get back, an' he acted like they'd probably still be here then."

Smoke got quiet as he thought, refilling his coffee cup and building himself another cigarette. As he smoked, he went over the possibilities in his mind.

"What do you think he has in mind, Johnny? Did he give you any idea at all?" Smoke asked, tilting his head as smoke trailed from his nostrils.

"Nope, none a'tall."

"Well, it can't be a bank robbery. There isn't a bank in the territory that would warrant using fifty men, or that would make more than a few rich."

"Heck, Smoke, if'n he robbed the entire town of Big Rock of everything in it, it wouldn't be worth enough for that many men," George said.

"Likewise," Sally said, a thoughtful look on her face, "it can't be cattle or land. And there's no big army around here with a large payroll to rob."

Smoke shook his head. "We need to get someone on the inside to see what Cain has in mind. Did he seem to trust you, Johnny?"

"Yeah. He thinks I'm still on the owlhoot trail, sellin' my gun to the highest bidder."

"Wait a minute, Johnny," George said, a frightened look on his face. "Yore forgittin' 'bout Bob Blanchard."

"Who?" Smoke asked.

"Yeah, you're right, George," Johnny said. Then to Smoke, "Bob Blanchard is the bartender over at Fontana, an' seemed right friendly with Cain an' his men."

"Who is he?"

"He's a man who was on the fringes of the Tilden Franklin thing a few year ago. He wasn't directly involved, but when you shot up Fontana an' ran off or kilt all the gunnies, he sort'a stayed around. Word is he's lived almost like a hermit up there ever since."

"So?"

"Well, if'n he was in the know 'bout what happened then, George thinks sooner or later he's gonna remember that you an' I sort'a became friends, an' that I settled down up here an' hung up my guns. If he does, then Cain'll know I ain't no friend of his."

"George is right, Smoke," Sally said. "It's much too dangerous to ask Johnny to go back to Fontana. If those men even suspected he wasn't what he claimed, they'd kill him without a second thought."

"You're right, Sally. It is too dangerous to even think about sending Johnny back there. We've got to find someone else that they won't suspect."

"Trouble is, Smoke, too many of the folks around here were mixed up in that Franklin fracas," Johnny said. "Blanchard'd be sure to recognize most of 'em."

"Yes. We need someone from out of town, and they need to be handy with a gun to fit in with that group."

"How 'bout Joey Wells, Smoke?" George asked. "You think he'd do it if'n you asked him to?"

Smoke nodded slowly, thoughtfully. "That's not a bad idea, George, not a bad idea at all."

"Smoke, you can't ask Joey to do that," said Sally. "He's settled down now, and I got a wire not too long ago from Betty saying they'd had another baby."

Smoke turned in his chair to look up at her. "I know it's risky, Sally. But think of the damage fifty hard men under the leadership of a crazy man can do to this county. Think of how many innocent people may get killed if we don't find out what they're up to."

"Why not just call in the army?" she asked. "Monte says he's a wanted man, and probably most of those with him are, too. The army could just come in and arrest them all."

Johnny North shook his head. "It won't work, Miss Sally. Cain is an old rebel raider. He's gonna have pickets posted all around that town who'll warn him if any threat is comin'. The army'd never even get close to him."

"Johnny's right, Sally. It's going to take just one man, the right man, to do the job."

"Poor Betty," Sally said, a wistful look in her eyes. "Just when she thinks her man is settling down for good, something like this has to happen."

"Then you think he'll come?" Smoke asked her.

She gave him a look, her eyes soft. "Yes, Smoke, because he's just like you. You two are cut from the same bolt of cloth. If a friend needs you, no matter how dangerous it is, you're going to go. Same with Joey. If you ask, he'll come."

Smoke nodded. "I'll wire him in the morning. See if he'll come for a visit so I can explain what's happening and see what he thinks."

"You'd better mention for him to steer clear of Fontana on his way down here," Johnny said. "It wouldn't do for Cain to talk to him 'fore you get a chance to explain things."

"Right. I'll ask him to come the back way and not to let anyone see him."

"That ought'a be easy for him, since the entire Union Army looked for him for over two years an' couldn't find him," Johnny said, with a grin.

15

A week later, Cal was giving Smoke and everyone else around him fits. The young man was tired of being confined to bed and wanted to get out and about.

Cal looked up from trying to pull his boots on to see Sally Jensen standing in the doorway to the bunkhouse, hands on hips, a frown on her pretty face.

"Uh oh," he muttered.

"Uh oh is right, young man!" Sally said through gritted teeth. "How many times do I and Dr. Spalding have to tell you to stay in bed? If that lung wound gets infected, you'll die. Do you want that?"

Cal pulled his foot out of his boot and swung his legs back up under the covers on the bed. "No ma'am," he said in a low, dispirited voice. "It's just that I'm 'bout to go crazy if'n I don't get outta this room. The walls're closing in on me an' I feel all cramped up, kind'a like I cain't hardly breathe."

Sally's voice softened as she approached the bed. "I know how hard it is for you, Cal, but it's for your own good."

Suddenly, she snapped her fingers. "I know! I'll fix up a chair with a footrest on the porch of our cabin. That way you can get some fresh air and look out over the Sugarloaf and watch Pearlie and the other hands working cattle."

Cal's face brightened. "That'd be great, Miz Sally. Not as good as gettin' back in the saddle, but almost."

Sally smiled and walked back to the cabin she shared with Smoke. As she was piling some sheets and blankets on a chair on the porch, getting it ready for Cal, Smoke rode up to the front of the cabin.

He dismounted and tied Joker's reins to the hitching rail. When he got to the porch, he wrapped his big arms around Sally and gave her a gentle kiss.

"Um-m-m," she said in a low voice. "What was that for?"

He shrugged and smiled. "Nothing. Just a hello kiss."

She reached up and pulled his face back down and kissed him again. "Hello," she said.

He glanced at the chair she was fussing over. "What's that for?"

"So Cal can sit out here and get some fresh air. He says he's going crazy staying in bed for so long."

Smoke nodded. "I don't blame him. That's one of the hardest things about being wounded, the recovery time."

"What did you find out in Big Rock? Any news of the gang of bandits?"

"No. Monte says no one's come into Big Rock from Fontana way since Johnny told us they were holed up there."

"Did he contact the U.S. Marshals or the army?"

"Yes. They said they'd get here eventually, 'cause Cain and some of the men riding with him are wanted, but the marshals are way up in the northern part of the territory and won't be available for some time."

"What about the army?"

He shook his head. "The commanding officer of the nearest fort wired back they could only intervene if the governor requested it due to the gang causing massive civil disturbance, which they're not."

"So, what you're telling me is that we're on our own to deal with them."

"That's about the size of it."

"You look pleased," she said, staring into his eyes. "You

really didn't want the marshals or the army to come here, did you?"

"Nope. This is our problem, and it was our friend they shot down in cold blood on our ranch. I'd just as soon take care of the snakes myself."

"But Smoke, there are more than fifty men in that gang."

He nodded. "I know. I didn't say I was going to do it all by myself. There are plenty of men around here who will be glad to help rid the county of that pond scum over in Fontana."

"Speaking of help, when do you expect Joey Wells?"

"I don't know. I haven't had an answer to my wire, but it's only been a few days."

"Do you think he'll come?"

"It all depends on how civilized his wife has made him. Sometimes, settling down raising a family changes a man, takes all the spirit out of him. He may not even consider picking up his guns again."

She laid her hand on his cheek, a wistful expression on her face. "It didn't change you, Smoke."

"Aren't you glad?" he asked with a grin. "You're not the kind of lady who wants a lapdog for a husband."

"You're right," she said with a sigh. "Life with you is many things, but boring is definitely not one of them."

She finished fixing the chair, adjusting the ottoman so Cal could stretch out in a semi-reclining position.

"Smoke, would you go get Cal and help him over here? I'll fix a fresh pot of coffee while you do that."

Smoke walked over to the bunkhouse and through the door.

"Hey, Smoke," Cal said, his face lighting up to have company.

"Get your boots on, boy. We're taking you for a trip over to the cabin."

After Cal struggled into his boots, refusing to let Smoke do it for him, he got shakily to his feet.

Smoke stood next to him. "Here, Cal, put your arm around my shoulders."

"I can do it on my own," Cal said.

Smoke looked at him. "Listen, Cal, I know you can, but Sally told me to help you over to the cabin. Do you want to go out there and tell her you don't need any help?"

"Uh . . . not really."

"Neither do I, so make it easy on both of us and just kind'a throw your arm around me so's she'll think we're both doing what she says."

With some effort they finally made it across the yard and onto the porch. Cal realized he really needed Smoke's help, the bedrest and wound having made him weaker than he thought.

He eased into the chair, sweat on his forehead from the effort to walk, and pulled the blankets up to his waist.

"How's that, Cal?" Sally asked.

"Great. I got me a good view of the whole Sugarloaf from here."

"Would you like some coffee? I made a fresh pot."

"Sure."

While she was gone, Smoke built himself a cigarette.

"Could I have one of those?" Cal asked.

Smoke frowned, but pitched the cloth packet of Bull Durham to Cal, along with his papers.

After they both had their cigarettes lighted, Sally appeared on the porch with two cups of steaming, aromatic coffee.

"Just what do you think you're doing, Cal?" she asked, looking at the cigarette in his hand.

"Uh—"

"You know you shouldn't be smoking with that lung wound."

"Sally," Smoke said gently, "quit babying him. If he's old enough to get shot trying to defend our ranch, he's old enough to decide if he wants a smoke."

"But it's not good for him."

"Life out here is dangerous, dear. In the greater

scheme of things, smoking is low risk compared to most of what we do."

She shook her head and whirled around to disappear back in the cabin.

As they smoked and drank their coffee, both men looked out over the rolling hills and green pastures of the Sugarloaf, enjoying the view and the day.

16

The next morning Cal was in his chair on Smoke's front porch as soon as breakfast was over.

Pearlie, on his way to do the day's chores, stopped by to chat.

"Well, how do it feel to be the king of the ranch, lazybones?" Pearlie asked in his soft drawl.

"Actually, not so good," Cal answered, his face serious. "I just know that without me out there to make sure things get done right, I'm gonna have to do 'em all over again once I'm back on my feet."

"Oh, is that so? By the looks of things, by the time you're back on your feet it'll be smack in the middle of winter, an' there won't be all that much left to do."

Cal started to answer. When, out of the corner of his eye, he spotted something on the horizon.

"Uh oh," he muttered. "Smoke, you better get out here. Looks like company comin'," he hollered.

When Smoke and Sally walked out onto the porch, Cal pointed off in the distance. A lone figure could be seen riding toward the cabin, taking his time, keeping his horse in a ground-covering lope.

"Who do you think that is?" Cal asked.

Smoke's lips curled in a smile. "Unless I miss my guess, that's Joey Wells."

"Mr. Wells?" Cal asked, his voice rising in excitement.

Since Cal's first meeting with the man he'd read about in hundreds of dime novels, Joey had been a hero to him.

"Yeah. I guess he decided to just show up instead of wiring me back."

Sally turned and started back into the cabin. "I guess I'd better cook up another batch of eggs and some bacon. He's going to be mighty hungry after riding all the way here from Pueblo."

As the figure slowly got larger, Smoke thought back to the day Joey arrived at Longmont's Saloon, looking for him. . . .

The batwings were thrown wide and a man entered slowly, stepping to the side when he got inside so that his back was to a wall. He stood there, letting his eyes adjust to the darkened interior of the saloon. Louis recognized the actions of an experienced pistoleer, saw how the man's eyes scanned the room, flicking back and forth before he proceeded to the bar. The cowboy was short, about five feet nine inches, Louis figured, and was covered with a fine coat of trail dust. He had a nasty looking scar on his right cheek, running from the corner of his eye to disappear in the edge of his handlebar mustache. The scar had contracted as it healed, shortening and drawing his lip up in a perpetual sneer. His small gray eyes were as cold and deadly as a snake's, and he wore a brace of Colt .44s on his hips, tied down low, and carried a Colt Navy .36 in a shoulder holster. Louis, an experienced gunfighter himself, speculated he had never seen a more dangerous hombre in all his years. *He looks as tough as a just-woke grizzly,* he thought.

As hair on the back of his neck prickled and stirred, Louis shifted slightly in his seat, straightening his right leg and reaching down to loosen the rawhide thong on his Colt, just in case.

The stranger flipped a gold Double-Eagle on the bar, took possession of a bottle of whiskey, and spoke a few words in a low tone to the bartender. After a moment, the barman inclined his head toward Louis, then busied himself wiping the counter with a rag, casting worried glances at Louis out of the corner of his eye.

The newcomer turned, leaning his back against the bar, and stared at Louis. His eyes flicked up and down, noting the way Louis had shifted his position and how his right hand was resting on his thigh near the handle of his Colt. His expression softened and his lips moved slightly, turning up in what might have been a smile in any other face. He evidently recognized Louis as a man of his own kind, a brother predator in a world of prey.

Louis watched the gunman's eyes, thinking, *This man has stared death in the face on many occasions, and has never known fear.* With a slow deliberate motion, his gaze never straying, Louis picked up his china coffee cup with his left hand and drained it to moisten his suddenly dry mouth, wondering just what the stranger had in mind, and whether he had finally met the man who was going to beat him to the draw and put him in the ground.

The pistoleer grabbed his whiskey with his left hand and began to saunter toward Louis, his right hand hanging at his side. As he passed one of the poker tables, a puncher threw his playing cards down and jumped up from the table with a snort of anger. "Goddamned cards just won't fall for me today," he said, as he turned abruptly toward the bar, colliding with the stranger.

The cowboy, too much into his whiskey to recognize his danger, peered at the newcomer through bleary, red-rimmed eyes, spoiling for a fight. "Why don't you watch where yer goin', shorty?" he growled.

The gunman's expression never changed, though Louis thought he detected a kind of weary acceptance in his eyes, as if he had been there many times before. In a voice smooth with soft consonants of the South in it, he replied, "I believe ya' need a lesson in manners, sir."

The drunken cowboy sneered, "And you think yore man enough to give me that lesson, asshole?"

In less time than it took Louis to blink, the pistoleer's Colt was drawn and cocked, and the barrel was pressed under the puncher's chin, pushing his head back. "Unless ya' want yore brains decoratin' the ceiling I'd suggest ya' apologize to the people here fer yore poor upbringin', and fer yore Mamma not never teachin' ya' any better than to jaw at yore betters."

The room became deathly quiet. One of the other men at the table moved slightly and the stranger said without looking at him, "Friend, 'less ya' want that arm blown plumb off, I'd haul in yore horns 'til I'm through with this'n."

Fear-sweat poured off the cowboy's face and his eyes rolled, trying to see the gun stuck in his throat. "I'm . . . I'm right sorry, sir. It was my fault, and I . . . I apologize fer my remarks."

The gunman stepped back, holstered his Colt, and glanced at a wet spot on the front of the drunk's trousers. "Apology accepted, sir." His eyes cut to the man at the table who had frozen in position, afraid to move a muscle. "Ya' made a wise choice not ta' buy chips in this game, friend. It's a hard life ta' go through with only one hand." Without another word, he ambled over to stand next to Louis's table, his back to the wall where he could observe the room as he talked.

"Ya' be Mr. Longmont?"

Louis nodded, eyebrows raised. "Yes sir, I am. And to whom do I have the pleasure of speaking?"

"I be Joseph Wells, 'though most calls me Joey."

At the mention of his name, the men at the poker table got hastily to their feet and grabbed their friend by his arm and hustled him out the door, looking back over their shoulders at the living legend who had almost curled him up.

Louis didn't offer his hand, but smiled at Wells. "Pleased to make your acquaintance, Mr. Wells." He nodded at an empty chair across the table from him. "Would you care to take a seat and have some food?"

Wells scanned the room again with his snake eyes before he pulled a chair around and sat, his back still to a wall. "Don't mind if'n I do, thank ye kindly."

Louis waved a hand and a young black waiter came to his table. "Jeremiah, Mr. Wells would like to order."

"Yes sir," the boy replied as he looked inquiringly at Wells.

"I'll have a beefsteak cooked jest long enough ta' keep it from crawling off'n my plate, four hen's eggs scrambled, an' some tomaters if'n ya' have any."

The boy nodded rapidly and turned to leave.

"An' some *cafécito,* hot, black, and strong enough to float a horseshoe," Wells added.

Louis grinned. "I like to see a man with a healthy appetite." He glanced at a thick layer of trail dust on Wells's buckskin coat. "You have the look of a man a long time on the trail."

"That's a fact. All the way from Mexico. Pretty near a month, now."

The waiter appeared and placed a coffee mug on the table, filled it with steaming black coffee from a silver server, and added some to Louis's cup before setting the pot on the table. Wells pulled a cork from his whiskey bottle and poured a dollop of amber liquid into his coffee. He offered the bottle to Louis, who shook his head.

Wells shrugged, blew on his coffee to cool it, and drank the entire cup down in one long draught. He leaned back and took his fixings out and built himself a cigarette. Striking a lucifer on his boot, he lit the cigarette and stuck it in the corner of his mouth. He left it there while he spoke, squinting one eye against the smoke. "That's mighty good coffee." He refilled his cup and again topped it off with a touch of whiskey. "Shore beats that mesquite bean coffee I been drinking fer the last month."

Louis nodded, reviewing in his mind what he had heard about the famous Joey Wells. Wells had been born in the foothills of Missouri. He was barely in his teens when he fought in the Civil War for the Confederate Army. Riding with a group called The Missouri Volunteers, he became a fearless, vicious killer, eagerly absorbing every trick of guerilla warfare known from the mountain men and hillbillies he fought with. After Lee's surrender at Appomattox, Wells's group attempted to turn themselves in. They reported to a Union Army outpost and handed over their weapons, expecting to be sent home, as other Confederate soldiers had been. Instead, the entire group was assassinated—all except Wells and a few others who were late getting to the surrender site. From a hill nearby, they watched their unarmed comrades being gunned down. Under the code of the Missouri Feud, they vowed to fight the Union to the death.

After Joey and his men perpetrated several raids upon unsuspecting Union soldiers and camps—killing viciously to fulfill their vow of vengeance—a group of hired killers and thugs known as the Kansas Redlegs were assigned to hunt down the remaining Missouri Volunteers. After several years of raids and counter-raids, Joey was the last surviving member of his renegade group. It took him another year and a half, using every trick he had learned, to track down and kill all of the remaining Redlegs, over a hundred and fifty men. Along the way, he became a legend, a figure mothers used to scare their children into doing their chores, a figure men whispered about around campfires at night. With each telling his legend grew, magnified by penny dreadfuls and dime novels, until there was no place left in America for him to run to.

After the last Redleg lay dead at his feet, Joey was said to have gone to Mexico and set up a ranch there. Rumor had it Texas Rangers had struck a bargain with him, vowing to leave him in peace if he stayed south of the border.

Louis fired up another cigar, sipped his coffee, and wondered what had happened to cause Wells to break his truce and head north to Colorado. Of course, he didn't ask. In the West, sticking your nose in another's business was an invitation to have someone shoot it off.

After his food was served, Wells leaned forward and ate with a single-minded concentration, not speaking again until his plate was bare. He filled his empty coffee cup with whiskey, built another cigarette, and leaned back with a contented sigh. Smoke floated from the butt in his mouth and caused him to squint as he stared at Louis from under his hat brim. "A while back, I met some fellahs down Chihuahua way tole me 'bout a couple 'a friends of theirs in Colorado. One was named Longmont."

Louis motioned to the waiter to bring him some brandy, then nodded, waiting for Wells to continue. "Yep. Said this Longmont dressed like a dandy and talked real fancy, but not to let that fool me. This Longmont was a real bad pistoleer and knew his way around a Colt, and was maybe the second fastest man with a short gun they'd ever seen."

Louis dipped the butt of his stogie in his brandy, then stuck it in his mouth and puffed, sending a cloud of blue smoke toward the ceiling. "These men say anything else?" he asked, eyebrows raised.

"Uh huh. Said this Longmont would do ta' ride the river with, and if'n he was yore friend he'd stand toe-ta'-toe with ya' against the devil hisself if need be."

Louis threw back his head and laughed. "Well, excusing your friends for engaging in a small amount of hyperbole, I suppose their assessment of my character is basically correct."

Wells's lips curled in a small smile. "Like they said, ya' talk real purty."

"And who was the other man your friends mentioned?"

"*Hombre* named Smoke Jensen. They said Jensen was so fast he could snatch a Double-Eagle off'n a rattler's head and leave change 'fore the snake could strike."

Louis drowned his quiet smile in coffee. "Your friends have quite a way with words, themselves. Might I ask what their names are?"

"'Couple'a Mex's named Louis Carbone and Al Martine. Got 'em a little *rancho* down near Chihuahua." Wells dropped his cigarette on the floor and ground it out with his boot. "They be pretty fair with short guns theyselves, fer Mex's."

Louis nodded, remembering the last time he had seen Carbone and Martine. The pair had hired out their guns to a rotten, no good back-shooter named Lee Slater. Slater bit off more than he could chew when he and his men rode through Big Rock, shooting up the town and raising hell. Problem was, they also wounded and almost killed Sally Jensen, Smoke's wife. Smoke went after them, and in the end he faced down the gang in the very streets of Big Rock where it all started. . . .

Lee Slater stepped out of the shadows, his hands wrapped around the butts of Colts, as were Smoke's. "I'm gonna kill you, Jensen!" he screamed.

A rifle barked, the slug striking Lee in the middle of his back and exiting out the front. The outlaw gang leader lay dead on the hot dusty street.

Sally Jensen stepped back into Louis's gambling hall and jacked another round into her carbine.

Smoke smiled at her and walked down the boardwalk.

"Looking for me, *amigo?*" Al Martine spoke from the shadows of a doorway. His guns were in leather.

"Not really. Ride on, Al."

"Why would you make such an offer to me? I am an outlaw, a killer. I hunted you in the mountains."

"You have a family, Al?"

"*Sí.* A father and mother, brothers and sister, all down in Mexico."

"Why don't you go pay them a visit? Hang up your guns for a time?"

The Mexican smiled and finished rolling a cigarette. He lit it and held it to Smoke's lips.

"Thanks, Al."

"Thank you, Smoke. I shall be in Chihuahua. If you ever need me, send word. Everybody knows where to find me. I will come very quickly."

"I might do that."

"*Adios, compadre.*" Al stepped off the boardwalk and was gone. A few moments later, Sheriff Silva and a posse rode up in a cloud of dust.

"That's it, Smoke," the sheriff announced. "It's all over. You're a free man, and all these other yahoos are gonna be behind bars."

"Suits me," Smoke said, and holstered his guns.

"No it ain't over!" The scream came from up the street.

Everybody looked. Pecos stood there, his hands over the butts of his fancy engraved .45s.

"Oh crap!" Smoke said.

"Don't do it, kid!" Louis Carbone called from the boardwalk. "It's over. He'll kill you, boy."

"Hell with you, you greasy son of a bitch!" Pecos yelled.

Carbone stiffened. Cut his eyes to Smoke.

"Man sure shouldn't have to take a cut like that, Carbone," Smoke told him.

Carbone stepped out into the street, his big silver spurs jingling. "Kid, you can insult me all day. But you cannot insult my mother."

Pecos laughed and told him what he thought about Carbone's sister, too.

Carbone shot him before the kid could even clear leather. The Pecos Kid died in the dusty street of a town that would be gone in ten years. He was buried in an unmarked grave.

"If you hurry, Carbone," Smoke called, "I think you can catch up with Martine. Me and him smoked a cigarette together a few minutes ago, and he told me he was going back to Chihuahua to visit his folks."

Carbone grinned and saluted Smoke. A minute later he was riding out of town, heading south. . . .*

* * *

* *Code of the Mountain Man*

Louis grinned at the memory. Carbone and Martine had been killers who had been given a second chance at life through the generosity of Smoke Jensen. He hoped they had taken advantage of it. "How are Carbone and Martine doing?"

Wells shrugged. "Pretty fair. Ain't much fer ranchin', though. Spend most of their time drinkin' tequila and shaggin' every *señorita* within a hundred miles—most of the *señoras,* too, I s'pect."

Louis laughed again. "That would certainly be like Al and Louis, all right."

"They said they owed you and Jensen a debt of honor fer how you all helped them out a while back." Wells reached into a leather pouch slung over his shoulder on a rawhide thong.

Louis tensed, his hand moving toward his Colt. Wells noticed the motion and shook his head slightly. "Don't you worry none, Mr. Longmont. I ain't here to do you or your'n any harm. I'm jest deliverin' somethin' fer Carbone and Martine. A token a' their 'preciation, they called it."

He opened his pouch and took out a set of silver spurs, with large, pointed star-rowels and hand-tooled leather straps, and a large, shiny Bowie knife with a handle inlaid with silver and turquoise. "The knife's fer Jensen, the spurs are fer you."*

When Smoke arrived at the saloon a few moments later, he and Joey had taken to each other as if they'd known each other for years. They had shared so many common experiences, it would have been unusual for them not to become close friends.

*Honor of the Mountain Man

17

As Joey dismounted, Pearlie whispered under his breath, "Boy, that's 'bout the most dangerous-lookin' man I ever did see."

Smoke nodded, taking in the scar on the right cheek, the brace of Colt .44s in twin holsters on his hips, and the ever-present Colt Navy .36 in his shoulder holster. Smoke realized Joey hadn't changed a bit in the couple of years since he'd seen him.

"Hey, old friend," Smoke said as they shook hands. "Having a passel of babies and becoming a rancher don't seem to have tamed you any."

"Not enough so's you can tell it," Joey replied with a smile. "Cal, Pearlie," he said, nodding in greeting.

"Howdy, Mr. Wells," Cal said, his hero worship showing in his eyes.

"Naw, it's still just Joey to my friends, Cal. What happened to you to get you all bundled up in that chair?"

"That's what I want to talk to you about, Joey," Smoke said. "Come on into the house and tell Sally hello. I suspect she's got breakfast all ready for you by now."

"Good. My wife said to tell her hello, and to say she was right. The second young'un's a whole lot easier to raise than the first."

Later, Smoke and Cal and Pearlie and Joey sat on the porch, drinking after-breakfast coffee and smoking.

"Now that we got the eatin' an' helloin' behind us, why don't you tell me what's stuck in your craw, Smoke?"

Smoke went on to tell Joey about Lazarus Cain and his gang, how they'd shot Cal and were holed up in Fontana, sitting and waiting.

"What do you think they're waitin' fer?" Joey asked.

Smoke shook his head. "God only knows, but one thing's for sure, they're up to no good."

"You can make bet on that," Joey said. "I heared 'bout Cain whilst I was still fightin' the Redlegs. He was a bastard clear through then, an' I'm bettin' he ain't changed enough so's you can tell it."

"That's what I need your help for, Joey. I need someone Cain will trust to ride on over to Fontana, stay a while, and see if they can find out what his plans are."

Joey's lips curved up in a half-sneer and half-smile. "I think I know someone who'll be glad to do that fer you, Smoke."

"It'll be dangerous. He might talk to someone who'll know we rode together a few years back."

Joey shrugged. "So what? I've rode with plenty of men I've later had to kill. How'll he know it'd matter to me one way or t'other?"

"You may have to prove yourself to him," Smoke said.

Another shrug. "No matter. I've been doin' that since I was knee-high to a toad."

Smoke leaned forward, his elbows on his knees. "Since it'd be too dangerous for you to come here to report, here's how we'll handle it . . ."

Joey rode into Fontana just before dusk, after circling around to enter from the north instead of the south.

The town was already jumping, with music and shouting and hollering coming from the only saloon in town.

Smoke was right, he thought as he looked in the batwings. There had to be at least forty or fifty hard cases sitting around the place, drinking as if the bartender was giving it away free.

He hitched up his holsters and walked into the room, pausing a moment as he always did to size up the place and get his bearings in case of sudden trouble.

After a moment, the room quieted as the men inside noticed him standing there. One, a six-and-a-half-foot-tall man who'd had too much to drink to sense the danger in Joey's eyes, walked over to him.

"Hey, mister. We don' much like strangers 'round here," the man slurred, his voice thick with too much whiskey.

Joey started to brush past him, saying, "Sit down before I plant you, bigmouth."

The man grabbed Joey by the shoulder and whirled him around, pulling his arm back with his fingers curled into a fist.

Before anyone could blink, both Joey's hands were filled with iron. Without a moment's hesitation, he brought the barrel of one of his big Army .44s crashing down on the man's skull, dropping him like a sack of flour.

In another second, both pistol hammers were eared back, and Joey faced the room, as calm as if he were alone.

"Anybody else got somethin' to say?" he asked in a harsh voice.

From the corner of the table, a tall, lean, hawk-faced man stood up. "Well, I'll be damned," he said, a broad smile on his face. "I do believe that's Joey Wells who just joined us, boys."

A low murmur swept the room. There wasn't anyone living west of the Mississippi who hadn't heard of the feats of Joey Wells, and to those south of the Mason-Dixon line he was more than a hero—he was a living legend.

"A couple of you boys drag Max out and put his head in a horse trough, an' you can tell him how lucky he is to be alive after bracin' Joey Wells," Cain called.

After two men grabbed the fallen man by his boots and shoulders and half-carried, half-dragged him out the front door, Cain turned to Joey and held out his hand.

Joey hesitated just a second or two, looking Cain in

the eye to show he wasn't intimidated, then took the hand.

"My name's Lazarus Cain, Joey. I heard about you when I rode with Bill Quantrill's raiders after the war."

"Yeah? Well, we all did some ridin' after the war. Seemed like the thing to do at the time."

Joey turned his back on Cain and sauntered over to the bar. "Gimme a whiskey, an' use that bottle with the label on it in the corner there," he said, pointing.

Bob Blanchard quickly grabbed the bottle Joey pointed at, jerked the cork out, and placed it and a clean glass on the bar in front of him.

As Joey filled the glass, Cain sidled up next to him. "I heard you had some marshal trouble over near Pueblo."

Joey downed his drink and poured another. He glanced at Cain out of the corner of his eyes. "Johnny North tole me he'd been by here. He's not bad with a gun, but he's got a big mouth."

"He tell you I have some work you might be interested in?"

Joey sipped this drink instead of bolting it, and turned to face Cain. "I heared about you when you rode with Quantrill, Cain. I heared you was crazy, always spoutin' off 'bout God an' the Bible an' such. Are you crazy, Cain? 'cause I don't much cotton to workin' fer a crazy man, no matter how good he is with a gun."

Lazarus's cheeks burned, and his eyes narrowed at being called crazy. He stood there a moment, muscles rigid, fists clenched, thinking on what Joey had said. Then, suddenly, he burst out laughing. "You know, Joey, I probably was a little crazy back then. The war did that to some people, all the killin' an' dyin' an' knowin' that if we'd had more guns an' ammunition, the blue-bellies wouldn't've had a chance against us."

Joey nodded slowly. Cain was right about that. The war was crazy, and it made everyone who survived it just as crazy as it was. But this man was more than that. His eyes were burning with an inner fire, and it was clear if you studied him, as Joey did people, that he was filled with

372   *William W. Johnstone*

inner demons of some sort. He was plain off-kilter. Joey
had no doubt about that. He would have to be careful,
'cause this man might just do anything, for any reason
whatsoever.

"So, if I decide to work with you, what's the job and
what's my cut liable to be?"

Lazarus stared at Joey for a moment with those insane
eyes, then held out his hand to Blanchard, who stuck a
whiskey glass in it. Lazarus held it out, and Joey poured
it full from his bottle.

"There's a local rancher whose land is plumb covered
with gold. The man has no interest in it, but won't let
anyone else try to mine it. We"—he pointed over his
shoulder at the men in the room—"plan to kill him and
his hands and take the gold for ourselves."

"What's this rancher's name that don't have no interest in gold? He sounds even crazier than you, Cain."

Lazarus smiled. It was refreshing to have someone
around who didn't walk on eggshells with him . . . who
would speak his mind in front of him. Wells was prov-
ing to be every bit as interesting as he'd heard he was.

"His name's Smoke Jensen."

Joey let his eyes widen a bit in mock surprise. "Jensen,
huh? I rode with him a few years back. He helped me . . .
take care of some *bandidos* who shot up my family."

Lazarus's face turned suspicious. "You rode with
Jensen? What'd you think of him?"

"Fastest man with a six-gun I've ever seed, 'ceptin' fer
me, of course."

"So you and he were friends?"

Joey's eyes turned hard and cold as stone, though his
expression didn't change. "Let me git this straight, Cain.
I don't have no friends, an' that includes you. Just 'cause
I ride with a man don't give him no claim on my friend-
ship later. If'n I decide to ride with you, I'll do what I'm
paid to do. But, when the job's over don't make the mistake of thinkin' I owe you anythin' else, 'cause you might
be my next job—understand?"

"You're a man after my own heart, Joey. Hard as nails and tough as a just-woke grizzly bear."

Joey let his lips curl in a half-smile. "So I've been told."

"What do you think of the job offer?"

"I'll have to do some thinkin' on it. Jensen is mighty tough, an' he's got lots of friends in Big Rock. How do you plan to handle them?"

Lazarus held up his hand. "I'll tell you the details after you decide whether you're gonna ride with us or not."

Joey emptied his glass. "Well, then, how 'bout some grub? You got anythin' worth eatin' in this dump?"

"Only if you like enchiladas an' beans," Lazarus said with a smirk.

He inclined his head at Blanchard, who yelled at the Mexican cook in the kitchen to get another plate ready.

Joey picked up his bottle and glass and walked to the nearest table against a wall. The three men sitting there looked up from their drinks, scowls on their faces.

"Whatta you want, Wells?" one asked.

"I need yore table. I'm fixin' to sit down an' eat."

"You can kiss my butt, runt," the other man snarled. "We ain't afraid of you, or your reputation."

Joey turned and handed the glass and bottle to Lazarus, and when he turned back around, a long knife was in his left hand. Quick as a wink the blade was against the snarling man's throat and a tiny trickle of blood was running down his neck. The cowboy's eyes were wide and frightened.

"Excuse me. I don't hear so well," Joey whispered. "Just what was it you said to me?"

At a movement from one of the other men at the table, Joey filled his right hand with iron before the other man could get his pistol half out of its holster.

"Do you really want to ante up in this game, mister?" Joey asked, eyebrows raised.

"Uh . . . no . . . I was just gittin' up to leave the table," the man said, his voice harsh with fear.

Both the other occupants of the table scraped back their chairs and hurried out the batwings. Joey looked back into the eyes of the scared man with the knife against his throat.

"I'm sorry, but I didn't hear you answer my question. You said somethin' 'bout not bein' afraid of me—isn't that right?"

"No . . . no . . . I was just kiddin'. You can have the table if'n you want it, Mr. Wells," said the man, his voice breaking from fear.

"Why, thank ye kindly," Joey said in a low voice. "That's right neighborly of you."

He pulled the knife back, wiped the blood off its blade on the man's cheek, then slipped it in a scabbard on the back of his belt as the man bolted from the saloon.

By the time Joey sat down, he could hear the man's horse galloping out of town.

He glanced up at Lazarus, who was smiling down at him. "Looks like you lost a man."

"It wasn't any great loss. I don't need any cowards ridin' with me."

Joey shook his head. "That man wasn't a coward. He just knew his limitations. I don't call that yellow. I call it smart."

"Well, smart or yellow, he's gone," Lazarus said, "and good riddance to him."

"You got any peppers fer these enchiladas?" Joey asked. "They're a mite bland."

18

Lazarus Cain sat at the table and drank as Joey ate. "Say, Joey, what happened to those *bandidos* Jensen helped you go after?"

Without looking up Joey replied, "They died."

"You mind tellin' me about it?" Lazarus asked.

"Why?"

"Because I've been stuck here in this one-horse town for nigh onto three weeks waitin' for enough men to show up to take down Jensen and maybe even the town of Big Rock, an' I ain't had nobody with anything interestin' to say to talk to the entire time." He gave a small shrug of his shoulders. "I'll understand if'n you don't want to talk about it, but I'd be obliged if you would, just to pass the time."

Joey paused to slab a thick coat of butter onto a tortilla. After he rolled it up and bit off half of it, he sat back in his chair and pulled out his makin's. He built a cigarette, stuck it in the corner of his mouth, and lighted it.

He squinted one eye against the smoke curling up, and let the cigarette bob up and down as he talked in his soft, Southern accent, taking an occasional sip of whiskey without removing the butt from his mouth.

"The gang of *bandidos* had joined up with a man name of Murdock, an' Jensen and his men and me went to war with 'em. We'd managed to kill or wound most of 'em when the leader of the *bandidos,* a man called *El Machete,* 'cause of his habit of choppin' people to death with one, and Murdock ran off to Murdock's ranch. I'd taken some lead in the shoulder, but me an' Jensen took off after 'em. . . ."

Smoke put a hand on Joey's arm and helped him climb up on Red, then he stepped into the saddle on Horse. They rode off toward the Lazy M and Murdock and Vasquez at an easy canter.

After a few miles, Smoke noticed fresh blood on Joey's shoulder and a tight grimace of pain on his lips.

"This ride too much for your wound, Joey? If it is, we can go back and wait a few days for the stitches the doc put in to knit together."

Joey shook his head, looking straight ahead. "I want to end this business, Smoke. All my life it seems I've been livin' with hate—first during the war, then after, when I was chasin' Redlegs." He took a deep breath. "The only time I've been at peace was with Betty, and then when little Tom came I thought my life was complete and all that anger was behind me."

He pulled a plug of Bull Durham out and bit off the end. As he chewed, he talked. "Since Vasquez and his men rode into my life, I've found all that hate and more back in my heart." He looked over at Smoke. "At first, I thought I'd missed all the excitement of the chase, an' the killin'. But I've found that the hate festers inside of ya', an' I'm afraid if I don't git shut of it soon I won't be fit ta' go back to Betty. She's just too fine a woman ta' have to live with a man all eat up inside with hate and bitterness."

Smoke smiled gently. "I don't think you have to worry about that, Joey. You've just been doing what any man would do, fighting to protect your family and your home." He slowed Horse and bent his head to light a cigar. When he had it going good, he caught up with Joey. "When you see the end of Vasquez and Murdock, things'll go back like they were. The only hate I can see

inside you is anger at the men who hurt your loved ones,
and that's a good thing. A man who won't stand up for
his family is no good."

Joey gave a tight grin. "You ought to be a preaching'
man, Smoke. You sure know the right things ta' say."

Smoke laughed until he choked on his cigar smoke. After
he finished coughing, he said, "Now that's a picture to think
on—Smoke Jensen, holding Sunday-go-to-meeting revivals."

They stopped at the riverbed and watered their
mounts in one of the small pools. "What are you going
to do about the river, once this is over?" Joey asked.

Smoke gave him a look he didn't quite understand
and said, "Oh, I think I'll leave that to the new ramrod
of the Rocking C. It'll be his decision to make."

Another hour of easy riding brought them to the outskirts of the Lazy M. They could see two horses in the
distance, tied up to a hitching rail near the corral, away
from the house. Smoke pulled Puma Buck's Sharps .52
from his saddle boot and began to walk toward a group
of trees about a hundred yards from the house, keeping the trees between him and the house so Murdock
and Vasquez wouldn't be able to see him coming.

Joey walked alongside, carrying a Henry repeating
rifle in his right hand, hammer thong loose on his Colt.

Murdock was in his study, down on hands and knees
in front of his safe, shoveling wads of currency into a
large leather valise.

He and Vasquez had arrived back at his ranch at three
in the morning and had taken a nap, planning to leave
the territory early the next morning. They had slept
longer than intended, and were now hurrying to make
up for lost time.

Vasquez was sitting at Murdock's desk, his feet up on
the leather surface, a bottle of Murdock's bourbon in
one hand and one of his hand-rolled cigars in the other.

"What you do now, *Señor* Murdock? Where you go?"

Murdock looked back over his shoulder, his hands full of cash. "I plan to head up into Montana. There's still plenty of wild country up there, a place where a man with plenty of money, and the right help, can still carve out a good ranch."

"What about Emilio?" Vasquez asked, his right hand inching toward his *machete*. He was looking at the amount of cash in the safe, thinking it would last a long time in Mexico. He could change his name, maybe grow a beard, and live like a king for the rest of his life.

Murdock noticed the way Vasquez was eyeing his money, so he pulled a Colt out of the safe and pointed it at the Mexican. "Just keep your hands where I can see 'em, Emilio. I was planning on taking you with me. I can always use a man like you." He raised his eyebrows. "But now I'm not so sure that's a good idea. I don't want to have to sleep with one eye open all the way to Montana to keep you from killing me and taking my money."

Vasquez smiled, showing all his teeth, "But *señor*, you have nothings to fear from Emilio. I work for you always."

Murdock had opened his mouth to answer when he heard a booming explosion from in front of his house and a .52 caliber slug plowed through his front wall, tore through a chest of drawers, and continued on to imbed itself in a rear wall.

Murdock and Vasquez threw themselves on the floor behind his desk, Vasquez spilling bourbon all over both of them in the process.

"*Chinga* . . ." Vasquez grunted.

"Jesus!" said Murdock.

Smoke hollered, "Murdock, Vasquez! Come out with your hands up and you can go on living . . . at least until the people of Pueblo hang you."

The two outlaws looked at each other under the desk. "What do you think?" Murdock asked.

Vasquez shrugged. "Not much choice, is it? I think I rather get shot than hang. You?"

Murdock nodded. "Maybe I can buy our way out."

Vasquez gave a short laugh. "*Señor,* you not know mens very well. Jensen and Wells not want money, they want our blood."

Murdock didn't believe him. Everyone wanted money. It was what made the world go round. "Jensen, Wells. I've got twenty thousand in here, in cash. It's yours if you turn your backs and let us ride out of here!" Murdock called.

His answer was another .52 caliber bullet tearing through the walls of his ranch house. It seemed nothing would stop the big Sharps slugs.

Murdock said, "I guess you're right."

Vasquez answered, "Besides, after they kill us they take moneys, anyway."

Murdock scrambled on hands and knees to the wall, where he took his Winchester '73 rifle down off a rack. He grabbed a Henry and pitched it across the room to Vasquez. "Here, let's start firing back. Maybe we'll get lucky."

Vasquez chuckled to hide the fear gnawing at his guts like a dog worrying a bone. "And maybe horse learn to talk. But I do not think so."

They crawled across the floor and peeked out the window. They could see nothing. Then a sheet of flame shot out of a small group of trees in front of the house and another bullet shattered the door frame, knocking the door half open and leaving it hanging on one hinge.

"Goddamn!" Murdock yelped. He rose and began to fire the Winchester as fast as he could work the lever and pull the trigger. He didn't bother to aim, just poured a lot of lead out at the attackers.

"Vasquez," he whispered, "see if you can sneak out the back and circle around 'em. Maybe you can get them from behind."

"Hokay, *señor,*" the Mexican answered. He crawled through the house, praying to a God he had almost forgotten existed that he'd make it to his horse. He wasn't about to risk trying to sneak up on Jensen and Wells. If he got to his horse he was going to be long gone before they knew it.

He eased the back door open and stuck his head out. Good, there was no one in sight and no place to hide behind the cabin.

Crouching low, he ran in a wide circle to where he and Murdock had left their horses. He slipped between the rails on the far side of the corral and crawled on his belly across thirty yards of horseshit to get to his mount's reins. He reached up and untied the reins and stood up next to his bronc, his hand on the saddle horn, ready to leap into the saddle and be off.

"Howdy, *El Machete,*" he heard from behind him.

He stiffened, then relaxed. It was time to make his play. Maybe, as Murdock said, he would get lucky.

He grabbed iron and whirled. Before his pistol was out of its holster, Joey had drawn and fired, his bullet taking the Mexican in the right shoulder. The force of the slug spun Vasquez around, threw him back against his horse, then to the ground. He fumbled for his gun with his left hand, but couldn't get it out before Joey was standing over him.

"Okay, *Señor* Wells. I surrender."

Joey's eyes were terrible for the Mexican to behold. They were black as the pits of hell, and cold as those of a rattler ready to strike.

Joey leaned down and pulled Vasquez's machete from its scabbard on his back. "I don't think so, Vasquez."

He held the blade up and twisted it, so it gleamed and reflected sunlight on its razor-sharp edge. Joey looked at him and smiled. "Guess what, *El Machete?*"

Suddenly, Vasquez knew what the cowboy had in mind. "No . . . no . . . *por favor,* do not do this, *señor!*"

Joey pursed his lips, "Try as I might, Vasquez, I cain't think of a single reason I shouldn't."

With a move like a rattler's strike, Joey slashed with the machete, severing Vasquez's right arm at the elbow. The Mexican screamed and grabbed at his stump with his left hand.

"Remember Mr. Williams, *El Machete?*"

As Vasquez looked up through pain-clouded, terror-filled eyes, the machete flashed again, severing his left arm at the elbow.

Vasquez screamed again and thrashed around on the ground, trying to stanch the blood as it spurted from his ruined arms by sticking the stumps in the dirt. It didn't work.

Joey stood and watched as Vasquez bled to death, remembering his wife and son lying in their own blood because of this man.

Smoke continued peppering the house with the Sharps until one of the slugs tore open the potbellied stove, setting the house on fire.

As flames consumed the wooden structure, Murdock began to scream. Just before the roof caved in he came running out of the door, his clothes smoldering and smoking, holding a leather valise in one hand and a Colt in the other. He was cocking and firing wildly at Smoke, who stood calmly, ignoring the whine of the slugs around his head.

"This is for Puma Buck," he whispered, and put a slug between Murdock's eyes. His head exploded, and he dropped where he stood, dead and in hell before he hit the ground.

Smoke walked over and picked up the valise, looked in it, smiled, and hooked the handles on his saddle horn.

He helped Joey up on Red, climbed on Horse, and they headed home. . . .*

Joey'd had to replace his cigarette twice by the time he finished the story, but he had Lazarus's full attention.

"So, did you and Jensen split the money in the valise?" Lazarus asked.

*Honor of the Mountain Man

Joey hesitated. Smoke had given him the money to help him build a new life in the Colorado territory, but he didn't feel he could tell Lazarus that.

"Actually, no. I took some to cover my expenses, but Jensen gave the rest to some ranchers who'd been burned out by Murdock an' his men."

"I guess what I've heard is right, that Jensen don't have no desire to get rich."

Joey shrugged his shoulders. "He feels he is rich, with his ranch an' wife an' friends. He just don't love money, or the gettin' of money, like the rest of us do."

"You two seemed to be awfully close friends in your story. Are you sure goin' after him won't cause you any second thoughts?"

"I done explained that to you, Cain. You got any second thoughts 'bout invitin' me in, I can leave any time. It's your call."

Lazarus shook his head. "No, I'll take your word for it, Joey. But," he paused and his eyes got hard, "make no mistake about it. I don't never forget if somebody crosses me, an' I don't rest until I've paid 'em back for their treachery."

Joey opened his mouth in a prodigious yawn, as if Lazarus's words meant nothing to him. "Warnin' noted, Cain. Now, this town got anyplace a man can get some sleep? I been on the trail so long my feet're probably growed to my boots."

Lazarus got to his feet. "Come on, I'll take you over to the hotel. I can't promise you clean sheets, but at least they'll have a bed you can bunk in."

Joey gave a half-smile. "Hell, I'm so tired I could sleep standin' up leanin' again a wall."

19

It was just after three o'clock in the morning when Joey slipped out of his bed and pulled his boots on. He stepped to the window and glanced at the sky. The moon had set, and the night was as black as the bottom of a well.

Easing the window open, he slipped through it and out onto the balcony. He crawled over the rail and hung by his hands for a moment, then dropped the ten feet to the ground, landing with a soft thud in the dirt of the alleyway.

Slowly, looking over his shoulder as he went, he made his way to the livery stable. He knew from his years in the war that the hours between three and four in the morning were the hardest for sentries on guard duty. For some reason, the mind and body seem to shut down and not work well in those hours.

He peeked in the window of the livery office and saw a man sitting at a desk with his head on his arms, fast asleep. Of course, the empty whiskey bottle on the desk next to him explained his condition, as well as the hour.

Inside, Joey slipped a halter on Red but didn't bother with a saddle. He walked the big horse out the door and down the street a ways before he jumped up on his back. He continued to walk the mount until he was past the town limits, then he put the stud into a lope, using the stars as his guide through the inky blackness of the night.

Smoke had told him to ride straight east and he'd find the place he was to meet Pearlie.

Sure enough, after about an hour's ride he saw a huge rock sticking up out of the relatively flat land around it. On the side away from town, he could see some smoldering coals where a small campfire had been laid.

He slid to the ground and walked over to the figure lying in a blanket next to the fire. He reached out with his foot and gently nudged the form.

"Hold it right there, mister," called a voice from behind him.

Joey's hand went toward his pistol, then he recognized Pearlie's drawl.

He held his hands out and turned. "You wouldn't shoot an old friend, would you, Pearlie?" Joey said.

He heard the click of Pearlie earing down the hammer on his Colt as a shadow separated itself from the rock and moved toward him.

"Howdy, Joey. I couldn't tell for sure if'n it was you or not, so I figured better be safe than sorry."

"You did right, Pearlie. I was fixin' to jump your butt about sleepin' on the job when I saw that blanket next to the fire."

"You want some coffee? I believe it's still warm."

Joey squatted next to the bed of coals and held his hands out to warm them. The night was chilly, with the temperature almost down to the freezing level.

"Sure would hit the spot," he said.

He made a cigarette and stuck it in the corner of his mouth while he drank his coffee.

"What did you find out about Cain's plans?" Pearlie asked.

"Not much. He still doesn't trust me enough to give me the details. But I did find out he's plannin' to come after Smoke at the ranch."

Pearlie's voice rose a little in alarm. "When?"

Joey shook his head. "That I don't know. What I can't figure out is why he's got so many men. It sure wouldn't take fifty men to raid the Sugarloaf if they weren't expectin' any trouble."

"Why does he want to come after Smoke?"

"For the gold on his land. He's heard there's enough there to make a lot of men very rich."

Pearlie nodded. He, like most of the people around the area, had forgotten all about the gold buried on the Sugarloaf. In the aftermath of the Tilden Franklin affair, a prospector had come out of the hills around Smoke's ranch loaded to the gills with fool's gold. Smoke had just let people believe that's what Franklin had found—fool's gold. Only a few people knew the truth, that the Sugarloaf was covered with the real stuff. Evidently, someone who knew the truth had been talking to Cain.

"Only thing I *can* figure," Joey continued, "is that after he takes out Smoke and the men on the ranch, he's gonna try and tree Big Rock to keep it under control while he gets the gold."

"That's crazy," Pearlie said. "Nobody's ever treed a Western town."

"I agree, but I don't believe Cain's playin' with a full deck of cards. The man seems to think he can't be beaten by anybody, no matter what the odds."

"And you don't have any idea when all this is gonna take place?"

"No, so you have to warn Smoke to be ready at any time. If'n I can, I'll try an' get away in time to warn you, but that may not be possible."

"All right. You ride with your guns loose, Joey. You're in a nest of snakes over there. Be sure you don't get bitten."

"*Adíos,* partner," Joey said as he climbed up on Red. "Tell Smoke I'll see him soon, one way or another."

Joey turned to walk away, then snapped his fingers and looked back over his shoulder. "Oh, an' tell Smoke to expect some visitors in the next couple'a days."

"Who's that?" Pearlie asked.

Joey gave a smirky grin. "Smoke'll know 'em when they git here. They is old acquaintances of his. When he wired me that he needed help, I figured if it was bad enough for Smoke to ask for me, it wouldn't do no harm to have a couple'a extra guns around . . . just in case."

Smoke nodded as Pearlie told him what Joey had said. "Damn, I wish there wasn't any gold on the Sugarloaf. Just the mention of the word is enough to drive men out of their minds with greed."

"He also said to expect some more help in the next few days. He wired some old friends of yours that you might need a couple of guns."

"I wonder who that could be?" Smoke said, a puzzled expression on his face.

"Well, I don't much care. If'n we're gonna be facin' fifty guns, we're gonna need all the help we can git," Pearlie said.

"I know. All right, here's what we'll do: They most probably won't hit us during the day, so I want you to have all the hands rest during daylight. Soon as night falls, they're all going to need to be on guard."

Pearlie looked worried. "Smoke, you know all the hands are loyal as can be, an' if'n you asked 'em they'd stick they hands in a fire for you, but I don't know just how much help they're gonna be in a real fight. Most of those men've never fired a gun in anger or at another person."

"I know. But it can't be helped. I want you to give all the men a choice. If they don't want to stay and help, I'll understand. They can stay in Big Rock until this is over and then come back to their jobs when it's done, no hard feelings."

"How about askin' Mr. Longmont or Sheriff Carson for some help?"

Smoke shook his head. "No. Out here, a man saddles his own horse and kills his own snakes. It's my home and my job to defend it."

"What else do you want me to do?"

"Head on into Big Rock. We're going to need plenty

of supplies—some dynamite and gunpowder and lots of ammunition."

"Anything else?"

"Yeah. You need to tell Monte what Joey said, that Cain might try to attack Big Rock after he's done here."

Pearlie rode the buckboard into town, so he'd have a way to bring the supplies back to the Sugarloaf. In spite of some protestations from Sally, Cal rode with him. Smoke intervened and said it was time for Cal to get more active, or he'd turn to stone lying in the bed for so long.

"How're you feelin', Cal?" Pearlie asked when he noticed Cal's face screw up in pain whenever the buckboard bounced over a rock in the road.

"Not too bad, considerin' you've hit just 'bout every rock 'tween the Sugarloaf and town," Cal answered with a sideways glance at his friend.

Pearlie shook his head. "Well, it's your own damn fault. Drawin' down on that many men without ol' Pearlie to back you up."

Cal grunted. "You'd've done the same thing, Pearlie. Don't you go denyin' it, neither."

Pearlie gave a lopsided grin. "Yeah, but I'd've gotten more'n two of the bastards."

"'Course, their bullets would've probably killed you, since you ain't had near the practice bein' shot as I have," Cal replied.

"That's the truth, boy, I'll admit it. You have been shot more times than I can shake a stick at." He looked at Cal out of the corner of his eye. "I guess you won't hardly be wearin' a shirt at all, this summer. You'll be paradin' around showin' that teensy scar to all the girls in Big Rock."

"Teensy scar?" Cal said with mock anger. "Hell, any bigger an' it'd cover my whole chest!"

As they pulled into Big Rock, Pearlie slowed the wagon and stood up, the reins in his hands.

"What're you doin'?" Cal asked.

"Just lookin' to make sure ain't nobody doin' any

target practice. The way you attract lead, we're both liable to get shot by accident."

He pulled the wagon up before the general store and jumped down to the ground. "Let me take this list in to the store, an' then we'll mosey on over to Longmont's for a bite to eat while they get the supplies ready."

"Hell, Pearlie, you just ate lunch no more'n two hour ago. You hungry already?"

Pearlie got a pained expression on his face. "It ain't a matter of bein' hungry. It's a matter of eatin' when you get the chance. The way things been goin' 'round here lately, no tellin' when I'll next get to chow down."

He came out of the store a few minutes later and walked around the buckboard. When he reached up to help Cal climb down, Cal shook his head.

"Don't even think about it, Pearlie. I'm a growed man, an' I can do it on my own."

"You ain't all that growed up, pup. You just stubborn, is all."

Once Cal got down, they walked side by side up the street to Longmont's saloon. As they went through the batwings, Pearlie heard a voice with a strong Mexican accent growl, "Stick up those hands, *gringo!*"

As both boys crouched, their hands falling to their pistol butts, Al Martine let out a loud guffaw, followed shortly by the staccato braying of Louis Carbone.

Cal and Pearlie straightened up, sheepish grins on their faces.

"Al, Louis, when did you two reprobates get into town?" Pearlie asked, walking over to shake their hands.

"On this morning's train, *compadre,*" Al answered.

"What are you doing up here?" Cal asked. "Last we heard you were down near Chihuahua chasin' the girls and pretendin' to be respectable ranchers."

Louis shrugged, holding his hands out and tilting his head in the Mexican manner. "*Señor* Joey wired us that Smoke might need some help, so we got on first train this way, an' here we are."

He threw his arm over Cal's shoulder, raising his eyebrows when Cal grunted in pain.

"What happen, little bronco?" he asked. "You sore?"

"It's nothin', Louis."

"Nothin', hell!" Pearlie said. "He took two bullets from a galoot named Lazarus Cain 'bout three weeks ago."

"Is that the trouble *Señor* Joey was talking about?" Al asked as they walked over to Louis Longmont's table and took their seats.

Pearlie nodded. "Yep. Seems this gent has got 'bout fifty or so men gathered up over at Fontana, an' he's plannin' on ridin' on the Sugarloaf in the next few days."

Longmont paused, a cigar halfway to his lips. "What was that, Pearlie? I hadn't heard that."

Pearlie told them about his meeting with Joey Wells out on the prairie near Fontana. "Joey says he don't know exactly when it's gonna take place, but he says they're comin' for Smoke for sure an' certain."

Al pulled a half-smoked, chewed up cigar butt out of his shirt pocket and stuck it in his mouth, leaning over to accept a light from Longmont. "Then it is settled. We ride today for Smoke's *ranchito*. He will need our help."

Louis Longmont stood up. "You boys eat all you want, on the house. I have a few very important errands to run, so I'll see you later."

20

After getting the buckboard loaded up, Pearlie told Al and Louis to climb aboard and they headed for the Sugarloaf. Al sat on the front seat with Pearlie and Cal, while Louis propped his back up against a couple of bags of flour right behind them.

As they left the city limits, Al leaned back against the seat of the hurricane deck and lighted a long, smelly, black cigar. He glanced sideways at Pearlie, a sly grin on his lips. "*Señor* Pearlie, Louis and me, we hear the rumors of a *grande* fight from when *Señor* Joey was here before."

Pearlie looked at him. "You mean you heard 'bout that little fracas all the way down in Chihuahua?"

"*Sí. El Machete* was *muy famoso*, how you say . . . famous, in Mexico. Many of the *vaqueros* who visit speak of the time he was beaten by the outlaw Joey Wells and his compadre, Smoke Jensen."

Pearlie chuckled. "It was some how-de-do, let me tell you. First off, this rancher Murdock had hired himself a bunch of the most dangerous outlaws around, and he was set on bringing Smoke and Joey down. All we had to help us was a passel of men who barely knew which end of a gun the bullet comes out of, along with Louis Longmont, Monte Carson, and an old sheriff named Ben Tolson."

"Go on, Pearlie," Louis called from the back of the

wagon, "only speak louder. The wheels they squeak *muy* loud."

"Well, we were holed up in this little ranch, an' Smoke had us prepare some surprises for Murdock an' his men, to kind'a even out the odds a mite. Smoke had set up some men in the cabin, an' others in some trees off to the left. Then he said he an' Louis an' Joey an' Cal an' me was gonna ride like cavalry, attackin' the raiders on hossback when they came ridin' in. . . ."

Smoke said, "Then let's shag our mounts, boys. I want to get a little ways away from the ranch house so we can ride and attack without getting shot by our own men."

Smoke and Louis and Joey waited while Cal and Pearlie mounted up and then rode toward Murdock's ranch at an easy trot. Smoke had Colts on both legs, a Henry Repeating rifle in one saddle boot, and a Greener 10-gauge scattergun in the other.

Louis rode with one pistol in a holster on his right leg and had two sawed-off American Arms 12-gauges in saddle boots on either side of his saddle horn. The two-shot derringer behind his belt would be useful only in very close quarters.

Joey had his Colt in his right hand holster, his Navy in his shoulder holster, and two short-barreled Winchester rifles, one in a saddle boot and one he carried across his saddle horn.

Cal had the twin Navy Colt .36 caliber pistols Smoke had given him that he'd used while riding with Preacher. He also carried a Henry Repeating rifle slung over his shoulder on a rawhide strap.

Pearlie had double-rigged Army Colt .44s and a Greener 12-gauge shotgun with a cut-down barrel for close-in work.

Joey glanced around at his compatriots and laughed. "Hell, boys, if Lee'd had this much firepower at Appomattox he wouldn't have had to surrender."

The riders from the Lazy M came galloping toward

Smoke's spread like an invading horde of wild men. They started shouting and hollering and firing their weapons toward the cabin while still well out of range.

Smoke, Joey, Louis, Cal, and Pearlie were bent low over their saddle horns behind a small rise in a group of pine trees, waiting for them to pass.

As they rode by, Joey cut a chunk of Bull Durham and stuck it in his mouth. He chewed a moment, then spat, a disgusted look on his face. "Guess those assholes are tryin' to scare us to death with all that yelping like Injuns."

Cal, whose heart had hammered when he saw the number of men who rode by, took a deep breath, praying he wouldn't disgrace himself or Smoke in the upcoming battle.

Pearlie glanced at him and saw the sweat beginning to bead his forehead in spite of the chilliness of the early evening air. He reached over and punched Cal in the shoulder. "Don't worry none, partner, we're gonna teach these galoots a lesson they'll never forget."

Cal nodded, relaxing a little bit, knowing he was among friends who would fight with him, side by side, against the devil himself if necessary.

When Smoke heard gunfire being returned from the area of the cabin, he put his reins in his teeth, took his Greener 10-gauge in his left hand and his Colt .44 in his right, and spurred Horse forward, guiding the big Palouse with his knees.

Joey looped his reins over his neck, took his short-barreled Winchester rifle in his hands, jacked the lever down to feed a shell into the chamber, and rode after Smoke.

Louis filled both his hands with his American Arms express guns, eared back the hammers on all four barrels, and leaned forward, urging his mount over the hill.

Pearlie winked at Cal as he grabbed his Greener cut-down shotgun in his left hand and drew his Colt with his right. Before he put the reins between his teeth, he said, "Come on cowboy, it's time to make some history of our own!"

Cal drew both his Navy .36s and took off after the others, teeth bared in a grin of both exhilaration and fear.

Murdock's men were in the trap Smoke had devised for them, caught with the shotgun brigade hidden among boulders at their rear, off to their left, hidden in the setting sun, the men with rifles, and to the front, the cabin with its contingent of men who, though not accurate with their weapons, were pouring lead into the outlaws at a furious rate, hitting some by mere chance.

Cal and Pearlie had scattered a series of twenty small piles of kerosene-soaked wood across the clearing where Murdock's men were trapped, and those were now lighted, making the area look like an army camp with its campfires.

Just before Smoke and his band arrived from the bandits' right side, completing their boxing-in maneuver, Monte Carson, leaning out of an upstairs window, did as he had been instructed.

He began to fire his Henry repeating rifle, fitted with a four power scope, at the base of the small fires. The wood had been piled by Cal and Pearlie over cans of black powder, put in burlap sacks with horseshoe nails packed around them.

When Monte's molten lead entered the cans of powder, they exploded, sending hundreds of projectile-like nails in all directions and spreading smoke and cordite in a dense cloud to blind and confuse the enemy.

Men and horses went down by the dozens. Those not killed outright were severely wounded by both explosions and nails.

Other traps began to become effective. Several trenches had been dug, with sharpened spikes stuck in the bottoms. As first horses, then men on foot, began to step into the trenches, horrible screams of pain from both men and animals began to ring out in the gathering darkness.

Curly Rogers and his group of bounty hunters were directly behind Vasquez and Murdock as they approached the cabin. Rogers was firing his Colts at the ranch house as he and his men passed the pile of boulders. A sudden explosion came from between two of the rocks, and Rogers felt as if someone had kicked him in the side. He was blown out of his saddle, three buckshot pellets in his hide. He bounced and quickly scrambled to his feet, barely managing to avoid being trampled by his fellow outlaws.

Rogers clamped his left arm to his side, pulled out another gun, and ran toward the cabin, hoping to find another horse. His feet went right through one of the deadfalls and his legs fell onto two sharpened spikes, sending agony racing through Rogers' body like a fire. He screamed, "Help me . . . oh dear God, somebody help me!" As he flopped on the ground, wooden stakes impaled his legs, and a bullet from the cabin, aimed at another rider, missed its intended target and severed his spine, ending his pain and leaving him lying paralyzed on the ground.

Cates, seeing the amount of resistance at the ranch, tried to veer his horse off to the left and escape. As he passed between two pine trees, the baling wire Cal had strung nine feet off the ground caught him just under the chin. Horse and rider rode on, but Cates's head stayed behind to fall bouncing on the ground like overripe fruit.

Trying to escape the withering fire from the cabin and the trees, the half-breeds Sam Silverwolf and Jed Beartooth whirled their horses and headed for the boulders, intending to take cover there among the rocks.

Tyler and Billy Joe, leaders of the shotgun brigade, saw them coming and stepped into the open, shotguns leveled. Silverwolf got off two shots with his pistol, taking Tyler in the chest and gut, doubling him over. Billy Joe, twenty-two years old and never having fired a gun in anger before, stood his ground as slugs from the two half-breed killers and rapists pocked stone and ricocheted around him. He sighted down the barrel, waited until they were in range, and pulled both triggers at the same time. The double blast from the shotgun exploded and kicked back, knocking Billy Joe on his butt.

When he scrambled to his feet, breaking the barrel open to shove two more shells in, he saw the breeds' riderless horses run past. He squinted and looked up ahead of him on the ground. What he saw made him turn his head and puke. Silverwolf and Beartooth had been literally shredded by the twin loads of buckshot. There wasn't much left of the two murderers that would ever be identified as human, just piles of blood and guts and limbs and brains lying in the dirt.

Juan Jimenez was jumping his horse over one of the small fires when Monte fired into it. Horse and rider were blown twenty feet into the air. Protected from most of the nails by his mount's body, Jimenez survived the blast, but both his legs were blown off below the knees, the stumps cauterized by the heat of the explosion. He landed hard, breaking his left arm in two places, white bone protruding from flesh.

When Jimenez looked down and saw both his legs gone, he screeched and yelled and began to tear at his hair, his mind gone. His agony ended moments later when Ben Tolson took pity on him and shot him from the doorway to the cabin.

The Silverado Kid, Blackie Bensen, and Jerry Lindy were riding next to each other. When the Kid realized the trap they were in, he yelled at his men to pull their mounts to the left. "Rush the trees over yonder—it's our only chance to get away!" he hollered.

The three men rode hard at the trees, guns blazing, lying low over saddle horns. Mike and Jimmy were lying behind a log, their Henrys resting on it as they fired. Jimmy drew a bead on Blackie Bensen and fired. His first shot took Blackie in the left shoulder, spinning him sideways in the saddle. This caused Jimmy's next shot to pierce Blackie's right shoulder blade, entering his back and boring through into his right lung. The ruptured artery there poured blood into Blackie's chest, causing him to drown before he had time to die from loss of blood.

The Silverado Kid fired his Colts over his horse's head, two shots hitting home—one in Mike's chest, killing him instantly, the second careening off a tree to imbed itself in Josh's thigh, throwing him to the ground.

Todd raised his Winchester '73 and pumped two slugs into Jerry Lindy, flinging the outlaw's arms wide before the twin hammer-blows catapulted him out of his saddle to fall under the driving hoofs of the Kid's mount, shattering his skull and putting out his lights forever.

Jimmy's next shot grooved the Kid's left chest, causing him to rethink his objective. The Kid jerked his reins to the side and pulled his horse's head around to head back into the melee around the cabin. He'd had enough of the rifle brigade.

Explosions were coming one on top of another. Billowing clouds of gunpowder and cordite hung over the area like groundfog on a winter morning. The screams of men hit hard and dying and those just wounded mingled to create a symphony of agony and despair.

Into this hell rode Smoke and his friends. Joey screamed his rebel yell at the top of his lungs—"Yee haw!"—striking fear into the hearts of men who knew it to be a call for a fight to the death.

Smoke answered with a yell of his own, and soon all five men charging the murderers and bandits were screaming and firing shotguns and pistols and rifles into the crowd as they closed ranks with them.

The mass of men broke and splintered as Smoke and Joey and Louis and Cal and Pearlie cut a swath of death through it with their blazing firepower and raw courage.

Smoke saw Horton and Max shooting at the cabin from horseback, while Gooden, Boots, and Art South were nearby on foot, their broncs lying dead at their feet, pierced by hundreds of horseshoe nails.

Smoke glanced at Louis and yelled, "Remember them?" and pointed at the group of men. Louis nodded, his eyes flashing. "Damn right," he said. Louis had been one of the men who rode up into the mountains to stand with Smoke against the bounty hunters in the Lee Slater fracas.

Louis bared his teeth in a wide grin. "Let's do it!" he

yelled, and rode hard and fast at the killers with Smoke at his side.

Horton and Max saw the two men coming, Colts blazing, and screamed in fear. "Oh Jesus," Horton shouted, "it's Jensen and that devil, Longmont." He whirled his horse and tried to run. A slug from Louis's Colt hit him between the shoulder blades, throwing him off his horse. It took him ten minutes to die, ten minutes of blazing pain.

Max, less a coward than Horton, turned his mount toward Smoke and Louis and charged them, firing his pistols with both hands. Smoke fired twice with the Colt in his right hand, missing both times. Then he triggered the 10-gauge Greener he held in his left hand. It slammed back, throwing Smoke's arm in the air, making him wonder momentarily if his wrist was broken.

The load of buckshot and nail heads met Max head on. The lead exploded his body into dozens of pieces, scattering blood and meat over a ten-square-yard area.

Smoke stuck the Greener in his saddle boot and pulled his left-hand Colt. He began to alternate, firing right, then left, then right again, as he continued his charge over Max's body toward Gooden, Boots, and Art South.

Gooden snap-shot at Louis and hit home, the slug tearing into the gambler's left thigh but missing the big artery there.

Louis returned the favor, punching a slug into Gooden's gut which doubled him over and knocked him to the ground. "Oh, no," he screamed, "not the stomach again!" He lay there, trying to keep his intestines in his abdomen, but they kept spilling out. Finally, Gooden gave up and lay back and died.

Art South fired at Louis and missed, but nailed his horse in the right shoulder, knocking Louis tumbling to the ground. He rolled and sprang to his feet, left hand pushing his wounded left leg to keep him upright.

Art South stepped closer to Louis and extended his hand, pointing his Colt between Louis's eyes. "Any last words, Longmont?" South asked, grinning.

"No," Louis said, and he pulled his derringer out from behind his belt and shot both .44 barrels into South's chest, blowing him backward to land at Boots's feet.

Boots swung his pistol toward the now unarmed and defenseless Louis, who merely stared unflinchingly back at the outlaw.

Boots's lips curled up in a snarl, until they disappeared into the hole Smoke blew in his face with his .44s. The bullets entered on either side of Boots's nose, blowing his cheekbones out the back of his head.

Smoke grabbed the reins of a riderless horse while Louis bent and picked up the Colt Boots had dropped. Smoke reached down and picked Louis up with one arm and swung him into the saddle.

"Thanks, partner," Louis shouted.

Smoke just smiled and rode off, looking for other prey.

Cal and Pearlie had emptied their guns and were reloading, trying to keep their mounts from shying while they punched out empty brass casings and stuffed in new ones.

The Silverado Kid galloped over to where Bill Denver and Slim Watkins were riding, firing up into the cabin. Bill Denver shot into the second story window, his slug hitting Monte Carson in the side of the head and taking out a chunk of his scalp as it knocked him unconscious and blew him back out of sight. Two of the punchers in the room rolled Monte over and began dressing his wound while a third picked up his rifle and took his place at the window.

The Kid shouted, "Denver, Watkins, look over there!"

He pointed toward Cal and Pearlie, off to the side of the fracas, surrounded by dead gunnies they had killed. "There's only those two young'uns between us and freedom. Let's dust the trail on outta here, boys," he cried.

Denver and Watkins nodded and wheeled their mounts to follow the Kid's lead. The three desperadoes spurred their broncs into a gallop, right at Cal and Pearlie.

Cal shouted, "Look out, Pearlie, here they come!"

With no time to reload his pistols, Cal dropped them and swung the Henry repeating rifle off his back and jerked the lever, firing from the hip without bothering to aim.

Pearlie holstered his still empty pistols and shucked his Greener 12-gauge with the cut-down barrel from his saddle boot. He eared back the hammers and let 'em down as Cal began to fire.

The Silverado Kid, scourge and killer of women and children, the man too tough for Tombstone, took three .44 caliber slugs from Cal's rifle, two in the chest and one in the left eye. The entire left side of him disappeared as he back-flipped over his horse's rump to land spread-eagled and dead in the dust.

Denver and Watkins got off four shots with their pistols. The first shot took Cal in the right hip, above the joint, and punched out his right flank, blowing him out of the saddle.

The next shot missed, but the third and fourth both hit Pearlie, one burning a groove along his neck, and the other skimming his belly, tearing a chunk of fat off but not hitting meat.

Pearlie gave a double grunt and doubled over, then straightened up and let both his hammers down, one after the other. Denver took a full load of .00-buckshot in the face, losing his head in the bargain, and Watkins right arm and right chest were disintegrated in a hail of hot lead from Pearlie's express gun.

Both men were dead before they hit the ground.

Pearlie jumped out of his saddle and sat cradling Cal's unconscious body in his arms while he reloaded his pistols. No one else was going to hurt his friend as long as he was alive to prevent it.

Jerry Jackson, train robber from Kansas, rode his horse at the cabin, screaming curse words at the top of his lungs, a blazing torch in one hand and Colt in the other.

Ben Tolson stepped out of his doorway and onto the porch, his shotgun blasting back at Jackson.

Jackson was blown off his mount at the same time his

.44 slug tore into Tolson's right chest, spinning him around and back through the door he gave his life to defend.

Joey, his pistols and both Winchester rifles empty, stood up in his stirrups, looking for Cal and Pearlie. He wanted to make sure they were all right.

He heard a yell from behind him and looked over his shoulder to see Colonel Waters riding at him, his sword held high above his head, blood streaming from a wound in his left shoulder.

"Wells, prepare to die, you bastard!" Waters screamed as he bore down on the ex-rebel.

Joey bared his teeth, let out his rebel yell again, and pulled his Arkansas Toothpick from its scabbard. He wheeled Red around and dug his spurs in, causing the big roan to rear and charge toward the Union man.

They passed, the sword flashing toward Joey's head. He ducked and parried with his long knife, deflecting Waters's blade, sending sparks flying in the darkness. Both horses were turned, and again raced toward each other. At the last minute, Joey nudged Red with his legs and the huge animal veered directly into Waters's smaller one, knocking both horse and rider to the ground.

Joey swung his leg over the saddle horn and bounded out of the saddle. He crouched, Arkansas Toothpick held waist-high in front of him and waited for Waters to get to his feet.

The Colonel stood, sleeving blood and sweat off his face. "You killed my men, every one, Wells, and now you are going to die."

Joey spit tobacco juice at Waters's feet. "Yore men, like you, Waters, were cowards who killed defenseless boys who'd given up their guns. They didn't deserve ta' live, an' neither do you."

Joey waved the blade back and forth. "Come an' taste my steel, coward!"

Waters lunged, his sword outstretched. Joey leaned to his right, taking the point of the sword in his left shoulder while striking underhanded at Waters.

Joey's blade drove into Waters's gut just under his ribs and angled upward to pierce the officer's heart. The two men, gladiators from a war long past, stood there chest to chest for a moment. Then light and hate faded from Waters's eyes and he fell dead before the last of The Missouri Volunteers.

Murdock saw they were losing the battle and shouted at Vasquez, "Emilio, let's get out of here!"

The two men, who had managed to stay on the periphery of the gunfight, wheeled their horses and galloped back toward the Lazy M. They were able to escape Smoke's trap only because of the heavy layer of smoke and dust in the air. By the time the men in the boulders saw them coming they were by and out of range of their shotguns.

The fracas lasted another twenty minutes before all of the gunnies were either dead or wounded enough to be out of commission.

It was full dark by now, and the punchers in the cabin lighted torches and joined with men from the trees and boulders and began to gather their wounded and dead. The injured who worked for Smoke were brought into the cabin and were attended to by Andre and the others. Their gunshot wounds were cleaned and dressed and they were given hot soup and coffee—those in pain, whiskey.

Smoke bent over Monte Carson, checking his bandages to make sure they were tight. Carson drifted in and out of consciousness, but Smoke was sure he would survive.

Andre fussed over Louis's leg wound, cleaning and re-cleaning it until finally Louis said, "Just put a dressing on it, Andre. There're others here who need you more than I do."

Smoke glanced at Louis, a worried look on his face. "Have you seen Cal or Pearlie or Joey, Louis?"

Louis looked up quickly, "Aren't they here?"

Smoke shook his head. "No."

Louis struggled to his feet, using a rifle as a cane. "Let's go. They may be lying out there wounded." He glanced at Smoke, naked fear in his eyes. "Or worse."

The two men walked among the dead and dying outlaws, ignoring cries for help and mercy as they looked for their friends. The outlaws deserved no mercy. They had taken money to kill others, and would now have to face the consequences of their actions. A harsh judgment, but a just one.

Finally, Smoke spied the horse Pearlie had been riding, standing over near a small creek that ran off to the side of the cabin. "Over here," he called to Louis and ran toward the animal, praying he would find the young man alive.

He stopped short at what he saw. Joey, his left shoulder wrapped in his bloodstained shirt, was trying to dress Pearlie's neck and stomach wounds, but Pearlie wouldn't let go of Cal to give him access. The young cowboy had one hand holding his wadded-up shirt against a hole in Cal's flank to stop the bleeding, while he held his Colt in the other, hammer back, protecting his young friend from anyone else who might try to harm him.

Smoke heard Joey say, "Come on, Pearlie, the fight's over. Let me take care of where ya' got shot. Then we kin git Cal over to the cabin fer treatment."

Pearlie shook his head. "I'm not movin' from here 'til I see Smoke. I promised him I was gonna watch over Cal, and I aim to do just that!"

Smoke chuckled as Louis hobbled up beside him. "Would you look at that, Louis. Like a mother hen with her chick."

Louis grinned. "If I ever find a woman who'll take care of me like that, I'll give up gambling and settle down."

"Pearlie, you've done a good job," Smoke said as he knelt by Cal. "Now let Joey fix you up while I take Cal to the cabin so Andre can patch his wounds."

Pearlie lifted fatigue-ridden eyes to stare at Smoke. "Smoke, you got him?"

Smoke lifted Cal in his arms. "Yes, Pearlie, I've got him."

Pearlie mumbled, "Good." Then he let his pistol fall to the dirt and passed out. . . .*

* * *

Honor of the Mountain Man

Al Martine shook his head as Pearlie finished recounting the events of that night two years ago. "I can see *es muy peligroso*—very dangerous—to ride with you, Pearlie. From what I hear, every time Cal does so he ends up shot."

"It's like I said, Al," Pearlie said, watching Cal as his cheeks burned red, "that boy draws lead like honey draws flies."

21

Lazarus Cain looked up as Joey Wells walked through the batwings of the Dog Hole Saloon in Fontana. When Joey walked straight to a table across the room and sat down by himself without so much as looking at Lazarus or saying hello, the bandits' leader leaned over to speak in a low tone to Blackie Jackson.

"Blackie, what do you think of Wells? Can he be trusted?"

The ex-blacksmith stared at Joey for a moment before answering. "I don't know, boss. He's a strange one, all right. Don't never enter into no conversation with the boys, nor join in with the whores in the back room." He shook his head. "I just don't have any clear idea of what's goin' on in his head most of the time."

Lazarus began to talk in the stilted manner he always used when quoting the Bible. "But let him ask in faith, with no doubting, for he who doubts is like a wave of the sea driven and tossed by the wind. If he is a double-minded man, unstable in all his ways, as a flower in the field he will pass away."

Blackie looked at Lazarus, his eyebrows raised. "What's that mean, boss?"

"That is from the Epistle of James, Blackie, an' it means if Joey is playin' both ends against the middle I'll cut him down like a weed."

"You got any reason to suspect he's gonna go agin us?"

"No . . . but then again, he ain't exactly acted over-joyed to be with us, either. I want you to keep a close eye on Wells, Blackie, an' let me know if he does anything outta line."

"Sure thing, boss. How about I get one of the boys to watch his room at night, an' make sure he don't leave without sayin' good-bye or nothin'?"

"That'll be just fine, Blackie."

Lazarus got to his feet and walked over to Joey's table, where he sat eating scrambled eggs and *chorizo*.

"Mornin', Joey."

Joey looked up and nodded, but continued to chew his food without speaking.

Lazarus pulled out a chair and sat down. "Some of the boys been complainin', Joey. They say you ain't actin' very friendly. Matter of fact, they say you been outright rude."

Joey cut his eyes at Lazarus, the cold deadliness of them making the hair on the back of the preacher's neck stand up. Since his days in the Civil War, Lazarus had never met a man who could make him taste the bitter flavor of fear, until Wells.

"Get to the point, Lazarus. I know you don't give a damn what the boys think or say," Joey growled around a mouthful of sausage and eggs.

"I've been kind'a wonderin' myself, Joey, if you're committed to this little enterprise I got planned, or if you're having second thoughts about it."

Joey swallowed and pushed his plate away, pulled out his Arkansas Toothpick, and shaved a sliver of wood off the edge of the table. He holstered his knife and used the piece of wood to pick bits of meat from between his teeth.

"Lazarus, if'n I decide not to go along with you on your plan, I'll pack my gear an' leave. I certainly won't hang around here, enjoyin' the . . . delightful company you've gathered together in this garden spot of a town."

Lazarus gave a short laugh at the wry tone of Joey's

voice. "They do leave something to be desired in a conversation, don't they?" he asked.

"Only if'n you want to talk 'bout somethin' other than whiskey, women, or who's killed the most men in their lives. I quit talkin' to 'em when the conversation always seemed to get around to who's fastest on the draw."

"Oh?"

"Yeah. I tried to tell the first couple'a men who brought it up that it ain't who's fastest that counts, it's who's left on his feet when the smoke clears. Any galoot can practice again' tin cans 'til he's fast as greased lightnin'. But when you're standing across from a man whose eyes tell you he's gonna kill you, and your bowels are turning to liquid and gurglin' in your stomach, it do make a difference in your perspective on the matter of gunfightin'."

Lazarus threw back his head and laughed out loud. "Joey, I couldn't've said it better myself. Speed with a gun is only one part of winning a duel. The willingness to go ahead, knowin' you're gonna take some lead an' maybe die, but knowin' also you're gonna drop that son of a bitch facin' you, is more important than speed."

Joey reached across and poured a couple of fingers of whiskey into his glass. He held up the glass and looked into the liquid, speaking as if to himself. "Hell, facin' death is easy, Lazarus. It's facin' life that's hard." As he finished speaking, he drank his glass empty and then stood up.

"If'n you're through askin' me questions, I'm gonna go take a walk."

"Sure, Joey. Go right ahead," Lazarus said, a wide smile on his face. "Go anywhere you want."

Joey glanced back at him with a smirk as he turned to leave. "I wasn't askin' your permission, Cain, I was just lettin' you know."

Lazarus's face turned a bright red as Joey sauntered out of the room. Damn, but that man could be infuriatingly smug. *After all this is over,* Lazarus promised himself, *I'll wipe that smart alec expression off his face for good.*

As Joey strolled down the rotting boardwalks of Fontana, he noticed out of the corner of his eye that Blackie Jackson walked out of the batwings of the Dog Hole just after he did.

He decided to turn down a side street and see if the man was following him or if it was just a coincidence that he'd left at the same time.

After covering fifty yards, Joey stopped in front of an old storefront that still had a couple of panes of glass in the windows. He stood there, pretending to look inside, and watched the reflection in the glass.

Sure enough, he saw Blackie peek around the corner at the end of the street, evidently interested in just where Joey was going and what he was going to do.

Damn, Joey thought, *Cain must be suspicious to have sicced his trained dog on me like this. I'm gonna have to be careful when I go to meet Pearlie, that is if Cain ever lets it slip when he's planning on having his little party out at Smoke's place. It just won't do to have him dog my steps, so I'll just have to discourage his curiosity a mite.*

Joey put his hands in his pockets and continued to stroll the streets, as if he had nothing on his mind other than passing the time of day with a little exercise.

Eventually he came to the livery stable and entered. He walked over to where Red was stabled and took a bucket of oats and poured a generous helping into the bucket hung on a nail in front of his mount. Better let the big stud stock up on some grain, 'cause he was going to need all the stamina he could muster if push came to shove and Joey had to travel fast and far. Grass and hay were okay for general purposes with a horse, but nothing improved their bottom like grain, and plenty of it.

22

Smoke came out on the porch when he heard the sound of the buckboard coming up the road to the cabin. He was surprised, and delighted to see the two Mexicans riding with Pearlie and Cal.

As they climbed down, he walked over and held out his hand. *"Compadres!"* he called. *"¡Buenos días!"*

"Señor Smoke," Al said as he took Smoke's hand. "Your Spanish has improved since our last meeting."

Smoke laughed. "Well, I haven't had much occasion to use it since you and your partner headed south, *amigo.*"

"It has been most boring in Chihuahua, without you to liven up the lives of the occupants of our little town," Louis said, shaking Smoke's hand with both of his.

"I take it you two are the surprise Joey said he'd arranged for me?"

"Sí. Señor Joey said you might need some help, so we came as fast as the Union Pacific could bring us," Al said.

Sally stepped out on the porch and waved. "Hello, men," she said.

Both men bowed and took off their hats. *"Buenos días, Señora* Sally," they said in unison.

"I figure you've already eaten, but I've got some hot apple pie on the stove, if you're interested."

Al immediately turned and put his hand up against Pearlie's chest. "Only if someone will restrain this man whose stomach is larger than the Grand Canyon. Otherwise, there will not be enough left for us to eat," Al teased.

"We'll put Pearlie at the end of the line," Smoke said.

"I think I should get first shot at that pie," Cal said, "since the doctor tole me I need to keep my strength up by eatin' as much as possible."

As he walked rapidly toward the cabin, Smoke laughed. "Seems to me you're pretty spry for someone who's supposed to be recovering from a gunshot wound."

He called back over his shoulder as he disappeared into the house, "Miss Sally's food has done wonders for my healin'."

Later, Al leaned back in his chair and eyed the empty pie tin on the table in front of the cowboys. "That was most wonderful, *Señora* Sally. I have not had such food in many months."

Sally brought the pot from the stove and refilled coffee cups all around, except for Cal, who was drinking fresh cow's milk.

"I'm glad you enjoyed it. Since you're going to be staying a while, I'll cook up some more, just in case you get hungry later."

Smoke took his cup and walked out onto the porch so he could smoke a cigarette. As he built one and lighted it, he said, "You boys know what you're getting into here?"

Both men nodded. "*Sí*," said Louis. "Pearlie told us about the *bandido*, Cain, and his plans to attack your *rancho*."

"Are you aware of how much he's got us outnumbered?"

Al Martine shrugged. "Numbers, they do not matter so much, Smoke, as the men who make up the fight."

"*Sí*," Louis agreed. "It is what is inside a man, here," he said, pointing to his chest, "not how many guns he has in his hands."

Smoke nodded. "You're right. And with this group, I think Cain may have bitten off more than he can chew."

Pearlie, hearing the sound of hoofbeats in the distance,

stood up and shaded his eyes with his hand as he peered out over the Sugarloaf.

"Company comin', Smoke," he said, resting his hand on the butt of his pistol.

Immediately the men on the porch got out of their chairs and drew guns, wondering if somehow Cain and his men were already coming.

After a moment, Pearlie relaxed. "You won't believe this, Smoke. It looks like Louis Longmont is bringin' us more reinforcements."

Sure enough, within minutes four riders came into view. Louis Longmont, accompanied by George Hampton, Johnny North, and Monte Carson rode toward the cabin.

They dismounted and tied their horses to the hitching rail nearby and walked to the porch.

Smoke shook his head, a tight smile on his face. "What have we here?" he asked as Longmont approached.

"Hello, Smoke, boys," he said.

"What's going on, Louis?"

"After talking with Pearlie and Al and Louis, I got to thinking that perhaps you might have need of some more firepower, Smoke. So, I spoke to Monte, and then we rode out to North's place to see if he'd be willing to take a hand in this little poker game."

He spread his hands wide. "As you can see, you now have a few more guns available when Cain decides to make his move."

"Sally," Smoke called, "better put another pot on the stove. It seems there are some more men here who have more loyalty than brains."

Pearlie went into the cabin and brought out four additional chairs and everyone sat down. Soon Sally brought cups and coffee for their guests.

"How do you want to play this, Smoke?" Johnny North asked. "You think it'd be better to set up an ambush here at the Sugarloaf, or plan on makin' our play somewheres else?"

Smoke glanced around at the terrain surrounding the cabin, slowly shaking his head. "If at all possible, if we have enough time, I don't think we ought to let them get this far. The area around the cabin is too difficult to defend. Too many trees and boulders that would give the attackers cover."

Monte Carson nodded in agreement. "You're right, Smoke. If they get this far, I don't know if eight of us, nine counting Joey, could stand 'em off without taking the chance of losing the cabin to fire or dynamite."

"Our best chance, when faced with as many men as Cain has riding for him, is to set up an ambush somewhere where we have the advantage of good cover or high ground," Louis Longmont said, pulling a cigar out of his pocket and firing it up.

Smoke agreed. "A lot will depend on how much time we have to prepare. Pearlie's supposed to meet with Joey tonight to see if he's heard anything definite about the time Cain plans to attack."

"Cicero, when writing about the campaigns of the Roman army, made mention of the fact that the best defense is a good offense," Longmont said. "We had good luck once before when faced with a similar situation by attacking the gunmen while they were still in Fontana."

"That is *un bueno* plan, *Señor* Longmont," Al Martine said. "That way, the *bandidos* will not be ready for the fight, which will give us an advantage."

"It'll also help keep the ranch safe. No tellin' how many head of cattle an' fences and things you'll lose if the battle takes place on the Sugarloaf," Johnny North added.

Smoke looked at Monte Carson. "We had a few more men last time we took on Fontana. Do you think nine of us is enough to do the deed, Monte?"

Monte shrugged. "Better nine against fifty when they're not expectin' us an' fightin' in a town where there's plenty of cover, than tryin' to outfight 'em on horseback on the plains."

"Yeah, Smoke," Cal added. "If'n we can do it late at night, an' catch 'em whilst they're all asleep, they're liable to be shootin' each other in all the confusion, while we'll know where each other is."

"What do you mean *we*, Cal?" Pearlie asked. "You ain't in no shape for another fracas just yet."

Cal's eyes narrowed and his lips grew tight. "Just try an' stop me, Pearlie. I ain't about to miss a chance to get back at those men who shot me."

"Here's what I propose," Smoke said. "There's a hill overlooking Fontana, just to the south. I'll sneak up there and make a sketch of the town. When Pearlie meets with Joey, we'll have him try to find out where most of the gang is bunking down. Then we'll make a plan of attack to make the most out of the element of surprise."

Louis Longmont nodded. "With any luck, we'll be able to take out a significant portion of the gang with our initial attack, which will help even out the odds quite a bit."

"What if Pearlie is unable to talk to Joey?" Louis Carbone asked. "Perhaps Al an' me might go into the town to find out what you want to know."

Smoke wagged his head. "No, Louis, but thanks. That'd be much too dangerous. I suspect the nearer Cain gets to the attack the more suspicious of strangers he'll be, and we can't afford to lose your guns before the battle. We'll just have to hope Pearlie can meet with Joey and find out where the gang is staying in the town and the date of the attack."

23

That night, Pearlie arrived at the place where he was supposed to meet with Joey and built a small fire. He made a pot of coffee and huddled there in the chilly blackness, waiting.

In Fontana, Joey eased out of his bed and began to slip his trousers on. As he glanced out of a window, he noticed a flare of light across the street from the hotel, followed by an intermittent glowing red spot.

Damn, he thought, *Cain has somebody watching the hotel. Probably makin' sure I don't go anywhere.*

He sat on the edge of his bed and thought for a few minutes. He really didn't have any news for Smoke, so risking his place with the outlaws just to have a meeting was foolish. He finally decided to go back to sleep and give it one more day trying to find out the date of the attack.

By five o'clock in the morning, Pearlie gave up any hope of seeing Joey. He kicked dirt over the smoldering coals of his fire and climbed wearily on Cold and began the long ride back to the Sugarloaf, hoping nothing had happened to his friend.

* * *

At breakfast the next morning Joey decided to force the issue with Lazarus. He finished his eggs and sausage, wiped his mouth on his sleeve, and stood up from the table.

Sauntering over to where Lazarus was sitting at his corner table with Blackie Jackson and Curly Joe Ventrillo, Joey flipped a twenty dollar gold piece onto the middle of the table.

Lazarus looked up, surprised. "What's that for, Joey?"

"Fer my room an' board the past week. I figger that'll 'bout cover it."

"What do you mean?"

"I'm leavin'. I'm bored sittin' 'round here doin' nothin' all day, with no prospects of any action in the near future."

"I told you, it won't be long now. Settle down and be patient," Lazarus said.

Joey leaned forward, his hands on the table. "That ain't all of it, Cain. I also ain't used to bein' treated like a hired hand, not bein' told what's goin' on an' expected to sit around waitin' fer my orders. I don't much like it."

Blackie Jackson glared at Joey. "Who cares what you like an' don't like, Wells? You'll wait for Mr. Cain's orders an' do like he says, just like everbody else."

Joey slowly turned his head to stare into Jackson's eyes, his gaze deadly as a rattler's just before it strikes.

"I don't recall addressin' your boy, Cain. But you better tell him 'fore he antes up in this hand, he'd best have enough chips to back up his big mouth."

As he finished talking, Joey straightened up and loosed the hammer thong on his Colt. He turned to face Jackson, his hands hanging limp at his sides, his eyes flat and cold.

"You want to try an' give me some more orders, boy?" he asked Jackson.

Blackie's face blanched white, and sweat began to bead on his forehead in spite of the coolness of the morning. He licked suddenly dry lips and glanced at Cain, his eyes begging for help.

The saloon became dead quiet as the men in it noticed what was happening. They all watched, wanting to see if Wells's deadly reputation was accurate.

Finally, Lazarus brought an end to it. "Men," he said, "take it easy. There's no need for this. Sit down, Joey, an' I'll tell you what you want to know."

Joey relaxed, the stiffness going out of his muscles and a small grin turning up the corners of his mouth. He turned away from Blackie, showing his contempt for the man in his manner.

"So, what the hell's goin' on? Are we gonna go after Smoke Jensen, or sit here until winter comes?"

Lazarus leaned forward and spoke in a low voice, so none of the others in the room could hear. "Give me two more days, Joey. I'm expecting the last wagonload of supplies in today or tomorrow. It's got the gunpowder for my cannons, an' enough ammunition to start our own war."

"And after we kill Jensen, what are your plans then?"

"I told you. We'll make a run on Big Rock an' shoot it to hell. Even if we don't destroy the town, we'll cause so much confusion no one will even notice that Jensen's ranch has been taken over. By the time anyone gets on to us, we'll all be rich from the gold we take out of his land."

Joey smiled coldly. "I must say, I do like the sound of that word rich, Cain." He reached over and picked up his twenty dollar gold piece and put it in his pocket. "I'll stick for two more days."

Lazarus nodded. "Good, Joey. You won't regret it."

Two of Cain's men riding sentry duty crested a small hill south of town. Mario Lopez, a man on the run from the Federales in Mexico for murder, rape, and cattle theft, noticed a glint of sun on metal just off to the left.

"Hey, Johnny, you see that?" he asked.

His riding partner, Johnny Crow, a half-breed Mescalero Apache, glanced over at him. Johnny's eyes were red-rimmed and swollen, showing he'd had a rough night the night before—as he did most nights, drinking enough whiskey for any two men.

"No, what'd you see?"

"Sunlight reflectin' off metal . . . right over there."

"It's probably nothin'," the Indian mumbled, wondering if his head was going to explode. He figured he must've gotten some bad whiskey, cause he'd never had a hangover like this one before.

"Let's go see, *muchacho*," Mario said as he jerked his horse's head around and spurred it forward.

"Damn," Johnny said, fearing he was going to puke if he got his horse into a gallop.

As they crested the ridge, Mario saw something he couldn't understand. A tall man wearing buckskins was standing before a wooden framework, drawing on a large sheet of paper. He rode over to him, Johnny following.

"Hey mister, what you doin'?" Mario asked, his hand resting on the butt of his pistol.

Smoke Jensen looked up, showing no apparent concern at being seen. "Why, I'm drawing a sketch of Fontana."

"You what?" Mario asked again, not having any idea what a sketch was.

"Drawing a picture of Fontana," Smoke repeated. "Would you like to see it?"

"Why you do that?"

Smoke put his charcoal pencil down and turned to face the two men on horseback, a smile on his lips. "Because, there's a bunch of lowlifes staying in the town, and some friends of mine and me are going to ride in there soon and kill them."

Mario's eyes widened and he jerked at his pistol. Before he got his gun halfway out of his holster, Smoke's hand appeared in front of him, filled with iron. The Colt barked once, spitting a slug that took Mario full in the chest, shattering his breastbone and tearing a hole the size of a man's fist in his heart. He was blown backward off his horse, dead before he hit the dirt.

Having a couple of extra seconds, Johnny managed to

get his gun clear of its holster, but never managed to raise the barrel before Smoke's second shot hit him in the forehead. The back of his head exploded, filling his hat with pieces of bone and brain as he tumbled off his horse to land facedown on the ground.

"That's two we won't have to worry about when we come calling," Smoke mumbled to himself.

Whistling a low tune, he gathered up his easel and drawing and packed them on Joker. After he was packed and ready to leave, he arranged the two bodies facing each other about three feet apart. He took a deck of cards from his saddlebag and scattered it between the two men, along with the few dollars he found in their pockets.

Joey was at the bar having a beer when one of the outlaws burst through the batwings. It was Boots Hemphill, so called because he wore expensive, knee-high leather boots which he spent hours each day keeping shiny.

"Boss . . . Mr. Cain . . . it's Johnny an' Mario! I found 'em dead off to the south."

Lazarus got quickly to his feet, motioning Blackie and Curly Joe to follow him as he went to the door.

"Mind if'n I tag along?" Joey asked, curious about what was happening.

"Suit yourself," Lazarus growled.

It took them about thirty minutes to find the bodies, laid out as Smoke had left them.

Lazarus got down off his horse and walked over to stand before them.

"It appears the fools were playing poker, an' one or the other got angry," he said, shaking his head.

Joey looked at the bodies and noticed something, but he kept his mouth shut. He knew it hadn't happened as Lazarus figured. The man named Mario was holding his pistol all right, but the hammer was still eared back. If he'd shot the half-breed, his gun wouldn't be cocked.

Joey had to turn his head to hide his smile. He recognized Smoke Jensen's handiwork, two bullets perfectly placed, two dead men who probably hadn't even gotten off a shot. He hoped Cain wouldn't think to check their pistols to see if they'd been fired.

Lazarus didn't. The men were low on his list of assets, so he just got on his horse and started to ride off.

"What about the bodies, Mr. Cain?" Boots asked.

"Take what you want, an' leave 'em for the buzzards an' wolves. Serves the bastards right for playin' cards while they were supposed to be on guard duty."

That evening, just after supper, Joey drank a glass of whiskey, then gave a wide yawn and started to walk out of the saloon.

Lazarus intercepted him just outside the batwings. "Where you goin', Joey?" he asked.

"Over to the hotel. It's been a long day. I think I'll turn in early tonight."

"Yeah, you do that. We got a big day tomorrow if that shipment gets here."

Joey nodded and touched the brim of his hat as he walked to his room.

Lazarus spoke over his shoulder to Blackie. "Have one of the boys watch him. I still got a funny feelin' about Mr. Joey Wells."

Joey gathered his few possessions together into his saddlebags, threw them over his shoulder, and slipped from his hotel room. Trying to stay close to buildings in shadows and out of the moonlight, he made his way to the livery stable.

He put a saddle on Red and cinched it down tight, flipped the saddlebags behind the saddle, and began to lead the big stud toward the door.

The sound of a pistol hammer being eared back stopped him in his tracks.

"Just where do you think you're goin', Wells?" came a voice from out of the darkness.

"I thought I'd take a little ride in the moonlight," Joey answered, his voice cool though his heart was racing.

Boots Hemphill walked out into the meager light streaming through a nearby window. "Mr. Cain told me to keep an eye on you. I guess it's a good thing he did."

Joey's eyes fell to the Colt Hemphill was holding in his right hand.

"Come on, let's go see what he has to say about your little moonlight ride," Hemphill said sarcastically.

"All right," Joey said. "Just let me get my saddlebags."

He turned and made to reach for the bags, but let his hand fall to his waist and grab the handle of his Arkansas Toothpick.

As he pulled the saddlebags off Red, he made a quick backhand motion. The knife turned over one and a half times before it imbedded itself in Boots's throat.

He dropped his pistol and grasped the knife's handle, gurgling and choking on his own blood.

Falling to his knees, he finally managed to get the knife free, only to watch as his blood pumped out three feet in front of him from a severed carotid artery. He cast pleading eyes up at Joey for a few seconds, then he fell facedown in a pool of his own blood, dead.

Joey took his Arkansas Toothpick from the dead hands and wiped it on Boots's shirt, then slipped it back in his scabbard.

Figuring he might need the edge of a little getaway time, Joey bent over and grabbed Boots under the armpits and dragged him to a pile of hay in the corner of the livery. He used a pitchfork to dig a deep hole in the hay and rolled the dead man into it, covering him with a thick layer of straw.

Afterward, he used his boot to spread dirt over the thick pool of blood where the body had fallen, covering up all traces of the fight.

He led Red out the door of the livery and closed it behind him. As he climbed in the saddle, Joey sighed, thinking about the man he'd just killed. "A man should always know his own limitations," he whispered, walking his horse down the street and out of town.

Once clear of the town, he leaned forward in the saddle and urged the stud on, racing for the Sugarloaf to tell Smoke of the impending attack the next day.

He hoped Al and Louis had made it. They were going to need all the guns they could find to hold off Cain and his gang.

24

Cal had insisted on riding with Pearlie out to where he was supposed to meet Joey, vowing that if their old friend didn't show up tonight he was going to ride into Fontana to make sure he was all right.

Pearlie just shook his head. "Ya cain't do that, boy. You wouldn't make it ten yards inside the town limits 'fore you'd be blown clear outta your saddle."

"I know, but that's what I want'a do."

Pearlie reined his horse to a stop next to the boulder. "Here, use up some of that energy makin' us a fire. It's gonna get plumb cold tonight 'fore long."

After Cal had the fire going and a pot of coffee cooking next to it, he settled down on his ground blanket and built himself a cigarette. Lighting it off a burning piece of wood, he squinted through the smoke at Pearlie sitting across from him.

"You remember the story Al and Louis told us 'bout how they met Smoke?"

Pearlie grinned. "Sure. It was just after Lee Slater an' his gang shot up Big Rock, an' some of the bullets hit Miss Sally."

Cal nodded, "Yeah, they signed on to fight with Slater agin' Smoke an' his friends."

"That's when they had that big shootout at the town of Rio," Pearlie said. Leaning back against his saddle, his hands behind his head, he stared at the stars and thought about what it must have been like, and how much the next few days were going to be like it when they attacked Lazarus Cain in Fontana.

Cal handed him a cup of coffee and squatted next to him, his forearms on his thighs. "Al said Smoke had killed just about all the outlaws, an' Miss Sally put the final bullet in Lee Slater, when Al decided to make his move. . . ."

A man stepped out of the shadows. Lee Slater. His hands were wrapped around the butts of Colts, as were Smoke's hands. "I'm gonna kill you, Jensen!" he screamed.

A rifle barked, the slug striking Lee in the middle of his back and exiting out the front. The outlaw gang leader lay dead on the hot dusty street.

Sally Jensen stepped back into Louis's gambling hall and jacked another round into her carbine.

Smoke smiled at her and walked on down the boardwalk.

"Looking for me, *amigo?*" Al Martine spoke from the shadows of a doorway. His guns were in leather.

"Not really. Ride on, Al."

"Why would you make such an offer to me? I am an outlaw, a killer. I hunted you in the mountains."

"You have a family, Al?"

"*Sí.* A father and mother, brothers and sister, all down in Mexico."

"Why don't you go pay them a visit? Hang up your guns for a time?"

The Mexican smiled and finished rolling a cigarette. He lit it and held it to Smoke's lips.

"Thanks, Al."

"Thank you, Smoke. I shall be in Chihuahua. If you ever need me, send word, everybody knows where to find me. I will come very quickly."

"I might do that."

"*Adiós, compadre.*" Al stepped off the boardwalk and was gone.

Smoke finished the cigarette, grateful for the lift the tobacco gave him. His eyes never stopped moving, scanning the buildings, the alleyways, the street.

He caught movement on the second floor of the saloon, the hotel part. Sunlight off a rifle barrel. He lifted a .44 and triggered off two fast rounds. The rifle dropped to the awning, a man following it out. Zack fell through the awning and crashed to the boardwalk. He did not move.

Rich Coleman and Frankie stepped out of the saloon, throwing lead, and Smoke dived for the protection of a water trough.

"I got him!" Frankie yelled.

Smoke rose to one knee and changed Frankie's whole outlook on life—what little remained of it.

Rich turned to run back into the saloon and Smoke fired, the slug hitting him in the shoulder and knocking him through the batwings. He got to his boots and staggered back out, lifting a .45 and drilling a hole in the water trough as he screamed curses at Smoke.

Smoke finished it with one shot. Rich staggered forward, grabbing anything he could for support. He died with his arms around an awning post.

The thunder of hooves cut the afternoon air. Sheriff Silva and a huge posse rode up in a cloud of dust.

"That's it, Smoke," the sheriff announced. "It's over. You're a free man, and all these other yahoos are gonna be behind bars."

"Suits me," Smoke said, and holstered his guns.

Luttie Charles stepped out of the saloon, a gun in each hand, and shot the sheriff out of the saddle. The possemen filled Luttie so full of lead the undertaker had to hire another man to help tote the casket.

"Dammit!" Sheriff Silva said, getting to his boots. "I been shot twice in my life, and both times in the same damn arm!"

"No, it ain't over!" The scream came from up the street.

Everybody looked. Pecos stood there, his hands over the butts of his fancy engraved .45s.

"Oh, crap!" Smoke said.

"Don't do it, kid!" Carbone called from the boardwalk. "It's over. He'll kill you, boy."

"Hell with you, Carbone, you greasy son of a bitch!" Pecos yelled.

Carbone stiffened. Cut his eyes to Smoke.

"Man sure shouldn't have to take a cut like that, Carbone," Smoke told him.

Carbone stepped out into the street, his big silver spurs jingling. "Kid, you can insult me all day. But you cannot insult my mother."

Pecos laughed and told him what he thought about Carbone's sister, too.

Carbone shot him before the kid could even clear leather. The Pecos Kid died in the dusty streets of a town that would be gone in ten years. He was buried in an unmarked grave.

"If you hurry, Carbone," Smoke called, "I think you could catch up with Martine. Me and him smoked a cigarette together a few minutes ago, and he told me he was going back to Chihuahua to visit his folks."

Carbone grinned and saluted Smoke. A minute later he was riding out of town, heading south. . . .*

Cal finished retelling the story both he and Pearlie had heard several times, and Pearlie grinned.

"I can see why they both came so fast when Joey wired them Smoke needed help," Pearlie said. "He let them live when most men would have shot 'em down or at least put 'em in jail."

Cal nodded. "That's why Smoke has so many good friends. He don't judge a man as bad by his reputation, only by how he is to Smoke. If'n someone don't do him no harm, then Smoke'd just as soon let 'em be."

Code of the Mountain Man

Their conversation was interrupted by the sound of hoofbeats coming toward them at a fast clip.

Pearlie jumped to his feet, his gun in his hand. "Sounds like somebody's comin' in a hurry. We better be ready for trouble, Cal."

Cal pulled his pistol and the men went to peer around the boulder, trying to make out who was approaching in the darkness.

"Yo, the camp," called a voice they recognized as belonging to Joey.

Pearlie and Cal holstered their weapons. "Come on in, Joey," Pearlie called.

He walked over to the fire and poured a fresh cup of coffee and handed it to Joey as he jumped down off Red.

"Thanks," Joey said, rolling the cup between his palms to warm them. "It's gettin' a mite chilly out there on the plain 'tween town an' here."

Cal nodded. "That's 'cause there's nothin' to break the wind comin' down off'n the peaks of the mountains over yonder."

Pearlie, impatient to find out what Joey knew, interrupted. "Did you learn when Cain's plannin' on attackin' the Sugarloaf?"

Joey grinned a sly grin. "Yeah. Tomorrow or the next day. He's waitin' fer a wagonload of dynamite an' gunpowder an' ammunition to come in. Then he's gonna make his play."

"That don't give us much time," Cal said.

"You got that right, boy," Joey answered.

"You headed back to Fontana?" Pearlie asked.

Joey wagged his head. "Nope. Done burnt my bridges there, boys. Cain must'a suspected somethin', 'cause he had me followed to make sure I didn't leave town."

"How'd you get away?" Cal asked.

Joey patted his Arkansas Toothpick. "I just showed the man my blade, up close like, an' then I got on Red an' rode on out."

"Do you need to rest, or can we head for the Sugarloaf now?" Pearlie asked.

Joey emptied his coffee cup. "Naw, I'm all right. Red is easy-gaited. Ridin' him's like sittin' on a porch in a rockin' chair. Let's shag our mounts, boys. We're burnin' time, an' we ain't exactly got a surplus of it to waste."

As Pearlie and Cal saddled their horses, Cal looked over his shoulder and said, "By the way, Al Martine and Louis Carbone arrived the other day."

Joey smiled. "Good. They once said if Smoke ever needed 'em they'd come runnin', but you never know if someone will really do it or not 'til you ask 'em."

"I don't think they thought twice about it," Pearlie said. "From the way they talked, they got on a train the same day they got your wire."

"It'll be good to see 'em again," Joey said. "Now, let's quit jawin' an' ride!"

25

Lazarus Cain was enjoying his breakfast in the Dog Hole Saloon until Blackie Jackson approached his table.

"I can tell by the look on your face you got bad news for me," Lazarus said, spearing another piece of sausage and shoving it into his mouth.

"That's right, boss. I just got back from the hotel. Wells's room is empty. He must've cleared out during the night."

"What about Boots Hemphill? He was supposed to be watching Joey. Where is he?"

Before Jackson could answer, Lazarus pointed a finger at him. "If the bastard fell asleep and let Joey walk out of town, I'll crucify him."

Jackson shook his head. "Hemphill's missin' too, Lazarus. I can't find hide nor hair of him anywhere."

Lazarus washed down his food with a deep drink of coffee, then wiped his mouth with the back of his sleeve. He got to his feet, pulled out his Colt, and banged on the table with its butt until he had everyone's attention in the saloon.

"Listen up, everybody. I want all of you to comb the town. Boots Hemphill is missing, and so is Joey Wells. I don't have to tell you how much harder our job is gonna be if somebody tips Jensen off that we're comin' after him. Now, get lookin'!"

He glanced up at Jackson. "Blackie, did you look in Hemphill's hotel room?"

"Yep. All his clothes an' saddlebags an' gear is still there. If he left followin' Wells, or with him, he left all his belongings behind."

Lazarus rubbed his beard stubble for a minute, thinking. "That's an idea. I want you to go check out the livery, see if Hemphill's horse is still there. Seems there are only three possibilities of what happened."

"What're those, boss?"

"If Hemphill's horse is gone it means *he's* gone, either as Wells's partner, or followin' him like I asked. If Hemphill's horse is still there, then he's in town someplace, an' we need to find him and ask why he didn't stop Wells from leavin'."

"Yes sir."

After Blackie left, heading for the livery, Lazarus threw his coffee cup across the room in frustration. Nothing, absolutely nothing, was going right on this job. First, the wagon with the extra dynamite and ammunition was late in arriving, and now one of his best men had disappeared—either to warn Jensen, or just because he got impatient and wanted to be elsewhere. Lazarus knew it was crucial to his plans to find out why Joey had left. It would make a big difference in how he approached Jensen's ranch if he knew they were coming.

He walked over to the bar and poured himself a tall whiskey. To hell with coffee. The way things were going he needed something more substantial in his gut.

Blackie was back in less than an hour, the scowl on his face showing Lazarus the news wasn't going to be good.

"Well, is Hemphill's horse in the stable?"

"Yeah, an' so is Boots."

"What do you mean, so is Boots? Why didn't you bring him with you?"

"'Cause I didn't want to drag him the whole way over here, that's why."

"You mean he's dead?"

"Deader than the cow that made his boots."

"How?"

"Looks like he took a knife, a big knife, in the throat. He was hid in the hay an' I'd never of found him 'cept the ground was muddy from all the blood he spilt."

"Damn!" Lazarus spit, slamming his hand palm down on the bar. "That means he must've caught Joey trying to leave, an' Joey killed him."

Blackie nodded. "Most likely the way it went down, all right."

Lazarus cut his eyes to Blackie. "If Joey wanted to leave bad enough to kill to get out quietly, he must be plannin' to tell Jensen what's goin' on."

"I'd bet my hoss on it."

"Call the men together. We've got to get movin' before Jensen has time to plan a defense against us. Even if Joey warns him this mornin' it'll take him a few days to round up enough men to cause us any problems. If we get the ammunition wagon today, we can hit him tonight!"

Blackie had the entire gang assembled in the saloon within thirty minutes. Lazarus had them sit at the tables, while he stood at the bar, addressing them.

He looked out over the crowd, thinking about the men he'd gotten involved in this.

At one table sat seven men, all bank robbers and members of assorted gangs that read like a Most Wanted list. The leader of this particular group was Three-fingers Sammy Torres. He was a tall, over six-foot Mexican with a large mustache and smallpox scars on his face. It was said he'd lost the two fingers of his left hand in a fight, when his opponent bit them off. Torres reportedly made the man swallow them, then cut his throat and gut and reclaimed the digits. He carried the mummified fingers in a small leather pouch hung on a strip of rawhide around his neck.

Two of his confederates, Dick Wheeler and Billy
Baugh, were said to have ridden with the James gang
until Jesse got mad 'cause they made eyes at his wife. It
was a testament to their toughness that he didn't kill
them but allowed them to leave the gang.

The remaining four men were from the Dalton gang.
Having survived the shootout that broke up the gang in
Coffeeville, Kansas, they'd headed north and joined up
with Lazarus. They went by Jimmy, Jake, Sonny, and
Clyde. He didn't know their last names, and didn't much
care as long as they did what they were supposed to.

At the table next to them were four Mexicans in dirty
clothes. They had come from somewhere down near Del
Rio. They were called Pedro Gonzalez, Jaime Sanchez,
Coronado Vallentine, and Perro Gutierrez. He hadn't
asked how the man got the name Perro, which meant
dog in English. They'd ridden with a local *bandido* on the
Mexican border who'd just recently been strung up by
the Texas Rangers—who they said had followed them
over halfway here before heading back to Texas. The
Mex's rarely bathed, and the other men didn't much
like them in the saloon, saying the smell ruined their appetites. 'Course, it didn't seem to do much to lessen
their thirst for whiskey. The Mexicans would be good
cannon fodder if needed. He'd have them rush the
ranch first to see how well defended it was.

Behind the Mex's were the Rebels, as they called
themselves. Ex-Confederate soldiers, they still wore the
tattered remains of their uniforms, as if it made any kind
of difference at this late date. Bobby Barlow, Christopher
Tucker, Riley Samuels, Danny Donnahue, and Willie
Bodine were all from some backwoods place in Arkansas
named Dogsnot, or some such hillbilly name. They
weren't very intelligent, but Lazarus didn't plan to let
them do any thinking. As long as they could ride and
shoot and didn't turn yellow on him, he figured they'd
do all right.

There were a couple of black men in the group. Ordi-
narily, Lazarus didn't have much use for men of darker

color, but he figured they'd be useful, especially if there
was much digging to be done for the gold. Nigras were
good at digging. Whether they lasted until time came
to divvy up the proceeds was another matter, entirely.
Bartholomew Winter and Jedediah Jones were full-on
black, and they rode with a man with a heavy reputation named Cherokee Bill, a half-black and half-Indian
who'd been terrorizing the ranches up near the Indian
Nations for some time. They'd joined up because the
U.S. Marshals had finally gotten around to trying to
roust them out of their mountain hideouts up there.
Cherokee Bill said they planned to stay around until the
marshals went back to Oklahoma Territory. Then they'd
head back to the Nations. That is, Lazarus thought, if he
decided to let them live that long. At least they seemed
to know their place and never tried to sit with the white
folks in the saloon.

Lazarus continued to review the men under his command in this manner for a few more minutes, then
decided the time had come.

"Men," he called, raising his hands to stop the chat-
ter and noise in the room so he could be heard. "There's
a good chance we'll be ridin' on the Jensen ranch in the
next day or so. I want you to go easy on the whiskey until
this is over."

He scowled at the loud groan that arose from the men
in the room, some of whom openly laughed at his sug-
gestion.

He gave a cold smile. "All right, I realize temperance
is something none of you are exactly used to. But know
this—if any of you mess up because you're drunk or
hungover, I'll personally put a bullet in your gut and
leave you to rot to death on the trail. Have I made myself
perfectly clear?"

The noise quieted down and some of the men dropped
their eyes. He knew he had their full attention now.

"Jimmy, I want you and Jake and Sonny and Clyde to
get to work puttin' fuses in the dynamite we've got
stacked up over at the store. I know you Dalton riders

liked to use explosives in your bank jobs, so I figure you're the ones who'd do the best at gettin' it ready to use."

Jimmy nodded his head after glancing at his companions. "No problem, boss. We'll get on it first thing in the morning."

Lazarus shook his head. "No, Jimmy. You'll get on it right now, as soon as I'm through talkin'.

"I want the rest of you to get on over to the store an' pick up as many boxes of shells for your guns as you think you'll need. Put 'em in your saddlebags an' have 'em ready to travel by tomorrow. When it comes time to leave, I want everything and everybody ready to go."

"Why the sudden rush, Cain? We been sittin' around here for two weeks or more, an' now you act like there's a fire in your britches," said Donny Donnahue, one of the rebel riders.

"We may have a slight problem. Joey Wells took off last night. I fear he may have gone to warn Jensen we're comin'."

As they all looked around at each other, Lazarus could see the fear this caused in some of the men.

"You mean we might not just be fightin' Smoke Jensen, one of the toughest hombres in the area, but may also have to go up agin' Joey Wells, *the* toughest hombre anywhere?" asked Three-fingers Sammy Torres.

"That's right, Three-fingers. You got a problem with that?" Lazarus asked.

Torres shrugged. "Not particularly. It will no doubt mean there will be less men left to share in the loot after we kill them," he answered with a laugh.

Lazarus nodded. "There is that to consider. Now you men get on over to the store and pick up your bullets and dynamite, like I told you."

He turned to Bob Blanchard. "Bob, the bar is closed for the rest of the day."

Lazarus ignored the groan from the men and walked over to his table, signaling his leaders to join him.

After the others had left, he looked around at Blackie

Jackson, Tom Cartwright, Curly Joe, Pig Iron Carlton, Jeremy Britt, and King Johannson.

"Men, we're gonna stick together through all this. Let the other fools take the front of the charge and do the dangerous work. We'll hang back and finish off any survivors at the ranch after the others have broken through the defenses."

Jeremy Britt frowned. "I say, Lazarus, that doesn't sound very sporting."

Lazarus cut his eyes at Jeremy. "I don't think you realize who we're dealing with here, Jeremy. Wells and Jensen are two of the best men with guns we could pick to go up against. I only put our odds of beatin' 'em, even with a ten to one advantage in numbers, at about fifty-fifty. If for some reason they turn out to be too tough for this bunch, I want us to survive to fight another day."

Jeremy shrugged. "You're the boss, boss," he said with a smile. "But I want a piece of Joey Wells. I don't like traitors."

Lazarus's face grew cold as a gravedigger's shovel. "For that, my friend, you're gonna have to stand in line."

"Did you mean it, Lazarus, 'bout the bar bein' closed the rest of the day?" asked Curly Joe Ventrillo.

"Not for us, boys, only for the cannon fodder," Lazarus answered with a grin.

Tom "Behind the Deuces" Cartwright got to his feet and walked over to the bar.

"Bob, gimme that bottle of Kentucky bourbon over there and some clean glasses. We got a little more drinkin' to do 'fore the day's over."

Blanchard looked over at Lazarus, saw him nod, and handed Cartwright the bottle and glasses.

After he filled everyone's glass, Lazarus stood up and held his glass high. "Boys, a toast. To gold, and all the things it can buy!"

26

After Lazarus and his men finished their drinks, he sent them after the others to make ready for the attack on Smoke Jensen's ranch.

He walked over to the bar and held out his glass for a refill.

Bob Blanchard poured more whiskey into the glass, a worried look on his face.

"What is it, Bob? You look like you got somethin' on your mind," Lazarus said.

"There's something I ought'a tell you, Mr. Cain. After all, you been awfully good to me, payin' me for the whiskey an' food an' such your men are usin'."

"Go on, Bob, I'm listenin'."

"I couldn't help but overhear you talkin' to your men just now, 'bout goin' on down the road an' tryin' somethin' else if the attack on Smoke Jensen don't work out."

"Yeah, so what?"

"How much do you really know about Smoke Jensen, Mr. Cain?"

"Just what everybody else does, that he's a famous shootist and ex-outlaw, and a mighty tough hombre."

Blanchard shook his head. "You don't know near enough, then. See, Jensen's an old mountain man, trained by the most famous mountain man of all, Preacher."

"So what? We ain't gonna be fightin' him up in the mountains, Bob."

"That's not it, Mr. Cain. The mountain men lived by a code, a code of vengeance. Once you done one of them wrong, he'd not never give up 'til he'd repaid you, double."

"I don't see what—"

"I'm just telling you this so you won't think you're gonna be able to ride away from this after it's over if Jensen is still alive."

Blanchard took down a glass and poured himself a drink and refilled Lazarus's.

"Let me tell you a story 'bout what happened to the men who kilt Smoke's dad, just after they got here to Colorado. . . .

"Smoke's dad, Emmett, came back from the War Between the States in the summer of eighteen sixty-five. Smoke, who was known as Kirby then, was only about fourteen or fifteen years old. Emmett sold their scratch-dirt farm in Missouri, packed up their belongin's, and they headed north by northwest. Long about Wichita, they met up with an old mountain man who called himself Preacher. For some reason, unknown even to the old-timer, he took them under his wing when he saw they was as green as new apples, and they traveled together for a spell.

"Soon they was set upon by a band of Pawnee Injuns, an' Smoke kilt his first couple of men. The story goes that Preacher couldn't hardly believe it when he saw him draw that old Navy Colt. Says he knew right off the boy was destined to become a legend—if he lived long enough, that is. That's when Preacher gave young Kirby Jensen his nickname—Smoke—from the smoke that came outta that Navy Colt, and from the color of his hair.

"Right after that, Emmett told Preacher that he had set out lookin' for three men who killed Smoke's brother and stole some Confederate gold. Their names were Wiley Potter, Josh Richards, and Stratton—I don't remember his first name. Emmett went on to tell Preacher that he was goin' gunnin' for those polecats, and if'n he didn't come back he wanted Preacher to take care of Smoke until he was growed up enough to do it for himself. Preacher told Emmett he'd be proud to do that very thing.

"The next day Emmett took off and left the old cougar to watch after his young'un. They didn't hear nothin' for a couple of years, time Preacher spent teaching the young buck the ways of the West and how to survive where most men wouldn't. Preacher later told people that during that time, though Smoke was about as natural a fast draw and shot as he'd ever seen, the boy spent at least an hour ever day drawing and dry-firin' those Navy Colts he wore.

"About two years later, at Brown's Hole in Idaho, an old mountain man found Smoke and Preacher and told Smoke his daddy was dead, and that those men he went after'd killed him. Smoke packed up, an' he and Preacher went on the prod.

"They got to Pagosa Springs—that's Indian for healin' waters—just west of the Needle Mountains, and stopped to replenish their supplies. Then they rode into Rico, a rough-an'-tumble mining camp that back then was an outlaw hangout."

Blanchard halted in his tale to build himself a cigarette and stick it in his mouth, then continued telling Lazarus about the legend of Smoke Jensen's early years. . . .

Smoke and Preacher dismounted in front of the combination trading post and saloon. As was his custom, Smoke slipped the thongs from the hammers of his Colts as soon as his boots hit dirt.

They had bought their supplies and turned to leave when the hum of conversation suddenly died. Two rough-dressed and unshaven men, both wearing guns, blocked the door.

"Who owns that horse out there?" one demanded, a

snarl in his voice, trouble in his manner. "The one with the SJ brand?"

Smoke laid his purchases on the counter. "I do," he said quietly.

"Which way'd you ride in from?"

Preacher had slipped to his right, his left hand covering the hammer of his Henry, concealing the click as he thumbed it back.

Smoke faced the men, his right hand hanging loose by his side. His left hand was just inches from his left-hand gun. "Who wants to know—and why?"

No one in the dusty building moved or spoke.

"Pike's my name," said the bigger and uglier of the pair. "And I say you came through my diggin's yesterday and stole my dust."

"And I say you're a liar," Smoke told him.

Pike grinned nastily, his right hand hovering near the butt of his pistol. "Why . . . you little pup. I think I'll shoot your ears off."

"Why don't you try? I'm tired of hearing you shoot your mouth off."

Pike looked puzzled for a few seconds; bewilderment crossed his features. No one had ever talked to him in this manner. Pike was big, strong, and a bully. "I think I'll just kill you for that."

Pike and his partner reached for their guns.

Four shots boomed in the low-ceilinged room, four shots so closely spaced that they seemed as one thunderous roar. Dust and bird droppings fell from the ceiling. Pike and his friend were slammed out the open doorway. One fell off the rough porch, dying in the dirt street. Pike, with two holes in his chest, died with his back against a support pole, his eyes still open, unbelieving. Neither had managed to pull a pistol more than halfway out of leather.

All eyes in the black, powder-filled and dusty, smoky room moved to the young man standing by the bar, a Colt in each hand. "Good God!" a man whispered in awe. "I never even seen him draw."

Preacher moved the muzzle of his Henry to cover the men at the tables. The bartender put his hands slowly on the bar, indicating he wanted no trouble.

"We'll be leaving now," Smoke said, holstering his Colts and picking up his purchases from the counter. He walked out the door slowly.

Smoke stepped over the sprawled, dead legs of Pike and walked past his dead partner in the shooting.

"What are we 'posed to do with the bodies?" a man asked Preacher.

"Bury 'em."

"What's the kid's name?"

"Smoke."

A few days later, in a nearby town, a friend of Preacher's told Smoke that two men, Haywood and Thompson, who claimed to be Pike's brother, had tracked him and Preacher and were in town waiting for Smoke.

Smoke walked down the rutted street an hour before sunset, the sun at his back—the way he had planned it. Thompson and Haywood were in a big tent at the end of the street, which served as saloon and café. Preacher had pointed them out earlier and asked if Smoke needed his help. Smoke said no. The refusal came as no surprise.

As he walked down the street a man glanced up, spotted him, then hurried quickly inside.

Smoke felt no animosity toward the men in the tent saloon—no anger, no hatred—but they'd come here after him. *So let the dance begin,* he thought.

Smoke stopped fifty feet from the tent. "Haywood! Thompson! You want to see me?"

The two men pushed back the tent flap and stepped out, both angling to get a better look at the man they had tracked. "You the kid called Smoke?" one said.

"I am."

"Pike was my brother," said the heavier of the pair. "And Shorty was my pal."

"You should choose your friends more carefully," Smoke told him.

"They was just a-funnin' with you," Thompson said.

"You weren't there. You don't know what happened."

"You callin' me a liar?"

"If that's the way you want to take it."

Thompson's face colored with anger, his hand moving closer to the .44 in his belt. "You take that back, or make your play."

"There is no need for this," Smoke said.

The second man began cursing Smoke as he stood tensely, legs spread wide, body bent at the waist. "You're a damned thief. You stolt their gold, and then kilt 'em."

"I don't want to have to kill you," Smoke said.

"The kid's yellow!" Haywood yelled. Then he grabbed for his gun.

Haywood touched the butt of his gun just as two loud gun-shots blasted in the dusty street. The .36 caliber balls struck Haywood in the chest, one nicking his heart. He dropped to the dirt, dying. Before he closed his eyes and death relieved him of the shocking pain by pulling him into a long sleep, two more shots thundered. He had a dark vision of Thompson spinning in the street. Then Haywood died.

Thompson was on one knee, his left hand holding his shattered right elbow. His leg was bloody. Smoke had knocked his gun from his hand, then shot him in the leg.

"Pike was your brother," Smoke told the man. "So I can understand why you came after me. But you were wrong. I'll let you live. But stay with mining. If I ever see you again, I'll kill you."

The young man turned, putting his back to the dead and bloody pair. He walked slowly up the street, his high-heeled Spanish riding boots pocking the air with dusty puddles.*

*The Last of the Mountain Man

27

Lazarus stopped Blanchard's story long enough to pull a cigar out of his pocket, light it, and get his glass refilled.

"How old was Jensen when this happened?" he asked the bartender.

"I don't know exactly. 'Bout eighteen or so, I guess."

Lazarus nodded, his eyes narrowed. "Go on, Bob."

"After Smoke shot and killed Pike, his friend, and Haywood, and then wounded Pike's brother, Thompson, he and Preacher went after the other men who kilt Smoke's brother and stole the Confederates' gold. They rode on over to *La Plaza de los Leones*, the plaza of the lions. It was there that they trapped a man named Casey in a line shack with some of his *compadres*. Smoke and Preacher burnt 'em out and captured Casey. Smoke took him to the outskirts of the town and hanged him."

Lazarus's eyebrows shot up. "Just hanged him? Without a trial or notifying the authorities?"

Blanchard flicked ash off his cigarette without taking it out of his mouth. "Yes sir. Smoke likes to take care of his enemies himself. Why, I'll bet that even if he knows you and your men are coming after him, he won't ask nobody else for any help."

Blanchard hesitated. Then, remembering where he left off, he continued. "Anyway, Jensen knew that town would never of hanged one of their own just on the word of Smoke Jensen."

Blanchard snorted. "Like as not they'd of hanged Smoke and Preacher instead. Anyway, after that the sheriff of that town put out a flyer on Smoke, accusing him of murder. Had a ten thousand dollar reward on it, too."

"Did Smoke and Preacher go into hiding?" Lazarus asked, figuring that's what he would have done.

"Nope. Seems Preacher advised it, but Smoke said he had one more call to make. They rode on over to Oreodelphia, lookin' for a man named Ackerman. They didn't go after him right at first. Smoke and Preacher sat around doin' a whole lot of nothin' for two or three days. Smoke wanted Ackerman to get plenty nervous. He did, and finally came gunnin' for Smoke with a bunch of men who rode for his brand. . . ."

At the edge of town, Ackerman, a bull of a man with small, mean eyes and a cruel slit for a mouth, slowed his horse to a walk. Ackerman and his hands rode down the street, six abreast.

Preacher and Smoke were on their feet. Preacher stuffed his mouth full of chewing tobacco. Both men had slipped the thongs from the hammers of their Colts. Preacher wore two Colt .44's—one in a holster, the other stuck behind his belt. Mountain man and the young gunfighter stood six feet apart on the boardwalk.

The sheriff closed his office door and walked into the empty cell area. He sat down and began a game of checkers with his deputy.

Ackerman and his men wheeled their horses to face the men on the boardwalk. "I hear tell you boys is lookin' for me. If so, here I am."

"News to me," Smoke said. "What's your name?"

"You know who I am, kid. Ackerman."

"Oh yeah!" Smoke grinned. "You're the man who helped kill my brother by shooting him in the back. Then you stole the gold he was guarding."

Inside the hotel, pressed against the wall, the desk clerk listened intently, his mouth open in anticipation of gunfire.

"You're a liar. I didn't shoot your brother. That was Potter and his bunch."

"You stood and watched it. Then you stole the gold."

"It was war, kid."

"But you were on the same side," Smoke said. "So that not only makes you a killer, it makes you a traitor and a coward."

"I'll kill you for sayin' that!"

"You'll burn in hell a long time before I'm dead," Smoke told him.

Ackerman grabbed for his pistol. The street exploded in gunfire and black powder fumes. Horses screamed and bucked in fear. One rider was thrown to the dust by his lunging mustang. Smoke took the men on the left, Preacher the men on the right side. The battle lasted no more than ten to twelve seconds. When the noise and the gunsmoke cleared, five men lay in the street, two of them dead. Two more would die from their wounds. One was shot in the side—he would live. Ackerman had been shot three times: once in the belly, once in the chest, and one ball had taken him in the side of the face as the muzzle of the .36 had lifted with each blast. Still Ackerman sat in his saddle, dead. The big man finally leaned to one side and toppled from his horse, one boot hung in the stirrup. The horse shied, then began waking down the dusty street, dragging Ackerman, leaving a bloody trail.

Preacher spat into the street. "Damn near swallowed my chaw."

"I never seen a draw that fast," a man spoke from his storefront. "It was a blur."

The editor of the paper walked up to stand by the sheriff. He watched the old man and the young gunfighter walk down the street. He truly had seen it all. The old man had killed one man, wounded another. The young man had killed four men, as calmly as if picking his teeth.

"What's that young man's name?"

"Smoke Jensen. He's a devil."

"What did they do next, Bob?" Lazarus asked, sipping his whiskey slowly, considering what he was learning about the character of Smoke Jensen.

"Well, they both had some minor wounds, and there was a price on Smoke's head, so they took off to the mountains to lay up for a while and lick their wounds and let the heat die down."

Blanchard stubbed out his cigarette. "Except it didn't work out exactly that way. They chanced upon the remains of a wagon train that'd been burned out by Indians, and rescued a young woman. Nicole was her name. She was the lone survivor of the attack. There wasn't nothin' else they could do, so they took her up into the mountains with them, where they planned to winter.

"Smoke built them a cabin out of adobe and logs, and they spent two winters and a summer in that place, up in the high lonesome. After the first year, Smoke and Nicole had a kind of unofficial marrying, and by the second winter she had Smoke a son."

"I didn't know Jensen had a son."

Blanchard shook his head. "He doesn't, now. When the boy was about a year old, Smoke had to go lookin' for their milk cow that wandered off. When he came back, he found some bounty hunters had tracked him to the cabin and were in there with Nicole and the baby. . . ."

Some primitive sense of warning caused Smoke to pull up short of his home. He made a wide circle, staying in the timber back of the creek, and slipped up to the cabin.

Nicole was dead. The acts of the men had grown perverted, and in their haste her throat had been crushed. Felter sat by the lean-to and watched the valley in front of him. He wondered where Smoke had hidden the gold.

Inside, Canning drew his skinning knife and scalped Nicole, tying her bloody hair to his belt. He then skinned a part of her, thinking he would tan the hide and make himself a nice tobacco pouch.

Kid Austin got sick to his stomach watching Canning's callousness, and went out the back door to puke on the ground. That moment of sickness saved his life—for the time being.

Grissom walked out the front door of the cabin. Smoke's tracks had indicated he had ridden off south, so he should probably return from that direction, but Grissom felt something was wrong. He sensed something, his years on the owlhoot back trails surfacing.

"Felter?" he called.

"Yeah?" He stepped from the lean-to.

"Something's wrong."

"I feel it. But what?"

"I don't know." Grissom spun as he sensed movement behind him. His right hand dipped for his pistol. Felter had stepped back into the lean-to. Grissom's palm touched the smooth wooden butt of his gun as his eyes saw the tall young man standing by the corner of the cabin, a Colt .36 in each hand. Lead from the .36s hit him in the center of the chest with numbing force. Just before his heart exploded, the outlaw said, "Smoke!" Then he fell to the ground.

Smoke jerked the gun belt and pistols from the dead man. Remington Army .44s.

A bounty hunter ran from the cabin, firing at the corner of the building. But Smoke was gone.

"Behind the house!" Felter yelled, running from the lean-to, his fists full of Colts. He slid to a halt and raced back to the water trough, diving behind it for protection.

A bounty hunter who had been dumping his bowels in the outhouse struggled to pull up his pants, at the same time pushing open the door with his shoulder. Smoke shot him twice in the belly and left him to scream on the outhouse floor.

Kid Austin, caught in the open behind the cabin, ran for the banks of the creek, panic driving his legs. He leaped for the protection of a sandy embankment, twisting in the air, just as Smoke took aim and fired. The ball hit Austin's right buttock and traveled through the left cheek of his butt, tearing out a sizable hunk of flesh. Kid Austin, the dreaming gun-hand, screamed and fainted from the pain in his ass.

Smoke ran for the protection of the woodpile and crouched there, recharging his Colts and checking the .44s. He listened to the sounds of men in panic, firing in all directions and hitting nothing.

Moments ticked past, the sound of silence finally overpowering gunfire. Smoke flicked away sweat from his face. He waited.

Something came sailing out the back door to bounce on the grass. Smoke felt hot bile build in his stomach. Someone had thrown his dead son outside. The boy had been dead for some time. Smoke fought back sickness.

"You wanna see what's left of your woman?" a taunting voice called from near the back door. "I got her hair on my belt and a piece of her hide to tan. We all took a time or two with her. I think she liked it."

Smoke felt rage charge through him, but he remained still, crouched behind the thick pile of wood until his anger cooled to controlled, venom-filled fury. He unslung the big Sharps buffalo rifle Preacher had carried for years. The rifle could drop a two thousand pound buffalo at six hundred yards. It could also punch through a small log.

The voice from the cabin continued to mock and taunt Smoke, but Preacher's training kept him cautious. To his rear lay a meadow, void of cover. To his left was a shed. He knew that was empty, for it was still barred from the outside. The man he'd plugged in the butt was to his right, but several fallen logs would protect him from that direction. The man in the outhouse was either dead or passed out. His screaming had ceased.

Through a chink in the logs, Smoke shoved the muzzle of the Sharps and lined up where he thought he had seen a man move, just to the left of the rear window, where Smoke had framed it out with rough pine planking. He gently squeezed the trigger, taking up slack. The weapon boomed, the planking shattered, and a man began screaming in pain.

Canning ran out the front of the cabin, to the lean-to, sliding down hard beside Felter behind the water trough. "This ain't workin' out," he panted. "Grissom, Austin, Poker, and now Evans is either dead or dying. The slug from that buffalo gun blowed his arm off. Let's get the hell outta here!"

Felter had been thinking the same thing. "What about Clark and Sam?"

"They growed men. They can join us or they can go to hell."

"Let's ride. They's always another day. We'll hide up in them mountains, see which way he rides out, then bushwhack him. Let's go." They raced for their horses, hidden in a bend of the creek, behind the bank. They kept the cabin between themselves and Smoke as much as possible, then bellied down in the meadow the rest of the way.

In the creek, in water red from the wounds in his butt, Kid Austin crawled upstream, crying in pain and humiliation. His Colts were forgotten—useless, anyway. The powder was wet—all he wanted was to get away.

The bounty hunters left in the house, Clark and Sam, looked at each other. "I'm gettin' out!" Sam said. "That ain't no pilgrim out there."

"The hell with that," Clark said. "I humped his woman, and I'll kill him and take the ten thousand."

"Your option." Sam slipped out the front and caught up with the others.

Kid Austin reached his horse first. Yelping as he hit the saddle, he galloped off toward the timber in the foothills.

"You wife don't look so good now," Clark called out to Smoke. "Not since she got a haircut and one titty skinned."

Deep silence had replaced the gunfire. The air stank of black powder, blood, and relaxed bladders and bowels, death-induced. Smoke had seen the men ride off into the foothills. He wondered how many were left in the cabin.

Smoke remained still. His eyes, burning with fury, touched the stiffening form of his son. If Clark could have read the man's thoughts, he would have stuck the muzzle of his .44 into his mouth and pulled the trigger, guaranteeing himself a quick death instead of what waited for him later on.

"Yes, sir," Clark taunted him. He went into profane detail about the rape of Nicole and the perverted acts that followed.

Smoke eased slowly backward, keeping the woodpile in front of him. He slipped down the side of the knoll and ran around to one wall of the cabin. He grinned. The bounty hunter was still talking to the woodpile, to the muzzle of the Sharps stuck through the logs.

Smoke eased around to the front of the cabin and looked in. He saw Nicole, saw the torture marks on her, saw the hideousness of the scalping and the skinning knife. He lifted his eyes to the back door, where Clark was crouching just to the right of the closed door.

Smoke raised his .36 and shot the pistol out of Clark's hand. The outlaw howled and grabbed his numbed and bloodied hand.

Smoke stepped over Grissom's body, then glanced at the body of the armless bounty hunter, who had bled to death.

Clark looked up at the tall young man with the burning eyes. Cold slimy fear put a bony hand on his shoulder. For the first time in his evil life, Clark knew what death looked like.

"You gonna make it quick, ain't you?"

"Not likely," Smoke said, then kicked him on the side of the head, dropping Clark unconscious to the floor.

When Clark came to his senses, he began screaming.

He was naked, staked out a mile from the cabin, on the plain. Rawhide held his wrists and ankles to thick stakes driven into the ground. A huge ant mound was just inches from him. And Smoke had poured honey all over him.

"I'm a white man," Clark screamed. "You can't do this to me." Slobber sprayed from his mouth. "What are you, half-Apache?"

Smoke looked at him, contempt in his eyes. "You will not die well, I believe."

He didn't.*

Lazarus shook his head, his brow furrowed with thought. "I see what you mean, Bob. If we fail in our attack, Jensen will hunt us down one by one until he's killed all of us or one of us kills him."

"That's about the size of it, Mr. Cain. I just didn't want you going up against him until you knew what kind of man he is."

"Thanks for the warning, Bob. I guess the only thing to do is make sure we kill Jensen when we get the chance."

Blanchard nodded. "It's that, or spend the rest of your life looking back over your shoulder, waitin' on him to show up."

*The Last Mountain Man

28

About five miles outside of Fontana, Smoke reined Joker to a halt. "If what I've heard about Cain is true, with his military background he's gonna have sentries posted around Fontana that'll warn him we're coming."

"What do you want to do, Smoke?" Louis Longmont asked.

"Since Joey and I have the most experience at this, we'll take out the sentries. I want the rest of you to ride in a wide circle around the town and try to intercept that wagon of dynamite and ammunition Cain's expecting to arrive today. It should be coming from the north, from Pueblo."

After the others rode off, Smoke pulled his Colts out and began to check his loads, while Joey did the same.

"It's gonna seem like old times ridin' with you, Smoke," Joey said.

Smoke grinned. "Yeah, let's hope it turns out as well this time as it did last time . . ."

Smoke and Joey began to ride a circuit around Fontana, keeping their eyes peeled for any approaching riders. It didn't take them long to attract a couple.

Two men rode up, each carrying Winchester rifles in

their hands, the butts resting on their thighs as they reined up in front of Smoke and Joey.

One of the men, dark-skinned with several days' growth of beard, spoke up. "Where you gents headed?"

Smoke glanced at Joey, his lips curled in a lazy smile. "The man wants to know where we're headed, partner."

Joey, his face deadly serious, replied, "Yeah, I heard the nosy son of a bitch."

He looked directly at the man who'd spoken. "What's your name, mister?" he asked.

The dark-skinned man glanced at the man sitting on the horse next to him, then back at Joey. "What's it to you?"

Joey shrugged. "I just thought it'd be nice to have somethin' to carve on the cross over your grave, assumin' anybody cares enough 'bout your sorry butt to come out here and bury you."

"Why you . . ." the man growled and started to lower his rifle barrel.

Twin explosions erupted almost simultaneously from Smoke and Joey's hands, which were full of Colts. The two men were blown backward off their horses before they could ear back the hammers on their long guns.

The silent one struggled to get to his feet. Then a bullet from Smoke put him down for good.

Smoke cut his eyes to Joey. "I feel kind'a bad not offering them a chance to quit this madness and go on about their way."

Joey shook his head. "That kind of thinkin's gonna git you kilt, partner. There's not a one of the bunch ridin' with Cain who's worth two seconds of thought. They's all murderers an' thieves an' such, an' don't deserve the time of day, much less a chance to shoot us while they's decidin' whether to stay or leave."

"I guess you're right," Smoke said.

"Ain't I always?" Joey said, this time grinning.

The next two sentries, perhaps because they'd heard the shots or perhaps because they were just more ornery than the first pair, didn't bother to accost Smoke and Joey. They just started blasting away with long guns as soon as they saw them riding by.

Luckily for Smoke and Joey, the pair were abysmal shots, and the first volley of bullets whined by harmlessly, other than startling the two gunmen out of a year's growth.

"Damn!" Joey shouted even as he leaned far over Red's neck and spurred the big stud toward the distant men firing at them.

The two men, sitting on their horses, stopped shooting for a moment when they realized the men they were aiming at were doing something crazy. Instead of trying to get away from the hail of bullets, they were galloping at full speed *toward* them.

Pete Garcia looked at Julio Cardenez with disbelief. "Julio, the mens are *stupido!*"

Julio didn't bother to reply, since the men were getting closer by the second and he could see pistols in their hands.

Julio and Pete continued to fire, the explosions of their rifles making their horses jump and dance in fear, which did nothing to improve their already terrible aim.

Joey, who'd spent considerable years after the Civil War riding and shooting from horseback, was under no such handicap.

While he was still fifty yards from the attackers, his first slug whipped the bandit's hat off. The second took the man in the left chest, just above his heart. The force of the bullet twisted the man around in his saddle, but didn't knock him to the ground.

Julio Cardenez tried to put his rifle to his shoulder, but then he noticed his left arm wouldn't work right.

"Damn, Pete," Julio said, wonderment in his voice as if he'd never expected something like this to happen. "I am hit!"

Pete glanced at Julio while levering his Winchester as fast as he could. When he turned his head to the left, a slug from Smoke's pistol entered the right side of his face and exited out the left, blowing his lower jaw completely off in a split second.

Pete tried to scream at the terrible pain, but could only gurgle as his blood poured down his throat and into his windpipe.

By the time Julio looked up from his useless left arm, Joey was twenty yards away, staring at him over the sights of a Colt Army .44 caliber pistol.

"No!" screamed Julio, holding out his good right arm as if that could shield him from Joey's bullets.

It didn't. The next one passed through the meat of Julio's forearm and hit him in the right eye, exploding his skull and killing him instantly.

Smoke, seeing the terrible mess his bullet had made of Pete's face, withheld his fire, watching the man strangle and drown in his own blood. Pete fell out of the saddle, his skin the color of night, gasping like a fish out of water as he died.

Smoke and Joey rested their broncs as they punched out empty cartridges and reloaded their pistols.

"How many left, do you think?" Smoke asked.

Joey pursed his lips for a moment, thinking. "If'n he's goin' by the rules the rebels used to follow, he's got eight sentries surroundin' his camp. Two on each point of the compass."

Smoke slipped his pistol into his holster. "That means we've got four more to deal with."

Joey nodded. "At least."

Louis Longmont was the first to spy the wagon. "There it is," he called to the others, pointing up the road.

A man could be seen driving a buckboard, a saddled horse following along behind on a dally rope.

Monte Carson was the first to speak as they signaled the wagon to a halt. "Howdy, mister. My name's Monte Carson, an' I'm the sheriff around here. What's in the back of your wagon?"

The driver looked worriedly around at the faces of the

men surrounding him. "Uh, some supplies from Garrett's General Store over in Pueblo."

"What kind'a supplies?" Louis Longmont asked.

The man stared at Louis Carbone and Al Martine, who looked like Mexican *bandidos* with their large, silver spurs, crossed bandoliers of shells on their chests, and twin Colt pistols on their hips.

"What business is it of yours?" he asked.

Al drew his pistol and crossed his arms on his saddle horn, leaning forward, the barrel of the gun pointing down. "*Señor*, the man he asked you very nice. Why you not answer his question, *muy pronto?*"

"I'm carryin' dynamite, gunpowder, an' about two hundred boxes of shells, forty-fours, forty-fives, an' a few thirty-six caliber bullets."

Monte let his face look puzzled. "You figurin' on goin' to war, mister?"

"No. These are for a Mr. Cain, in the town of Fontana," the driver answered belligerently. "Now, why don't you just let me ride on into town and do what I'm bein' paid to do?"

"I can't do that," Monte said. "The town of Fontana is under quarantine."

"Quarantine?" the man asked.

"Yeah. Seems they's a disease in that town that's gonna kill everybody in it," said Pearlie, a smirk on his face.

"What is it? The pox?"

"No," answered Louis Longmont. "It is a disease called greed. It is being spread by Lazarus Cain, and it has infected everyone in the town."

"Greed ain't fatal," the driver persisted, not getting the joke.

Al Martine cocked his pistol with a loud metallic sound. "It is in this case, my friend," he growled.

"Uh, if you gentlemen will allow me, I'll just get on my horse and head on back to Pueblo."

"That'll be just fine," Monte said. He smiled, looking around at the group of men with him. "My friends and I will make sure Mr. Cain gets all of the bullets and dynamite in your wagon, one way or another." He hesitated and grinned at the others riding with him. "You have my word on it."

Nate Bridges and Will Calloway were riding sentry for Lazarus when Nate stopped his horse and pulled a small canvas sack out of his shirt pocket and began to build himself a cigarette. Will stopped his horse, too, and pulled out his canteen to get a drink of water.

As Nate dipped his head to lick the paper around his tobacco, there came a sudden sound from behind him, like a sledgehammer hitting a side of beef, and Nate back-flipped off his horse.

"What the hell?" Will said, glancing down at his partner as a booming sound echoed from across the valley.

He saw a spreading stain of crimson on the front of Nate's shirt, then looked back over his shoulder in time to see a puff of smoke come from a tiny figure on horseback over fifteen hundred yards away.

He jerked his reins and whirled his horse, saving his life as the bullet from Joey's Sharps Big Fifty hit him in the shoulder.

The force of the slug almost unseated Will, but he managed to keep his balance and leaned over the neck of his mount and spurred it toward Fontana as fast as the animal could run.

"Damn! Missed the second one," Joey muttered as he reloaded the Sharps.

"That might not be so bad," Smoke said. "Let him tell Cain what happened, and when the other sentries don't show up and he realizes what happened to them, it'll cause him some confusion."

"Why is that good? I thought we wanted the element of surprise."

"We did. But that wasn't going to happen with us having to kill all the sentries. Sooner or later he was going to realize he was under attack, anyway. Now we'll let him stew on it a while, wondering just who and how many are after him."

"Well, if that's the plan, then we need to git those other two sentries pronto," Joey said.

After he put the Sharps in his saddle boot they rode north, the direction of the remaining two sentries.

Bill Boudreaux and Francois Tibbido, two friends on the run from New Orleans for killing five men in a riverboat gambling feud, were riding the northern sentry post.

"Say, Bill," drawled Francois, "here come two men." He pointed off to the west.

"Uh huh," Bill replied.

"What you want to do?"

"Let them come. Then when they get here we kill them, *mon ami*," Bill said.

"Why not just tell them to leave?" Francois asked, his face glum.

"'Cause Monsieur Cain, he be plenty mad if he find out. He say kill anyone who come, so we kill these two mens." Bill hesitated, then asked, "Unless you want to go to Monsieur Cain an' tell him you be too soft for this job?"

"No! I agree. They must die."

As soon as Smoke and Joey got within thirty yards of the two men they were approaching, they saw the men go for their guns.

Without hesitating, Smoke and Joey filled their hands with iron, firing on the two sentries before they could clear leather.

Smoke hit Bill Boudreaux in the heart and throat with two shots that sounded almost simultaneous. The bullets tore into Boudreaux, killing him before he had time to scream.

Joey's shots hit Francois in the stomach and left arm, doubling him over his saddle horn with a loud grunt.

After a few seconds, he toppled to the side to fall to the ground, moaning in pain and writhing in the dirt.

"Help me . . . oh dear God, help me . . ." he cried.

Joey rode over to look down at the dying man. "You got a gun. Help yourself," he said. Then he and Smoke rode off toward Fontana's town limits, where they were to meet with their friends.

29

Will Calloway made it to just in front of the Dog Hole Saloon in Fontana before impending shock from loss of blood caused him to faint and fall off his horse.

Donny Donnahue was just coming from the outhouse when he saw Will hit the dirt.

"Hey, everbody, come quick!" he yelled as he ran to help the fallen man.

When he got next to Will, Donny saw almost his entire shirt soaked with blood. "Jesus," he muttered, having never seen anyone lose that much blood and survive.

Several cowboys burst out of the batwings of the Dog Hole and ran to stand over Will. Finally, Three-fingers Sonny Torres, who had seen and treated more gunshot wounds than most doctors, knelt next to Will and pulled out a large knife. He stuck the blade in the front of Will's shirt and sliced it open.

After Torres peeled off the shirt, several of the men standing watching gave low whistles. There was a hole as big as a man's fist in the front of Will's shoulder. Most of the bleeding had stopped or at least slowed to a slow trickle, and there were no arterial spurters.

Sonny Torres rolled Will up on his side and looked at his back.

"Here's where the bullet enter," he said, pointing to a

small hole just behind Will's shoulder, next to his shoulder blade.

He let him roll back. "And that is where she exit," he said, indicating the huge hole in the front of Will's chest.

"What the hell kind'a gun did that?" asked Donny.

Torres shrugged. "A large calibre, maybe a buff'lo gun of some sort, like a Sharps."

Lazarus Cain came striding through the crowd of men, parting them with his hands as if he were Moses parting the Red Sea.

"What the hell's goin' on here?" he asked.

"'Pears one of our men went an' got hisself shot," answered Willie Bodine.

"Is that Will Calloway lyin' there?" Lazarus asked.

"Yes sir," answered Donny. "I's just comin' outta the shitter when I saw him fall off'n his horse."

Torres glanced up from where he still kneeled next to Will. "Looks like he was shot with a long gun of some kind, Mr. Cain. Prob'ly a Sharps or somethin' like it."

"Damn!" Lazarus stepped back and looked around the town. "Has anyone seen any of the other sentries? Who was ridin' with Will, anyway?"

"I believe it was Nate Bridges," Billy Baugh drawled in his low, Southern accent. "Leastways, I seen the two of 'em ridin' outta town together this mornin'."

Lazarus started pointing. "I need some men to ride out and check on the sentries. Wheeler, you ride north. Gonzalez, you take the south end. Tucker, you go east, and Samuels, I want you to ride to the west."

He hesitated. "Men, I don't know if this means anything or not, but ride with your guns loose and watch your backsides. We may have some problems comin' our way."

Within two hours, Lazarus had gotten the bad news and was having a meeting with his most trusted men in the Dog Hole. They were seated at their favorite table in the corner, and several bottles of whiskey were being passed around.

Lazarus looked at his men. "We've got some trouble. The men I sent out found every one of our sentries dead, bodies scattered all over the countryside."

"Were all of 'em kilt with long guns?" asked Curly Joe Ventrillo.

Lazarus shook his head. "No. It appeared as if some were shot at close range with pistols."

"Did they find any other bodies, other than our chaps?" asked Jeremy Brett.

Lazarus shook his head slowly.

"That means whoever did this is good," said Blackie Jackson. "Those sentries were hard men. I don't see some pilgrims ridin' up an' killin' ever one without getting a least a little shot up."

"You're right, Blackie. Whoever is out there is a force to be reckoned with."

"Cain't hardly be the army, then," opined Pig Iron Carlton. "Them boys are so green they'd've probably shot one or two of their own men theyselves."

"No, I don't think this is the authorities," said Lazarus, a thoughtful expression on his face as he stared out the window. "If it was the army or marshals, we'd've heard from them by now."

He wagged his head. "This is something different."

"Well then, who could it be, boss?" asked Tom "Behind the Deuces."

"I don't know."

"Do you suspect it could be Smoke Jensen? Maybe Joey Wells warned him, after all," said King Johannson, absently fingering the handle of the machete hanging on his belt.

Lazarus frowned. "I doubt it. If Jensen knew we were comin' an' that we had over fifty men, why wouldn't he just notify the army or the territory marshals? There'd be no need for him to even get involved."

Jeremy Brett removed the Colt pistol from his shoulder holster and flipped open the loading gate as he began to check his loads. "I fear you may have underestimated this Jensen gentleman. From what I have heard and read, he is a man who does not suffer tribulation well."

"What's that supposed to mean, Jeremy?" asked Lazarus. "Speak English, will you?"

Jeremy smiled. "I believe we were on Mr. Jensen's ranch the day we arrived here."

"So?"

"Do you remember what happened that day?"

Lazarus thought a minute, then looked slowly up at Jeremy. "We shot some young ranchhand."

"It is merely my supposition that perhaps Mr. Smoke Jensen did not take kindly to us killing one of his men. Perhaps this is his way of telling us that."

"Do you really think a man of Jensen's reputation would go to war over losing one of his hired hands?" asked Lazarus.

"From what I've heard, though the stories are admittedly exaggerated, Jensen would go to war if you scuffed his boots."

Lazarus rubbed his chin whiskers as he thought. "If this is Jensen an' his men, it won't be so bad. As a matter of fact, it's probably better if he comes to us rather than us fightin' him on his own ground."

"What do you mean?" asked Curly Joe.

"This way there won't be no chance of us ridin' into no traps or ambushes."

"Wonder how many men he's got ridin' with him," said Blackie Jackson.

"It really doesn't matter, old chap," said Jeremy Brett. "Once they ride into town, they're all as good as dead."

"I want you men to get the boys scattered out all over town," ordered Lazarus. "Have 'em get ready for an attack. Post some on roofs, some in high placed rooms where they have a good line of fire. You know the drill. Tell 'em to get ready. Smoke Jensen's coming to town, and we're gonna throw him a party."

30

Smoke and Joey circled around Fontana until they found where their friends were waiting. They'd made a campfire and were cooking some beans and fatback and heating up some biscuits Sally had sent along in a paper sack.

Louis Longmont looked up from his coffee cup and smiled. "I see the sentries were no match for the team of Jensen and Wells."

"Not even close," Joey said. "Them boys just thought they knew how to fight 'til they ran into a twister called Smoke Jensen."

Smoke inclined his head at Pearlie, who was sitting on his haunches next to the fire, a plate piled high with food on his knees. "I might'a known you boys would be eating, since Pearlie's riding with you."

"Golly, Smoke," Pearlie mumbled around a mouthful of food, "ya just never know when you're gonna next git a chance to eat when you're fightin' outlaws an' such. I figgered it'd be best to eat while there weren't nothin' goin' on."

Smoke walked over to the kettle on the trestle over the fire and scooped out a helping for himself. "Don't worry, Pearlie, I was just funning with you. It is always a good idea to eat before a fight. You're right. There's no telling just how long we're going to be tied up in this little fracas."

Joey built himself a cigarette and stuck it in the side of his mouth, then proceeded to drink coffee without disturbing the butt.

"We may have a little trouble, boys," he said.

"How's that, Joey?" Sheriff Monte Carson asked.

"One of the sentries got away. He was carryin' some of my lead in him, but we figure he might've made it back to Fontana to warn the others we're comin'."

"Damn!" said Louis Carbone. *"Es muy malo!"*

Longmont shrugged. "It's not all that bad, Louis. In fact, it really won't make a hell of a lot of difference. Even if they suspect someone has targeted them, they won't know who or how many, nor will they have much time to make preparations for our arrival."

Smoke nodded. "That's the way I figure it, Louis. In fact, it might be better if they have a little time to worry about just who's on their trail."

"Yeah," Monte Carson agreed. "Worried men don't always think as good as men without a lot on their mind." He smiled a grim smile. "I'd a lot rather trail a man who knows he's bein' trailed an' is spendin' a lot of his time lookin' back over his shoulder instead of thinkin' 'bout how he can get the drop on me."

Smoke walked over to the wagon and began to peer inside it. "What've we got here?"

Longmont stepped over to lean on the edge of the buckboard. "Looks like Cain was planning on going to war with you and the town of Big Rock, Smoke. He's got enough ammunition and gunpowder and dynamite in this wagon to cause quite a ruckus."

Cal added, "If he'd managed to get it, that is."

"You boys did a good job," Smoke said approvingly. "If Cain had been able to acquire this wagon we'd've had our hands full, all right."

"Now, our only problem," Monte said, "is to figure out how we can make the best use of this stuff ourselves."

Smoke's lips curled up in a wide grin. "Oh, I think I have some ideas on that subject, Monte."

He took his sketch of Fontana out of his saddlebag and spread it on top of the boxes in the buckboard. With a pencil, he pointed to various areas of the town as he talked, dividing up his forces as commanders had been doing before upcoming battles for centuries.

"Louis," he said, addressing Carbone, "you and Al are used to working as a team. I want you two to approach the town from the south. Take as much dynamite as you can carry, tied together two sticks at a time. When you begin your approach, light a cigar and keep it in your mouth to set the fuses off when you're ready to toss the dynamite."

"Cal, I want you and Pearlie to stay together. You're still not up to full strength, so I don't want you to try anything too strenuous. I'm gonna station you on the road out of town, in case some of the outlaws decide it's getting too hot in Fontana and try to make tracks for someplace cooler."

Cal's face fell. "You mean you're gonna keep me outta the action so I won't get shot again, don't ya?"

Pearlie turned to face Cal. "That's not it at all, Cal. Smoke's got to put each man where he can do the best for the team, 'cause we're so outnumbered."

"Pearlie's right, Cal. Your job is just as important as anyone else's. If any of the gunnys get away, they're liable to come back later and do us damage. Your job, and Pearlie's, is to make sure that doesn't happen."

Smoke turned to the remainder of the men. "Louis, I'd like you and Monte to attack from the north, and Johnny and George to come in from the east."

He hesitated. "Joey and I will go in first from the west, from the back of town."

"What do you mean, go in first?" Monte asked.

Smoke pointed to the tins of gunpowder lying in the buckboard. "We're gonna sneak in and plant a few of those where they'll do the most good. Your signal to attack will be when you see them go off."

"What if Cain's men manage to get you before that happens?" Johnny North asked.

Joey shrugged. "Then, you'll hear the gunshots. Either way, it'll be time for you to do your best to blow those bastards to hell and gone."

31

Smoke took a tin of bootblack out of his saddlebag and scooped some out on his fingers before handing the can to Joey.

"Put some of that on your face, Joey. It'll help keep us from being seen while we skulk around tonight."

Smoke smeared boot polish around his eyes and mouth until his face was as black as the night. "If things go well," he said to the others, "Joey and I should have the gunpowder set up within about thirty minutes. Give us ten minutes more, just in case. If you haven't heard from us by then, come in with your guns blazing."

Joey finished applying the bootblack and looked up. "Just be careful. If'n you see a couple'a fellows with black faces, make sure you don't blast 'em 'til you see who they are."

Smoke turned to his saddle boot and removed his Greener 10-gauge sawed-off shotgun. He slipped the rawhide strap over his neck so that the gun hung down just under his right arm. He took out a box of shells and filled his buckskin jacket pockets.

While he was doing this, Joey did the same thing with his Winchester rifle, filling his pockets with shells, as well.

Finally, Smoke took two black dusters from his saddle-bag. He threw one to Joey and put the other one on. As the two men stepped into their saddles, Pearlie touched the brim of his hat. "Luck, Smoke, Joey."

Joey smiled sarcastically. "Son, luck don't have nothin' to do with it . . . it's who's the meanest gonna survive. The others gonna be buzzard bait."

Smoke and Joey slipped off their horses and left them ground-reined fifty yards from the first buildings on the outskirts of Fontana. Smoke glanced at the sky. Luckily, though there was a half moon the fall weather had brought storm clouds scudding in from over the mountaintops which kept the moonlight to a minimum.

Smoke handed Joey one of the canvas bags full of tins of gunpowder, and he threw another over his shoulder. Stepping lightly and crouching over to minimize their outline against the horizon, they walked quickly into town. With their dark faces and the black dusters flaring out behind them, they looked like strange, malevolent shadows moving in the night.

Slipping down an alleyway, Smoke peered around a corner of the building he was behind and looked toward the Dog Hole Saloon.

"Uh oh," he whispered.

"What is it?" Joey asked.

"It's just past seven o'clock, and I don't see any activity at the saloon."

He could just make out Joey's head in the semi-darkness when he nodded. "That means they're expectin' us," Joey said. "Otherwise they'd all be in there gettin' liquored up."

Smoke took one of the tins of gunpowder out of his sack and placed it next to the corner of the building. While getting ready for this evening, he'd had Pearlie and Cal put blasting caps and fuses into the cans, and Louis Longmont had tied white strips of cloth to the tops of the cans so they'd be easily visible from a distance.

Easing out of the alley, keeping close to the buildings,

Smoke and Joey went in separate directions, each planting tins of the black powder along the way.

Bobby Barlow turned to Christopher Tucker. "Hey, Chris. You got any tobaccy?"

The two men had been riding together since Manassas, and Bobby had been smoking Chris's tobacco since before then.

"You know we ain't supposed to smoke whilst we're on guard duty, Bobby."

"Guard duty, hell! There ain't nobody comin' tonight. It's all in Cain's head."

Chris passed over a small sack with his Bull Durham in it. The two were sitting in a darkened room that used to be the town doctor's office, watching out the front window. They'd been placed there by Blackie Jackson to keep an eye on the main street of Fontana.

Bobby struck a lucifer on his pants leg and lighted his cigarette. As he blew smoke out of his nostrils, he squinted and tapped Chris on the shoulder.

"Looky there, Chris. There goes one of those darkies, walkin' down the boardwalk as bold as brass."

Chris shrugged. "So?"

"So? Didn't Blackie Jackson tell us everbody was gonna be under cover tonight, waitin' fer the attack?"

"Yeah, he did."

Bobby got to his feet. "I'd better tell that dumb ass to get off'n the street, then."

He stepped to the door and called softly, "Hey, Bartholomew, it that you?" He figured it had to be Bartholomew Winter, who was the shortest of the three black men riding with them.

The black-faced figure turned his head and took two quick steps toward Bobby, muttering something the man couldn't understand.

"What'd you say?"

Bobby saw something flash in the meager moonlight

and then felt a horrible burning pain in his chest as twelve inches of Arkansas steel pierced his heart.

When Bobby grunted in surprise and pain, Chris called, "Anything wrong, Bobby?"

The short man stepped back from Bobby and let him fall to the floor. Before he hit the ground, Joey's Arkansas Toothpick was slicing across Christopher Tucker's throat, killing him without a sound.

He walked to the window and placed one of the tins of powder on the windowsill, where it could be seen from the street. Then he vanished silently into the darkness.

As Smoke straightened from placing his last tin of gunpowder next to a wall, a harsh voice came from the blackness behind him.

"What do you think you're doin', nigger?" asked Riley Samuels, smiling as he stood there next to Donny Donnahue in the doorway to the old dry goods store.

"Yeah," added Donnahue, "you boys too ignorant to know we supposed to be off the streets tonight?"

The two ex-Confederate soldiers were grinning, their teeth glowing white in the scant moonlight as they took out some of their frustration on what appeared to be one of the black men riding with Cain.

When the figure stood up, Riley's mouth dropped open. None of the Negro troops were this big. This man had to be well over six feet tall.

Donny pointed to the figure's midsection. "What you got there, boy?" he asked.

The black man's teeth gleamed in a wide smile. "It's called a Greener, *boy*," Smoke answered, and let the hammers down.

The gun kicked back, turning him half around as a two-foot-long tongue of flame leapt out of the barrels toward the rednecks. Six ounces of molten lead spread out in a tight pattern, opening the men's chests and exploding their hearts into tiny pieces.

Before the echoes of the explosion of the shotgun had

faded Smoke lit a cigar, touched it to a fuse sticking out of the can of gunpowder on the floor next to him, and calmly walked out of the room.

Willie Bodine, the last of the rebels with Cain, came running down the stairs from where he'd been keeping watch out of a second floor window.

"Donny, Riley, what the hell's goin' on down here?" he asked just as he noticed the burning fuse in the corner of the room next to the bodies of his friends.

"God!" he managed to get out as the gunpowder exploded, blowing his right arm and leg off and tearing his stomach open to expose his guts as he was thrown out the front window. What was left of Willie Bodine landed in the middle of the street, his blood pooling around his dead body in the dirt.

South of Fontana, Louis Carbone leaned over and lit the cigar sticking out of Al Martine's mouth when he heard the shotgun blast followed closely by the explosion of the gunpowder.

"Well, *amigo,* it is time to ride."

Al nodded. "Time to ride and kill, *compadre.*"

They leaned over the necks of their mounts and put spurs to their flanks, heading into hell.

In the north, Louis Longmont stuck out his hand to Monte Carson. "You ready, partner?" he asked.

Monte took his hand and nodded. "It'll be a pleasure to do battle with you, Mr. Longmont."

The two gunfighters rode toward the town at an easy canter, their hands filled with iron and their eyes flicking back and forth, looking for targets.

On the east side of town Johnny North looked at George Hampton as they moved their horses toward town. "Johnny, don't you go gettin' yourself killed tonight. My daughter'd never forgive me if I let that happen."

Johnny shook his head, smiling grimly. "George, neither would I, neither would I."

* * *

Lazarus Cain jerked his head to the side when he heard the shotgun blast and the explosion of the gunpowder. "Damn! It's begun," he said to Blackie Jackson, who sat next to him in the saloon.

Blackie nodded and reached over to turn off the lantern hanging on the wall next to them, plunging the room into darkness.

The rest of Cain's personal team were scattered around the saloon and on the second floor and roof of the building, waiting for the attack.

As Al and Louis rode into town, Pedro Gonzalez and Jaime Sanchez rose up on the roof of a boardinghouse and began to fire down at them. Pedro's second shot hit Al's horse in the neck and he somersaulted, throwing Al to the ground.

Louis put the fuse on a bundle of dynamite to his cigar, and when it ignited he threw it onto the roof behind the shooters.

It exploded, sending the two gunmen catapulting off the roof as if they'd been shot out of a cannon. Jaime Sanchez landed on his head not five feet from where Al lay, snapping his neck and breaking his back in three places.

Al glanced back over his shoulder at Louis. "Careful, *amigo*, you almost landed him on top of me."

Pedro Gonzalez's headless body slammed into the ground twenty yards away, and still moved, writhing in the dirt, as if it were alive for several seconds.

Al scrambled on hands and knees, grabbed his sack of dynamite off his saddle horn, and then ran toward the nearest building, trying to get off the street.

Two black men stepped out of the building, guns in their hands.

"Hold it, mister," Bartholomew Winter said, in his soft Southern accent. "Drop that bag and raise your hands."

"Sure . . . sure . . . only, don't shoot me," Al begged as he complied with the man's orders.

When he saw their eyes follow the bag as he dropped it, his hands flashed to his pistols, drawing and firing before the two men saw him move.

His left-hand gun shot Bartholomew Winter in the throat, blowing out his spine and almost decapitating him. His right-hand gun shot Jedediah Jones in the middle of his chest, shattering his sternum and piercing his heart, killing him before his finger could tighten on the trigger.

Cherokee Bill, notorious outlaw, watched this happen from the building where he and Bartholomew and Jedediah had been stationed. He shook his head. *This ain't my fight,* he thought. He quietly slipped out the back door of the room and got on his horse. He spurred the animal into a gallop and headed south out of town as fast as he could ride back toward the Indian Nations in Oklahoma Territory. He didn't know it, but he was riding toward a date with a hangman's noose, in less than a year.

On the east side of town, Coronado Vallentine and Perro Gutierrez were holed up in a barn next to the livery stable with Dick Wheeler and Billy Baugh. They watched silently as buildings began to explode and burn all over town.

"Damn!" Dick Wheeler muttered, watching through his window as the flames leapt toward the sky.

"Hey, here comes two men ridin' down the street," said Billy Baugh, pointing his rifle out his window.

Wheeler was just about to tell the other men to hold their fire until they got closer when Perro Gutierrez snapped off a shot with his pistol.

The bullet took George Hampton in the right chest, spinning him around and knocking him to the ground.

Johnny North, fearing the worst, spurred his horse directly toward the barn as fast as he could ride. He rode into the building through the doors, both hands full of iron.

Perro Gutierrez whirled around, firing blindly.

Johnny shot him in the face, exploding his head and throwing him backward over a bale of hay.

Thumbing his hammers back and firing as fast as he could from the back of his rearing, screaming horse, Johnny was deadly accurate.

Dick Wheeler didn't get off a shot before he was hit in the neck and chest. Billy Baugh managed to fire twice, one of his bullets notching Johnny's left ear, before Johnny shot him in the gut, doubling him over and knocking him to his knees, where he knelt as if in some sort of grotesque prayer.

Coronado Vallentine aimed his shotgun at Johnny's back, earing back the hammers and grinning over the sights. Just before he pulled the trigger a shot rang out from behind him, and he felt a blow between his shoulder blades.

He whirled around in time to see George Hampton standing there, blood all over his shirtfront, looking at him over the barrel of a Colt .45 that was still smoking.

Vallentine coughed, spitting blood, and found he didn't have the strength to pull the triggers on his shotgun. He grinned, and died, falling facedown on the straw-covered floor.

Johnny jumped down off his horse and ran to grab George just as he began to fall.

"Thanks, George, you saved my life," Johnny said.

Three-fingers Sammy Torres was holed up in the hotel building with the ex-Dalton gang members, Jimmy, Jake, Sonny, and Clyde. They were on the second floor, stationed at windows in various rooms where they had a good view of the street.

When Three-fingers Sammy saw two black-clad figures running across the street toward the saloon, he opened fire, pocking dirt around the running men but missing with all his shots.

Luckily, Monte and Louis Longmont saw the muzzle flash from his rifle and reined up their horses before they got to the hotel. Jumping to the ground, they pulled pistols and eased down an alley and around the corner and into the back door of the building.

Finding no one on the first floor, they began to climb the stairs, eyes staring upward for any sign of a hostile body.

They just reached the second floor landing when Jake stepped out of a doorway, checking his pistol to see if it was fully loaded. He looked up to find four barrels pointed at him.

He snapped his loading gate shut and started to raise his pistol. Two bullets, one each from Louis and Monte, took him in the chest, blowing him back into the room he'd just come out of so hard that he backpedaled and hit the window, shattering it, and fell out onto the street below.

When Sonny and Clyde burst out of their doors, Monte and Louis crouched and began to fire away. Monte blew Clyde to hell, but not before one of Clyde's slugs pierced his abdomen, exiting out his flank after burrowing through six inches of fat and muscle. Monte doubled over, pressing his elbow to the wound to slow the bleeding, but keeping his eyes open for more enemies.

Louis shot Sonny in the face, shattering his buckteeth and blowing them out the back of his head.

Jimmy peered around the edge of a doorway, trying to see through the smoke and haze before he ventured out. Monte snapped off a shot, grazing the boy's head and making him duck back out of sight behind the door. Monte put two more bullets through the door, and Jimmy slowly fell out into the hall, his eyes showing surprise at the events of the evening.

Three-fingers Sammy Torres walked out of his room, his hands held high.

"I give up. I surrender," he said, grinning cockily, as if he hadn't a care in the world.

Louis shook his head. "Uh uh, mister. It is not going to be that easy. You dealt yourself into this hand, so ante up, or die where you stand."

"You wouldn't shoot a man who surrendered, would you?" Torres asked.

Monte, from down the hall, grunted, "If he won't, I sure as hell will. Fill your hand, outlaw, or I'll shoot you down like a dog."

Torres scowled and grabbed for his pistol. He managed to get it half raised and fire a shot before Louis shot him between the eyes, snapping his head back and flinging him spread-eagled onto his back on the floor.

"I must be getting too old for this," Louis mumbled, looking down at his thigh, where a spreading pool of crimson was appearing.

"Yeah," Monte agreed, "me too," and he sat down with his back to a wall.

Cain peered out a front window of the saloon, watching as the town was destroyed around him. Al Martine and Louis Carbone were walking down the street, calmly throwing dynamite onto roofs and into windows, blowing men and pieces of men to hell and gone.

Johnny North, after dressing George Hampton's wound and making him lie down in the barn, was walking down the street from the other direction, using a rifle to fire into the tins of gunpowder Joey and Smoke had secreted along the boardwalk. Buildings on both sides of the street were exploding in flames, which were spreading, fueled by fall winds blowing in from the mountains.

Monte Carson and Louis Longmont, leaning on each other for support, managed to make it out onto the street before Al Martine shot into the gunpowder in the lobby, collapsing the building and throwing more dead men from the roof.

Floyd Devers, Walter Blackwell, Tad Younger, and Johnny Samson, all ex-members of Bloody Bill Anderson's gang, were hiding in one of the boardinghouses.

"Men, it don't look good out there. Half the damn town's burning already," Devers said.

"Yeah," answered Tad Younger. "Let's get the hell out of here."

"You got my vote," agreed Samson.

The four men ran out the back door and jumped on their horses and rode down a back road, out of town.

Joey and Smoke made their way toward the saloon, figuring that was where Cain and his cadre of picked men would hole up.

King Johannson and Pig Iron Carlton leaned over the parapet of the saloon roof, searching for someone to shoot.

Johannson leveled his rifle at Carbone, taking aim. A bullet plowed into the board he was resting his elbow on, sending a shower of splinters several inches long into his face.

He screamed and stood up, clawing at his right eye, which had a long piece of wood protruding from it. Joey levered another shell into his rifle and fired again, taking Johannson just under the hairline, the bullet blowing the top of his skull off and knocking him back out of sight.

Carlton leaned over and fired twice at Joey, his second slug gouging a chunk of meat from Joey's left shoulder before Smoke leveled his Greener and fired both barrels.

The buckshot took half the roof off as it tore through Carlton, shredding his left arm to bloody pulp and flinging him out off the roof. He landed on his back on a water trough, his spine snapping with an audible crack.

In the saloon, Blackie Jackson leaned over and whispered to Lazarus, "It don't look good, boss. Let's hightail it out of town and live to fight another day."

"Have you got the horses tied out back like I told you?" Jackson nodded.

Lazarus jumped to his feet and hurried toward the door. "Then let's make tracks."

* * *

Curly Joe Ventrillo, Tom "Behind the Deuces" Cartwright, and Jeremy Brett were left to face Smoke and Joey alone in the saloon.

Smoke and Joey slipped through the batwings and stepped to the side, each with their backs against the wall, letting their eyes adjust to the gloom in the room.

Ventrillo, Brett, and Cartwright walked out onto the second floor landing, looking down at Smoke and Joey over the railing.

"I don't suppose you chaps would allow us to ride out of here, would you?" Brett asked, a sardonic smile on his face.

"Not likely," Joey growled, his hands hanging next to his pistol.

Ventrillo spread his hands wide. "But, we have you outnumbered. You don't have a chance of killing all three of us before one of us gets you."

"You fellows called this dance, now someone's got to pay the band. Jerk that sixkiller and go to work."

The five men drew, Smoke and Joey's hands moving so fast it was almost a blur.

Four shots rang out before any of the outlaws on the landing cleared leather.

Smoke put one in Brett's chest and another in Carlton's neck. Joey put a slug in Ventrillo's face and another in Carlton's stomach.

As smoke billowed and the men fell to the floor, Smoke heard hoofbeats from the back of the saloon.

"Cain's getting away," he said.

Smoke and Joey ran toward the livery to get horses to follow the outlaw leader.

32

Pearlie and Cal were watching the sky over Fontana turn orange and red in the reflected glow of burning buildings.

"Dammit, Pearlie," Cal said, "we oughta be there to help Smoke out."

"Yeah, I know, Cal, but I aim to do what Smoke said, as hard as it is to miss the action."

"Sh-h-h," Cal whispered. "I hear horses comin'."

The two men got down off the buckboard where they'd been sitting and slipped the hammer thongs off their pistols.

Four riders came galloping up, reining in when they saw the road blocked by the wagon, and the two men standing in front of it.

Walter Blackwell called out, "Get your wagon outta our way!"

Cal gave a low laugh. "You know who that galoot is, Pearlie?"

"No," Pearlie shook his head.

"It's the man who shot his friend, Bloody Bill Anderson, in the back, to save his own skin."

Pearlie nodded. "Looks like he's turning tail and runnin' from another fight, don't it, Cal?"

"Sure does," Cal answered.

Sweat began to form on Blackwell's forehead. "You

men get out of our way or we'll be forced to gun you down!" he yelled.

Both Cal and Pearlie grinned. "Let's dance!" Pearlie said.

Six men went for their guns simultaneously.

Cal was a shade faster than Pearlie and got off the first shot, hitting Blackwell in the chest before he cleared leather.

Pearlie shot a fraction of a second later, his slug taking Johnny Samson in the left eye, blowing out the side of his skull and breaking his neck.

Floyd Devers fired once, just as Cal's second shot hit him in the stomach, doubling him over his saddle horn with a grunt of pain. Cal fired again, into his right ear, knocking him out of the saddle and onto the ground.

Tad Younger and Pearlie fired at the same time, Younger taking one in the neck and Pearlie taking one in the left shoulder.

As cordite and gunsmoke swirled in a thick cloud and echoes of gunfire reverberated off distant mountains, Pearlie and Cal looked at each other.

"Well, I'll be darned," Pearlie muttered, glancing down at his shoulder. "Looks like some of your natural attraction for lead has rubbed off onto me."

Cal removed his hat and stuck his finger through the hole Devers's bullet had left in it. "Yeah, thank goodness." He sighed.

Blackie Jackson and Lazarus Cain slowed their horses to a walk, letting them blow after their long ride from Fontana.

"You think any of the boys got out alive?" Jackson asked.

Lazarus shook his head. "Doubtful. Not if Jensen's as good as they say he is."

A voice came from the darkness behind them. "He is, and they didn't," Joey Wells said.

Jackson and Cain whirled around to find Smoke Jensen and Joey Wells sitting on horses just behind them.

"Well, well," Lazarus said. "So it comes down to this, huh?"

"That's right," Smoke said. "You came after me, and now you've found me. Let's settle this."

Blackie Jackson, thinking Smoke's attention was fixed on Lazarus, went for his pistol. Two shots rang out almost as one, both hitting Jackson in the chest an inch apart, right over his heart. When he hit the dirt his gun was still in its holster, untouched.

Lazarus eyed the tall figure dressed in buckskins as they faced each other across the mountain meadow. His hands tensed above the walnut grips of his holstered revolvers, pistols that had killed dozens of times before.

"You're no match for me, Jensen. I'll kill you before you can clear leather."

"That hasn't been decided yet," a stony voice replied, a cold stare fixed on Lazarus. "You reach for them guns, an' one of us is gonna die."

Something stirred inside Lazarus Cain, a chilly feeling he'd never known before, forming a knot in his belly. He looked down at Blackie Jackson, lying dead as a stone where Smoke Jensen and Joey Wells had killed him as casually as swatting a fly.

"You can't be that good," Lazarus spat at the mountain man. His mouth went dry as he said it, yet he refused to believe the taste on his tongue might be fear.

"Only one way to find out," Smoke Jensen replied evenly, no change in his tone or expression. "Go for your guns and we'll settle this. I'm tired of all this banter. You're wastin' a helluva lot of my time."

Lazarus gave Jensen a false grin, ready to make his play. "I never was one to let a feller back me down . . ."

As he grabbed for his gun he saw Jensen's hand move almost faster than his eye could follow.

His gun was half out of his holster when Lazarus heard an explosion and felt as if he'd been kicked in the chest by a mule.

The next thing he knew, he was flat on his back looking up at stars and a moon half hidden behind scurrying clouds.

He reached into his coat pocket, over his heart, and took out the Bible his father had given him. Just above the bullet imbedded in it was a hole. He smiled grimly, then died.

On the way back to Fontana, Joey glanced over at Smoke. "We're gonna have to get together more often, Smoke," he drawled. "Life's been gettin' plumb dull without you around."